ALSO BY MICHAEL CONNELLY

FICTION

The Black Echo

The Black Ice

The Concrete Blonde

The Last Coyote

The Poet

Trunk Music

Blood Work

Angels Flight

Void Moon

A Darkness More Than Night

City of Bones

Chasing the Dime

Lost Light

The Narrows

The Closers

The Lincoln Lawyer

Echo Park

The Overlook

The Brass Verdict

The Scarecrow

Nine Dragons

The Reversal

The Fifth Witness

The Drop

The Black Box

The Gods of Guilt

The Burning Room

The Crossing

The Wrong Side of Goodbye

The Late Show

Two Kinds of Truth

NONFICTION

Crime Beat

EBOOKS

Suicide Run

Angle of Investigation

Mulholland Dive

The Safe Man

Switchblade

DARK SACRED NIGHT

DARK SACRED NIGHT

MICHAEL CONNELLY

Little, Brown and Company
New York   Boston   London

Little, Brown and Company
Hachette Book Group
1290 Avenue of the Americas, New York, NY 10104
littlebrown.com

First Edition: October 2018

Little, Brown and Company is a division of Hachette Book Group, Inc. The Little, Brown name and logo are trademarks of Hachette Book Group, Inc.

The publisher is not responsible for websites (or their content) that are not owned by the publisher.

The Hachette Speakers Bureau provides a wide range of authors for speaking events. To find out more, go to hachettespeakersbureau.com or call (866) 376-6591.

ISBN 978-0-316-48480-0 (hardcover) / 978-0-316-52672-2 (large print) / 978-0-316-42154-6 (signed edition) / 978-0-316-42155-3 (B&N signed edition)
LCCN 2018945140

10 9 8 7 6 5 4 3 2 1

LSC-C

Printed in the United States of America

For Detective Mitzi Roberts,
Renée's inspiration

BALLARD

1

The patrol officers had left the front door open. They thought they were doing her a favor, airing the place out. But that was a violation of crime scene protocol regarding evidence containment. Bugs could go in and out. Touch DNA could be disturbed by a breeze through the house. Odors were particulate. Airing out a crime scene meant losing part of that crime scene.

But the patrol officers didn't know all of that. The report that Ballard had gotten from the watch lieutenant was that the body was two to three days old in a closed house with the air-conditioning off. In his words, the place was as ripe as a bag of skunks.

There were two black-and-whites parked along the curb in front of Ballard. Three blue suits were standing between them, waiting for her. Ballard didn't really expect them to have stayed inside with the body.

Up above, an airship circled at three hundred feet, holding its beam on the street. It looked like a leash of light tethering the circling craft, keeping it from flying away.

Ballard killed the engine but sat in her city ride for a moment. She had parked in front of the gap between two houses and could look out at the lights of the city spreading in a vast carpet below. Not many people realized that Hollywood Boulevard wound up into the mountains, narrow and tight, to where it was strictly residential and far in all ways from the glitz and grime of the Hollywood Boulevard tourist mecca, where visitors posed with costumed superheroes and sidewalk stars. Up here it was money and power and Ballard knew that a murder in the hills always brought out the department's big guns. She was just babysitting. She would not have this case for long. It would go to West Bureau Homicide or possibly even Robbery-Homicide Division downtown, depending on who was dead and what their social status was.

She looked away from the view and tapped the overhead light so she could see her notebook. She had just come from her day's first callout, a routine break-in off Melrose, and had her notes for the report she would write once she got back to Hollywood Division. She flipped to a fresh page and wrote the time—01:47 a.m.—and the address. She added a note about the clear and mild weather conditions. She then turned the light off and got out, leaving the blue flashers on. Moving to the back of the car, she popped the trunk to get to her crime scene kit.

It was Monday morning, her first shift of a week running solo, and Ballard knew she would need to get at least one more wear out of her suit and possibly two. That meant not fouling it with the stink of decomp. At the trunk she slipped off her jacket, folded it carefully, and placed it in one of the empty cardboard evidence boxes. She removed her crime scene coveralls from a plastic bag and pulled them on over her boots, slacks, and blouse. She zipped them up to her chin and, placing one boot and then the other up on the bumper, tightened the Velcro cuffs around her ankles. After she did the same around her wrists, her clothes were hermetically sealed.

Out of the kit she grabbed disposable gloves and the breathing mask she'd used at autopsies when she was formerly with RHD, closed the trunk, and walked up to join the three uniformed officers. As she approached, she recognized Sergeant Stan Dvorek, the area boss, and two officers whose longevity on the graveyard shift got them the cushy and slow Hollywood Hills beat.

Dvorek was balding and paunchy with the kind of hip spread that comes with too many years in a patrol car. He was leaning against the fender of one of the cars with his arms folded in front of his chest. He was known as the Relic. Anybody who actually liked being on the midnight shift and lasted significant years on it ended up with a nickname. Dvorek was the current record holder, celebrating his tenth year on the late show just a month before. The officers with him, Anthony Anzelone and Dwight Doucette, were Caspar and Deuce. Ballard, with just three years on graveyard, had no nickname bestowed upon her yet. At least none that she knew about.

"Fellas," Ballard said.

"Whoa, Sally Ride," Dvorek said. "When's the shuttle taking off?"

Ballard spread her arms to display herself. She knew the coveralls were baggy and looked like a space suit. She thought maybe she had just been christened with a nickname.

"That would be never," she said. "So whadda we got that chased you out of the house?"

"It's bad in there," said Anzelone.

"It's been cooking," Doucette added.

The Relic pushed off the trunk of his car and got serious.

"Female white, fifties, looks like blunt-force trauma and facial lacerations," he said. "Somebody worked her over pretty good. Domicile in disarray. Could've been a break-in."

5

"Sexual assault?" Ballard asked.

"Her nightgown's pulled up. She's exposed."

"Okay, I'm going in. Which one of you brave lads wants to walk me through it?"

There were no immediate volunteers.

"Deuce, you've got the high number," Dvorek said.

"Shit," said Doucette.

Doucette was the newest officer of the three, so he had the highest serial number. He pulled a blue bandanna up from around his neck and over his mouth and nose.

"You look like a fucking Crip," Anzelone said.

"Why, because I'm black?" Doucette asked.

"Because you're wearing a fucking blue bandanna," Anzelone said. "If it was red, I'd say you look like a fucking Blood."

"Just show her," Dvorek said. "I really don't want to be here all night."

Doucette broke off the banter and headed toward the open door of the house. Ballard followed.

"How'd we get this thing so late, anyway?" she asked.

"Next-door neighbor got a call from the victim's niece back in New York," Doucette said. "Neighbor has a key and the niece asked him to check because the lady wasn't responding to social media or cell calls for a few days. The neighbor opens the door, gets hit with the funk, and calls us."

"At one o'clock in the morning?"

"No, much earlier. But all of PM watch was tied up last night on a caper with a four-five-nine suspect and on a perimeter around Park La Brea till end of watch. Nobody got up here and then it got passed on to us at roll call. We came by as soon as we could."

6

Ballard nodded. The perimeter around a robbery suspect sounded suspect to her. More likely, she thought, the buck had been passed shift to shift because nobody wants to work a possible body case that has been cooking in a closed house.

"Where's the neighbor now?" Ballard asked.

"Back home," Doucette said. "Probably taking a shower and sticking VapoRub up his nose. He's never going to be the same again."

"We gotta get his prints to exclude him, even if he says he didn't go in."

"Roger that. I'll get the print car up here."

Snapping on her latex gloves, Ballard followed Doucette over the threshold and into the house. The breathing mask was almost useless. The putrid odor of death hit her strongly, even though she was breathing through her mouth.

Doucette was tall and broad-shouldered. Ballard could see nothing until she was well into the house and had stepped around him. The house was cantilevered out over the hillside, making the view through the floor-to-ceiling glass wall a stunning sheath of twinkling light. Even at this hour, the city seemed alive and pulsing with grand possibilities.

"Was it dark in here when you came in?" Ballard asked.

"Nothing was on when we got here," said Doucette.

Ballard noted the answer. No lights on could mean that the intrusion occurred during the daytime or late at night, after the homeowner had gone to bed. She knew that most home invasions were daytime capers.

Doucette, who was also wearing gloves, hit a wall switch by the door and turned on a line of ceiling lamps. The interior was an open-loft design, taking advantage of the panorama from any spot in the living room, dining room, or kitchen. The staggering view was counterbalanced on the rear wall by three large paintings that were part of a series depicting a woman's red lips.

Ballard noticed broken glass on the floor near the kitchen island but saw no shattered windows.

"Any sign of a break-in?" she asked.

"Not that we saw," Doucette said. "There's broken shit all over the place but no broken windows, no obvious point of entry that we found."

"Okay."

"The body's down here."

He moved into a hallway off the living room and held his hand over the bandanna and his mouth as a second line of protection against the intensifying odor.

Ballard followed. The house was a single-level contemporary. She guessed it was built in the fifties, when one level was enough. Nowadays anything going up in the hills was multilevel and built to the maximum extent of code.

They passed open doorways to a bedroom and a bathroom, then entered a master bedroom that was in disarray with a lamp lying on the floor, its shade dented and bulb shattered. Clothes were strewn haphazardly over the bed, and a long-stemmed glass that had contained what looked like red wine was snapped in two on the white rug, its contents spread in a splash stain.

"Here you go," Doucette said.

He pointed through the open door of the bathroom and then stepped back to allow Ballard in first.

Ballard stood in the doorway but did not enter the bathroom. The victim was faceup on the floor. She was a large woman with her arms and legs spread wide. Her eyes were open, her lower lip torn, and her upper right cheek gashed, exposing grayish pink tissue. A halo of dried blood from an unseen scalp wound surrounded her head on the white tile squares.

A flannel nightgown with hummingbirds on it was pulled up over the hips and bunched above the abdomen and around the breasts. Her feet were bare and three feet apart. There was no visible bruising or injury to the external genitalia.

Ballard could see herself in a floor-to-ceiling mirror on the opposite wall of the room. She squatted down in the doorway and kept her hands on her thighs. She studied the tiled floor for footprints, blood, and other evidence. Besides the halo that had pooled and dried around the dead woman's head, an intermittent ribbon of small blood smears was noticeable on the floor between the body and the bedroom.

"Deuce, go close the front door," she said.

"Uh, okay," Doucette said. "Any reason?"

"Just do it. Then check the kitchen."

"For what?"

"A water bowl on the floor. Go."

Doucette left and Ballard heard his heavy footsteps move back up the hallway. She stood and entered the bathroom, stepping gingerly alongside the wall until she came up close on the body, and squatted again. She leaned down, putting a gloved hand on the tiles for balance, in an attempt to see the scalp wound. The dead woman's dark brown hair was too thick and curly for her to locate it.

Ballard looked around the room. The bathtub was surrounded by a marble sill holding multiple jars of bath salts and candles burned down to nothing. There was a folded towel on the sill as well. Ballard shifted so she could see into the tub. It was empty but the drain stopper was down. It was the kind with a rubber lip that creates a seal. Ballard reached over, turned on the cold water for a few seconds, and then turned it off.

She stood up and stepped over to the edge of the tub. She had put in enough water to surround the drain. She waited and watched.

"There's a water bowl."

Ballard turned. Doucette was back.

"Did you close the front door?" she asked.

"It's closed," Doucette said.

"Okay, look around. I think it's a cat. Something small. You'll have to call Animal Control."

"What?"

Ballard pointed down at the dead woman.

"An animal did that. A hungry one. They start with the soft tissue."

"Are you fucking kidding me?"

Ballard looked back into the tub. Half of the water she had put in was gone. The drain's rubber seal had a slow leak.

"There's no bleeding with the facial injuries," she said. "That happened postmortem. The wound on the back of the head is what killed her."

Doucette nodded.

"Someone came up and cracked her skull from behind," he said.

"No," Ballard said. "It's an accidental death."

"How?" Doucette asked.

Ballard pointed to the array of items on the bathtub sill.

"Based on decomp, I'd say it happened three nights ago," she said. "She turns out the lights in the house to get ready for bed. Probably that lamp on the floor in the bedroom was the one she left on. She comes in here, fills the tub, lights her candles, gets her towel ready. The hot water steams the tiles and she slips, maybe when she remembered she left her glass of wine on the bed table. Or when she started pulling up the nightgown so she could get in the tub."

"What about the lamp and the spilled wine?" Doucette asked.

"The cat."

"So, you just stood here and figured all this out?"

Ballard ignored the question.

"She was carrying a lot of weight," she said. "Maybe a sudden redirection as she was getting undressed—'Oh, I forgot my wine'—causes her to slip and she cracks her skull on the lip of the tub. She's dead, the candles burn out, the water slowly leaks down the drain."

This explanation only brought silence from Doucette. Ballard looked down at the dead woman's ravaged face.

"The second day or so, the cat got hungry," Ballard concluded. "It went a little nuts, then it found her."

"Jesus," Doucette said.

"Get your partner in here, Deuce. Find the cat."

"But wait a minute. If she was about to take a bath, why's she already in a nightgown? You put the nightgown on after the bath, don't you?"

"Who knows? Maybe she comes home from work or dinner out, gets into nightclothes, gets comfortable, maybe watches TV...then decides to take a bath."

Ballard gestured to the mirror.

"She also was obese," she said. "Maybe she didn't like looking at herself naked in the mirror. So she comes home, gets into nightclothes, and stays dressed until it's time to get in the tub."

Ballard turned to go past Doucette and step out of the room.

"Find the cat," she said.

2

By three a.m. Ballard had cleared the scene of the death investigation and was back at Hollywood Division, working in a cubicle in the detective bureau. That vast room, which housed the workstations of forty-eight detectives by day, was deserted after midnight and Ballard always had her pick of the place. She chose a desk in the far corner, away from spillover noise and radio chatter from the watch commander's office down the front hallway. At five seven she could sit down and disappear behind the computer screen and the half walls of the workstation like a soldier in a foxhole. She could focus and get her report writing done.

The report on the residential break-in that she had rolled on earlier in the night was completed first and now she was ready to type up the death report on the bathtub case. She would classify the death as undetermined pending autopsy. She had covered her bases, called in a crime scene photographer, and documented everything, including the cat. She knew a determination of accidental death might be second-guessed by the victim's family and maybe even her superiors. She was confident, however, that the autopsy would find no indications of foul play and the death would eventually be ruled accidental.

She was working alone. Her partner, John Jenkins, was on bereavement leave. There were no replacements for detectives who worked the late show. Ballard was halfway through the first night of at least a week going solo. It all depended on when Jenkins came back. His wife had endured a long, painful death from cancer. It had torn him up and Ballard told him to take all the time he needed.

She opened her notebook to the page containing the details she had written about the second investigation and then called up a blank incident report on her screen. Before beginning, she dipped her chin and pulled the collar of her blouse up to her nose. She thought she picked up the slight odor of decomposition and death but couldn't be sure if it had permeated her clothes or was simply an olfactory memory. Still, it meant that her plan to wear the suit again that week was not going to work out. It was going to the cleaners.

While her head was down, she heard the metal-on-metal bang of a file drawer being closed. She looked up over the workstation divider to the far side of the bureau, where four-drawer file cabinets ran the length of the room. Every pair of detectives was assigned a four-drawer stack for storage.

But the man Ballard saw now opening another drawer to check its contents was not a detective she recognized, and she knew them all from once-a-month squad meetings that drew her to the station during daylight hours. The man who was checking the cabinets seemingly at random had gray hair and a mustache. Ballard instinctively knew he didn't belong. She scanned the entire squad room to see if anybody else was there. The rest of the place was deserted.

The man opened and closed yet another drawer. Ballard used the sound to cover getting up from her chair. She squatted down and, with the row of work cubicles as a blind, moved to the central aisle, which would allow her to come up behind the intruder without being seen.

She had left her suit jacket in the cardboard box in the trunk of her car. This gave her unfettered access to the Glock holstered on her hip. She put her hand on the grip of the weapon and came to a stop ten feet behind the man.

"Hey, what's up?" she asked.

The man froze. He slowly raised his hands out of the open drawer he was looking through and held them so she could see them.

"That's good," Ballard said. "Now you mind telling me who you are and what you're doing?"

"Name's Bosch," he said. "I came in to see somebody."

"What, somebody hiding in the files?"

"No, I used to work here. I know Money up front. He told me I could wait in the break room while they called the guy in. I sort of started wandering. My bad."

Ballard came down from high alert and took her hand off her gun. She recognized the name Bosch, and the fact that he knew the watch commander's nickname gave her some ease as well. But she was still suspicious.

"You kept a key to your old cabinet?" she asked.

"No," Bosch said. "It was unlocked."

Ballard could see the push-in lock at the top of the cabinet was indeed extended in the unlocked position. Most detectives kept their files locked.

"You got some ID?" she asked.

"Sure," Bosch said. "But just so you know, I'm a police officer. I have a gun on my left hip and you're going to see it when I reach back for my ID. Okay?"

Ballard brought her hand back up to her hip.

"Thanks for the heads-up," she said. "Tell you what, forget the ID for now. Why don't we secure the weapon first? Then we'll—"

"There you are, Harry."

Ballard looked to her right and saw Lieutenant Munroe, the watch commander, entering the squad room. Munroe was a thin man who still walked with his hands up near his belt like a street cop, even though he rarely left the confines of the station. He had modified the belt so it carried only his gun, which was required. All of the other bulky equipment was left in a drawer of his desk. Munroe wasn't as old as Bosch but he had the mustache that seemed to be standard with cops who came on in the seventies and eighties.

He saw Ballard and read her stance.

"Ballard, what's going on?" he asked.

"He came in here and was going through the files," Ballard said. "I didn't know who he was."

"You can stand down," Munroe said. "He's good people—used to work homicide here. Back when we had a homicide table."

Munroe turned his gaze to Bosch.

"Harry, what the hell were you doing?" he asked.

Bosch shrugged.

"Just checking my old drawers," he said. "Sort of got tired of waiting."

"Well, Dvorek's in the house and waiting in the report room," Munroe said. "And I need you to talk to him now. I don't like taking him off the street. He's one of my best guys and I want him back out there."

"Got it," Bosch said.

Bosch followed Munroe to the front hallway, which led to the watch office and the report-writing room, where Dvorek was waiting. Bosch looked back at Ballard as he went and nodded. Ballard just watched him go.

After they were gone, Ballard stepped over to the file drawer Bosch had last been looking in. There was a business card taped to it. That's what everybody did to mark their drawers.

Detective Cesar Rivera
Hollywood Sex Crimes Unit

She checked the contents. It was only half full and the folders had fallen forward, probably while Bosch was leafing through them. She pushed them back up so they were standing and looked at what Rivera had written on the tabs. They were mostly victim names and case numbers. Others were marked with the main streets in Hollywood Division, probably containing miscellaneous reports of suspicious activities or persons.

She closed the drawer and checked the two above it, remembering that she had heard Bosch open at least three of them.

These were like the first, containing case folders primarily listed by victim name, specific sex crime, and case number. At the front of the top drawer she noticed a paper clip that had been bent and twisted. She studied the push-button lock on the top corner of the cabinet. It was a basic model and she knew it could easily have been picked with a paper clip. Security of the records themselves was not a priority, because they were contained in a high-security police station.

Ballard closed the drawers, pushed in the lock, and went back to the desk she had been using. She remained intrigued by Bosch's middle-of-the-night visit. She knew he had used the paper clip to unlock the file cabinet, and that indicated he had more than a casual interest in the contents of its drawers. His nostalgic story about checking out his old files had been a lie.

She picked up the coffee cup on the desk and walked down the hall to the first-floor break room to replenish it. The room was empty, as usual. She refilled and carried the cup over to the watch office. Lieutenant Munroe was at his desk, looking at a deployment screen that showed a map of the division and the GPS markers for the patrol units out there. He didn't hear Ballard until she came up behind him.

"Quiet?" she asked.

"For the moment," Munroe said.

Ballard pointed to a cluster of three GPS locators in the same spot.

"What's happening there?"

"That's the Mariscos Reyes truck. I've got three units code seven there."

It was a lunch break at a food truck at Sunset and Western. It made Ballard realize she had not taken a food break and was getting hungry. She wasn't sure she wanted seafood, however.

"So, what did Bosch want?"

"He wanted to talk to the Relic about a body he found nine years ago. I take it Bosch is looking into it."

"He said he's still a cop. Not for us, right?"

"Nah, he's a reserve up in the Valley for San Fernando PD."

"What's San Fernando got to do with a murder down here?"

"I don't know, Ballard. You shoulda asked him while he was here. He's gone now."

"That was quick."

"Because the Relic couldn't remember shit."

"Is Dvorek back out there?"

Munroe pointed to the three-car cluster on the screen.

"He's back out, but code seven at the moment."

"I was thinking about going over there, getting a couple shrimp tacos. You want me to bring you back something?"

"No, I'm good. Take a rover with you."

"Roger that."

On the way back to the D bureau she stopped in the break room and dumped the coffee in the sink and rinsed out the cup. She then pulled a rover out of the charging rack and headed out the back door of the station to her city car. The mid-watch chill had set in and she got her suit jacket out of the trunk and put it on before driving out of the lot.

The Relic was still parked at the food truck when Ballard arrived. As a sergeant, Dvorek rode in a solo car, so he had a tendency to hang with other officers on break for the company.

"Sally Ride," he said, when he noticed Ballard studying the chalkboard menu.

"What's up, Relic?" she said.

"Halfway through another night in paradise."

"Yeah."

Ballard ordered one shrimp taco and doused it liberally with one of the hot sauces from the condiment table. She took it over to Dvorek's black-and-white, where he was leaning against the front fender and finishing his own meal. Two other patrol officers were eating on the hood of their car, parked in front of his.

Ballard leaned against the fender next to him.

"Whatcha get?" Dvorek asked.

"Shrimp," Ballard said. "I only order off the chalkboard. Means it's fresh, right? They don't know what they'll have until they buy it at the docks."

"If you think so."

"I need to think so."

She took her first bite. It was good and there was no fishy taste.

"Not bad," she said.

"I had the fish special," Dvorek said. "It's probably going to take me off the street as soon as it gets down into the lower track."

"T.M.I., Sarge. But speaking of coming in off the street, what did that guy Bosch want with you?"

"You saw him?"

"I caught him snooping in the files in the D bureau."

"Yeah, he's kind of desperate. Looking for any angle on a case he's working."

"In Hollywood? I thought he worked for San Fernando PD these days."

"He does. But this is a private thing he's looking into. A girl who got killed here nine years ago. I was the one who found the body, but damn if I could remember much that helped him."

Ballard took another bite and started nodding. She asked the next question with her mouth full of shrimp and tortilla.

"Who was the girl?" she asked.

"A runaway. Name was Daisy. She was fifteen and putting it out on the street. Sad case. I used to see her on Hollywood up near Western. One night she got into the wrong car. I found her body in an alley off of Cahuenga. Came in on an anonymous call—I do remember that."

"Was that her street name?"

"No, the real thing. Daisy Clayton."

"Was Cesar Rivera working the sex table back then?"

"Cesar? I'm not sure. We're talking nine years ago. He coulda been."

"Well, do you remember Cesar having anything to do with the case? Bosch picked his file cabinet."

Dvorek shrugged.

"I found the body and called it in, Renée—that's it," he said. "I had no part in it after that. I remember they sent me down to the end of the alley to string tape and keep people out. I was just a slick sleeve."

Uniformed cops got a hash mark on their sleeves for every five years of service. Nine years ago, the Relic was a near-rookie. Ballard nodded and asked her last question.

"Did Bosch ask you anything I didn't just ask?"

"Yeah, but it wasn't about her. He asked about Daisy's boyfriend and whether I ever saw him on the street again after the murder."

"Who was the boyfriend?"

"Just another runaway throwaway. I knew him by his graffiti handle: Addict. Bosch said his name was Adam something. I forget. But the answer was no, I never saw him after that. Guys like that come and go."

"Was that all it was—a boyfriend-girlfriend thing?"

"They ran together. You know, for protection. Girl like that, she needed a guy out there. Like a pimp. She worked the street, he watched out for her, and they split the profits. Except that night, he dropped the ball. Too bad for her."

Ballard nodded. She guessed that Bosch wanted to talk to Adam/Addict as the person who would know the most about who Daisy Clayton knew and interacted with, and where she went on the last night of her life.

He could also have been a suspect.

"You know about Bosch, right?" Dvorek asked.

"Yeah," Ballard said. "He worked in the division way back when."

"You know the stars out on the front sidewalk?"

"'Course."

There were memorial stars on the sidewalk in front of Hollywood Station honoring officers from the division who were killed in the line of duty.

"Well, there's one out there," Dvorek said. "Lieutenant Harvey Pounds. The story on him was he was Bosch's L-T when he worked here, and he got abducted and died of a heart attack when he was being tortured on a case Bosch was working."

Ballard had never heard the story before.

"Anybody ever go down for it?" she asked.

"Depends on who you talk to," Dvorek said. "It's supposedly 'cleared-other,' but it's another mystery in the big bad city. The word was that something Bosch did got the guy killed."

"Cleared-other" was a designation for a case that was officially closed but without an arrest or prosecution. Usually because the suspect was dead or serving a life sentence for another crime, and it was not worth the time, expense, and risk of going to trial on a case that would not result in additional punishment.

"Supposedly the file on it is sealed. High jingo."

"High jingo" was LAPD-speak for when a case involved department politics. The kind of case where a career could be diverted by a wrong move.

The information on Bosch was interesting but not on point. Before Ballard could think of a question that would steer Dvorek back toward the Daisy Clayton case, his rover squawked and he took a call from the watch office. Ballard listened as Lieutenant Munroe dispatched him to a Beachwood Canyon address to supervise a team responding to a domestic dispute.

"Gotta go," he said as he balled up the foil his tacos had come in. "Unless you want to ride along and back me up."

It was said in jest, Ballard knew. The Relic didn't need backup from the late show detective.

"I'll see you back at the barn," she said. "Unless that goes sideways and you need a detective."

She hoped not. Domestics usually ended up being he-said-she-said deals in which she acted more as a referee than a detective. Even obvious physical injuries didn't always tell the tale.

"Roger that," Dvorek said.

3

Day watch detectives were all about traffic patterns. Most days the majority of daysiders got to the bureau before six a.m. so they could split by midafternoon, missing the traffic swell both coming and going. Ballard counted on this when she decided she was going to ask Cesar Rivera about the Daisy Clayton case. She spent the remainder of her shift waiting on his arrival by pulling up and studying the electronic records available on the nine-year-old murder.

The murder book, a blue binder full of printed reports and photos, was still the bible of a homicide investigation in the Los Angeles Police Department, but as the world turned digital, so did the department. Using her LAPD password, Ballard was able to access most of the reports and photos from the case that had been scanned into the digital archives. The only thing missing would be the handwritten notes detectives usually shoved into the back sleeve of the murder book.

Most important, she was able to view the chronological record, which was always the spine of the case, a narrative of all moves made by investigators assigned to it.

Ballard determined immediately that the murder was officially classified as a cold case and assigned to the Open-Unsolved

Unit, which was part of the elite Robbery-Homicide Division working out of headquarters downtown. Ballard had once been assigned to the RHD and knew many of the detectives and associated players. Included in that number was her former lieutenant, who had pushed her up against a wall and tried to force himself on her in a bathroom at a squad Christmas party three years earlier. Her rejection of him and subsequent complaint and internal investigation was what landed her on the night shift at Hollywood Division. The complaint was determined to be unfounded because her own partner at the time did not back her up, even though he had witnessed the altercation. Department administrators decided that it would be for the good of all involved to separate Ballard and Lieutenant Robert Olivas. He stayed put in RHD and Ballard was moved out, the message to her clear. Olivas got by unscathed, while she went from an elite unit to a posting no one ever applied or volunteered for, a slot normally reserved for the department's freaks and fuckups.

In recent months, the irony of this was not lost on Ballard as the country and the Hollywood entertainment industry in particular were awash in scandals involving sexual harassment and worse. The chief of police even instituted a task force to handle all the claims pouring in from the movie industry, many of them decades old. Of course, the chief's task force was composed of RHD detectives, and Olivas was one of its supervisors.

The history with Olivas was not far from Ballard's mind as her curiosity about Bosch and the case he was working sent her into the department's digital channels. Technically she was not breaking any rules by pulling up the old reports, but the case had been moved from Hollywood when its homicide team was disbanded and placed with the Open-Unsolved Unit, which was part of the Robbery-Homicide Division and Olivas's domain.

Ballard knew that her moves in the department database would leave a digital trail that Olivas might become aware of. If that happened, he would have the opportunity to be spiteful and initiate an internal investigation into what she was doing with an RHD case.

The threat was there but it wasn't enough to stop her. She hadn't been afraid of Olivas when he followed her into the bathroom at the Christmas party three years ago; she had shoved him back and he'd fallen into a bathtub. She wasn't afraid of him now.

While the chronological record was the most important part of a case review, Ballard started with a quick survey of the photos. She wanted to see Daisy Clayton in life and in death.

The photo packet included crime scene and autopsy photos but also a posed shot of the girl in what looked to Ballard to be a private school uniform—a white blouse with a monogram over the left breast that said SSA. She was smiling at the camera, her blond hair midlength, makeup covering acne on her cheeks, a distant look already in her eyes. The back of the photo had been scanned as well and it read "Grade 7, St. Stanislaus Academy, Modesto."

Ballard decided to leave the crime scene photos for later and went to the chrono, first scrolling to see the latest moves on the case. She quickly learned that outside of annual due-diligence checks, the investigation had largely been dormant for eight years, until it was assigned six months earlier to a cold case detective named Lucia Soto. Ballard didn't know Soto but she knew of her. She was the youngest female detective ever assigned to RHD, beating the record Ballard had previously held by being eight months younger when appointed.

"Lucky Lucy," Ballard said out loud.

Ballard also knew that Soto was currently assigned to the Hollywood Sexual Harassment Task Force because the powers that be in the department—mostly white men—knew that putting as many women on the task force as possible was a prudent move. Soto, who already had a media profile and nickname because of an act of heroism that led to her RHD posting, was often used as the face of the task force for press conferences and other media interactions.

This knowledge now gave Ballard pause. She put together a quick chronology. Six months earlier, Soto either requested or was assigned to the unsolved Daisy Clayton case. Shortly afterward, she was reassigned from the Open-Unsolved Unit to the harassment task force. Then Bosch shows up at Hollywood Station to ask questions about the case and attempt to get a look at the files of a sex crimes detective.

There was a connection there that Ballard didn't yet have. She quickly found it and started to understand things better when she conducted a new search of the department database and called up all cases that listed Bosch as a lead investigator. She zeroed in on the last case he handled before leaving the LAPD. It was a multiple-victim murder involving an arson of an apartment building in which several victims, including children, died of smoke inhalation. On several of the reports associated with the case, Bosch's partner was listed as Lucia Soto.

Ballard now had the connection—Soto took the Clayton case on and then somehow drew her former partner Bosch into it, even though he was no longer with the department. But Ballard didn't have the reason, meaning there was no explanation as to why Soto would go outside the department for help with the investigation, especially when she was moved out of Open-Unsolved for the task force.

Unable to answer that question for the moment, Ballard went back to the case files and started reviewing the investigation from the start. Daisy Clayton was deemed a chronic runaway who repeatedly left her own home as well as the temporary group homes and shelters she was placed in by the Department of Children and Family Services. Each time she ran, she ended up on the streets of Hollywood, joining other runaways in homeless camps and squats in abandoned structures. She abused alcohol and drugs and sold herself on the streets.

The first record of a police interaction with Daisy was sixteen months before her death. It was followed by several more arrests for drugs, loitering, and solicitation for prostitution. Because of her age, the early arrests only resulted in her being returned to her single mother, Elizabeth, or to DCF authorities. But nothing seemed to stop the cycle of her returning to the streets and of being under the influence of Adam Sands, a nineteen-year-old former runaway with his own history of drugs and crime.

Sands was interviewed at length by the original investigators on the case and was eliminated as a potential suspect when his alibi was confirmed: he was being held in the Hollywood Division jail at the time of Daisy Clayton's murder.

Cleared as a suspect, Sands was questioned extensively about the victim's routines and relationships. He claimed to have no information on who she had met with on the night of her murder. He revealed that her routine was to loiter near a shopping plaza on Hollywood Boulevard near Western Avenue that included a mini-market and a liquor store. She would solicit men as they were leaving the stores and then have sex with them in their cars after they drove into one of the many nearby alleys for privacy. Sands said he often stood lookout for her during the transactions but on the night in question he had been grabbed by police on a warrant for not appearing in court on a misde-meanor drug charge.

Daisy was left on her own at the shopping plaza and her body was found the next night in one of the alleys she used for her tricks. It was naked and there were indications of violent sexual assault and torture. Afterward, it had been cleaned with bleach. None of the victim's clothes were ever found. Detectives deter-mined that as many as twenty hours had passed between the time she was last seen at the shopping plaza soliciting johns and when police received an anonymous call about a body being seen in a dumpster in an alley off Cahuenga and Officer Dvorek was dispatched to roll on the call. The missing hours were never ac-counted for but it was clear from the bleaching of the body that Daisy had been taken somewhere and then used and murdered, and her body was carefully cleaned of any evidence that might lead to her killer.

The one clue that the original detectives puzzled over throughout the investigation was a bruise on the body that they were convinced was a mark left by the killer. It was a circle two inches in diameter on the upper right hip. Within the circle was a crossword with the letters A-S-P arranged horizontally and vertically with the S in common.

The letters of the crossword were backwards on the victim's body, indicating that they read correctly on the device or tool used to make the mark. The circle around the crossword appeared to be a snake eating itself but the blurring of the bruising in the tissue made this impossible to confirm.

Many hours of investigative work were expended on the crossword's meaning but no definitive conclusion was reached. The case was originally investigated by two homicide detectives assigned to the Hollywood Division and then reassigned to Olympic Division when the regional homicide teams were consolidated and Hollywood lost its fabled murder unit. The investigators' names were King and Carswell, and Ballard knew neither of them.

Time of death was established during the autopsy at ten hours after the victim was last seen and ten hours before the body was found.

The coroner's report listed the cause of death as manual strangulation. It further refined this conclusion by stating that marks left on the victim's neck by the killer's hands indicated that she was strangled from behind, possibly while being sexually assaulted. Tissue damage in both the vagina and anus was listed as both pre- and postmortem. The victim's fingernails were removed postmortem, a move viewed as an attempt by the killer to make sure no biological evidence was left behind.

The body also showed postmortem abrasions and scratches that investigators believed occurred during an effort to clean the victim with a stiff brush and bleach, which was found in all orifices including the mouth, throat, and ear canals. The medical examiner concluded that the corpse had been submerged in bleach during this cleaning process.

This finding coupled with the time of death led investigators to conclude that Daisy had been taken off the street and to a hotel room or other location by the killer where a bleach bath could be prepared for cleaning the body.

"He's a planner," Ballard said out loud.

The conclusions about the bleach led the original investigators to spend much of their time during the initial days of the investigation on a thorough canvass of every motel and hotel in the Hollywood area that offered direct access to rooms off the parking lot. The school photo of Daisy was shown to employees on all shifts, housekeepers were quizzed about any reports of a strong odor of bleach, and trash bins were searched for bleach containers. Nothing came of the effort. The location of the murder was never determined, and without a crime scene, the case was handicapped from the start. Six months into the investigation the case went cold with no leads and no suspects.

Ballard finally came back to the crime scene photos and this time carefully studied them despite their grim nature. The victim's age, the marks on her body and neck showing the overwhelming strength of her killer, her final naked repose on a spread of trash in a commercial trash bin...it all drew a sense of horror in Ballard, a sad empathy for this girl and what she had been through. Ballard had never been the kind of detective who could leave the work in a drawer at the end of shift. She carried it with her and it was her empathy that fueled her.

Before being assigned to the night beat, Ballard had been working toward a specialization in sexually motivated homicide at RHD. Her then-partner, Ken Chastain, was one of the premier investigators of sex killings in the department. Both had taken classes from and been mentored by Detective David Lambkin, long considered the department expert, until he pulled the pin and left the city for the Pacific Northwest.

That pursuit was largely sidelined by her transfer to the late show, but now as she reviewed the Clayton files, she saw a sexual predator hiding behind the words and reports, a predator unidentified for nine years now, and she felt a deep tug inside. It was the same pull that had first led her to thoughts of being a cop and a hunter of men who hurt women and left them like trash in the alley. She wanted in on whatever it was that Harry Bosch was doing.

Ballard was pulled out of these thoughts when she heard voices. She looked up from the screen and over the workstation wall. She saw two detectives taking off their suit jackets and draping them over their chairs, readying for a new day of work.

One of them was Cesar Rivera.

4

Ballard packed up her things and left her borrowed workstation. She first went into the print room to gather the reports she had fed into the communal printer after typing them up earlier. The detective squad lieutenant was old school and still liked hard-copy reports from her in the morning, even though she also filed them digitally. She separated the reports on the death investigation and the earlier burglary call, stapled them, and then walked them to the inbox on the desk of the lieutenant's adjutant so they were ready for his arrival. She then sauntered over to the sex crimes section and came up behind Rivera as he was sitting at his station and preparing for the day by dumping an airline-size bottle of whiskey into a mug of coffee. She didn't let on that she had seen this when she spoke.

"Hail, Cesar."

Rivera was another mustache guy, his almost white against his brown skin. He matched this with flowing white hair that was a little long by LAPD standards but acceptable on an old detective. He jolted a bit in his seat, afraid his morning routine had been seen. He swiveled his chair around but relaxed when he saw it was Ballard. He knew she would not make any waves.

"Renée," he said. "What's up, girl? You got something for me?"

"No, nothing," she said. "Quiet night."

Ballard kept her distance in case she smelled like decomp.

"So what's up?" Rivera asked.

"About to leave," Ballard said. "I was wondering, though. You know a guy used to work out of here named Harry Bosch? He worked homicide."

She pointed to the corner of the room where the homicide squad was once located. It was now used by an anti-gang team.

"Before I got here," Rivera said. "I mean, I know who he is—everybody does, I think. But no, I never dealt with the guy. Why?"

"He was in the station this morning," Ballard said.

"You mean on graveyard?"

"Yeah, he said he came in to talk to Dvorek about an old homicide. But I found him looking through your stack."

She pointed toward the long row of file cabinets running along the wall. Rivera shook his head in confusion.

"My stack?" Rivera said. "What the fuck?"

"How long have you been at Hollywood Division, Cesar?" Ballard asked.

"Seven years, what's that got to—"

"You know the name Daisy Clayton? She was murdered in '09. It's an open case, classified as sexually motivated."

Rivera shook his head.

"That was before my time here," he said. "I was at Hollenbeck then."

He got up and walked over to the row of file cabinets and pulled a set of keys out of his pocket to open the top drawer of his four-drawer stack.

"Locked now," he said. "Was locked when I left last night."

"I locked it after he left," Ballard said.

She said nothing about finding the bent paper clip in the drawer.

"Isn't Bosch retired?" Rivera said. "How'd he get in here? He keep his nine-nine-nine when he split?"

Every officer was given what was called a 999 key, which unlocked the back door of every station in the city. They were distributed as a backup to the electronic ID keys, which were prone to malfunction and failure during power outages. The city was not scrupulous about collecting them when officers retired.

"Maybe, but he told me Lieutenant Munroe let him in so he could wait for Dvorek to come in off patrol," Ballard said. "He wandered, and that's when I saw him looking in your files. I was working over in the corner and he didn't see me."

"He's the one who mentioned the Daisy case?"

"Daisy Clayton. No, actually Dvorek said that's what Bosch wanted to talk to him about. Dvorek was first officer on scene with her."

"Was it Bosch's case back then?"

"No. It was worked by King and Carswell initially. Now it's assigned to Open-Unsolved downtown."

Rivera walked back to his desk but stayed standing while he grabbed his coffee cup and took a long drink out of it. He then abruptly pulled the cup away from his mouth.

"Shit, I know what he was doing," he said.

"What?" Ballard asked.

There was a sense of urgency in her voice.

"I got here just as they were reorganizing and moving homicide over to West Bureau," Rivera said. "The sex table was expanding and they brought me in. Me and Sandoval were add-ons, not replacements. We both came from Hollenbeck, see."

"Okay," Ballard said.

"So the lieutenant assigned me that cabinet and gave me the key. But when I opened the top drawer to put stuff in there, it was full. All four drawers were full. Same with Sandoval—his four were filled up as well."

"Filled with what? You mean with files?"

"No, every drawer was filled with shake cards. Stacks and stacks of them crammed in there. The homicide guys and the other detectives had decided to keep the old cards after the department went digital. They stuck them in the file drawers for safekeeping."

Rivera was talking about what were officially called field interview cards. They were 3 x 5 cards that were filled out by officers while they were on patrol when they encountered people on the streets. The front of each card was a form with specific identifiers regarding the person interviewed, such as name, date of birth, address, gang affiliation, tattoos, and known associates. The back of each card was blank, and that was where the officer could write any ancillary information about the subject.

Officers carried stacks of blank FI cards on their person or in their patrol cars—Ballard had always kept hers under the sun visor in her car when she had worked patrol in Pacific Division. At the end of shift, the cards were turned in to the divisional watch commander and the information on them was entered by clerical staff into a searchable database. Should a name that was run through the database produce a match, the inquiring officer or detective would have a ready set of facts, addresses, and known associates to start with.

The American Civil Liberties Union had long protested the department's use of the cards and the collection of information from citizens who had not committed crimes, calling the practice

35

unlawful search and seizure and routinely referring to the Q&As as shakedowns. The department had fended off all legal attempts to stop the practice, and many of the rank and file referred to the 3 x 5 cards as shake cards, a not-so-subtle dig at the ACLU.

"Why were they keeping them?" Ballard asked. "Everything was put into the database and would be easier to find there."

"I don't know," Rivera said. "They didn't do it that way at Hollenbeck."

"So, what did you do, clear them out?"

"Yeah, me and Sandy emptied the drawers."

"You threw them all out?"

"No, if I've learned anything in this department, it's not to be the guy who fucks up. We boxed them and took them to storage. Let it be somebody else's problem."

"What storage?"

"Across the lot."

Ballard nodded. She knew he meant the structure at the south end of the station's parking lot. It was a single-level building that had once been a city utilities office but had been turned over to the station when more space was needed. The building was largely unused now. A gym for officers' use and a padded martial arts studio had been set up in two of the larger rooms, but the smaller offices were empty or used for nonevidentiary storage.

"So, this was seven years ago?" she asked.

"More or less," Rivera said. "We didn't move it all at once. I cleared one drawer out, and when it got filled and I had to go down to the next, I'd clear that one. It went like that. Took about a year."

"So what makes you think that Bosch was looking for shake cards last night?"

Rivera shrugged.

"There would have been shake cards in there from the time of the murder you're talking about, right?"

"But the info on the shake cards is in the database."

"Supposedly. But what do you put in the search window? See what I mean? There's a flaw. If he wanted to see who was hanging around Hollywood at the time of the murder, how do you search the database for that?"

Ballard nodded in agreement but knew that there were many ways to pull up info on field interviews in the database such as by geography and time frame. She thought Rivera was wrong about that but probably right about Bosch. He was an old-school detective. He wanted to look through the shakes to see who the street cops in Hollywood were talking to at the time of the Clayton murder.

"Well," she said, "I'm out of here. Have a good one. Stay safe."

"Yeah, you too, Ballard," Rivera said.

Ballard left the detective bureau and went up to the women's locker room on the second floor. She changed out of her suit and into her sweats. Her plan was to head out to Venice, drop off laundry, pick up her dog at the overnight kennel, and then carry her tent and a paddleboard out to the beach. In the afternoon, after she had rested and considered her approach, she'd deal with Bosch.

The morning sun blistered her eyes as she crossed the parking lot behind the station. She popped the locks on her van and threw her crumpled suit onto the passenger seat. She then saw the old utilities building at the south end of the lot and changed her mind about leaving right away.

She used her key card to enter the building and found a couple other denizens of the late show working out before heading home after the morning rush hour. She threw a mock salute at them and went down a hallway that led to former city offices now used for storage. The first room she checked contained items recovered in one of her own cases. The year before, she had taken down a burglar who had filled a motel room with property from the homes he had broken into or had bought with the money and credit cards he had stolen. Now a year later, the case had been adjudicated and much of the property had still not been claimed. It had been returned to Hollywood Station for when the division organized an annual open house for victims as a last chance for them to claim their property.

The next room down was stacked with cardboard boxes containing old case files that for various reasons had to be kept. Ballard looked around here and moved several boxes in order to get to others. Soon enough, she opened a dusty box that was filled with FI cards. She had hit pay dirt.

Twenty minutes later she had culled twelve boxes of FI cards and lined them along the wall in the hallway. By individually sampling cards from each of the boxes, she was able to determine that the cards spanned the years from 2006, when the digitizing initiative began, to 2010, when the homicide section was moved out of Hollywood Division.

Ballard estimated that each of the boxes held up to a thousand cards. It would take many hours to comb through them all thoroughly. She wondered if that was what Bosch was expecting to do, or if he was planning a more precise search for one card or one night in particular, perhaps the night Daisy Clayton was taken off the street.

Ballard wouldn't know the answer until she asked Bosch.

She left a note on the row of boxes in the hallway, saying that they were on hold for her. She returned to the parking lot and got into her van after checking the straps holding her boards to the roof racks. Shortly after she had been assigned to Hollywood Division and word leaked that she was involved in an internal harassment investigation, there were some in the station who attempted to retaliate against her. Sometimes it was basic bullying, sometimes it went deeper. One morning at the end of her shift, when she stopped her van at the station lot's electric gate, her paddleboard slid forward off the roof and crashed against the gate, splintering the nose's fiberglass. She repaired the board herself and started checking the rack straps every morning after her shift.

She took La Brea down to the 10 freeway and headed west toward the beach. She waited until a few minutes after eight o'clock to call the number for RHD that she still had programmed into her phone. A clerk answered and Ballard asked for Lucy Soto. She said the name with a clipped familiarity that imparted the idea that this was a cop-to-cop call. The transfer was made without question.

"This is Detective Soto."

"This is Detective Ballard, Hollywood Division."

There was a pause before Soto responded.

"I know who you are," she said. "How can I help you, Detective Ballard?"

Ballard was used to detectives she wasn't personally acquainted with knowing about her. With female detectives, there was always an awkward moment. They either admired Ballard for her perseverance in the department or believed her actions had made their own jobs more difficult. Ballard always had to find out which it was, and Soto's opener gave no hint as to which camp she was in. Her repeating Ballard's name out loud might have been a move to let someone like a partner or supervisor on the task force know who she was talking to.

Not being able to read her yet, Ballard just pressed on.

"I work the late show here," she said. "Some nights it keeps me running, some nights not so much. My L-T likes me to have a hobby case to kind of keep me busy."

"I don't understand," Soto said. "What's this have to do with me? I'm sort of in the middle of —"

"Yeah, I know you're busy. You're on the harassment task force. That's why I'm calling. One of your cold cases — that you're not working because of the task force — I was wondering if I could take a whack at it."

"Which case?"

"Daisy Clayton. Fifteen-year-old murdered up here in —"

"I know the case. What makes you so interested?"

"It was a big case here at the time. I heard some blue suiters talking about it, pulled up what I could on the box, and got interested. It looked like with this task force thing you weren't doing much with it at the moment."

"And you want to give it a shot."

"I make no promises but, yeah, I'd like to do some work on it. I would keep you in the loop. It's still your case. I'd just do some street work."

Ballard was on the freeway but not moving. Her weeding through the boxes in the storage room had pushed her into the heart of rush hour. She knew the morning breeze would also be in full effect on the coast. She'd be paddling against it and the chop it would kick up. She was missing her window.

"It's nine years later," Soto said. "I'm not sure the street's going to produce anything. Especially on graveyard. You'll be spinning your wheels."

"Well, maybe," Ballard said. "But they're my wheels to spin. You okay with this or not?"

There was another long pause. Enough time for Ballard to move the van about five feet.

"There's something you should know," Soto said. "There's somebody else looking into it. Somebody outside the department."

"Oh, yeah?" Ballard said. "Who's that?"

"My old partner. His name's Harry Bosch. He's retired now but he...he needs the work."

"One of those, huh? Okay. Anything else I should know? Was this one of his cases?"

"No. But he knows the victim's mother. He's doing it for her. Like a dog with a bone."

"Good to know."

Ballard was now getting a better sense of the lay of the land. It was the true purpose of her call. Permission to work the case was the least of her concerns.

"If I come up with anything, I'll feed it to you," Ballard said. "And I'll let you get back to the reckoning."

Ballard thought she heard a muffled laugh.

"Hey, Ballard?" Soto then added quietly. "I said I knew who you were. I also know who Olivas is. I mean, I work with him. I want you to know I appreciate what you did and I know you paid a price. I just wanted to say that."

Ballard nodded to herself.

"That's good to know," she said. "I'll be in touch."

BOSCH

5

From the San Fernando Courthouse it was only a block's walk back to the old jail where Bosch did his file work. He covered the distance quickly, a spring in his step caused by the search warrant in his hand. Judge Atticus Finch Landry had read it in chambers and asked Bosch a few perfunctory questions before signing the approval page. Bosch now had the authority to execute the search and hopefully find the bullet that would lead to an arrest and the closing of another case.

He took the shortcut through the city's Public Works yard to the back door of the old jail. He pulled the key to the padlock as he moved toward the former drunk tank, where the open-case files were kept on steel shelves. He found that he had left the lock open and silently chastised himself. It was a breach of his own as well as departmental protocol. The files were to be kept locked up at all times. And Bosch liked to keep the matters on his desk secure too, even during a forty-minute search-warrant run to the courthouse next door.

He moved behind his makeshift desk—an old wooden door set across two stacks of file boxes—and sat down. Immediately, he saw the twisted paper clip sitting on top of his closed laptop.

He stared at it. He had not put it there.

"You forgot that."

Bosch looked up. The woman—the detective—from the night before at Hollywood Station was straddling the old bench that ran between the freestanding shelves full of case files. She had been out of his line of sight as he came into the cell. He looked over at the open door where the padlock dangled from its chain.

"Ballard, right?" he said. "Good to know I'm not going crazy. I thought I had locked up."

"I let myself in," Ballard said. "Lock Picking 101."

"It's a good skill to have. Meantime, I'm kind of busy here. Just got a search warrant I need to figure out how to execute without my suspect finding out. What do you want, Detective Ballard?"

"I want in."

"In?"

"On Daisy Clayton."

Bosch considered her for a moment. She was attractive, maybe midthirties, with brown, sun-streaked hair cut at the shoulders and a slim, athletic build. She was wearing off-duty clothes. The night before, she had been in work clothes that made her seem more formidable—a must in the LAPD, where Bosch knew female detectives were often treated like office secretaries.

Ballard also had a deep tan, which to Bosch was at odds with the idea of someone who worked the graveyard shift. Most of all he was impressed that it had been only twelve hours since she had surprised him at the file cabinets in the Hollywood detective bureau and she already appeared to have caught up to him and what he was doing.

"I talked to your old partner, Lucy," Ballard said. "She gave me her blessing. It is a Hollywood Station case, after all."

"Was—till RHD took it," Bosch said. "They have standing now, not Hollywood."

"And what's your standing? You're out of the LAPD. Doesn't seem to be any link to the town of San Fernando that I could see in the book."

In his capacity as an SFPD reserve officer for the past three years, Bosch had largely been working on a backlog of cold cases of all kinds—murders, rapes, assaults. But the work was part-time.

"They give me a lot of freedom up here," Bosch said. "I work these cases and I also work my own. Daisy Clayton's one of my own. You could say I have a vested interest. That's my standing."

"And I have twelve boxes of shake cards at Hollywood Station," Ballard said.

Bosch nodded. He was even more impressed. She had somehow figured out exactly what he had gone to Hollywood for. As he studied her, he decided it wasn't all a tan. She had a mix of races in her skin. He guessed that she was probably half white, half Polynesian.

"I figure between the two of us, we could get through them in a couple nights," Ballard said.

There was the offer. She wanted in and would give Bosch what he was looking for in trade.

"The shake cards are a long shot," he said. "Truth is, I've run the string out on the case. I was hoping there might be something in the cards."

"That's surprising," Ballard said. "I heard you're the kind of guy who never lets the string run out—your old partner called you a dog with a bone."

Bosch didn't know what to say to that. He shrugged.

Ballard got up and walked toward him down the aisle between the shelves.

"Sometimes it's slow, sometimes it isn't," she said. "I'm going to start looking through the cards tonight. Between calls. Anything in particular I should look for?"

Bosch paused but knew he needed to make a decision. Trust her or keep her on the outside.

"Vans," he said. "Look for work vans, guys who carry chemicals maybe."

"For transporting her," she said.

"For the whole thing."

"It said in the book the guy took her home or to a motel. Some place with a bathtub. For the bleaching."

Bosch shook his head.

"No, he didn't use a bathtub," he said.

She stared at him, waiting, not asking the obvious question of how he knew.

"All right, come with me," he finally said.

He got up and led her out of the cell and back to the door to the Public Works yard.

"You looked at the book and the photos, right?" he said.

"Yes," she said. "Everything that was digitized."

They walked into the yard, which was a large open-air square surrounded by walls. Along the back wall there were four bays delineated by tool racks and workbenches where city equipment and vehicles were maintained and repaired. Bosch led Ballard into one of these.

"You saw the mark on the body?"

"The A-S-P?"

"Right. But they got the meaning of it wrong. The original detectives. They went down a spiral with it and it was all wrong."

He went to a workbench and reached up to a shelf where there was a large, translucent plastic tub with a blue snap-on top. He brought it down and held it out to her.

"Twenty-five-gallon container," Bosch said. "Daisy was five-two, a hundred and five pounds. Small. He put her in one of these, then put in the bleach as needed. He didn't use a bathtub."

Ballard studied the container. Bosch's explanation was plausible but not conclusive.

"That's a theory," she said.

"No theory," he said.

He put the container down on the floor so he could unsnap the top. He then lifted the tub up and angled it so she could see into it. He reached inside and pointed to a manufacturer's seal stamped into the plastic at the bottom. It was a two-inch circle with the A-S-P reading horizontally and vertically in the center.

"A-S-P," he said. "American Storage Products or American Soft Plastics. Same company, two names. The killer put her in one of these. He didn't need a bathtub or a motel. One of these and a van."

Ballard reached into the container and ran a finger over the manufacturer's seal. Bosch knew she was drawing the same conclusion he had. The logo was stamped into the plastic on the underside of the tub, creating a ridged impression on the inside. If Daisy's skin had been pressed against the ridges, the logo would have left its mark.

Ballard pulled her arm out and looked up from the tub to Bosch.

"How'd you figure this out?" she asked.

"I thought like he did," Bosch said.

"Let me guess, these are untraceable."

"They make them in Gardena, ship them to retailers everywhere. They do some direct sales to commercial accounts but as far as individual sales go, forget it. You can get these at every Target and Walmart in the country."

"Well, shit."

"Yeah."

Bosch snapped the top back on the tub and was about to return it to the high shelf.

"Can I take it?" Ballard asked.

Bosch turned to her. He knew he could replace it and that she could easily get her own. He guessed it was a move to draw him further into a partnership. If he gave her something, then it meant they were working together.

He handed the tub over.

"It's yours," he said.

"Thank you," she said.

She looked at the open gate to the Public Works yard.

"Okay, so I start tonight on the shakes," she said.

Bosch nodded.

"Where were they?" he asked.

"In storage," Ballard said. "Nobody wanted to throw them out."

"I figured. It was smart."

"What were you going to do if you found them still in the file cabinets?"

"I don't know. Probably ask Money if I could hang around and look through them."

"Were you just going to look at cards from the day or week of the murder? The month maybe?"

"No, all of them. Whatever they still had. Who's to say the guy who did this didn't get FI-ed a couple years before or a year after?"

Ballard nodded.

"No stone uncovered. I get it."

"That make you change your mind? It'll be a lot of work."

"Nope."

"Good."

"Well, I'm gonna go. Might even go in early to get started."

"Happy hunting. If I can come by, I will. But I have a search warrant to execute."

"Right."

"Otherwise, call me if you find something."

He reached into a pocket and produced a business card with his cell number on it.

"Copy that," she said.

Ballard walked off, holding the container in front of her by the indented grips on either side. As Bosch watched, she made a smooth U-turn and came back to him.

"Lucy Soto said you know Daisy's mother," she said. "Is that the standing you said you had?"

"I guess you could say that," Bosch said.

"Where's the mother—if I want to talk to her?"

"My house. You can talk to her anytime."

"You live with her?"

"She's staying with me. It's temporary. Eighty-six-twenty Woodrow Wilson."

"Okay. Got it."

Ballard turned again and walked off. Bosch watched her go. She made no further U-turns.

6

Bosch went back into the jail to get the search warrant and to close and lock the cold-case cell. He then crossed First Street and entered the SFPD detective bureau through the side door off the parking lot. He saw two of the unit's full-time detectives at their workstations. Bella Lourdes was the senior detective most often paired with Bosch when his investigations took him out into the streets. She had a soft, motherly look that camouflaged her skills and toughness. Oscar Luzon was older than Lourdes but the most recent transfer to the detective unit. He had a sedentary thickness settling in and liked wearing his badge on a chain around his neck like a narc instead of on his belt. Otherwise, it might not be seen. Danny Sisto, the third member of the team, was not present.

Bosch checked Captain Trevino's office and found the door open and the detective commander behind his desk. He looked up from some paperwork at Bosch.

"How'd it go?" Trevino asked.

"Signed, sealed, delivered," Bosch said, holding the warrant up as proof. "You want to get everybody in the war room to talk about how we do this?"

"Yeah, bring Bella and Oscar in. Sisto's out at a crime scene, so he won't make it. I'll pull somebody in from patrol."

"What about LAPD?"

"Let's figure it out first and then I'll call Foothill and make it a captain-to-captain thing."

Trevino was picking up the phone to call the watch office as he spoke. Bosch ducked back out and used the warrant to signal Lourdes and Luzon to the war room. Bosch went in, took a yellow pad off the supply table and sat at one end of the oval meeting table. The so-called war room was really a multipurpose room. It was used for training classes, as a lunchroom, as an emergency command post, and on occasion as a place to strategize investigations and tactics with the whole detective squad — all five members of it.

Bosch sat down and flipped over the cover sheet of the warrant so he could reread the probable-cause section he had composed. It was drawn from a fourteen-year-old murder case. The victim was Cristobal Vega, fifty-two, who was shot once in the back of the head while he was walking his dog up his street to Pioneer Park. Vega was a veteran gang member, a shot caller for Varrio San Fer 13, one of the oldest and most violent gangs in the San Fernando Valley.

His death was a shock to the tiny town of San Fernando because he was well known within the community after having publicly adopted a Godfather-like presence, deciding neighborhood disputes, contributing major funds to local churches and schools, and even delivering food baskets to the needy during the holidays.

It was a good-guy disguise that cloaked a thirty-plus-year run as a gangster. On the inside of the VSF, he was notoriously violent and known by the moniker Uncle Murda. He moved with two bodyguards at all times and rarely strayed from SanFer turf, because he had been "green-lit" by all surrounding gangs as a result of his leadership position and planning of violent forays into other turf. The Vineland Boyz wanted him dead. The Pacas wanted him dead. Pacoima Flats wanted him dead. And so on.

The killing of Uncle Murda was also surprising because Vega had been caught on the street alone. He had a handgun tucked into the waist of his sweatpants but had apparently thought he was safe to duck out of his fortified home and take his dog to the park shortly after dawn. He never made it. He was found facedown on the sidewalk a block short of the park. His assassin had approached so stealthily from behind that Vega had not even pulled the gun from his waistband.

Though Vega was a hood and a killer himself, the SFPD investigation into his murder had initially been intense. But no witness to the shooting was ever found and the only evidence recovered was the .38 caliber bullet removed during autopsy from the victim's brain. No competing gang from the area took credit for the kill, and graffiti that either lamented or celebrated Vega's demise offered no clue as to who or what gang had carried out the hit.

The case went cold and detectives who were assigned due-diligence checks on it each year did not muster a lot of enthusiasm. It was clearly a case where the victim's death was not seen as much of a loss to society. The world was doing just fine without Uncle Murda.

But when Bosch opened the files as part of his cold-case review, he took a different approach. He had always operated according to the axiom that everybody counts in this world or nobody counts. This belief dictated that he must give each case and each victim his best effort. The fact that Uncle Murda had gotten his moniker because of his willingness to carry out the deadly business of the VSF did not deter Bosch from wanting to find his killer. In Bosch's book, nobody should be able to come up behind a man on a sidewalk at dawn, put a bullet in his brain, and then disappear into the shadows of time. There was a murderer out there. He might have killed since and he might kill again. Bosch was coming for him.

The time of death was determined by various factors. Vega's wife said he had gotten up at six a.m. and taken the dog out the door about twenty minutes later. The coroner could only narrow it down to the 100 minutes between then and eight a.m., which was when his body was discovered by a resident near the park. Two canvasses by detectives in the neighborhood produced not a single resident who reported hearing the shot, leading to the conclusion that the shooter might have used a silencer on his weapon—or the entire neighborhood did not want to cooperate with police.

While there were many handicaps in the investigation of years-old cases—loss of evidence, witnesses, crime scenes—the element of time could also be advantageous. Bosch always looked for ways to turn time in his favor.

In the Cristobal Vega investigation, a lot had happened in the fourteen years since the murder. Many of the gangsters in the VSF and its rivals had gone to prison for various crimes, including murder. Some had gone straight and cut ties with the life. These were the people Bosch focused on, using database searches and conversations with gang unit officers in the SFPD and from nearby LAPD divisions to produce two lists of gangsters in prison or believed to be in the straight life.

Over the previous year, he had made numerous prison stops and conducted dozens of visits to the homes and workplaces of men who had left their gang affiliations behind. Each conversation was tailored to the circumstances of the man he was visiting but in each instance questioning casually moved toward the unsolved killing of Cristobal Vega.

Most of the conversations were dead ends. The subject either maintained the code of silence or had no knowledge of the Vega killing. But eventually pieces of information started to create the mosaic. When he heard more than three denials of involvement from members of the same gang he moved that gang off the suspect list. Eventually he had scratched every one of the SanFer rivals off the list. It wasn't conclusive but it was enough to turn his focus inward at Vega's own gang.

Bosch eventually struck pay dirt in the rear parking lot of a discount shoe store in Alhambra, east of Los Angeles. The store was where a man named Martin Perez, a reformed San-Fer, worked as an inventory manager far away from the turf he once trod. Perez was forty-one years old and had shed his gang affiliation twelve years earlier. Though he had been carried in gang unit intel files as a hard-core member of the SanFers since he was sixteen, he had escaped the life with several arrests on his record but no convictions. He had never been to prison and had spent only a few days here and there in county jail.

The files Bosch reviewed contained color photos of the tattoos that adorned most parts of Perez's body during his active years. Included in these was an RIP UNCLE MURDA ink job on his neck. This put him high on the list of men Bosch wanted to talk to.

Bosch staked out the shoe store's parking lot and spotted Perez stepping out back to smoke a cigarette while on a three p.m. break. Through a pair of binoculars Bosch confirmed that Perez still carried the tattoo on his neck. He noted the time of the break and then drove away.

The next day he came back shortly before break time. He was dressed in blue jeans and a denim work shirt with permanent stains on it and carried a soft pack of Marlboro reds in the breast pocket. When he saw Perez behind the shop, he casually joined him, holding a cigarette up and asking if he could borrow a light. Perez flicked a lighter and Bosch leaned in to ignite his smoke.

Leaning back away, Bosch mentioned the tattoo he had just seen up close and asked how Uncle Murda died. Perez responded by saying that Uncle Murda was a good man who had been set up by his own people.

"How come?" Bosch asked.

"Because he got greedy," Perez said.

Bosch pushed no further. He finished his cigarette—the first he had smoked in years—and thanked Perez for the light, then walked away.

That night, Bosch knocked on the door of Perez's apartment. He was accompanied by Bella Lourdes. This time he identified himself, as did Lourdes, and told Perez he had a problem. He pulled his phone and played a snippet of the conversation they had shared while smoking behind the shoe store. Bosch explained that Perez had knowledge about a gang murder but had deliberately withheld it from authorities. This was obstruction of justice—a crime—not to mention conspiracy to commit murder, which would be the charges he would face unless he agreed to cooperate.

Perez took the option of cooperating, but he did not want to go to the San Fernando Police Department lest he be spotted in the old neighborhood by someone he used to run with. Bosch made a call to an old friend who worked in the Sheriff's Department homicide unit in Whittier and arranged to borrow an interview room for a couple hours.

The threat of charges against Perez was largely a bluff by Bosch, but it worked. Perez was deathly afraid of the L.A. County jail and the California prison system. He said both were well stocked with members of the *eMe* — the Mexican Mafia — which had a strong alliance with the VSF and was known for its brutal crimes against those who snitched or were perceived to be vulnerable to law enforcement pressure to flip. Perez believed that he would be marked for death whether he snitched or not. He chose to put everything on the table in hopes of convincing Bosch and Lourdes that he was not the killer but knew who was.

The story Perez told was as old as the crime of murder itself. Vega had risen to a place of power in the gang, and absolute power corrupts absolutely. He was taking more than his share in proceeds from the SanFers' criminal enterprises and was also known to force sexual relations on young women associated with members on the lower tiers of the gang. Many of those young *vatos* despised him. One named Tranquillo Cortez plotted against him. According to Perez, he was the nephew of Vega's wife and was incensed by Vega's greed and very public infidelities.

Perez was in Cortez's clique within the gang and was privy to part of the planning but insisted he was not present when Cortez killed Vega. The case had long been considered the perfect hit within the SFPD, because no evidence other than a bullet had been left behind. So this was where Bosch and Lourdes pressed Perez, asking many questions about the gun, its ownership, and its present whereabouts.

Perez said the gun was Cortez's own gun but had no information on how Cortez came to own it. As far as what happened to the weapon after the murder, he had no idea because he soon separated himself from the gang and left the Valley. But Perez did provide a piece of information that gave Bosch his focus. He said that Cortez had equipped the gun with a homemade silencer. This fit with the original investigation.

Bosch zeroed in, asking how Cortez had made the silencer. Perez said that at the time, Cortez worked in an uncle's muffler shop in nearby Pacoima, and he had machined it out of the same piping and internal sound-suppressing materials used in motorcycle mufflers. He did this after hours and without his uncle's knowledge. Perez also acknowledged that he and two other fellow gang members were with Cortez in the shop when he tested his creation by attaching it to his gun and firing a couple of shots into the back wall of the muffler shop.

After the interview with Perez, the priority for the investigators became confirming as much of his story as possible. Lourdes was able to nail down the link between Cortez and Vega's wife. She was his father's sister. She also determined that Cortez's standing within the VSF had risen over the past fourteen years and he was now a shot caller like the man he was suspected of assassinating. Meanwhile, Bosch confirmed that Pacoima Tire & Muffler, located on San Fernando Road in Los Angeles, was previously owned by Helio Cortez, the suspect's uncle, and that the new owner's name was not in any gang intel files of the San Fernando and Los Angeles police departments. Other details were substantiated and it all added up to enough probable cause for Bosch to go see a judge for a search warrant.

He had that now and it was time to move the case forward.

Lourdes and Luzon were the first to enter the war room. Soon they were followed by Trevino and then Sergeant Irwin Rosenberg, a dayside watch commander. In accordance with department protocol, all search warrants were served with a uniformed presence, and Rosenberg, a veteran street cop with high people skills, would coordinate that side of things. Everyone took seats around the oval table.

"What, no doughnuts?" Rosenberg asked.

The table was usually where the spread of food donated by citizens ended up. Almost every morning there were doughnuts or breakfast burritos. Rosenberg's disappointment was shared by all.

"All right, let's get this going," Trevino said. "What've we got, Harry? You should bring Irwin up to speed."

"This is the Cristobal Vega case," Bosch said. "The murder of Uncle Murda fourteen years ago. We have a search warrant allowing us to enter Pacoima Tire & Muffler on San Fernando Road and search for bullets fired into the rear wall of the main garage fourteen years ago. This place is on LAPD turf, so we will coordinate with them. We want to do it as unobtrusively as possible so word doesn't get back to our suspect or anybody else with the SanFers. We want to keep this quiet until it's time to hopefully make an arrest."

"It's going to be impossible with the SanFers," Rosenberg said. "They have eyes all over the place."

Bosch nodded.

"We know that," he said. "Bella's been working on a cover story. We just need to buy a couple days. If we find slugs, then I have it greased down at the lab. They'll ASAP the comparison to the bullet that killed Vega. If there's a match, we'll be good to go at our suspect."

"Who is the suspect?" Rosenberg asked.

Bosch hesitated. He trusted Rosenberg but it was not good case management to discuss suspects—especially when there was an informant involved.

"Never mind," Rosenberg said quickly. "I don't need to know. So, do you want to keep this to one car, two uniforms?"

"At the most," Bosch said.

"Done. We've got the new SUV in the yard that just came in. Hasn't been decaled yet. We could use that, not advertise we're from SFPD. That might help."

Bosch nodded. He had seen the SUV in the Public Works yard by the old jail. It had arrived from the manufacturer in black-and-white paint but the SFPD identifiers had not been applied to its doors and rear hatch. It could blend in with the LAPD vehicles and help disguise that the search was part of an SFPD investigation. It would further insulate the investigation from the VSF.

"In case we have to take out the whole wall, we'll have a Public Works crew with us," Bosch said. "They'll be using an unmarked truck."

"So what's our cover?" Luzon asked.

"Burglary," Lourdes said. "If anybody asks, we say somebody broke in during the night and there's a crime scene. It should do it. The place is no longer owned by the suspect's uncle. As far as we can tell, the new owner is clean, and we expect his full cooperation with both the search and the cover story."

"Good," Trevino said. "When do we go?"

"Tomorrow morning," Bosch said. "Right when the place opens at seven. With any luck we'll be in and out before most gangsters in the neighborhood open their eyes for the day."

"Okay," Trevino said. "Let's rally here at six and be in Pacoima when they open the doors."

The meeting broke up after that and Bosch followed Lourdes back to her workstation.

"Hey, I had a visitor to my cell earlier," he said. "Did you send her over?"

Lourdes shook her head.

"No, nobody came in here," she said. "I've been doing reports all day."

Bosch nodded. He wondered about Ballard and how she knew where to find him. His guess was that Lucia Soto had told her.

He knew he would find out soon enough.

7

Bosch got home early. He smelled cooking as soon as he opened the door, and found Elizabeth Clayton in the kitchen. She was sautéing chicken in butter and garlic.

"Hey," Bosch said. "Smells good."

"I wanted to make you something," she said.

They awkwardly hugged while she was in front of the stove. When Bosch first met her, she was an addict trying to bury her daughter's murder under a mountain of pills. She had had a shaved head, weighed ninety pounds, and would have willingly traded sex for thirty milligrams of guilt- and memory-blurring oxycodone.

Seven months later, she was clean and had put on twenty pounds, and her sandy-blond hair was long enough to frame the pretty face that had emerged during recovery. But the guilt and memories were still there at the edge of darkness and threatening every day.

"That's great," he said. "I'm going to clean up first, okay?"

"It'll be a half hour," she said. "I have to boil the noodles."

Bosch walked down the hallway, past Elizabeth's room, and into his own. He took off his work clothes and got into the shower. As the water cascaded down on his head, he thought about cases and victims. The woman cooking his dinner was a victim of the fallout that comes from murder, her daughter taken in a way too horrible to contemplate. Bosch thought he had rescued Elizabeth the year before. He had helped her through addiction and now she was straight and healthy, but the addiction had been what buffered reality and kept that contemplation away. He had promised her he would solve her daughter's killing but now found that he could not talk to her about the case without causing her the kind of pain she used to vanquish with pills. He was left with the question of whether he had rescued her at all.

After showering he shaved, because he knew it might be a couple days before he got the next chance. He was finishing up when he heard Elizabeth call him to dinner.

In the months since Elizabeth had moved in, Bosch had returned the dining room to its rightful purpose. He had moved his laptop and the files from the cases he was working into his bedroom, where he had a folding table set up. He didn't think she should be constantly reminded of murder, especially when he wasn't around.

She had place settings across from each other at the table and the food on another plate between them. She served him. There were two glasses of water. No alcohol.

"Looks great," Bosch said.

"Well, let's hope it tastes great," she said.

They ate silently for a few minutes and Bosch complimented her. The chicken had a good garlic kick that tasted great going down. He knew it would kick back later on but didn't mention that.

"How was group?" he asked.

"Mark Twain dropped out," she said.

She always referred to others in her daily group therapy meetings by code names drawn from famous people they reminded her of. Mark Twain had white hair and a bushy mustache. There was a Cher, an Albert (as in Einstein), an OJ, a Lady Gaga, and a Gandhi, who was also referred to as Ben, as in Ben Kingsley, the actor who won an Oscar for portraying him.

"Permanently?" Bosch asked.

"Looks like it," she said. "He had a slip and went back into lockdown."

"That's too bad."

"Yeah. I liked hearing his stories. They were funny."

More silence passed between them. Bosch tried to think of something to say or ask. The awkwardness of the relationship had grown to be the main part of it. Bosch had long known that inviting her to use a room in his house had been a mistake. He wasn't sure what he had thought would come of it. Elizabeth reminded Bosch of his former wife, Eleanor, but that was only a physical resemblance. Elizabeth Clayton was a badly damaged person with dark memories to work through and a difficult path ahead.

It had been only a temporary invitation—an until-you-get-on-your-feet thing. Bosch had converted a large storage room off the hallway into a small bedroom and furnished it with purchases from Ikea. But it had been almost six months and Bosch was unsure that Elizabeth would or could ever stand on her feet alone again. The call of her addiction was always there. The memory of her daughter was like a malignant ghost that followed her. And she had nowhere to go, except maybe back up to Modesto, where she had lived until her world fell apart with a midnight call from the LAPD.

Meantime, Bosch had alienated his daughter, who had not been consulted before he extended the invitation. She was away at college and came home less and less already, but the addition of Elizabeth Clayton to the household served to stop all visitation. Now Bosch saw Maddie only when he ventured down to Orange County to grab a quick breakfast or late dinner with her. On the last visit, she had announced that she planned to stay the summer in the house she rented with three other students near campus. Bosch took the news as a direct reaction to having Elizabeth in his house.

"I have to work tonight," Bosch said.

"I thought you said you had that search warrant thing tomorrow morning," Elizabeth said.

"I do but this is something else. It's about Daisy."

He said nothing further until he could gauge her response. A few moments went by and she didn't try to change the subject.

"There's a Hollywood detective who's interested in the case," he said. "She came to me today and asked questions. She's on the late show and is going to work it when she has time."

"'The late show'?" Elizabeth asked.

"That's what they call the midnight shift at Hollywood Division, because of all the crazy stuff that happens there in the middle of the night. Anyway, she found some old records I'd been looking for: cards where patrol officers took names of people on the street, people they stopped or were suspicious of."

"Was Daisy one of them?"

"Probably, but that's not why I want to see them. I want to see who else was floating around Hollywood at that time. It could lead to something."

"Okay."

"Anyway, there are twelve boxes of them. We'll do what we can tonight and then I have the search warrant in the morning. It could be a couple nights going down there."

"Okay. I hope you find something."

"The detective—her name is Ballard—asked about you. She said she might want to meet with you. Would that be okay?"

"Of course. I don't really know anything that can help but I will talk to anybody about Daisy."

Bosch nodded. It had been more than they had said about the case in weeks and he worried it would send Elizabeth into a dark spiral of depression if he pushed it further.

He checked his watch. It wasn't quite eight o'clock.

"I might take a nap for a couple hours before I head down there," he said. "That okay?"

"Yes, you should," she said. "I'll clean all this up and try to be quiet."

"Don't worry about it. I doubt I'll sleep. I'll just rest."

Fifteen minutes later Bosch was on his back, looking up at the ceiling in his bedroom. He could hear the water running in the kitchen and the dishes being stacked in the rack next to the sink.

He had set an alarm but knew he wouldn't be able to sleep.

BALLARD

8

Ballard got to Hollywood Division three hours before her eleven p.m. shift started so she could begin work on the shake cards. She first entered the main station, grabbed the late show rover out of its charger, and took it with her back across the parking lot to the outbuilding, where she had left the boxes lined in the hallway. There was nobody in the gym or martial arts training room. She found a work space in one of the storage rooms where wooden desks predating the last renovation of the station were still stored. Despite what Bosch had said earlier, Ballard was tempted to go right to the box of field interview cards from the time of the Daisy Clayton murder. Maybe she would get lucky and an obvious suspect would emerge from a 3 x 5 card. But she knew that Bosch's plan was the right one. To be thorough she should start at the beginning and move chronologically forward.

The first box of shake cards had dates beginning in January 2006, fully three years before the Clayton murder. She put the box on the floor next to the desk she was using and started pulling out four-inch stacks at a time. She gave each card a quick glance front and back, focusing on the location and time of the stop, checking to see if the interviewee was a male, and then examining the details further if warranted.

It took her two hours to get through the first box. Out of all the cards she examined, she put aside three for follow-up and discussion with Bosch and one just for herself. In the process, she reaffirmed her long-held belief about Hollywood being a final destination for many of society's freaks and losers. Card after card contained records of interviews with individuals who were aimlessly roaming the streets, looking for whatever grim opportunity presented itself. Many were outsiders trying to buy drugs or sex, and the police stop was designed to dissuade them. Others were permanent denizens—whether predators or prey—of the Hollywood streets with no seeming plan to change their situation.

Along the way, Ballard got to know something about the cops who conducted the field interviews. Some were verbose, some were profoundly grammatically challenged, some used codes, like Adam Henry (asshole), to describe the citizens they were interviewing. Some obviously didn't care to write FI cards and kept things to a minimum. Some were able to keep their sense of humor despite the circumstances of their job and the view it gave them of humanity.

The blank side of the card was where the most telling information was found and Ballard read these mini-reports with an almost anthropological interest for what they said about Hollywood and society at large. She put one card aside for herself simply because she liked what the officer had written.

Subject is a human tumbleweed
Goes where the wind blows him
Will blow away tomorrow
Nobody will miss him

The officer was named on the cards as T. Farmer. Ballard found herself looking for his FI cards so she could read more of his elegiac street reports.

The three cards she set aside for follow-up were all for white males who were deemed "tourists" by the officers who made the stop. This meant they were outsiders who came into Hollywood to look for something, in the case of these three men, most likely sex. They had not committed any crime when stopped and interviewed, so the officers were circumspect in what they wrote. But it was clear from the location, time, and tenor of the interviews that the officers suspected the men were trolling for prostitutes. One man was on foot, one man was in a car, and the third was in what was described as a work van. Ballard would run their names and license plates through the computer and law enforcement databases to see if there was any record or activity that warranted a closer look.

Ballard was halfway through the second box when her rover squawked at exactly midnight. It was Lieutenant Munroe.

"I missed you at roll call, Ballard."

She was not required to attend roll call but she appeared so often that it was noticed when she didn't.

"Sorry about that. I'm working on something and I lost track of time. Anything I should know?"

"No, all quiet. But your boyfriend from last night is here. Should I send him back?"

Ballard paused before keying the mic and answering. She assumed her visitor was Bosch. She knew that complaining about Munroe calling him her boyfriend would be a complete waste of time and would cost her more than she would gain from it.

She keyed the mic.

"I'm not in detectives. Hold my 'boyfriend' there. I'll come get him."

"Roger that."

"Hey, L-T. We have a PO on Hollywood roster named T. Farmer?"

If Farmer was still in the division, he must work dayside now. She knew everybody on the night shifts.

It was a few moments before Munroe responded.

"Not anymore. He went EOW right before you got here."

End of watch. Ballard suddenly remembered that when she was reassigned to Hollywood three years earlier, the whole division was mourning the death of one of its officers. It had been a suicide. She now realized it had been Farmer.

Ballard felt an invisible punch to the chest. She keyed the mic.

"Copy that."

9

Ballard decided to keep the review of the field interview cards close to the source. She brought Bosch to the storage room and set him up at one of the old desks, where it was less likely that other Hollywood officers would see him working with her and raise questions about it. She called Lieutenant Munroe on the private watch office number and told him where she would be if needed.

Bosch and Ballard decided to split reading duties rather than have Bosch back-read the cards Ballard had already gone through. It was the first sign of trust between them, a belief that each could rely on the other's assessment of the cards. And it would make the process faster.

Ballard was at a desk positioned perpendicular to Bosch's and this allowed her to watch him head-on, while he would have to turn and be more obvious about attempting to observe her. At first she surreptitiously kept an eye on him and in doing so ascertained that his process was different. His rate of putting cards aside for further consideration was far quicker than hers. At some point, he noticed that she was watching him.

"Don't worry," he said without looking up from his work.

"I'm employing a two-step approach. First a big net, then a smaller net."

Ballard just nodded, a bit embarrassed that she had been caught.

She soon started her own two-step process and stopped paying attention to Bosch, realizing that she was only slowing her own work down by watching him. After a long stretch of silence and after putting a large stack of cards into the no-interest pile, Ballard spoke.

"Can I ask you something?" she began.

"What if I said no?" Bosch replied. "You'd ask anyway."

"How did Daisy's mother end up living in your house?"

"It's a long story, but she needed a place to stay. I had a room."

"So this is not a romantic thing?"

"No."

"But you let this stranger stay in your house."

"Sort of. I met her on an unrelated case. I helped her out of a jam and then I found out about Daisy. I told her I'd look into the case and she could use the room I had while I investigated. She's from Modesto. I assume that if we close this thing, I'll get my room back and she'll go home."

"You couldn't do that if you were with the LAPD."

"There's a lot I couldn't do if I were still with the LAPD. But I'm not."

They both went back to the cards but almost immediately Ballard spoke again.

"I still want to talk to her," she said.

"I told her that," Bosch said. "Anytime you like."

A half hour went by and they both managed to finish off the cards in their respective boxes. Bosch went out into the hallway and brought a fresh box in for Ballard and then repeated the process for himself.

"How long can you do this?" Ballard asked.

"You mean tonight?" Bosch asked. "Till about five thirty. I have a thing at six up in the Valley. It may run through most of the day. If it does, I'll be back tomorrow night."

"When do you sleep?"

"When I can."

They were ten minutes into their next boxes when Ballard's radio squawked. Ballard responded and Munroe told her that a detective was requested on the burglary of an occupied dwelling on Sunset Boulevard.

Ballard looked at the stack of FI cards in front of her and radioed back.

"You sure they need a detective, L-T?"

"They asked. You in the middle of something or what?"

"No, I'm rolling now."

"Roger that. Lemme know what you've got out there."

Ballard stood up and looked at Bosch.

"I need to go and I can't leave you here," she said.

"You sure?" he asked. "I'll stay here and keep chopping wood."

"No, you're not LAPD. I can't leave you here unsupervised. I'd take a hit for that if someone came in and found you here."

"Whatever. So, what do I do, go with you?"

Ballard thought about that. It would work.

"You can do that," she said. "Take a stack of those with you and sit in the car while I check this call out. Hopefully, it's not a long one."

Bosch reached down into the box next to his desk and used two hands to pull out a good-size stack of cards.

"Let's go," he said.

The burglary call was less than five minutes from the station. The address was familiar to Ballard but she did not place it until they arrived and saw that it was a strip bar called Sirens on Sunset. And it was still open, which made the question of burglary a bit baffling.

There was one patrol car blocking the valet zone. Ballard pulled in behind it. She knew two units had already responded and assumed the other car was in the alley behind the station.

"This should be interesting," Bosch said.

"Not for you," Ballard said. "You wait here."

"Yes, ma'am."

"I hope this is just bullshit and I'll be right back out. Start thinking about code seven."

"You're hungry?"

"Not right now but I'm gonna need a lunch break."

Ballard grabbed the rover out of the console charger and got out of the car.

"What's open?" Bosch asked.

"Almost nothing," she said.

She closed the door and headed toward the front door of Sirens.

The interior entry area was dimly lit in red. There was a pay station with a bouncer and cashier, and a velvet-roped channel that led to an arched doorway to the dance floor. Ballard could see three small stages outlined in red below faux Tiffany atrium ceilings. There were women in various stages of undress on the stages but very few customers. Ballard checked her watch. It was 2:40 a.m. and the bar was open until 4. Ballard badged the bouncer.

"Where are the officers?" she asked.

"I'll walk you back," the bouncer said.

He opened a door that matched the walls in red-velvet paisley and led her down a dark hallway to the open door of a well-lit office. He then headed back to the front.

Three officers were crowded into the small room in front of a desk where a man sat. Ballard nodded. The blue suiters were Dvorek in charge and Herrera and Dyson, whom Ballard knew well because they were a rare female team, and the women on the late show often took code seven together. Herrera was the senior lead officer and had four hash marks on her sleeves. Her partner had one. Both women wore their hair short to avoid having it grabbed and pulled by suspects. Ballard knew that most days they worked out in the gym after their shifts and their shoulders and upper arms showed the results. They could hold their own in a confrontation and the word on Dyson was that she liked to start them.

"Detective Ballard, glad you could make it," Dvorek said. "This is Mr. Peralta, manager of this fine establishment, and he requested your services."

Ballard looked at the man behind the desk. He was in his fifties, overweight, with slicked-back hair and long, sharply edged sideburns. He wore a garish purple vest over a black collared shirt. On the wall behind his chair was a framed poster of a naked woman using a stripper pole to strategically cover her privates, but not quite enough to hide that her pubic hair had been trimmed to the shape of a small heart. To his right was a video monitor that showed sixteen camera angles of the stages, bars, and exits of the club. Ballard saw herself in one of the squares from a camera over her right shoulder.

"What can I do for you, sir?" she asked.

"This is like a dream come true," Peralta said. "I didn't realize the LAPD was almost all women. You want a part-time job?"

"Sir, do you have a problem that requires police involvement or not?" Ballard replied.

"I do," Peralta said. "I've got a problem—someone is going to break in."

"Going to? Why would someone break in when they can walk in the front door?"

"You tell me. All I'm saying is, it's going down. Look at this."

He turned to the video monitor and pulled out a drawer beneath it, revealing a keyboard. He hit a few keys and the camera angles were replaced with a schematic of the premises.

"I've got every opening in the building wired," Peralta said. "Somebody's on the roof fucking with the skylights. They're going to come down through there."

Ballard leaned across the desk so she could see the screen better. It was showing breaches at two of the skylights over the stages.

"When did this happen?" she asked.

"Tonight," Peralta said. "Like an hour ago."

"Why would they break in?"

"Are you kidding me? This is a cash business, and I don't walk out of here at four thirty in the fucking morning with a cash bag under my arm. I'm not that stupid. Everything goes into the safe and then once, maybe twice, a week—in daylight—I come in to do the banking, and I have two guys you don't want to fuck with watching my back the whole time."

"Where's the safe?"

"You're standing on it."

Ballard looked down. The officers moved back toward the

walls of the room. There was an outline cut in the planked wood floor and a fingerhold for pulling open the trap door.

"Is it removable?" Ballard asked.

"Nope," Peralta said. "Set in concrete. They'd have to drill it—unless they knew the combo, and there are only three people who know that."

"So how much is in there?"

"I did the banking after the weekend, so it's going to be light tonight. About twelve thou in there right now and we'll get it up to sixteen when I close out the registers tonight."

Ballard assessed things, looked up, and caught Dvorek's eye and nodded.

"Okay," she said. "We're going to take a look around. Any cameras on the roof?"

"No," Peralta said. "Nothing up there."

"Any access?"

"Nothing from inside. You'd need a ladder on the outside."

"All right. I'll be back in after we check around. Where's the door to the alley?"

"Marv will take you."

Peralta reached under the desk and pushed a button to call his bouncer. Soon the big man from the velvet rope returned.

"Take them out the back, Marv," Peralta said. "To the alley."

A few minutes later Ballard was standing in the alley, assessing the roofline of the club. The building was freestanding with a flat roof about twenty feet up. There was no approach from the business on either side and no ladders or obvious means of getting up. Ballard checked behind her. The other side of the alley was contained by wood and concrete fences and bordered on a residential neighborhood.

"Can I borrow a light?" Ballard asked.

Dyson pulled her Pelican off her equipment belt and handed it to Ballard. It was a small but powerful flashlight. Ballard walked the length of the building, looking for upward access. She found a possible ascension point by the west corner. A cinder-block enclosure had been built to contain a row of city trash containers. It was about six feet high and was next to the downspout of a gutter that ran along the edge of the roofline. Ballard shone the light up the downspout and saw that it was secured to the exterior wall with brackets every few feet.

Dvorek came up behind her.

"There's your ladder," Ballard said.

"You going up?" Dvorek asked.

"Not on your life. I'm calling an airship. They'll light it up and if anybody's up there, we'll grab them coming down."

"Sounds like a plan."

"Put the sisters on the other corner just in case they have a ladder up there with them and decide to come down the other side. I'll get the air unit offline."

"Gotcha."

Ballard didn't want to radio for the airship, because a burglar could be monitoring LAPD frequencies. She had a working relationship with the tactical flight officer on the chopper that covered the city's west side on most nights. They often responded to the same calls. Ballard on the ground, Heather Rourke, the spotter, in the air with her pilot partner Dan Sumner. Ballard shot a text to Rourke.

You guys up?

Two minutes went by before there was a response.

Yup. Just cleared a pursuit of an H/R suspect. What's up RB?

Ballard knew that the Rourke-Sumner team would have high adrenaline after chasing down a car involved in a hit-and-run. She was glad they were free.

Need you to fly over Sirens strip bar 7171 Sunset. Light up the roof to see if we have suspects.
Roger that—ETA 3
Copy. Switch to Tac 5
Copy. Tac 5

In the event they had to speak by radio for expediency, the tactical channel was an unpublished frequency that wasn't readily obtained on the internet.

Ballard still had Dyson's light. She waved it to get the attention of the three officers at the other corner of the building. She put the light on her free hand and held up three fingers and twirled her hand in the air.

They waited. Ballard was pretty sure it was a fruitless exercise. If there had actually been someone up there, they most likely would have noticed the lights from the arrival of the patrol cars and made their escape when the officers entered the building. But checking out the roof with the airship should give some measure of satisfaction to Peralta. Ballard would then write up a recommendation to the detective commander to send out someone from the commercial burglary unit to check the roof in daylight for any signs of an attempted break-in.

Ballard heard the helicopter's approach and tucked in close to the rear wall of the building, next to the trash enclosure. She raised the rover and switched it to the tactical 5 frequency.

She waited. The alley smelled like booze and cigarettes. She breathed through her mouth.

Soon the powerful beam of the chopper washed over everything, turning night into day. Ballard raised the rover.

"Anything, Air six?"

She held the radio to her ear, hoping to hear the response over the sound of the airship rotor. She partially heard it. The tenor of Heather Rourke's voice told her more than the words she could make out. There was somebody on the roof.

"…suspects. Heading…corner…"

Ballard dropped the rover and pulled her weapon. She backed into the alley, raising her gun toward the roofline. The light from the chopper was blinding. Soon she saw movement and heard yelling, but she could not make out the words over the sound of the rotor. She saw someone sliding down the gutter's downspout. Halfway down he lost his grip and fell to the ground. Soon another body was coming down the pipe, and then another.

Ballard tracked the movement with her gun. Soon all three of the suspects started running down the alley.

"Police! Freeze it right there!"

Two of the fleeing figures stopped in their tracks. The third kept going and after reaching the end, turned left into the neighborhood.

Ballard started approaching the two who had stopped and already raised their hands. As she ordered them to their knees, Dyson blew by her, running, and continued down the alley after the third suspect. Herrera followed her younger partner but at a much slower pace.

As Ballard approached, her gun at the ready, she saw—

The two suspects kneeling on the ground were just kids.

"What the fuck?" Dvorek said as he came up next to her.

Ballard holstered her weapon and put her hand on Dvorek's arm to make him lower his. She walked around and shone the beam of Dyson's light on their faces. They were no older than fourteen. Both were white, both looked scared. They were wearing T-shirts and blue jeans.

She realized she had dropped her rover to the ground near the trash enclosure.

"I can't hear myself think," she called to Dvorek. "Advise the airship on tac five that we have a code four here and they can stay with A twenty-five's pursuit."

Dvorek went to his rover to make the call and soon the chopper headed south in the direction the third boy had run. Ballard held the light on the young faces in front of her. One boy lowered one of his hands to try to block the blinding light.

"Keep your hands up," Ballard ordered.

He complied.

Ballard looked at the two boys in front of her and had a good idea why they had been on the roof.

"You two almost just got yourselves killed, you know that?" she barked.

"We're sorry, we're sorry," one of them said meekly.

"What were you doing up there?"

"We were just looking around. We didn't—"

"Looking around? You mean looking down at naked women?"

In the cold, hard light of her beam Ballard could see their cheeks turn red with shame. But she knew it was shame at being caught and called on it by a woman, not shame at climbing onto a roof to look down through a skylight at women's bodies.

She glanced at Dvorek and saw a small smile on his face.

She realized that on some level he admired their ingenuity—boys will be boys—and she knew that in the world of men and women, there would never be a time when women were viewed and treated completely as equals.

"Are you going to have to tell our parents?" one of the boys asked.

Ballard lowered the light and headed back to pick up her rover.

"What do you think?" Dvorek asked her quietly as she passed him.

The question further revealed him.

"Your call," Ballard said. "I'm out of here."

10

There was one booth in Du-par's at the Farmers Market that afforded a view of the entire restaurant and its entrance. Ballard always took it when it was available, and most nights when she was able to get a real meal break, it was so late that the place was largely empty and she had her choice of the room.

She sat across from Bosch, who had ordered coffee only. He explained that there were almost always breakfast burritos or doughnuts at SFPD in the morning, and he intended to go there at six for a briefing before his team delivered the search warrant.

Ballard didn't hold back. She had skipped dinner the evening before and was famished. She matched Bosch's coffee but added a blue-plate special that included pancakes, eggs, and bacon. As she waited for the food, she asked about the stack of FI cards he had gone through in the car while she handled the call at Sirens.

"No keepers," Bosch said.

"You come across any written by a P.O. named Farmer?" she asked. "Good writer."

"I don't think so...but I wasn't checking too many names. Are you talking about Tim Farmer?"

"Yeah, you knew him?"

"I went to the academy with him."

"I didn't know he was that old."

Ballard immediately realized what she had said.

"Sorry," she said. "I mean, like, why was a guy who'd been around so long still on the street, you know?"

"Some guys can't give up the street," Bosch said. "Like some guys can't give up homicide work. You know he—"

"Yeah, I know. Why'd he do it?"

"Who knows? He was a month from retirement. I heard it was kind of a forced retirement—if he stayed, they were going to put him on a desk. So he put in his papers and during his last deployment period pulled the plug."

"That's a sad fucking story."

"Most suicides are."

"I liked the way he wrote. His observations on the shakes were like poetry."

"A lot of poets kill themselves."

"I guess."

A waiter brought her food and Ballard suddenly wasn't all that hungry. She was feeling sad about a man she had never met. She poured syrup over her short stack and started to eat anyway.

"So, did you stay in touch after the academy?" she asked.

"Not really," Bosch said. "We were close then, and there were class reunions, but we were on different tracks. It wasn't like now with social media and all of that Facebook stuff. He was up in the Valley and came to Hollywood after I'd left."

Ballard nodded and picked at her food. The pancakes were getting soggy and more unappetizing. She moved her fork to the eggs.

"I've been meaning to ask you about King and Carswell," she said. "I assume you or Soto talked to them at the start of this."

"Lucia did," Bosch said. "One of them, at least. King retired about five years ago and moved to East Bumfuck, Idaho— somewhere out in the woods with no phone and no internet. He went completely off the grid. She got the PO box where his pension checks go and sent him a letter asking for an interview on the case. She's still waiting for an answer. Carswell also retired and he took a gig as an investigator with the Orange County D.A. Lucia went down and talked to him but he wasn't a font of new information. He barely remembered the case and told her everything he did know was in the murder book. It didn't sound as though he wanted to talk about a case he didn't close. I'm sure you know the type."

"Yeah—'If I can't close it, nobody else can.' What about Adam Sands, the boyfriend. Either of you do a fresh interview?"

"We couldn't. He died in 2014 of an overdose."

Ballard nodded. It wasn't a surprising end for Sands but it was a disappointment because he could have been helpful in setting the scene that Daisy Clayton lived and died in and in providing the names of other runaways and acquaintances. Ballard was beginning to see why Bosch wanted to locate the field interview cards. It might be their only hope.

"Anything else?" she asked. "I take it Soto has the murder book. Anything not in the database that's important?"

"Not really," Bosch said. "King and Carswell weren't the extra-mile sort of guys. Carswell told Lucia they didn't put their notebooks in the murder book because everything was in the reports."

"I got that feeling about them when I was reading the book online."

"Speaking of which, I started a secondary book with what I've been doing."

"I'd like to see it."

"It's in my car. I'll bring it in when we get back. I guess you should keep it now that you have official standing."

"All right. I will. Thanks."

Bosch reached into an inside pocket of his jacket and pulled out a shake card. He slid it across the table for Ballard to read.

"I thought you said there were no keepers," she said.

"There weren't," he said. "That one's from earlier. Read it."

She did. The card was written at 3:30 a.m. on February 9, 2009, several months before Daisy Clayton's murder. The subject of the field interview was a man named John McMullen who was thirty-six years old at the time he was questioned at the intersection of Western and Franklin Avenues. McMullen had no criminal record. According to the card, he was driving a white Ford panel van marked with Bible quotes and religious sayings and registered to a city-licensed charitable foundation called the Moonlight Mission.

The card said the van was parked in a red zone while McMullen was on the nearby sidewalk accosting pedestrians and asking if they wanted to be saved by the grace of Jesus Christ. Those who demurred were treated to a verbal lashing that included dire predictions of their being left behind during the upcoming rapture.

There was more on the flip side of the card: "Subject refers to himself as John the Baptist. Cruises Hollywood in his van, looking for people to baptize."

Ballard flipped the card onto the table in front of Bosch.

"Okay," she said. "Why'd you wait to show me this now?"

"I wanted to check him out a little bit first," Bosch said. "I made some calls while you were in the strip club."

"And?"

"And the Moonlight Mission still exists and he's still there."

"Anything else?"

"The van—it's still registered to him and apparently still in service."

"Okay, but I have a stack back at the station of about twenty van stops. Why is this the one card you decided to steal?"

"Well, I didn't steal it. I'm showing it to you. How's that stealing?"

"I told you all the cards had to remain on LAPD property except that stack I let you take tonight."

"Okay, fine. I took one of the cards I read earlier because I thought maybe after your callout we'd cruise by the Moonlight Mission and see what it's all about. That's all."

She dropped her eyes to her plate and pushed the eggs around again with her fork. She didn't like the way she was acting, being so picky and by the book with Bosch.

"Look," Bosch said. "I know about you. I know you've been burned bad in the department. So was I. But I've never betrayed a partner, and over the years, I've had a lot of them."

Ballard looked up at him.

"Partner?" she said.

"On this case," Bosch said. "You said you wanted in. I let you in."

"It's not your case. It's an LAPD case."

"It belongs to whoever's working it."

Bosch took a sip of coffee, but she could tell by his reaction that it had gone cold. He turned to look back from the booth toward the kitchen, where the waitress was loitering, and held the mug up for more.

He then turned back to Ballard.

"Look, you want to work with me on it, then fine, let's work," he said. "If not, we work separately, and that would be too bad. But this territorial bullshit...that's why nothing ever gets done. Like the great man said, 'Can't we all just get along?'"

Ballard was about to bark back at him, but the waitress was suddenly at the table with the coffee pot, and she held her tongue while both mugs were topped off. In those few seconds she calmed and thought about what Bosch had just said.

"Okay," she said.

The waitress put a check down on the table and walked back toward the kitchen.

"Okay what?" Bosch said. "Which way do you want to go?"

Ballard reached over and grabbed the check.

"Let's go to the Moonlight Mission," she said.

When they got into Ballard's city ride, she used her cell to call Lieutenant Munroe and tell him she was back in service but pursuing an investigative lead and would be out of the station until further notice. Munroe asked what case she was working on and she put him off, saying it was just a loose end on a hobby case. She disconnected and started the car.

"You don't like him, do you?" Bosch said.

"I'm the only detective who has to report to a patrol lieu-tenant," Ballard said. "He's not really my boss but he likes to think he is. And look, about before? That callout to the strip club...it just sort of fired up my feral instincts. I shouldn't have said you stole the shake card, okay? I apologize."

"No need to. I get it."

"No, you don't. You couldn't. But I appreciate your saying so."

She pulled out of the empty Farmers Market parking lot onto Fairfax and headed north.

"Tell me about John the Baptist," she said. "Where are we go-ing and why?"

"The mission is on Cherokee near Selma—south of the Boulevard," Bosch said. "And something about this guy looking for people to baptize poked at me. Call it a hunch, whatever. But Daisy was washed in bleach. I'm not much into organized religion, but when you get baptized you get immersed in the waters of Jesus or whatever, right?"

"I'm not much into it either—organized religion. I grew up in Hawaii. My father chased waves. That was our religion."

"A surfer. And your mother?"

"Missing in action. Back to John the Baptist. How did you—"

Before finishing the question, Ballard looked over at the mobile data computer terminal mounted on the dashboard. It was on a swivel and she knew that the screen had been facing the driver's seat when they left the station earlier because she wasn't working with a partner all this week while Jenkins was out. The screen had been turned and now faced Bosch.

"You used the MDC?" she asked in an accusing voice. "To run McMullen?"

Bosch shrugged and she took that as a yes.

"How?" she demanded. "Did you steal my password?"

"No, I didn't," Bosch said. "I used my old partner's. She only changes the last two digits each month. I remembered."

Ballard was about to pull over and dump Bosch out of the car, but then she remembered that she had once used a former partner's password to log into the department database on the down-low. Her partner was even dead at the time. How could she jump on Bosch for the same thing?

"So, what did you find?" she asked.

"He's clean," Bosch said. "No record."

They drove in silence for a while. Ballard took Fairfax all the way up to Hollywood Boulevard and then turned east.

"It's a lucky break that John the Baptist still has the van," she said. "If Daisy was ever in it, there might still be evidence."

Bosch nodded.

"Exactly what I was thinking," he said. "A lucky break—but only if he's the guy."

11

The Moonlight Mission was located in an old Hollywood bungalow that had somehow survived the ravages of time. It was completely surrounded by commercial structures and pay lots that serviced Hollywood Boulevard a block to the north and Sunset Boulevard a block south. It stood like an orphan in its concrete surroundings, the last vestige of a period when Hollywood was primarily a residential suburb of downtown.

Ballard came down Cherokee from the Boulevard and turned left on Selma. The front of the two-story Victorian was on Cherokee but there was a gated drive-in entrance to the rear of the house on Selma. Through the gate, she glimpsed a white van.

"There's the van," she said. "Did you see any lights on inside?"

"A couple," Bosch said. "Doesn't seem like a lot of activity at the mission tonight."

Ballard pulled into an empty self-pay lot and turned the lights off but left the engine and the heater running. She checked her watch. It was almost five, and she knew Bosch would need to go soon.

"What do you think?" she said. "We could go back to the station and knock off some more cards before you head out."

"Let's take another run by the front," Bosch said. "See what we've got."

Ballard dropped the car into drive and headed out of the lot. This time when they went by, the property would be on Bosch's side and he would get the best look.

Ballard took it slow, and just as she passed the property on the Selma side, the lights of the van behind the gate came on.

"He's leaving," Bosch said excitedly.

"Did you see him?" Ballard asked.

"No, just the headlights. But somebody's leaving. Let's see who and where to."

Ballard crossed through the intersection and pulled to the curb, still on Selma. She turned the lights on the G-ride off.

"He probably made us," she said.

"Maybe not," Bosch said.

He slid down in his seat and leaned to his right. Ballard was much smaller but she did the same thing, leaning left like she was asleep but giving herself an angle on the sideview mirror.

She watched the van pull through the automatic gate and turn toward them on Selma.

"Here he comes," she said.

The van went by the detective car without hesitation. It continued down Selma to Highland Avenue. It stopped and then turned left. Once it was out of sight, Ballard put the lights on and headed down Selma.

There were so few cars on Highland that it was easy to track the van but hard not to be obvious about it. For several blocks they were the only two vehicles on the road. Bosch and Ballard were silent as they followed.

At Melrose the van made an abrupt U-turn and headed back up Highland.

"He made us," Ballard said. "What should we —"

She stopped when the van turned into a shopping plaza on the corner.

"Keep going a few blocks," Bosch said. "Then turn right and come back on Melrose."

Ballard followed his instructions. When they got back to the intersection of Melrose and Highland, they spotted the van parked in front of a twenty-four-hour Yum Yum Donuts store. Ballard knew it was a popular place with the late show crew.

"He's just getting donuts," Ballard said. "He'll then head back to the mission or he'll go give them out at the homeless encampments and see if he can pick up a few baptisms."

"Probably," Bosch said.

"You want to go get doughnuts and get a look at him?"

"I'd rather get a look inside the van, see what he's got in there."

"Gaslight him?"

Bosch checked his watch.

"Let's do it," he said.

Ten minutes later, after discussing a strategy, they were following the van back up Highland. They had seen a white man wearing what looked like a full-length bathrobe come out of Yum Yum with two twelve-packs of doughnuts and then hop behind the wheel of the van. As they crossed Sunset, Ballard put on the grille lights of the detective car and straddled the lane so the van's driver could see her in his sideview. She signaled him over and he complied, pulling to the curb at the corner of Highland and Selma.

Ballard and Bosch both got out and approached on either side of the van. Ballard flipped her jacket back and kept her hand on her holstered gun as she approached the driver's-side door. The window came down as she got there. She noticed that on the door just below the window was written JOHN 3:16. She guessed that McMullen had named himself after a Bible verse.

"Good morning," she said. "How are you today, sir?"

"Uh, I'm fine," he said. "Is there a problem, Officer?"

"It's Detective, actually. Can I get some identification from you, sir?"

The man already had his driver's license in his hand. Ballard checked it, her eyes flicking from the ID to the man behind the wheel, wary of any quick move. McMullen had a beard and long hair with gray streaks that had infiltrated since the ID photo was taken.

The DOB on the license put him at forty-five years old. The address corresponded with the Moonlight Mission bungalow. She handed the driver's license back.

"What brings you out on the street so early, sir?" Ballard asked.

"I went to get doughnuts for my people," McMullen said. "How come you're stopping me?"

"We got a report of a van that was being driven erratically. Suspected drunk driver. Have you been drinking, sir?"

"No, and I never drink. Alcohol is the work of the devil."

"Do you mind stepping out of the van so we can make sure?"

McMullen noticed Bosch staring at him through the passenger-side window. He turned his head back and forth between him and Ballard.

"I told you I don't drink," he protested. "Haven't had a drop in twenty-one years."

"Then it should be pretty easy to show us you're sober," Ballard said.

McMullen gripped the steering wheel until Ballard could see the points of his knuckles turn white.

"All right," he said. "But you're wasting your time."

He reached his hand down out of sight and Ballard gripped her gun, ready to go. She saw Bosch make a quick head shake, telling her everything was all right. Then she heard McMullen's seat belt come off. He opened the door and climbed out, then slammed it behind him. He was dressed the part of the missionary in sandals and a white tunic cinched at the waist by a braided rope. Over this he wore an ankle-length maroon robe with gold tassels on the sleeves.

"Is there anyone else in the van, sir?" Ballard asked.

"No," McMullen said. "Why should there be?"

"Officer safety, sir. My partner's going to check to make sure. Are you okay with that?"

"Whatever. The lock on the side door's broken. He can open it."

"Okay, sir, please step to the back of your vehicle, where it's safer."

Ballard nodded to Bosch, who was now standing at the front of the van. She followed McMullen to the rear and started putting him through old-school field sobriety testing. She began with the walk and turn so she could glance back while McMullen was walking a straight line away from her. She saw Bosch leaning into the van through the rear side door. It looked like nothing was amiss.

McMullen completed the maneuver without issue.

"I told you," he said.

"Yes, you did, sir," Ballard said. "I want you now to face me and raise your right leg and hold it up, standing only on your left foot. Do you understand? I then want you to count to ten while keeping your foot up."

"Not a problem."

McMullen raised his leg and stared at Ballard.

"Who are your people?" Ballard asked.

"What do you mean?" McMullen said.

"You said you just got doughnuts for your people."

"The Moonlight Mission. I have a flock."

"So you're a preacher. You can put your foot down."

"Of sorts. I just try to lead people to the Word of God."

"And they go willingly? Raise your other foot now and hold it."

"Of course they do. Or they can leave. I don't force anybody to do anything."

"You provide beds for people, or is it just prayer services?"

"We have beds. People can stay temporarily. Once they find the Word, they want to get off the streets and make something of their lives. We've saved many. We've baptized many."

While McMullen was speaking, Ballard heard Bosch slide the van's door closed. His footsteps came up behind her.

"Young girls?" Bosch said over her shoulder. "They part of your flock?"

McMullen lowered his foot to the ground.

"What is this?" he said. "Why'd you pull me over?"

"Because we're looking for a girl who went missing last night," Ballard said. "A witness said she got pulled into a van."

"Not my van," McMullen said. "It's been parked all night behind a gate. You saw. There's nothing in there."

"Not now," Bosch said.

"How dare you!" McMullen fired back. "How fucking dare you to try to impugn the good work of the mission! I am in the business of saving souls, not taking them. I've been going down these streets for twenty years and no one has ever accused me of anything improper. Anything!"

As McMullen spoke, tears filled his eyes and his voice grew tight and high.

"Okay, okay, sir," Ballard said. "You have to understand, we need to ask these questions. When a young girl disappears, we have to do what we need to do and sometimes we step on toes. You can go now, Mr. McMullen. Thank you for your cooperation."

"I want your names," McMullen demanded.

Ballard looked at Bosch. They had intentionally not identified themselves when they had first stopped McMullen.

"Ballard and Bosch," she said.

"I'll remember that," McMullen said.

"Good," Bosch said.

McMullen climbed back into the van as Ballard and Bosch watched. He roared the engine and took a sharp turn onto Selma.

"What did you see?" Ballard asked.

"A couple bench seats and not much else," Bosch said. "I took some photos I'll show you in the car."

"You mean no baptismal font full of bleach?" Ballard asked.

"Not quite."

"So what do you think?"

"Doesn't mean anything. I'm still interested. What do you think?"

"Something seems off but I don't know. It will be interesting to see if he files a complaint."

"If he's our guy, he doesn't file the complaint, because he won't want the follow-up."

They walked back to Ballard's car and got in. Ballard was silent as she pulled away from the curb. She was wondering if joining forces with Bosch had been a career-threatening mistake.

BOSCH

12

The search team was waiting outside Pacoima Tire & Muffler when the current owner opened up for a day of business. To say he was surprised by the police presence that greeted him was an understatement. After lifting the garage door, he held his arms aloft and stared wide-eyed at the vehicles amassed in front of him. Bosch was the first out of his car and the first to get to him.

"Mr. Cardinale?" he said. "You can put your hands down. I'm Detective Bosch with the San Fernando Police Department. We have a search warrant for these premises."

"What?" Cardinale said. "What are you talking about?"

Bosch handed him the warrant.

"It's a search warrant," he said. "Signed by a judge. And it allows us to search for specific evidence relating to a crime."

"What crime?" Cardinale said. "I run a clean business. I'm not like the guy who was here before."

"We know that, sir. The crime relates to the prior ownership of the business but we still need to search, because we believe the evidence may still be in place."

"I still don't know what you're talking about. There is no crime here."

It took Bosch several more exchanges before Cardinale seemed to understand what was happening. He was about fifty with a midlife paunch and gray thinning hair. His hands were scarred from a lifetime spent working on cars. He had blurred blue tattoos on his forearms that looked to Bosch like old military insignia.

"How long ago did you take over the business?" Bosch asked.

"Eight years," Cardinale said. "I bought it for cash. No loan. My own hard-earned money."

"When you bought it, did you make any changes inside?"

"A lot of changes. I brought in all new tools. I modernized. Cleared out the old shit."

"What about the structure of the building? Any changes?"

"I spruced things up. Patched and painted, the usual. Inside and out."

Bosch assessed the building. It was standard cinder-block construction. Solid on the outside.

"What did you patch?"

"Holes in the walls, broken windows. I can't remember everything I did."

"You remember any bullet holes?"

That gave Cardinale pause. His eyes drifted away from Bosch's as he remembered taking over the shop.

"Are you saying somebody got shot here?" he asked.

"No, not at all," Bosch said. "We're looking for bullets that were shot into the walls."

Cardinale nodded and seemed relieved.

"Yeah, there were bullet holes," he said. "I mean, they looked like bullet holes. I had 'em patched and painted over."

"Can you show me where?" Bosch asked.

Cardinale entered his garage and Bosch followed, signaling

Lourdes and Luzon to follow. The shop owner led them to the rear of the first garage bay.

"Back here," he said. "There were holes in this wall that looked like they were from bullets. I remember thinking that at the time. We patched them all up."

He pointed behind a workbench that was covered with tools and pipe-bending vises. The area fit with the description Bosch had gotten from the witness Martin Perez.

"Okay," Bosch said. "We're going to have to move this bench and the tools out of here. We need to open the wall."

"And who closes it back up?" Cardinale asked.

"We have a city crew here that will make the necessary repairs. I can't promise it will be all painted and back to normal by the end of the day, but we'll get it there."

Cardinale frowned. He didn't put much stock in the promise. Bosch turned to Lourdes.

"Let's get the city guys in here to clear this and then bring the metal detector first," he said. "Let's move fast, maybe get out of here before the neighborhood takes notice."

"Too late," Lourdes said.

She signaled Bosch over into a private conversation.

"We have a problem," she said in a whisper. "The LAPD guy says Tranquillo Cortez is across the street."

"Are you kidding?" Bosch said. "How'd he find out so fast?"

"Good question. He's out there with some of his boys."

"Come on."

Bosch walked quickly out of the garage, with Lourdes following. Across the street was a *lavandería* with a small front parking lot. The business had not yet opened for the day, but there was a car in the lot, a classic old Lincoln Continental with pearl-white paint and suicide doors. Its suspension had been dropped a few notches so that it would barely clear a speed bump. Three men were leaning against its side with their arms folded, their tattoo sleeves on full display. The man in the middle wore a flat-brimmed Dodgers cap and a long white T-shirt that went down to his thighs. He was the smallest of the three but presented as the man in charge. Bosch recognized him from a photo on a SanFers organizational chart at the SFPD gang unit office. Tranquillo Cortez.

Without hesitation Bosch crossed the street.

"Harry, what are we doing?" Lourdes whispered from behind.

"Just gonna ask him a few questions," Bosch said.

As they entered the laundry's parking lot, only Cortez pushed his hips off the car and stood tall to greet Bosch.

"Officer, how are you today?" he said.

Bosch didn't answer. He walked directly up to Cortez and leaned down to get in the shorter man's face. He noticed the diamond earrings on both sides and the two blue tears tattooed off the outside corner of his left eye.

"Cortez, what are you doing here?" he asked.

"I'm waiting for the laundry to open," Cortez said. "You know, wash my clothes, see how white my whites can be with Tide and all."

He picked at his T-shirt and adjusted it like he was looking in a mirror.

"Who told you we were coming here?" Bosch said.

"Hmm, that's a good question," Cortez said. "I'm not sure I remember. Who told you to come here?"

Bosch didn't answer. Cortez wore his hat up high. He had shaved sidewalls with "VSF" tattooed above his right ear and "13" above his left. He smiled and his dark eyes became slits.

"Get the fuck out of here," Bosch ordered.

"You arresting me if I don't?" Cortez challenged.

"Yeah, I'll have you arrested for interfering with a police investigation. Then, who knows, maybe they make a mistake and put you in the Pacoima Flats tank and we see what happens next."

Cortez flashed the smile again.

"That'd be fun," he said. "For me, but not them."

Bosch reached up and slapped the brim of Cortez's Dodgers cap, knocking it off his head to the ground. A dark anger momentarily invaded the gangster's eyes. But then it cleared and Cortez returned to his standard smirk. He glanced back at his seconds and nodded. They pushed off the car and one opened the back door of the Lincoln for Cortez while the other retrieved his fallen hat.

"Catch you later, homeboy," Cortez said.

Bosch didn't respond. He and Lourdes stood there until the Lincoln pulled out of the lot and headed down San Fernando Road.

"Harry, why'd you do that with the hat?" Lourdes said.

Bosch ignored the question and answered with his own.

"How'd he know about this?" he asked.

"Like Sergeant Rosenberg said yesterday," Lourdes said. "They've got eyes everywhere."

Bosch shook his head. He didn't believe that Cortez had shown up just because he got a message from someone who happened to see the police activity at the garage.

"We might as well pull out of here right now," he said.

"Harry, what are you talking about?" Lourdes said. "They're in there, getting ready to take down the wall."

"Cortez was gloating. Why else would he show up here? He must know there's no slugs in the wall and no case."

"I don't know. That seems like a stretch. He's not that smart."

"Really? Well, we're about to find out."

They crossed back over to the auto shop and Bosch was stopped by Tom Yaro, the LAPD detective from Foothill Division who was on hand to represent his department, since the search was being conducted on his city's turf. Yaro was dressed down for the occasion, wearing blue jeans and a black golf shirt. He had jet-black hair that didn't look natural and had deposited liberal amounts of dandruff on his shoulders. He was little more than a babysitter on this operation and seemed put out by it, as though he felt that the LAPD shouldn't take a back seat to the smaller SFPD. He had been given few details of the case, but he knew who Tranquillo Cortez was and had sounded the alarm about the gangster showing up across the street. He now wanted to know what was going on. Bosch gave him the short version.

"Our suspect somehow got wind of the search and got up early to come watch," he said.

"That's fucked up," Yaro said. "Sounds like you sprung a leak."

"If we did, I'll find it."

Bosch walked on past him and back into the garage. He watched as a metal detector usually used to find water mains was moved over the back wall. It easily picked up the lines of screws used to secure drywall to the interior studs, but no other alerts came up. The bullet that was fired into Cristobal Vega's head had been a metal-jacketed .38 slug. Similar slugs should have registered as easily as drywall screws.

Despite his feeling that the search for bullets was for naught, Bosch decided to follow through with the execution of the warrant and told the city workers to cut through the drywall and bring the wall down. He reasoned that while Cortez may have dug the slugs out of the wall long ago, the interior side of the drywall would still show where bullets had gone through and the wall had eventually been patched. It would be at least a minor confirmation of Perez's story. Most likely not enough to move the case closer to prosecution, but confirmation just the same.

The workers cut out floor-to-ceiling slices of the drywall between the studs. The inside surface of each sixteen-inch-wide cut was then examined by the detectives for indications of bullet entry.

The third cut had what they were looking for. It was clear that there had been two perforations—matching Perez's story. They were small, bullet-size perforations and there was no indication that any effort had previously been made to extract the slugs. This contradicted Bosch's theory about why Cortez had shown up across the street to gloat. Rather than knowing there were no bullets in the wall, he knew something else that made him confident enough to show up.

The shots were spread four inches apart on the drywall, an indicator that they were part of the same test firing that Perez had described. The unpainted cinder block corresponding to the drywall penetrations showed impact damage but no bullets. The team had borrowed an evidence technician from the L.A. County Sheriff's Department, which contracted with the tiny SFPD to do all lab work. It was his job to pick through the rat droppings, hair, and other debris at the bottom of the space created by the 2 x 4 framing between the drywall and the cinder-block wall. His name was Harmon and he used a metal pick to search through about six inches of debris that had built up inside the wall, spreading it all out on the floor of the shop.

Bosch recorded Harmon's efforts on his cell phone, knowing that at some point he might have to lead a jury through the steps he had taken in finding the evidence against Tranquillo Cortez.

"Got one," Harmon said.

He used the metal pick to knock a slug out of the packed debris and across the concrete floor. Bosch leaned down, still holding the phone out to record. When he saw the slug, his renewed hopes for the case took another tumble. The projectile had split its metal casing and pancaked upon impact with the cinder block inside the wall. Bosch would wait for the expert opinion but he had been around enough cases to know that the bullet was too damaged to be considered for comparison with the bullet that killed Cristobal Vega.

"And here's the other one," Harmon said.

He picked out the second slug with a gloved hand and held it up. Bosch's eyes went to it with urgency.

But this one was in even worse shape. It too had pancaked but it had also shattered. He was looking at about half of the bullet.

"There's more," he said, even though someone of Harmon's skill would already know this.

"Still looking," Harmon said.

Bosch felt his phone buzz with a call but he let it go to message so he could continue to video Harmon's search.

Harmon soon found the rest of the second bullet and it was in as poor shape as the others. He then went through evidence-collecting procedures. He spoke without looking up at Bosch.

"Detective, it looks like you've been around," he said. "You probably know what I'm going to tell you."

"No good, huh?" Bosch said.

"Not for comparison on a scope," Harmon said. "We'll be able to determine a brand match and there's more than enough for metal-alloy comparison, but you know how that goes."

"Right."

The content of the slugs could be determined and compared

to the bullet that killed Perez, possibly leading to a conclusion that the bullets came from the same manufacturing group and lending some credence to the witness's story, but it would be nowhere near as definitive as the marks left by the gun that fired them. It was the difference between saying that the bullets came from the same batch and that they were fired by the same weapon. The difference had reasonable doubt written all over it.

Bosch was seeing the case go away as he stood there.

"I want to do the metal-alloy testing anyway," he said.

It was a last desperate shot.

"I'll talk to the boss," Harmon said. "I'll tell him it's a good case for it and will let you know."

Bosch knew that when he would hear back was anyone's guess. The alloy testing would take money and time. The SFPD was usually last in line at the sheriff's lab. Any sort of special work would go on the when-we-can-get-to-it list.

Bosch backed away from the grouping at the wall, giving Lourdes a look that said this was going nowhere. He addressed the head man of the Public Works crew.

"Okay, we're going to need to put this place back together," he said. "We want to keep the one piece of wall where we found the bullet holes. So you'll have to replace that."

One of the men grunted his assent and they headed out to the truck for their tools and a fresh piece of drywall to replace the old one.

Lourdes huddled with Bosch.

"So, if there were bullets in the wall after all, what was Cortez so smug about?" she asked.

"I don't know," Bosch said. "He knew something, but I doubt he knew the slugs would be useless."

Lourdes shook her head and then stepped back as the city workers walked a large sheet of fresh drywall into the garage bay.

Bosch's phone started buzzing again, and he walked out of the garage as he pulled it out of his pocket. The caller ID was blocked but he took the call anyway.

"Bosch."

"Harry Bosch?"

"That's right, who's this?"

"Ted Lannark, Sheriff's Homicide. You got a minute?"

"What's up?

"What can you tell me about a guy named Martin Perez?"

All at once Bosch knew why Cortez had acted like he had the world on a string.

"He's a peripheral witness in a gang murder I'm working. What is he to you?"

"He's dead and I have to find out who killed him."

Bosch closed his eyes.

"Where?" he asked.

"His apartment," Lannark said. "Somebody put a round in the back of his head."

Bosch opened his eyes and looked around for Lourdes.

"Bosch, you wondering how I knew to call you on your cell?" Lannark asked.

"Yeah," Bosch said. "How?"

"Your business card with the cell handwritten on it was in his mouth. Like it was a message or something."

Bosch considered that for a long moment before responding.

"I'm on my way."

"We'll be here waiting."

13

It was almost as if the killer wanted to make it easy for the landlord to clean up and re-rent the place. Martin Perez had been made to kneel in a walk-in shower with yellowed tiles and a glass sliding door. He was then popped once in the back of the head. He crumpled forward and to his right, the splatter of blood and brains contained within the enclosure, some of it even conveniently dripping down the drain.

The forensics team had not yet removed the business card that had been snugged between Perez's two front teeth and was easily readable as it protruded from his mouth.

It was clear to Bosch that the weapon had not been a .38, as this bullet had gone through the victim's skull and exited explosively. Bosch saw chipped tile on the wall Perez had been facing as well as on the floor near the drain. The marks were clean white and not yellowed by time and grime.

"You find the round?" Bosch asked.

It was the first question he asked after five minutes of studying the crime scene. He had driven out to Alhambra with Lourdes. Sheriff's investigator Lannark and his partner, Boyce, had taken an initial debriefing on the Martin Perez investigation and then escorted them into the bathroom to view the crime scene. At the moment, it was interdepartmental cooperation at its finest.

"No," Lannark said. "But we haven't moved him. We think he could have it in the gut. Goes through his head, hits down-angle on the wall in front of him, bounces down to the floor and then up into him before he hits the ground. New meaning to the double-tap, huh?"

"Yeah," Bosch said.

"Seen enough? How 'bout we back on out of here and talk some more outside?"

"Sure."

They went outside to a courtyard in the center of the two-story apartment building. Boyce joined the huddle. Both of the sheriff's men were seasoned detectives, calm in demeanor, with eyes that never stopped moving and observing. Lannark was black and Boyce was white.

Bosch started with questions before they got the chance.

"Has TOD been established?" he asked.

"Another resident of this fair place heard voices, then a muf-fled shot about five this morning," Lannark said. "After that, she heard some more yelling and then running toward the street. At least two people."

"Two voices yelling after the shooting?" Bosch asked.

"Yes, after," Boyce said. "But this isn't about you asking us questions, Bosch. We're still asking you."

"Right," Bosch said. "Ask away."

"Number one," Boyce said, "if this guy was some kind of wit-ness in a case, why wasn't he under protection?"

"We thought he was protected," Bosch said. "*He* thought he was protected. He was out of the neighborhood, ten years re-moved from the gang. He said nobody knew where he was and he turned down physical protection or relocation. We didn't use his real name in reports or on the search warrant application."

"Besides that, we were early into his information and had not confirmed any of it," Lourdes said. "That was what the search we were conducting this morning was for."

Lannark nodded and looked from Lourdes to Bosch.

"When did you give him your business card?" he asked.

"At the end of the first interview," Bosch said. "I'll have to look up the exact date—about four weeks ago."

"And you're saying he was not associated with anybody from the old neighborhood?" Lannark asked.

"That's what he told me," Bosch said. "Confirmed by our gang intel guys."

"So, what's your gut on this?" Boyce asked.

"My gut?" Bosch said. "My gut is that we sprang a leak. Somebody on our side told somebody on that side about the search. It got to somebody who knew what we would find in the wall of that garage, so he took out the witness who could connect the dots."

"And that's this guy Tranquillo Cortez?" Boyce said.

"Somebody working for him," Bosch said.

"Cortez is a shot caller now," Lourdes said. "He's top rank in the gang."

The sheriff's men looked at each other and nodded.

"All right," Lannark said. "That's going to be it for now. We'll finish up here and I'm sure we'll be in touch soon."

On the way out of the center courtyard to the gated entrance, Bosch scanned the concrete, looking for blood drops. He didn't see any and soon was in the passenger seat of the city car assigned to Lourdes.

"So, what do you think?" Lourdes said as she pulled the car away from the curb. "Did we fuck up?"

"I don't know," Bosch said. "Maybe. Bottom line is Perez refused protection."

"You really think somebody leaked to the SanFers?"

"I don't know about that either. We'll look at it for sure. If there was a leak, we'll find it. It could have been Martin saying the wrong thing to the wrong person. We may never know how it happened."

Bosch thought about the judge who had signed the warrant. He had asked Bosch several questions about the unnamed source in the affidavit, but it seemed he was only being thorough, and he had never specifically requested the real name. Judge Landry had been on the bench at least twenty years and was a second-generation jurist, having run for the superior court spot his father had occupied for thirty years until his death. It seemed unlikely that information in the warrant or discussed in his chambers would somehow have gotten to Tranquillo Cortez or any of the SanFers. The leak, intentional or otherwise, had to have come from somewhere else. Bosch started thinking about Yaro, the LAPD gang detective assigned to be on hand for the search. All gang detectives had sources in the gangs. The steady flow of intel from the gang was vital and sometimes information had to be traded in exchange.

Lourdes was working her way up to the 10 freeway so they could head west and back toward San Fernando.

"It seemed like you were looking for something when we were walking out," she said. "Anything specific?"

"Yeah," Bosch said. "Blood."

"Blood? Whose blood?"

"The shooter's. Did you work out the ricochet angle in the shower?"

"No, I couldn't get in there because you men were clogging up the whole bathroom. I stood back. You think the shooter got hit with the ricochet?"

"It's possible. Might explain the yelling the witness heard after the shooting. The sheriffs were thinking it hit Perez, but the angles didn't look right to me. I'm thinking the bullet came low, went between Perez's legs and hit our shooter. Maybe in the leg."

"That would be good."

"As soon as they roll that body, they'll know, but we might have a chance at getting ahead of them on this. You think your boy J-Rod has an idea who the SanFers use these days to do their patching?"

"I'll ask him."

She pulled her phone and called her cousin Jose Rodriguez, who was the SFPD's resident gang intel expert. By law, every hospital emergency room and legitimate physician had to report to authorities any case involving a gunshot wound, even if the injury is claimed by the victim to be accidental. This meant that criminal organizations had illegitimate doctors on call whom they could rely on to do medical patchwork at any time of the day or night and to keep quiet about it afterward. If Martin Perez's killer was hit with the ricocheting bullet, then it was likely that he and his accomplices would have gone back to their own turf to seek medical attention. The SanFers' turf was wide-ranging in the north valley and there was no shortage of shady doctors and clinics an injured man could go to. Bosch was hoping that J-Rod would be able to point them in the right direction.

While Lourdes talked in Spanish to her cousin on the phone, Bosch considered for the first time the question that had been hanging since he'd gotten the call from Lannark. Had he gotten Martin Perez killed? It was the kind of weight no cop needed or wanted but it was a risk that came with every case. Asking questions could be dangerous. It could get people killed. Perez had been out of the gang for years, had a job, and was a productive member of society when Bosch approached him behind the shoe store and asked for a light. Bosch believed he had taken appropriate precautions but there were always variables and potential risks. Perez hadn't voluntarily pointed the finger at Tranquillo Cortez. Bosch had used age-old police tactics and squeezed the information out by threat. It was from that decision that Bosch's guilt came.

Lourdes finished her call and reported to Bosch.

"He's going to put together a list," she said. "He doesn't know how current it will be but it's doctors who have been go-to guys for the SanFers and the *eMe*."

"When do we get it?" Bosch asked.

"He'll have it for us by the time we get back to the station."

"All right, good."

They drove in silence for a while. Bosch kept going back to his decision to squeeze Martin Perez. His review of it had him still doing the same thing.

"You know the irony of this?" Lourdes said.

"What irony?" Bosch responded.

"Well, Perez led us to that garage and we found the bullets but they were no good for comparison purposes. The reinvestigation would have probably ended there this morning."

"True. Even if we got a metallurgy match, the D.A. wouldn't have gotten too excited about it."

"No way. But now with Perez getting taken out, there's a case. And if we get the shooter, it may get us to Cortez. That's the definition of irony, right?"

"I'd have to ask my daughter. She's good at that stuff."

"Well, it's like they say, the cover-up is worse than the crime. It always gets them in the end."

"Hopefully that's how it works here. I want to put the cuffs on Cortez for this."

Bosch's phone started buzzing and he pulled it out. The caller was unknown.

"They rolled the body," he predicted.

He accepted the call. It was Lannark.

"Bosch, we pulled the body out of the shower," he said. "Perez wasn't hit on the ricochet."

"Really," Bosch said, acting surprised.

"Yeah, so we're thinking, maybe the shooter got hit by his own bullet. Maybe the leg or the balls—if we're lucky."

"That would be true justice."

"Yeah, so we're going to do hospital checks, but we figure the gang behind this probably has its own people for situations like this."

"Probably."

"Maybe you could help us out and get us some names of people we can check on."

"We can do that. We're still on the road but we'll see what we can come up with."

"Call me back, okay?"

"As soon as we have something."

Bosch disconnected and looked over at Lourdes.

"No bullet in the victim?" she asked.

Bosch stifled a yawn. He was beginning to feel the effects of the all-nighter he had spent with Ballard in Hollywood.

"No bullet," he said. "And they want our help."

"Of course they do," Lourdes said.

BALLARD

14

Ballard awoke to the sound of panicked voices and an approaching siren so loud she could not hear the ocean. She sat up, registering that it was not a dream, and pulled the inside zipper down on her tent. Looking out, she reacted to the sharp diamonds of light reflecting off the dark blue surface of the ocean. Using her hand to shield her eyes, she looked for the source of the commotion and saw Aaron Hayes, the lifeguard assigned to the Rose Station tower, on his knees in the sand, huddled over a man's body lying supine on the rescue board. A group of people were standing or kneeling beside them, some onlookers, some the fretful and crying friends and loved ones of the man on the board.

Ballard climbed out of the tent, told her dog, Lola, to stay at her post in front of it, and walked quickly across the sand toward the rescue effort. She pulled her badge as she approached.

"Police officer, police officer!" she shouted. "I need everybody to stand back and give the lifeguard room to work."

No one moved. They turned and stared at her. She wore after-swim sweats and her hair was still wet from that morning's surf and shower.

"Move back!" she said with more authority. "Now! You are not helping the situation."

She got to the group and started pushing people into a semi-circle formation ten feet back from the board.

"You too," she said to a young woman who was crying hysterically and holding the drowning victim's hand. "Ma'am, let them work. They are trying to save his life."

Ballard gently pulled the woman away and turned her toward one of her friends, who grabbed her into a hug. Ballard checked the parking lot and saw two EMTs running toward them, a stretcher between them, their progress slowed by their work boots slogging through the sand.

"They're coming, Aaron," she said. "Keep it going."

When Aaron raised his head to get a breath, Ballard saw that the lips of the man on the board were blue.

The EMTs arrived and took over from Aaron, who rolled away and stayed on the sand, panting for breath. He was wet from the rescue. He watched intently as the EMTs worked, first intubating and pumping water out of the victim's lungs, then adding a breathing bag.

Ballard squatted next to Aaron. They had a casual romantic relationship, sometime lovers with no commitment beyond the time they were together. Aaron was a beautiful man with a V-shaped, muscular body and angular face, his short hair and eyebrows burned almost white by the sun.

"What happened?" she whispered.

"He got caught in a rip," Aaron whispered back. "Took me too long to get out of it once I got him on the board. Shit, the warning signs were out, up and down the beach."

Aaron sat forward when he saw the EMTs react to getting a pulse on the victim. They started moving quickly and transferred the man to the stretcher.

"Let's help them," Ballard said.

She and Hayes moved across the sand and took sides on the stretcher behind the EMTs. They lifted and moved quickly across the sand to the parking lot, where the ambulance waited. One of the EMTs carried his share of the weight one-handed while continuing to squeeze the air bag.

Three minutes later the rescue ambulance was gone and Ballard and Hayes stood there, hands on their hips and winded. Soon the family and friends caught up, and Aaron told them which hospital the victim was being taken to. The hysterical woman hugged him and then followed the others to their cars.

"That was weird to see," Ballard said.

"Yeah," Hayes said. "Third one for me this month. The riptides have been off the charts."

Ballard was thinking of something else, of a time many years before on a beach far away. The image of a broken surfboard carried in by the waves. Young Renée searching the diamonds on the surface for her father.

"You okay?" Hayes asked.

Ballard came out of the memory and noticed the strange look on his face.

"Fine," she said.

She checked her watch. Most days she tried to get six hours in the tent after a morning on the water, whether it be surfing or paddling. But the commotion from the rescue had gotten her up after just four. The adrenaline rush with the rescue and run across the beach guaranteed she would not be going back to sleep.

She decided on an early start to work. There was follow-up to do on John the Baptist and several boxes of shake cards still to get through, whether or not the man from the Moonlight Mission turned out to be a valid suspect.

"Don't you have a debriefing now or something?" she asked.

"Uh, yeah," he said. "The beach captain will come interview me and we'll write it up."

"Let me know if you need anything from me."

"Thanks. Will do."

She hesitantly gave him a hug, then turned and walked back toward her tent to collect her things and her dog. The memory of Hawaii returned as she looked out at the sea: her lost father and the need to be by the water's edge, waiting for something that could never be.

15

Before heading into the station, Ballard parked her van on Selma a half block from the Moonlight Mission. Through the iron bars of the gate surrounding the back parking area she could see John the Baptist's van. It meant he was presumably home.

Bosch had gotten a look inside the van during the traffic stop and had shared the cell phone photos he had taken. There had been nothing of an incriminating nature. Not that they would have expected it after nine years. But she had noticed that the parking enclosure at the rear of the mission house gave the van close access to the back door. If the van was backed in, a body could be transferred from it and into the house quickly with only a split-second exposure outside. Additionally, she was curious about the stand-alone garage on the other side of the parking apron. Both times she had seen the van, it had been in the driveway and not in the garage. Why wasn't the garage used? What was in there that prevented the van from being parked inside?

Ballard's instinct about John McMullen was that he wasn't the guy. He had seemed sincere in his defense and his complaint during their confrontation early that morning. Detectives develop a sixth sense about character and often had to rely on these fleeting takes to judge people. She had shared her take on McMullen with Bosch as they drove away following the roust. Bosch didn't disagree but said the preacher still needed to be cleared beyond a quick search of his van before they moved on.

Now she was sitting in her own van, looking at the Moonlight Mission and needing to get a look inside. She could wait and do it with Bosch but she had no idea when he would be available. She had sent him a text checking on his status but had gotten no reply.

Ballard's rover was in its charging slot back at the station. She didn't like the idea of going in alone and without that electronic link to the mother ship, but the option of waiting made her even more uncomfortable. Seeing the drowning man and being reminded of her father had put her on edge. She needed to crowd out those thoughts and knew that making this move would do it. Work was always the distraction. She could lose herself in the work.

She pulled her phone and called the inside line to the watch office. It was almost five and the PM watch shift was on. A lieutenant named Hannah Chavez picked up the call.

"It's Renée Ballard. I'm following up on something from the late show and don't have a rover with me. Just wanted to let you know I'm going to be code six at the Moonlight Mission at Selma and Cherokee. If you don't hear from me in an hour, can you send a backup?"

"Roger that, Ballard. But while I got you, you handled the DB up in the hills the other night, right?"

"Yeah, that was me. It was accidental."

"Right, what I heard. But we just got a B and E call from that location. The burglary table has checked out for the day and I was going to shelve it till tomorrow but now I'm thinking—"

"You might want me to handle it."

"Read my mind, Ballard."

"Not really, but I'll cruise over after I clear the mission."

"I'll tell my guys to hang till you get there."

"How'd we get the call?"

"The family had arranged for some bio cleaners to get in there after the death. They apparently found the place ransacked and called it in."

"Roger that. Remember, back me up in an hour if I don't hit you back."

"Moonlight Mission—you got it."

Ballard climbed out of the driver's seat and into the back of her van. Last week's dry cleaning was on hangers on an equipment hook. She changed into what she considered her third-string work outfit, a chocolate Van Heusen blazer with a chalk pinstripe over the usual white blouse and black slacks. She emerged from the back of the van, locked it, and headed down the street to the mission.

She just wanted to take a look around inside, get a sense of the place, and maybe brace McMullen again. The direct approach was called for. She walked in through the front gate and up the steps to the porch. A sign on the door said WELCOME, so she opened it and entered without knocking.

Ballard stepped into a wide entry area with arched passages to rooms to the right and left and a wide, winding staircase in front of her. She walked into the center and waited a moment, expecting McMullen or someone else to appear.

Nothing.

She looked through the archway to the right and saw that the room was lined with couches, with a single chair in the middle, where the facilitator of a group discussion might sit. She turned to check the other room. Banners with Bible quotations and images of Jesus hung side by side on the far wall. At the center of the room was what looked like a freestanding sink with a crucifix rising from the porcelain sill where a faucet was intended to be.

Ballard stepped into the room and looked into the sink. It was half filled with water. She looked up at the banners and realized that not all the images were of Jesus. At least two featured drawings of the man she had met that morning.

Ballard turned to go back into the entrance hall and almost walked into McMullen. She startled, stepped back, and then quickly recovered.

"Mr. McMullen," she said. "You snuck up on me."

"I did not," McMullen said. "And in here I am Pastor McMullen."

"Okay. Pastor McMullen."

"Why are you here, Detective?"

"I wanted to talk to you."

Ballard turned and gestured toward the sink.

"This is where you do your work," she said.

"It's not work," he said. "This is where I save souls for Jesus Christ."

"Well, where is everybody? The house seems empty."

"Each night I seek a new flock. Anyone I bring in to feed and clothe must be on their own by this time. This is just a way station on the journey to salvation."

"Right. Is there somewhere we can talk?"

"Follow me."

McMullen turned and headed out of the room. His heels kicked up from under his robe and Ballard saw that he was barefoot. They went around the staircase and down a short hallway into a kitchen with a large eating space taken up by a long picnic table and benches. McMullen stepped into a side room that might have been a servant's pantry when the house was originally built but now served as an office or perhaps a confessional. It was spartan, with a small table and folding chairs on either side of it. Prominent on the wall opposite the doorway was a paper calendar with a photo of the heavenly skies and a verse from the Bible printed on it.

"Please sit," McMullen said.

He took one chair and Ballard sat opposite him, leaving her right hand down by her hip and her weapon.

She saw that the wall behind McMullen was lined with cork. Pinned to it was a collage of photos of young people wearing layers of sometimes ragged clothing. Many had dirty faces, some were missing teeth, some had drug-glazed eyes, and all of them constituted the homeless flock that McMullen brought to his baptismal font. The people on the wall were diverse in gender and ethnicity. They shared one thing: each smiled for the camera. Some of the photos were old and faded, others were covered by new shots pinned over them. There were first names and dates handwritten on the photos. Ballard assumed these were the dates of their acceptance of Jesus Christ.

"If you are here to talk me out of a complaint, then you can save your words," he said. "I decided that charity would be more useful than anger."

Ballard thought about Bosch's saying that it would be suspicious if McMullen did not make a complaint.

"Thank you," she said. "I was coming to apologize if we offended you. We had an incomplete description of the van we were looking for."

"I understand," McMullen said.

Ballard nodded at the wall behind him.

"Those are the people you've baptized?" she asked.

McMullen glanced behind him at the wall and smiled.

"Just some of them," he said. "There are many more."

Ballard looked up at the calendar. The photo showed a gold and maroon sunset and a quote:

COMMIT YOUR WAY TO THE LORD. TRUST HIM AND HE WILL HELP YOU.

Her eyes scanned down to the dates and she noticed that a number was scribbled in each day's square. Most were single digits but on some days the number was higher.

"What do the numbers mean?" she asked.

McMullen followed her eyes to the calendar.

"Those are the numbers of souls who receive the sacrament," he said. "Each night I count how many people took the Lord and Savior into their hearts. Each dark sacred night brings more souls to Christ."

Ballard nodded but said nothing.

"What are you really doing here, Detective?" McMullen asked. "Is Christ in your life? Do you have faith?"

Ballard felt herself being pushed onto the defensive.

"My faith is my business," she said.

"Why not proclaim your faith?" McMullen pressed.

"Because it's private. I don't... I'm not part of any organized religion. I don't feel the need for it. I believe in what I believe. That's it."

McMullen studied her for a long moment before repeating a question.

"What are you really doing here?"

Ballard returned the penetrating look and decided to see if she could draw a reaction.

"Daisy Clayton."

McMullen held her eyes but she could see he was not expecting what she had said. She could also see that the name meant something to him.

"She was murdered," he said. "That was a long—Is that your case?"

"Yes," Ballard said. "It's my case."

"And what does it have to do with—"

McMullen stopped short as he apparently answered his own question.

"The stop this morning," he said. "The detective looked in my van. For what?"

Ballard ignored his question and tried to steer things in the direction she wanted to go.

"You knew her, didn't you?" she asked.

"Yes, I saved her," he said. "I brought her to Christ and then He called her home."

"What does that mean? Exactly."

"I baptized her."

"When?"

McMullen shook his head.

"I don't remember. Obviously before she was taken."

"Is she on the wall?"

Ballard pointed behind him. McMullen turned to study the collage.

"I think—Yes, I put her up there," he said.

He got up and moved to the corked wall. He started pulling pins and tacks and removing the outer layers of photos, which he gently put down on the table. In a few minutes he had taken off several layers and then stopped as he studied one.

"I think this is Daisy," he said.

He pulled down the photo and showed it to Ballard. It depicted a young girl with a pink blanket wrapped around her shoulders. Her hair had a streak of purple and was wet. Ballard could see some of the banners from the baptism room in the background. The photo was dated by hand four months before Daisy Clayton's murder. Instead of writing her name she had drawn a daisy on the corner of the photograph.

"It's her," Ballard said.

"She was baptized into the grace of Jesus Christ," McMullen said. "She's with Him now."

Ballard held up the photo.

"Do you remember this night?"

"I remember all of the nights."

"Was she alone when you brought her here?"

"Oh, well, that I don't remember. I would have to find my calendar from that year and look at the number on that date."

"Where would the calendar be?"

"In storage. In the garage."

Ballard nodded and moved past McMullen to look at the photos still on the corked wall.

"What about here?" she asked. "Are there others who were baptized the same night?"

"If they allowed their pictures to be taken," McMullen said.

He stepped next to Ballard as they scanned the images. He started taking down photos and checking the dates on the back, then pinning them back up to the side of the collage.

"This one," he said. "It has the same date."

He handed Ballard a photo of a dirty and disheveled man

who looked to be in his late twenties. Ballard confirmed that the date on the back matched the date of Daisy's baptism. The name etched in marker on the print said Eagle.

"Another," he said.

He handed her another photo, this one of a much younger man, with blond hair and a hard look in his eyes. The dates matched and the name on this print was Addict. Ballard took the print and studied it. It was Adam Sands, Daisy's supposed boyfriend and pimp.

"Looks like that's it for that date," McMullen said.

"Can we go look for the calendar?" Ballard asked.

"Yes."

"Can I keep these photos?"

"As long as I get them back. They're part of the flock."

"I'll copy and return them."

"Thank you. Follow me, please."

They went outside and McMullen used a key to open a side door on the freestanding garage. They entered a space crowded with stored furniture and wheeled racks of clothing. There were also several boxes stacked against the walls, some with the years marked on them.

Fifteen minutes later, McMullen unearthed the 2009 calendar from a dusty box. On the date corresponding to the photo of Daisy, the calendar recorded seven baptisms. Ballard then took the calendar and flipped it four months forward to look at the date when Daisy was abducted and murdered. She found no number in the calendar square for the date of the murder or the two days after it.

McMullen saw the empty spots on the calendar at the same time Ballard did.

"That's funny," he said. "I almost never take a night off from my work. I don't—Oh, I remember now. The van had to have been in the shop. It's the only reason I would miss so many days in a row."

Ballard looked at him.

"You're sure?" she asked.

"Of course," McMullen said.

"You think you have any record of that? Which shop it was, what was wrong with the van?"

"I can look. I think this was a transmission problem back then. I remember I took it to the place on Santa Monica by the cemetery. Santa Monica and El Centro. On the corner. It begins with a Z but I can't remember the name."

"Okay. You take a look at your records and let me know what you find. Can I keep this calendar? I'll copy and return it."

"I guess."

Ballard could have photographed the photos and the calendar but she needed to take the originals in case they became evidence in the investigation.

"Good," she said. "I need to go now. I have a call I need to respond to."

She pulled out a business card and handed it to McMullen.

"If you find the receipt for the repair work or remember anything about Daisy, give me a call."

"I will, I will."

"Thank you for your cooperation."

Ballard walked out of the garage and down a walkway to the front gate. She trusted her instincts that John the Baptist was not the killer of Daisy Clayton, but she knew she still had a long way to go before he was in the clear.

16

A white box truck with CCB painted on its side was parked
in front of the Hollywood Boulevard house where the
woman whose face was eaten by her cat had been found. There
was also a patrol car and two blue-suiters standing on the street
with a man in a white jumpsuit. This time there was no space
for Ballard, who was still driving her own van, so she drove by,
gave a wave, and parked in front of a garage two doors down.
Few houses on the edge side of the hills had driveways. The
garages were right at the curb, and blocking one involved risk-
ing the potential ire of a homeowner, especially when the culprit
was not obviously a police vehicle.

She walked back to the house in question and had to intro-
duce herself to all three waiting men. She had little experience
with day watch blue suiters. These two were named Felsen and
Torborg. Both were young and cut with military precision and
bearing. Ballard recognized the name Torborg and knew him
by reputation. He was a hard charger nicknamed Torpedo, who
had accumulated several one-day suspensions for overaggres-
sive enforcement and behavior. Female cops referred to these as
testosterone time-outs.

The man in the jumpsuit was named Roger Dillon. He

worked for CCB, a biohazard cleaning service. He had reported the burglary. Though he had told his story to Felsen and Torborg, he was prompted to repeat it to the detective, who would actually compose the burglary report.

Dillon said the dead woman's niece in New York hired his firm to clean and decontaminate the house after her aunt's body was removed and the premises were cleared as a possible crime scene. She overnighted him her key but it didn't arrive until the early afternoon, delaying his getting to the house to perform the job. He was under a deadline because the niece, whom Ballard had identified during the death investigation as Bobbi Clark, was due to arrive the following morning. She planned to stay in the house while she organized services and took stock of the property she would be inheriting as the dead woman's only living relative.

"So, I get here and I don't even need the key, because the door's unlocked," Dillon said.

"Unlocked and open?" Ballard asked. "Or unlocked and closed?"

"Unlocked and closed but so you could see that it wasn't pulled all the way. I pushed on the door and it opened."

Ballard checked his hands.

"No gloves on?" she asked. "Show me where you touched the door."

Dillon moved up the short walkway to the front door. Ballard turned back to Felsen and Torborg.

"Hey, I don't have my rover with me," she said. "Can one of you call the watch office and tell them I'm code six here and to cancel the one-hour backup at Moonlight Mission? I forgot about it."

"Got it," Felsen said as he keyed his shoulder mic.

140

"Moonlight Mission?" Torborg said. "Talking to John the Baptist? I knew that freak would act out someday. What did he do?"

"Just talking to him about a cold case," Ballard said. "It wasn't much."

She turned and followed Dillon to the door. Since Torborg obviously knew John McMullen, she wanted to talk to him about his interactions with and impressions of the street preacher, but she had to deal with Dillon and the case at hand first.

Dillon was tall and his white coveralls seemed to be a size too small. The cuffs on the pants just ticked the top of his work boots and the overall picture to Ballard was of a boy who had outgrown his clothes. Dillon, of course, was no boy. Ballard pegged him in his midthirties. He had a handsome, clean-shaven face, a full mane of brown hair, and a wedding ring on his finger.

He was poised at the door, his finger running a clockwise circle around a spot shoulder-high on it. Ballard pulled a pair of gloves from her blazer pocket and started putting them on.

"You pushed it open and went in?" she asked.

"Yes," Dillon said.

She opened the door and held her hand up to signal him to enter.

"Show me what you did next," she said.

Dillon pulled an air-filtering mask up from around his neck and over his mouth as he entered. Ballard looked back at Felsen and Torborg. Felsen had just finished the radio call to the watch commander.

"Can you see if the print car is available and get an ETA?" she asked.

"Roger that," Felsen said.

"And don't leave," she added. "I need you guys here."

"The L-T's already asking when we can clear," Felsen said.

"Tell her I need you here," Ballard said sternly.

She entered the house after Dillon. The odor of decay still hung in the air but it had dissipated since she had worked the death case two nights before. Still, she wished she had her air mask, but it was in her kit in her city ride. Along with her hermetically sealable coveralls. She knew her third-string suit would be toast after one wearing. Luckily, the suit she had dropped off at the dry cleaners the day before would be ready in the morning.

"Walk me through it," she said. "How'd you know it was a break-in? The place was already pretty messed up."

Dillon gestured over her shoulder to the front wall of the living room. Ballard turned and saw that the three side-by-side prints of red lips were gone. When Ballard had called Bobbi Clark to report that her aunt was dead, Clark had asked specifically about the well-being of the prints, mentioning that they were the work of Andy Warhol and were rare APs—artist's prints—that were worth over six figures each and even more when combined as a series.

"Ms. Clark told me to be careful of these red lip paintings that were supposed to be in the living room," Dillon said. "So, I come in and no red lips. I called you guys because this is why I rarely go into a house by myself. I don't want to get accused of anything. We usually work in twos but my partner's on another job and this lady Clark really wanted this done today. When she gets here, she doesn't want to see blood or anything else. She told me about what the cat did."

Ballard nodded.

"Is it your company or you just work for the company?" she asked.

"It's mine," Dillon said. "Two trucks, four employees, available twenty-four-seven. We're a small shop. You wouldn't think it, but it's a competitive business. A lot of companies cleaning up after murders and bad things."

"Well, this wasn't a murder. How'd Ms. Clark come to hire you from New York?"

"Recommendation from the M.E. I give out a lot of business cards. And gifts at the holidays. People recommend me. I'll give you a stack of cards if you'll take them."

"Maybe later. I don't do many crime scenes like this. Not a lot of murders in Hollywood these days and I'm usually on graveyard."

"They had that five-spot last year at the Dancers. I got that one. Worked four days cleaning up that mess and then they never reopened the joint."

"I know. I was there that night."

Dillon nodded.

"I think I saw you on TV for that," he said.

Ballard decided to get back on track.

"So, you come in, you see the prints are gone. Then what?" she asked.

"I backed out and called you guys," Dillon said. "Then I waited about an hour for them and then they waited an hour for you. I'm not getting any work done and Ms. Clark lands at ten tomorrow morning."

"I'm sorry about that, but we have to conduct the investigation—especially if we're talking about a major theft. We've hopefully got a print car coming soon and we'll need to get yours so we can exclude them. I'm going to ask you to step outside now and wait with the officers while I work in here."

"How long before I can go to work?"

"I'll get you cleared as soon as possible but I don't think you're getting in here today. Someone will have to do a walk-through in as-is condition with Ms. Clark after she arrives."

"Shit."

"Sorry."

"You keep saying that but I don't make money on sorries."

Ballard understood his concerns as the owner of the company.

"I'll tell you what, get me some of your cards, and I'll keep them handy down the line."

"I'd really appreciate that, Detective."

Ballard followed him out of the house and asked Felsen about the print car. He said the ETA was fifteen minutes and Ballard knew from experience that all waiting times on the print car should be doubled. The car was assigned to the entire West Bureau and was operated by a latent-print tech who responded to all needs, ranging from property capers to violent crimes. It was safe to say the print car tech never stopped working.

Technically, Ballard was supposed to follow a protocol in which she would first study the crime scene and look for likely spots where the suspect could have left prints. Only upon finding possibilities should she call for the print car. But in reality, when it came to property crimes, the practice was the opposite. Delaying in calling the print car added up to long waits. She always called first to get her case in line and then started looking at the scene. She could then call the car off if she didn't find any likely deposits.

Ballard knew she was pushing her luck with Dillon but took a shot anyway at asking if he had a spare breathing mask. He surprised her by saying yes.

He walked to the back of his truck and rolled up the door. The interior was stuffed with wet vacuums and other equipment. He pulled a box of throwaway masks out of a drawer in a tool chest and handed her one.

"The filter in there is good for a day," he said. "That's it."

"Thank you," Ballard said.

"And I've got my cards right here."

He reached into another drawer and took out a stack of about ten business cards. He gave them to Ballard, who saw that the small print under CCB was the company's formal name: Chemi-Cal Bio Services. She put the cards in her pocket and thanked Dillon, even though she knew her opportunities to recommend his services would be few.

She left him there and went back inside the house, pulling on the breathing mask as she went. She stood in the living room and took in the place, observing and thinking. The removal of the source of decomposition—the body—would explain the decrease in noxious odor. But Ballard had been in houses like this before in the days after death and she believed that more than the removal of the body had helped the process. She concluded that she was looking for an open window.

She moved to the far wall of glass and soon realized that the panels were on tracks that disappeared into a wall. The panels could be pushed into the wall, creating a wide opening onto the rear deck and giving the house an indoor-outdoor style. She slid open the first glass panel and stepped out onto the deck. She saw that it ran the length of the house behind the guest bedroom and the master. On the far end of the deck sat a rectangular air-conditioning unit. It had been removed from the wall below a window and left there. It must have been the burglar's access point and the opening from which some of the decomp stink had escaped.

Ballard walked down the deck to look at the opening. It

was at least two feet tall and three wide. The AC unit looked relatively new. The homeowner had probably added it to provide extra cooling in the bedroom during the hottest weeks of summer.

Ballard had the point of entry. Now the question was, how did the burglar get to it? The house was cantilevered over the steep hillside. She stepped to the guardrail and looked down. That was not the way. It would have been too difficult a trek, requiring ropes and hoists. That kind of planning conflicted with the fact that the air conditioner had been left out of its wall slot. This indicated the sloppy work of an opportunist, not a planner.

She looked up. The roof of the deck was supported in four places by ornate black ironwork that formed a repeating pattern of tree branches crossing between two risers. Whether intentional or not, each one created a makeshift ladder down from the roof.

Ballard stepped back into the house and went out the front door. Dillon was leaning against his truck. When he saw her, he straightened up and spread his arms wide questioningly.

"Where's the print car?" he asked. "When am I going to get out of here?"

"Soon," Ballard said. "Thank you for your patience."

She pointed to his truck.

"But in the meantime, I saw you had a ladder on the wall inside your truck," she said. "Could I borrow it for a few minutes? I want to get on the roof."

Dillon seemed happy to have something to do, especially if it further indebted the LAPD to him.

"No problem," he said.

While Dillon got the ladder, Ballard stepped out into the street and walked along the front of the house. The design of the structure was all geared toward the view out the other side. That's where the deck, windows, and glass doors were. This side, which was just three feet from the curb, was drab and monolithic save for the front door and one small window to the master bathroom. This fortresslike design was softened with alternating concrete planters containing bamboo stalks and vine-entwined lattices. Ballard studied the latticework and saw places where the vines had been damaged by someone using the connections as foot- and handholds for climbing. It was another improvised ladder.

Dillon banged an extension ladder against the house. Ballard looked over and he gestured with his hand: all yours.

While Dillon held the ladder steady, Ballard climbed to the flat roof. She walked toward the back edge, looking for footprints in the gravel or any other evidence of a burglar. There was nothing.

She got to the far edge and looked out at the view. It was getting dark and the setting sun was turning the sky red and pink. She knew it would be a good sunset at the beach. She momentarily thought of Aaron and wanted to check in on him to see if he had any news on the man he had pulled out of the riptide.

Turning her attention back to the case at hand, she was now sure she had found the burglar's path. He had climbed up the lattice in the front, crossed the roof and climbed down the ironwork on the back deck. After removing the air conditioner, he had entered and taken the three prints off the wall as well as whatever other property might be missing. At that point, he simply walked out the front door with the stolen goods, leaving the front door slightly ajar.

There were elements of genius mixed with naïveté. All aspects of the caper told her it had occurred under cover of darkness. That meant the burglary had happened on the night right after the discovery of the victim's death. Someone had acted quickly, most likely with knowledge of the artwork in the house and its value—as well as its owner's death.

She turned in a circle, scanning the immediate neighborhood. She knew it was a city of cameras. Finding them was always high on any investigative protocol. Nowadays you looked for video before witnesses. Cameras didn't lie or get confused.

Hollywood Boulevard curved in and out along the mountain's edge. The house she stood on was at a sharp bend around a blind curve. Ballard spotted a house on the curve that had a camera ostensibly aimed at a side stairway down to a landing below street level. But she knew that depending on the camera's angle, there was a chance its field of view included the roof she stood on.

The print car arrived as Ballard was descending the ladder, again with Dillon holding it steady for her. She first walked the tech through the house and deck, pointing out as possible spots for latents the wall where the three Warhols had been located as well as the AC unit left on the back deck. Then she stepped out front and introduced Dillon, asking the tech to take his prints first for exclusionary purposes. She thanked Dillon for his time and the use of his ladder and told him he was clear to leave as soon as he was printed.

"You sure I'm not going to be able to do the cleaning tonight?" he asked. "I'll wait around."

"It's not possible," Ballard said. "Ms. Clark is going to have to do the walk-through with somebody from dayside burglary. We don't want the place cleaned before that."

"Okay, thought I'd try."

"Sorry about that."

"No worries. Make sure you use those cards."

He gave a little wave and went to the back of his truck to close it. Ballard headed down the street in the direction of the camera she had spotted. Ten minutes later she was talking to the owner of the home around the blind curve and looking over his shoulder at the video playback from the camera located on the side of his house. It had a full but digitally murky capture of the entire roof of the home that had been burglarized.

"Let's start at midnight," Ballard said.

17

Ballard had her badge out and up when the door was opened. The man standing there looked concerned but not surprised. He was in sweats and one hand was in the front warmer of the sleeveless hoodie. Ballard could tell he was a "better living through science" guy. He had thick arms and the pronounced neck veins and hard eyes of a 'roid rider. His brown hair was slicked back over his head. His green eyes were glassy. He was shorter than Ballard but probably out-weighed her two to one.

"Mr. Bechtel? Theodore Bechtel?"

"It's Ted. Yes?"

"I'm Detective Ballard, LAPD. I would like to ask you a few questions. Can I come in?"

Bechtel didn't answer. He stepped back to allow her room to enter. Ballard walked in, turning slightly sideways as she passed him so she wouldn't lose direct sight of him. At this point, she considered him to be a burglar. She didn't want to give him the chance to add assault or murder to the list.

Bechtel reached over to close the door after she entered. She stopped him.

"Can we leave that open if you don't mind?" she said. "A couple of my colleagues will be coming."

"Uh, I guess so."

She turned in the circular entry area to look at him and accept further direction. But Bechtel just looked at her.

"You've come for the Warhols, right?" he asked.

She wasn't expecting that. She hesitated, then composed a response.

"Are you saying you have them?" she asked.

"I do," he said. "They're in my study. Where they're nice and safe."

He nodded as if to confirm a job well done.

"Can you show me?"

"Of course. Follow me."

Bechtel led Ballard down a short hallway into a home office. Sure enough, the three red lips prints were leaning against the wall. Bechtel spread his hands as if to present them.

"I think those are Marilyn Monroes," he said.

"Excuse me?" Ballard responded.

"The lips. Warhol used Marilyn's lips. I read it online."

"Mr. Bechtel, I need you to explain why these are in your house and not on the wall of the house across the street."

"I took them for safekeeping."

"Safekeeping. Who told you to do that?"

"Well, nobody told me to do it. I just knew somebody needed to do it."

"Why is that?"

"Well, because everybody knew she had them in there, and they were going to get stolen."

"So, you stole them first?"

"No, I didn't steal them. I told you. I brought them over here for safekeeping. To keep them for the rightful heir. That's all. I hear she had a niece in New York who gets everything."

"That's the story you want to go with? That this was some kind of neighborly act of kindness?"

"It's what happened."

Ballard stepped back from him and took stock of what she knew and what she had in terms of witnesses and evidence.

"What do you do for a living, Mr. Bechtel?"

"Nutrition. I sell supplements. I have a store down in the flats."

"Do you own this house?"

"I rent."

"How long have you been up here?"

"Three months. No, four."

"How well did you know the woman who lived across the street?"

"I didn't. Not really. Just to say hello to. That sort of thing."

"I think at this point I need to advise you of your rights."

"What? Are you arresting me?"

He looked genuinely surprised.

"Mr. Bechtel, you have the right to remain silent. Anything you say can and will be used against you in a court of law. You have the right to an attorney to represent you. If you can't afford an attorney, one will be provided for you. Do you understand these rights as I have explained them?"

"I don't understand. I was being a good neighbor."

"Do you understand your rights as I have recited them to you?"

"Yes, shit, I understand. But this is completely unnecessary. I have a business. I didn't do—"

"Sit down in that chair, please."

Ballard pointed to a chair that was against the wall. She kept pointing until Bechtel reluctantly sat down.

"This is amazing," he said. "You try to do a good thing and you get hassled for it."

Ballard pulled her phone and speed-dialed the watch office. Before knocking on Bechtel's door, she had requested backup because Felsen and Torborg had been sent to another call while she had been down the street looking at video. Now she was facing a situation where she had to make a felony arrest without backup. Her call wasn't answered for six rings. While she waited, she casually took a few steps farther back from Bechtel so she would have more time to react should he decide he didn't want to be arrested.

Finally, her call was answered by a voice she didn't recognize.

"This is six-William-twenty-five, where's my backup?"

"Uh…I don't see that here on the board. You sure you called for backup?"

"Yes, fifteen minutes ago. Send it. Now. No delay. And keep this connection open."

Ballard barked the address into the phone, then refocused on Bechtel. She would find out about the missing backup later.

Bechtel was sitting with both hands in the front pocket of his hoodie.

"I want you to take your hands out of the hoodie and keep them where I can see them," she said.

Bechtel complied but shook his head like this whole thing was a misunderstanding.

"Are you really arresting me?"

"Do you want to explain why you climbed over the roof of the house across the street, broke in on the back deck, and took three artworks worth several hundred thousand dollars?"

Bechtel didn't speak. He seemed surprised by her knowledge.

"Yeah, there's video," Ballard said.

"Well, I had to get in there somehow," he said. "Otherwise, somebody else would've and then the paintings would be gone."

"They're prints, actually."

"Whatever. I didn't steal them."

"Did you take anything else besides the prints?"

"No, why would I do that? I just cared about the paintings. The prints, I mean."

Ballard had to decide whether to cuff Bechtel to neutralize the threat or to wait for backup, which now might be another ten to fifteen minutes away. It was a long time to wait with a suspect not fully controlled.

"The District Attorney's Office will decide whether a crime was committed. But I will be arresting you. Right now I want you—"

"This is such bullshit—"

"—to get up from the chair and face the wall. I want you to kneel on the floor and lace your fingers behind your head."

Bechtel stood up but didn't move any further.

"Kneel down, sir."

"No, I'm not kneeling down. I didn't do anything."

"You are under arrest, sir. Kneel down on the ground and lace your—"

She didn't finish. Bechtel started moving toward her. It was crystal clear in the moment that if Ballard pulled her gun, she would probably have to use it, and it would most likely be the end of her career, no matter how justified a shooting it would be.

But what wasn't clear was whether Bechtel was coming at her or trying simply to walk around her and leave the room.

He moved as if heading toward the door but then suddenly pivoted toward her. Ballard tried to use his advantage—his weight and muscles—against him.

As Bechtel advanced, Ballard placed a well-directed kick to his groin, then took two steps back and to the side as he doubled over and lurched forward, emitting a sharp groan. She grabbed his right wrist and elbow, pushed the wrist down and pulled the elbow up as she pivoted him over her leg. He went down face-first and she dropped all 120 pounds of her weight through her knees onto the small of his back.

"Don't fucking move!"

But he did. He groaned like a monster and attempted to rise, doing a push-up off the floor. Ballard drove a knee into his ribs and he dropped to the floor again with an *oof.* She quickly grabbed the cuffs off her belt and clasped one over his right wrist before he realized he was being cuffed. He struggled against the next one but Ballard had the leverage. She pulled the wrists together against his spine and closed the second cuff around the left. Bechtel was now controlled.

Ballard got up, exhausted but exhilarated that she had taken the much stronger man to ground.

"You're going to jail, motherfucker."

"This is all a big mistake. Come on, this is wrong."

"Tell it to the judge. They love hearing bullshit from guys like you."

"You'll regret this."

"Believe me, I already do. But it doesn't change anything. You're going to jail."

BOSCH

18

Bosch and Lourdes had spent the rest of the day watching Dr. Jaime Henriquez to see whether he would eventually make a house call. Henriquez was a native son of San Fernando. He was the kid who'd made good and stayed close. A UCLA-trained physician, he could have worked anywhere in the country. But he came home and now operated a busy general practice on Truman Avenue with two other doctors to handle the overflow of patients Henriquez drew. He was a San Fernando success story, having grown up in the barrio and now living in the lush Huntington Estates, the nicest and safest neighborhood in the city.

But while outwardly he was a pillar of success and respectability, his name was secretly carried in the SFPD's gang intel files. Both his father and grandfather had been SanFers, and loyalty—whether compelled or volunteered—ran deep. The secret of his life was that Henriquez was a suspected gang doctor, and Bosch and Lourdes were going to find out if he was treating the killer of Martin Perez. Lourdes's cousin J-Rod had put them onto Henriquez, saying he was one of three doctors on the gang unit's radar. But the other two had already drawn investigations from the state's medical board and it was J-Rod's interpretation that for this case—the killing of a witness—the SanFers would go to their top patcher, who lived a life that seemed beyond reproach.

Most of the day had been spent on surveillance of the busy medical office where Henriquez practiced. Both Bosch and Lourdes dodged calls from sheriff's detectives Lannark and Boyce. And as they watched the medical building and the Mercedes-Benz registered to Henriquez parked out front, they tried to figure out where the leak in the investigation had been.

One of two things had happened. Someone had tipped the SanFers to the fact that Martin Perez was cooperating with the police. Or Perez had made some slip with an acquaintance or family member and had given himself away.

Bosch and Lourdes believed it was most likely the former and they spent their time running down the possibilities, dismissing some and holding on to others.

Bosch had mentioned his suspicions about Tom Yaro, the LAPD detective assigned as interdepartmental liaison to the execution of the search warrant, but Lourdes pointed out that Yaro didn't have enough information about the case to set up the hit on Perez. Additionally, it had been Yaro who had alerted Lourdes to Cortez watching the morning's search from the parking lot of the laundry. But that could have been a sincere warning or part of a more devious plan to solidify Yaro as someone on the pro-Bosch team.

"Yaro was briefed for the search warrant," Lourdes said. "But we never discussed your source in the briefing, and Perez was a John Doe on the warrant. Yaro had no name, no location—it's a long shot, if you ask me."

This turned the conversation uncomfortably toward the SFPD. Many of the officers in the department were from San

Fernando, and it would have been virtually impossible to grow up in the two-square-mile town without knowing somebody who was in the SanFers. Still, that connection usually worked in a positive way. Many officers added to the gang intel files after street conversations with past acquaintances. Lourdes's cousin J-Rod was an example of this and she could not remember an incident in her history with the department when information had gone the other way.

That seemed to turn the conversation even more uncomfortably toward Bosch. What move had he made that might have revealed Perez's betrayal to the SanFers?

Bosch was at a loss. He acknowledged that he often left his laptop in the cell he used as an office. But the cell was always locked and the computer was password protected. He knew that both could be compromised but it still seemed like a remote possibility that a member of the SanFer gang would undertake such an intrusion.

"It's gotta be something else," he said. "Maybe we look at Perez again. Who knows? Maybe he called somebody, bragged about taking down Cortez. Nobody said he was very smart."

"Maybe," Lourdes said, but her tone implied that she was unconvinced.

Defeated in their efforts to figure it out or at least settle on a focus, they let silence fill the car until they spotted a man approaching Henriquez's Mercedes-Benz.

"Is that him?" Bosch asked.

Lourdes held up her phone where she had downloaded to her screen a photo of Henriquez from the DMV.

"It's him," she said. "Here we go."

They followed the doctor north and into the Huntington Estates, where he pulled into a garage next to a two-story home with columns out front. The garage was attached to the house, and the detectives lost sight of the doctor once the door automatically came down.

"Think that's it?" Lourdes said. "He's in for the night?"

"If he worked on the shooter this morning, then I think he's gotta check on the patient at some point," Bosch said.

"Unless he died."

"There's that."

"Or unless he's in that house."

"There's that, too."

"So we stay?"

"I'm staying. If you've got stuff to do, you can walk down the street and call an Uber. I'll let you know if he makes a move."

"No, I'm not leaving you here alone."

"Not a big deal. This is a long shot anyway."

"Not what partners do."

Bosch nodded.

"Okay," he said. "But one of us might have to Uber over to Route 66 to pick up dinner. Haven't eaten all day."

"Not a problem," Lourdes said. "If you like that stuff."

Bosch didn't take the bait. They'd had good-natured disputes about surveillance food in the past.

They were parked a half block from the doctor's house in the driveway of a home that was empty while under full renovation. Bosch had positioned his old Jeep Cherokee in front of a flatbed used for towing construction materials, and the old beater fit in. The windows were smoked, and as long as they didn't light themselves with phone screens, they would go unnoticed by the doctor or others in the neighborhood.

"Do you remember the music group Seals and Crofts?" Lourdes asked.

"Yeah," Bosch said. "Seventies, right? They were big."

"Before my time but I heard this is where they lived. The Estates."

"Hmm."

The small talk continued for almost two hours, until the discussion of food came up again in earnest. Lourdes wasn't interested in Bosch's hamburger-and-hot-dog joint and Bosch had long ago OD'd on all the Mexican restaurants in town. They were about to flip for it, when a car came down the street and killed its lights as it pulled into the driveway of the Henriquez house. It was full dark now but Bosch had identified the make of the car as it drove by the construction site. It was a white Chrysler 300.

"This is it," Bosch said.

No one got out of the car. It sat and idled, exhaust puffing from its twin pipes.

None of the house's exterior lights came on when a figure emerged from the side and got into the Chrysler.

"Is that the doctor?" Lourdes asked.

"Can't tell, but I'm betting it is," Bosch said.

The car took off from the Henriquez house and passed in front of Bosch's Jeep without slowing down. Bosch waited until it had turned a corner and then he pulled out.

The trick was following the Chrysler out of the residential neighborhood without being made. Once the surveillance was in the commercial district, it was easier to use other cars on the road as camouflage. Bosch and Lourdes followed it to San Fernando Road and then north into the Sylmar region of Los Angeles. At Roxford the Chrysler turned right and entered a neighborhood of middle-class ranch homes on quarter-acre properties.

Just past Herrick Street the Chrysler turned right into a driveway and parked. Bosch drove on by. Lourdes reported what she saw.

"Several men," she said. "They met the car and hurried him inside."

"Must've taken a turn for the worse," Bosch said.

"So, what do we do?"

"For now we wait."

"For what? This is L.A. We should call in LAPD SWAT and scoop them all up."

"We will. But let's wait till they get the doctor out of there. Now that we can prove he does work for the SanFers, I think your cousin might want to flip him and keep him on the hook the rest of his days."

Lourdes nodded. It was a good plan. Henriquez would more than likely be willing to trade information with the gang intel unit in exchange for avoiding the humiliation of being exposed as a gang doctor.

"Except we still don't know who snitched off Perez," Lourdes said. "That could make things very dangerous for the doctor if he turns informant too."

Bosch nodded.

"That we need to keep working on," he said. "But once we know who the shooter is, that might become clearer."

19

When Bosch entered his house, he was met with Elizabeth's suitcase sitting on the floor just inside the front door. It was actually his suitcase but he had brought it to her on the last day of rehab so she could pack her meager belongings. There had still been room in it for items they would shop for.

Through the back sliders he saw her on the deck on one of the lounges. He watched her for a moment, thinking she had not heard him come in. She was not reading or listening to music. She was not looking at her phone. She was simply staring into the pass, the never-ending movement of vehicles down on the freeway, like blood through the veins of the city. It was an aspect of the view that was always changing but always the same. In recent years, the only addition was the fireworks shot on special occasions from the Harry Potter ride at Universal Studios.

He crossed the living room, slid open one of the doors, and stepped out.

"Hey," he said.

"Hello," she said.

She smiled. He crossed the deck to the railing and leaned his back to it so he could look at her.

"You're limping," she said.

"Yeah," he said. "Guess I gotta go see Dr. Zhang."

The previous year Bosch had met Elizabeth while he briefly worked undercover on a case. He'd adopted a cane and limp as part of a pose as an opioid addict scamming shady pharmacies for prescriptions. The irony was that during a struggle with a murder suspect on a plane, he had strained a ligament in his already arthritic knee, and now he made monthly visits to Dr. Zhang, an acupuncturist he had met many years earlier on a case.

"I'll call her in the morning," he said.

He waited for her to say something but she didn't.

"I saw the suitcase," he said.

"Yes, I packed," she said. "I'm going to leave. But I didn't want to leave without telling you face-to-face. That just seemed wrong after all you've done."

"Where are you going?"

"I don't know."

"Elizabeth…"

"I'll find a place."

"You have one right here."

"Your daughter won't visit because I'm here. That's not fair to either of you."

"She'll change. Besides, I go down to see her."

"And she barely says a word to you. You told me. She doesn't even text you."

"We texted last night."

"You text good night and then she says the same back. That isn't a conversation. That isn't what you had before I came."

Bosch knew he could not win this angle of the argument, because she was right.

"We're getting close on the case," he tried. "This detective I told you about...I think she's all in. It's active. Just give us some time. We checked out a possible suspect last night."

"What does it matter?" Elizabeth asked. "It doesn't change anything. Daisy's been dead nine years."

"All I can tell you is that it matters," Bosch said. "It counts. You'll see when we get the guy."

He waited but she didn't respond.

"I'm sorry I'm so late," he said. "Did you eat something?"

"Yes, I made something," she said. "I put a plate in the refrigerator for you."

"I think I'm just going to go to sleep. I'm tired, my knee hurts. I'm going to get up early and go down to Hollywood Division to check in with Ballard before she goes home."

"Okay."

"Will you at least stay tonight? It's too late to go out there without a plan. We can talk about it tomorrow."

She didn't answer.

"I'll put the suitcase back in your room," he said.

Bosch turned momentarily to the view just as a single rocket trailing green light arced into the sky over Universal. It exploded with a flat bang, nothing like the real mortars he had heard in his life.

He headed toward the open slider.

"Daisy sent me a postcard from Universal once," Elizabeth said. "It was before they had Harry Potter. They still had the Jaws ride. The card showed the shark, I remember that. It was how I knew she was in L.A."

Bosch nodded.

"When I was sitting out here, I remembered a joke she told me when she was little. She heard it at school. You want to hear it, Harry?"

"Sure."

"What happens when you eat too much alphabet soup?"

"What?"

"You have a vowel movement."

She smiled at the punch line. Bosch smiled too, though he was sure his own daughter had told him the joke once, and it made Elizabeth's grief hit him deeper.

This had been the way he had learned more about Daisy. Elizabeth grieved and reminisced and then shared the stories, all from before the girl had run away. She told him about how the stuffed turtle she had won at Skee-Ball at a fair became her most prized possession until the seams wore out. She told him about Daisy splashing in rubber boots through the flooded pecan orchards near their home.

There were the sad stories, too. She told Bosch about the best friend who moved away, leaving her alone. She told him about Daisy growing up without a father. About the schoolyard bullying and the drugs. Good and bad, it all brought Bosch closer to both mother and daughter, made Daisy mean more to him than just her death and stoked the fire he warmed himself by as he pursued the case.

Bosch held at the door for a moment and then just nodded.

"Good night, Elizabeth. See you tomorrow."

"Good night, Harry."

He went in, noting that she did not say she would see him in the morning. He stopped in the kitchen but only to put ice into a Ziploc bag for his knee. He put her suitcase in the room she used, then went to his own room and closed the door. He stripped off his clothes and took a long shower until the hot water was gone. Afterward, he put on a pair of blue-plaid boxer shorts and a white T-shirt and used an ACE bandage from the medicine cabinet to wrap his knee and hold the ice bag to it.

He plugged his phone into its charger and set the alarm for four a.m. so he could get down the hill to Hollywood Station and work a few hours with Ballard on the shake cards before the end of her shift. He then turned out the light and gingerly climbed onto the bed, positioning himself on his back with one pillow under his head and the other propped under his knee as the slight bend this created in the joint helped ease the low hum of pain.

Still, the ice was uncomfortable and it kept him awake until he thought the knee pain was numbed to the point he could fall asleep. He unraveled the ACE bandage and put the ice bag into an empty champagne bucket he kept next to the bed in case the bag leaked.

Bosch was asleep soon and snoring lightly when the sound of his bedroom door opening woke him. He tensed for a moment but then saw the female silhouette in the doorway, outlined by oblique light from down the hall. It was Elizabeth. She was naked. She moved to the bed and climbed under the sheet that covered Bosch, straddling her legs over his hips. She leaned down and kissed him hard on the mouth before he could say anything, before he could remind her that he was old and might not be able to perform, let alone discuss the propriety of having a relationship with the mother of the girl whose death he was investigating.

Elizabeth kept her mouth on his and gently began to rock her hips. Bosch felt her warmth against him and reacted. Soon she was reaching to push down his shorts. Bosch's knee was no longer numb, but if there was pain, he wasn't feeling it. Elizabeth made all the moves and guided him inside her. Her hips worked in a steady rhythm and she put her hands on his shoulders and arched her back. The sheet fell aside. Bosch looked up at her in the dim light. Her head was thrown back like she was looking up at the ceiling. She was silent. Her breasts swayed above him. He put his hands on her hips to help lend his rhythm to hers.

Neither spoke, neither made a sound except for the deep exhalation of breath. First he felt her hips shudder, and soon after he desperately reached up and pulled her down into an embrace as his own body created that one moment that takes all other moments away—all fear, all sadness—and leaves just joy. Just hope. Sometimes love.

Neither moved, as though each one thought the fragile reverie might break with even the blink of an eye. Then she pushed her face further into the crook of his neck and kissed his shoulder. They'd had boundary lines. Bosch had told her that this was not his purpose in inviting her to stay with him, and she had said it would never come to that, because she had lost that part of herself—the capacity to connect.

But now here they were. Bosch wondered if this was her goodbye. If she would be gone tomorrow.

He put his hand on her back and moved his thumb and forefinger like an inchworm down her spine. He thought he heard a smothered giggle. If it was, he had never heard it before.

"I don't want you to go," he whispered. "Even if this never happens again. Even if it was a mistake. I don't want you to go. Not yet."

She raised herself up and looked at him in the darkness. He could see a slight glint in her dark eyes. He could feel her breasts against his chest. She kissed him. It was not a long, impassioned kiss like the one she had started with. It was a quick kiss on the lips and then she climbed off.

"Is that a champagne bucket?" she asked. "You knew I was coming in?"

"No," Bosch said quickly. "I mean, it is a champagne bucket but I use it for the ice pack for my knee."

"Oh."

"Why don't you stay in here tonight?"

"No, I like my bed. Good night, Harry."

She moved toward the door.

"Good night," Bosch whispered.

She closed the door behind her. Bosch stared at it in the darkness for a long time.

BALLARD

20

It was one a.m. and well into her official shift before Ballard completed the paperwork that went along with the arrest and booking of Theodore Bechtel on suspicion of breaking and entering and grand theft. After he was secured in a solo cell at the station, she walked through the parking lot to the storage rooms and retrieved a fresh box of shake cards. Once back in the detective bureau she set up in a back corner and soon was sifting through the reports on the human tumbleweeds, as Tim Farmer had called them, that drifted across the streets of Hollywood on a nightly basis.

After an hour she had put six cards aside for further consideration and follow-up. Several hundred did not make the cut. Her forward progress was slowed when she came across another card written by Farmer. His words and observations held her once again.

> *This kid knows nothing better than the street. If he was put into a one-bedroom apartment with a full kitchen he'd move into the closet and sleep on the floor. He's one of the rain people.*

She wondered who the rain people were in Farmer's estimation. People who couldn't fit in with the rest of society? People who needed the rain?

Her rover squawked and Lieutenant Munroe called her to the watch office. She took the long way, going down the rear hallway of the station and then up to the front. This allowed her to see who was in the station and maybe get a sense of what was happening before speaking to Munroe.

But the station was empty as it was on most nights. Munroe was standing behind his desk, looking down at the deployment screen, which showed the locations of cars and personnel in the field. He didn't look up but knew she had entered the room.

"Ballard, we've got a hot shot and I need you to get out there and honcho it," he said.

"What's the call?" Ballard asked.

"A woman calls in, says she's locked in the bathroom of a house up on Mount Olympus. Says she's been raped and managed to get to the bathroom with her cell phone. Says the guy's still there, trying to break the door down. I rolled two units and a sergeant. They get there and guess who the guy is? Danny fucking Monahan. It's a he-said-she-said, and I want you out there to make the call."

"Did they transport the victim to the rape center?"

"Nope. She's still there. She took a shower while she was in the bathroom."

"Shit. They should've transported her anyway."

"They're not sure she's a victim, Ballard. Just get out there and see for yourself. This should be right up your alley."

"What's that mean?"

"Whatever you want it to mean. Just get up there. And don't forget your rover."

He handed a slip of paper over the screen to her. It had the address written on it and the name and age of the person reporting the incident: Chloe Lambert, 22.

Ballard was in her city ride, heading back toward the hills within five minutes. She hated cases involving celebrities. Things always had a different reality to them. It wasn't normal life. Danny Monahan was a stand-up comic who had broken big in the last five years with podcasts and cable specials and now a growing string of hit movies that steadily broke the hundred-million-dollar mark at the box office. He was a triple threat and a major force to contend with in Hollywood. It seemed appropriate that he would live in a part of the Hollywood Hills known as Mount Olympus.

Ballard hit the blue lights and streaked down Sunset to Crescent Heights, where she turned north toward Laurel Canyon. The neighborhoods of Mount Olympus covered the front right shoulder of the canyon, with large homes that peeked at the lights of the city down in the flats. Ballard pulled into the driveway of a house on Electra Drive and parked behind one of the patrol cars.

She was met in the driveway by Sergeant Dvorek.

"Won't need a space suit tonight, Sally Ride," he said.

"Good," Ballard said. "What will I need?"

"The wisdom of Solomon, I guess. She says he's an ass bandit and he says she's setting him up for a MeToo moment."

"Why didn't you transport her to the RTC, Stan?"

Dvorek held his hands up as if to calm her.

"Just hold on, hold on. I didn't want to make the call on that because, if she gets transported, then there's a case number and this guy's life and career go down the toilet."

The male bias was no shock to Ballard. But now wasn't the time to call Dvorek on it.

177

"Okay, where are they?" she asked.

"I've got Monahan sitting snug as a bug in the home office, and the girl is…"

"The girl?"

"Woman, whatever. She's in the screening room on the other side of the house. Nobody's touched anything in the bedroom or talked to the suspect."

"Well, you did that right. I'm going to talk to the woman first. Show me."

Dvorek led the way into a massive home that appeared to be a conjoining of circular structures of different sizes. The center circle was the tallest. The entryway was at least two stories high.

"She's this way," Dvorek said.

They walked through a massive entertaining area with a small stage and microphone in one corner, where, Ballard guessed, Monahan practiced his stand-up routines or performed for invited guests and family. They then moved into a hallway and toward an open door where a blue suiter named Gina Gardner was standing post.

"G-G," Ballard said as she passed.

She entered a home theater with a large curtained screen at the front. Four rows of plush leather lounge chairs, twelve in all, were on stepped levels going toward the rear. Posters from Monahan's movies and in various languages lined the walls.

Sitting on the edge of one of the lounge chairs was a young woman wearing a man's bathrobe. She was blond with large doe eyes. Her cheeks were streaked with makeup that had run down her face with tears.

Dvorek presented the victim and then backed into the hallway with Gardner. Ballard held out her hand.

"Chloe, I'm Detective Ballard. I'm here to hear your story and to make sure you get whatever medical treatment you need."

"I just need to go home, but they won't let me. He's still here. I'm scared."

"You are perfectly safe. There are six police officers in the house and he's being held in a room on the other side. I just want to get some basic information from you and then we'll take you for medical examination and treatment. I'm going to record your statement."

"Okay."

Ballard sat on the edge of the lounge chair next to Chloe's and put the small digital recorder she always carried between them. Once she started to record, she identified herself and the victim and gave the time, date, and location of the interview.

"Chloe, how long have you known Danny Monahan?"

"Tonight was when I met him."

"Where was that?"

"At the Comedy Room. I went with my friend Aisha tonight and he was there. He did stand-up and then I met him at the bar in the back. He invited me up here."

"What about Aisha?"

"No, just me."

"Did you drive here in your own car?"

"No, I had Ubered. I mean to the Comedy Room. He drove me here in his car."

"Do you know what kind of car it was?"

"It was a Maserati but I don't know, like, which model it was."

"That's okay. So, you came here on an invitation. You were not forced."

"No, I even had sex with him and I wanted to. But then later he...god, this is so embarrassing..."

She started crying again.

"It's okay, Chloe. Nothing that happened is your fault. There is nothing to be embarrassed about. You are not the—"

"He rolled me over and raped me in the ass. I told him to stop but he wouldn't. I said no. I said no several times but he wouldn't stop."

She said it rapid-fire, like it was the one and only time she would be able to say it.

"Are you hurt, Chloe?"

"Yes, I'm bleeding."

"Okay, I have to ask you this question and I apologize ahead of time. Had you ever had anal sex before this occurred with Danny Monahan?"

"No, never. I think it's disgusting."

"Okay, Chloe, that's all for now. I'm going to get you to a rape treatment center where they're going to look for biological evidence and treat you for your injuries. They'll also be able to talk to you about counseling and what steps to take from there."

"I just want to go home."

"I know, but this is a necessary stage in the investigation. We need to do this. Okay?"

"Okay, I guess."

"Okay, you wait here. Officer Gardner is going to be outside the door at all times, and I'll be back soon."

When she stepped out through the door, Dvorek was gone. Gardner gave her a head wave and they walked up the hall so they could confer without Chloe hearing them. Gardner had ten years on the job, all of them at Hollywood Division. She was petite and wore her dark hair tied up in the back.

"She has her cell," Gardner said. "I heard her whispering on a call."

"Okay," Ballard said.

"Just so you know, I heard her say, 'This guy's going to pay. I'm going to be rich.'"

Ballard pointed to the body cam affixed to her uniform.

"You think that picked it up?"

"I don't know, maybe."

"Make sure I get the video file at end of shift. I want you to write up a report as well. Anything else?"

"No, just that."

"Thanks."

"Sure thing."

Ballard found Dvorek in the entertaining area and asked him to take her to the bedroom.

It was a large, round room with a round bed and a round mirror on the ceiling above it. Ballard kept her hands in her pockets as she leaned over the bed and looked down at the knot of sheets and pillows. She saw no blood or anything else that might constitute evidence. She went into the bathroom, which featured a large round Jacuzzi in the center. She inspected a large white-tiled shower stall but saw no blood or other evidence. In a waste-basket next to the toilet she saw a wad of blood-stained tissues.

"Okay, we're going to need to call out a field unit to collect everything," she said. "Can you make the call while I talk to the suspect?"

"You got it," Dvorek said. "I'll take you over to him first."

Danny Monahan was sitting behind a desk that was notable to Ballard because it wasn't big and it wasn't round. It was old and scratched, and that told her it had sentimental value to the comic genius sitting behind it.

"You notice the desk, huh?" he said. "I was a schoolteacher once. Not many people know that."

Monahan was midthirties, paunchy with success, his red hair too long, overly styled, and cut to look like he had just rolled out of bed and run his hands through it. A guy who cared about his looks but trying to appear that he didn't.

Ballard ignored the reveal about the desk.

"Mr. Monahan, I'm Detective Ballard. Has anyone read you your rights?"

"My rights? No. Come on, this is a shakedown. She wants money. She told me she would bleed me dry."

Ballard showed him her digital recorder and turned it on. She then recited the Miranda rights warning and asked Monahan if he understood them.

"Look, it might have gotten a little rough but it wasn't anything she didn't ask for," he said.

"Mr. Monahan," Ballard insisted. "If you want to talk to me and explain what happened, then you need to acknowledge that you understand the rights I have recited to you. If not, then we're done here and you are under arrest."

"Arrest? That is fucking absurd. This was completely consensual."

Ballard paused for a moment before speaking calmly and slowly.

"One more time," she said. "Do you understand your rights as they have been explained to you?"

"Yes, I understand my rights," Monahan said. "Happy now?"

"Do you want to talk to me about what happened here in your home tonight?"

"Sure, I'll talk, because it's all bullshit. It's a con—she wants money, Detective. You can't see that?"

Ballard put the recorder down on Monahan's old teaching desk. She again stated the time and location as well as Monahan's name and his agreement to give a recorded statement.

"Tell me what happened. This is your chance."

Monahan spoke matter-of-factly, as if describing what he had had for dinner.

"I met her at the club tonight and then I took her home and fucked her. That's what happened and it's what I do all the time. But this time, she gets up and runs into the bathroom, locks the door, and starts yelling rape."

"Did you try to break through the door to the bathroom?"

"Nope."

"Let's go back to the sex. Did she at any time say no or tell you to stop?"

"No, she stuck her ass up and said go for it. Anything else is a lie."

It was a classic he-said-she-said case, as Lieutenant Munroe had warned and as many rape cases reported to the LAPD were. But Ballard had seen the blood in the wastebasket and she knew that would tip consideration toward Chloe's side of the story. The results of the examination at the rape treatment center could also be probative if the victim's injuries were quantifiable. The blood in the basket seemed to indicate that they would be.

Arresting a celebrity in a celebrity town was risky business. The cases drew massive attention and the accused usually hired the best and brightest legal teams. The defense would do a deep dive into Ballard's life and career, and she knew as surely as she was standing there that her history as a complainant about sexual harassment in the department would be brought up and likely used to paint her as biased in favor of the female.

She realized she could back out at this point. The celebrity involvement would easily qualify this investigation as a downtown case. The newly formed sexual harassment task force should be called out. But Ballard also realized that the way the system worked could put other women in jeopardy. Her passing the buck here would result in a slow and methodical investigation during which Monahan would not be arrested or in any way removed from his life and routines. It might be weeks before the case was presented to the District Attorney's Office for charges.

But Monahan had just said he did this often—brought a woman up from the comedy clubs down below. Did he do what he did to Chloe to every woman he brought to the round bedroom? Ballard could not risk that her acting out of career caution or department protocol might lead to other women being victimized.

Ballard called Dvorek in from the hallway, then turned back to Monahan.

"Mr. Monahan, stand up," she said. "You're under arrest for—"

"Wait, wait, wait!" Monahan yelled. "Okay, okay. Look, I didn't want to do this but I can prove to you there was no rape. Just let me show you. There will be no arrest. I guarantee it."

Ballard looked at him for a moment, then glanced at Dvorek.

"You have five minutes," she said.

"We have to go to my bedroom," Monahan said.

"That's a crime scene."

"No, it's not a crime scene. I have the whole thing on video. You look at it, you'll see. No rape."

Ballard realized she should have seen that coming. The mirror on the ceiling. Monahan was a voyeur.

"Let's go," she said.

Monahan led the police procession to the bedroom, stating his case along the way.

"Look, I know what you're thinking, but I'm not a creep," he said. "But with all this MeToo stuff starting up last year, I thought I needed protection, you know?"

"You put in cameras," Ballard said.

"Damn right. I knew it might come to this. I didn't do it for me to watch—that would be sick. I just needed the protection."

In the bedroom he went to a remote control on a stand next to the bed and turned on a large screen that mirrored the curve of the wall. Soon the screen split into sixteen views from security cameras around the house. He highlighted one of the squares and expanded it. Ballard was now looking at an overhead view of the room that included her, Dvorek, and Monahan. Ballard turned to locate the camera and focused on the ornate frame of a painting on the wall near the head of the bed.

"Okay, now we just rewind," Monahan said.

Ballard turned back. Two minutes later, they were watching Monahan and Chloe Lambert have sex on the bed. There was no sound and thankfully it was a wide-angle lens. Ballard assumed that the action on the screen could be blown up, but that was not necessary for her to see what was obviously a consensual coupling.

"That was the first time we did it," Monahan said. "Then we took a little nap. You want me to fast-forward to the main event?"

"Please," Ballard said.

Monahan sped forward to the second round of sex, and it became clear through Lambert's body language and posturing that she had initiated the second go and the specific act of anal sex. When it was over, she walked calmly to the bathroom and closed the door.

Monahan started to fast-forward the playback again.

"So, here is where I hear her on the phone in there calling the cops."

He switched to normal playback and they watched as he jumped naked from the bed and rushed to the bathroom door. He leaned his head to the jamb like he was listening to the phone call Lambert was making, then started pounding the side of his fist against the door.

"You can turn it off," Ballard said. "I'm going to need a copy."

"No way," Monahan said. "Why?"

"Because it's evidence. I'm going to arrest her for filing a false report."

"I don't want her arrested. I just want you to get her the fuck out of here. You think I want every broad I've banged this year to know I have them on tape? Why do you think I didn't tell you about this from the start? I'm not pressing any charges. Just get her out of here."

"Mr. Monahan, it doesn't matter if you don't want to press charges. She made the false report to the police."

"Well, I won't cooperate and I'll hire the best fucking lawyer in the country to stop you from getting the video. You want that fight?"

"You know, sir, I could also charge you with recording a sexual encounter without both parties' knowledge and consent."

Monahan computed the ramifications of that for a few moments before speaking.

"Uh, don't you think decisions like this are above your pay grade, Detective?"

"You want me to call my commander? Or better yet, the sex harassment task force that leaks to the media like a sieve? If you

186

want, I'll call the chief of police at home. I'm sure everybody on the food chain will be totally discreet about this."

Monahan's face revealed that he was realizing the can of worms he was opening up.

"Sorry, my bad," he said. "I think you are probably perfectly capable of deciding how best to handle this."

Ten minutes later, Ballard returned to the home theater where Chloe Lambert was waiting. She dropped the clothes she had collected from the bedroom on the floor in front of her.

"You can get dressed," Ballard said.

"What's happening?" Lambert asked.

"Nothing's happening. You're going home. You're lucky you're not going to jail."

"Jail? What for?"

"Filing a false report. You weren't raped, Chloe."

"What the fuck? That guy's a predator."

"Maybe, but so are you. He has the whole thing on video. I watched it. So you can stop the act. Get dressed and I'll have you driven down the hill."

Ballard turned to leave but then hesitated and looked back.

"You know, it's women like you that…"

She didn't finish. She believed it would be lost on Chloe Lambert.

21

Ballard was depressed. She left the Monahan estate not knowing which of the two people she had interviewed was the more loathsome example of the human form. And yet neither would face consequences for their actions of the night. She decided to focus her enmity on Chloe as a betrayer of the cause. For every noble movement or advancement in the human endeavor across time, there were always betrayers who set everything a step back.

She tried to shake it off as she came through the back door of the station and headed down the hallway to the detective bureau. She had a half box of FI cards she wanted to finish before the end of her shift. She checked her watch. It was 4:15 a.m. Her plan was to write up a report on the callout to Electra Drive. She would pull no punches, naming all parties in the investigation and describing their actions, even though the investigation had come to nothing so far. She would file it in the detective commander's inbox and it would be someone else's decision from there. It might go down to the task force and it might even make it to the D.A.'s Office for consideration. Along the way, it might also get leaked to the media. No matter how it went, she was passing the buck on it, and that did not sit well with her. She could have arrested them both on the spot for different crimes, but such a move would have resulted in her actions being studied and questioned by a command staff that didn't like her or want her. Some fault would likely be found and she would be further buried by the department and pulled away from the one thing she needed most: her job on the late show.

She turned into the detective bureau and headed to the back corner where she had set up for work earlier. She was nearly there when she saw the familiar head of gray curly hair over one of the half walls of the workstation. Bosch.

When she got to him, she saw that he was looking through the last four-inch stack of cards from the storage box she had brought in.

"So, they just let you waltz in here anytime you like," she said by way of a greeting.

"To be honest, I sort of let myself in tonight," Bosch said. "They never took my nine-nine-nine key when I quit."

Ballard nodded.

"Well, I have to write a report. I won't be able to look at shake cards till I file."

"I'm on the last stack here. I'll go out back and get another box."

"I'd better go with you. Let's do it now before I settle in and start writing. I can tell you the latest on John the Baptist on the way."

They headed back through the station and out the rear door to the parking lot. Ballard updated Bosch on her return to the Moonlight Mission and interview with McMullen. She said that her gut instinct was still that McMullen wasn't their guy. She told him about the head count he kept on his calendars and the photo of Daisy she had found.

"So, you actually placed him with the victim," Bosch said. "He knew her."

"He baptized her several months before the murder," Ballard said. "But come on, she was a night dweller and he roams Hollywood at night, looking for souls to save. I would be surprised if they didn't cross paths. I still don't think there's anything there and I might have an alibi for McMullen's van."

She told him about the van being in the shop on the night of the abduction and murder.

"McMullen looked it up and left me a message about the place," she said. "As soon as they open this morning, I'm going to see if I can confirm that the van was there when Daisy got taken. If I do, then I think we move on from John the Baptist."

Bosch said nothing, indicating he was not ready to scratch the missionary man off the list of potential suspects.

"So, what's happening with your search warrant case?" Ballard asked.

"We got part of the way there," Bosch said. "We found the bullets we were looking for but they were no good for comparison. And then my source ended up dead out in Alhambra."

"Oh shit! And it's connected?"

"Looks that way. Done in by his own gang. LAPD SWAT arrested the shooter last night in Sylmar. He wasn't talking when I left but he's known to be tight with our suspect on the cold case. Sometimes when you blow the dust off an old investigation, bad things happen."

Ballard looked at him in the dim light of the parking lot. She wondered if that was some kind of warning about the Daisy Clayton case.

They walked silently the rest of the way to the storage facility. Once there, they each picked up a box of FI cards and headed back to the station. Ballard turned and assessed the boxes in the hallway before leaving. They were about halfway through.

Walking back across the lot, Bosch stopped for a breather and put his box on the trunk of a black-and-white.

"I've got a bad knee," he explained. "I get acupuncture when it acts up. Just haven't had the time."

"I've heard that knee replacements are better than the real thing these days," Ballard said.

"I'll keep that in mind. But that would take me out of the game for a while. I might never get back."

He picked up the box and pressed on.

"I was thinking," he said. "You remember the GRASP program—Were you here then?"

"I was on patrol," Ballard said. "'Get a GRASP on crime'—I remember. A PR stunt."

"Well, yeah, but I think that was still going strong when Daisy got taken. And I was wondering what happened to all that data they collected. I thought, if it was still around somewhere, we might get another angle on the lay of the land in Hollywood at the time of the murder."

GRASP was indeed a public relations ploy by a former chief who took the reins of the department and touted a law enforcement think-tank idea of studying crime through geography to help determine how people and facilities were targeted. It was revealed with much fanfare by the department but suffered a quiet death a few years later when a new chief with new ideas came in.

"I don't remember what it stood for," Ballard said. "I was on patrol in Pacific Division and I remember filling out the forms on the MDC. Geographic something or other."

"Geographic Reporting and Safety Program," Bosch said.

"The guys down in the ASS Office really worked some OT on it."

"Ass Office?"

"The Acronym Selection Section. You never heard of it? They got about ten guys down there full-time."

Ballard started laughing as she lifted her knee, held her box with one hand on her thigh, and used her key card to open the door of the station. She then opened it with her hip and let Bosch in first.

They walked down the hallway.

"I'll look into the GRASP files," she said. "I'll start at the ASS office."

"Let me know what you find."

Back at the workstation, Ballard noticed the blue binder that had been left at her spot. She flipped it open.

"What's this?" she asked.

"I told you I had started a new murder book for the reinvestigation," Bosch said. "I figured you would want to start adding to it, maybe do a chrono. I think it should stay with you."

There were only a few reports in the binder at the moment. One was Bosch's summary of his interview with a supervisor at American Storage Products about the container that he believed Daisy Clayton's body had been stuffed into.

"Good," she said. "I'll print out everything I have and put it in. I already have an online chrono going."

She flipped the binder closed and saw that it was old and the blue plastic faded. Bosch was recycling an old murder book and it didn't surprise her. She guessed that he had the records from several old cases in his home. He was that kind of detective.

"Did you close the one this came from?" she asked.

"I did," Bosch said.

"Good," she said.

They went back to work. There were no more callouts for Ballard that shift. She got her report writing finished and filed and then joined Bosch on the FI cards. By dawn they had made it through the two boxes they brought from storage. Fifty more cards were added to the stack that warranted a second look but did not rise to the level of requiring immediate action. As they worked through the cards, they had talked and Bosch had told her stories about his days in Hollywood Homicide in the 1990s. She noticed that he, or in some instances the media, had given names to many of his cases: the Woman in the Suitcase, the Man with No Hands, the Dollmaker, and so on. It was as though homicides back then were an event. Now it seemed that nothing was new, nothing shocked.

Ballard gathered their two stacks of keepers together along with the murder book.

"I'm going to put these in my locker and then go over to the auto repair shop," she said. "You want to go with me? To the shop, I mean."

"No," Bosch said. "I mean, I do, but I think I better get up to the Valley and see where we are on things. Maybe I'll see if I can get some pins stuck in my knee on the way."

"Let's check in later, then. I'll let you know what I get."

"That's a plan."

22

Ballard stopped for a latte after leaving the station. While waiting for it, she got a text from Aaron saying he was off all day. She took this to mean that the man he had pulled from the riptide had not survived and Aaron was given a "therapy day" to deal with it. She texted him back and said she had a stop to make before heading out toward the beach.

The two garage doors were open at Zocalo Auto Services when she got there. She had driven her van because she was not planning to go back to the station afterward.

A man stood in one of the open bays, wiping his already greasy hands on a rag and assessing the Ford Transit with the board racks. Ballard got out and quickly showed her badge to disabuse him of the idea that she was a potential client.

"Is the owner or manager here?" she asked.

"That's me," the man said. "Both. Ephrem Zocalo."

He had a strong accent.

"Detective Ballard, LAPD Hollywood Division. I need your help, sir."

"What can I do?"

"I'm trying to confirm that a particular van was here getting work done—a transmission possibly—nine years ago. Is that possible? Do you have records from '09?"

"Yes, we have records. But that is a very long time ago."

"You have computer records? Maybe just put in the name?"

"No, no computers. We have files and we keep, you know… we keep the papers."

It didn't sound too sophisticated but all Ballard cared about was that there were records of some sort.

"Are they here?" she asked. "Can I look? I have the name and dates."

"Yeah, sure. We have them in the back."

He led her to a small office adjacent to the repair bays. They passed a man who was working in a trench beneath a car, the high-pitched whine of a drill sounding as he removed the bolts of a transmission cover. He looked suspiciously at Ballard as she followed Zocalo to the office.

The office was barely big enough to hold a desk, chair, and three four-drawer file cabinets. Each drawer had a framed card holder on which a year was handwritten. This meant Zocalo had records going back twelve years, which gave Ballard hope.

"You said '09?" Zocalo asked.

"Yes," Ballard said.

He pointed a finger up and down the drawers until he found the one marked 2009. The labels were not in a clear chronological order and Ballard guessed that each year, he dumped the oldest set of records and started with a fresh drawer.

The 2009 drawer was the second drawer up in the middle row. Zocalo waved at it with an open hand as if saying it was all Ballard's to deal with.

"I'll keep everything in order," she said.

"Don't matter," Zocalo said. "You can use the desk."

He left her there and went back out into the garage. Ballard heard him saying something in Spanish to the other worker, but they spoke too fast for her to translate the conversation. But she heard the word *migra,* and her sense was that the man in the garage trench was worried that she was really an immigration agent.

She pulled the file drawer open and found it to be only a third full of receipts leaning haphazardly against the back panel. She reached down with both hands, pulled about half of them out, and carried them to the desk.

All surfaces of the desk seemed to be coated with a patina of grease. Zocalo clearly didn't visit the sink when he moved from doing repair work to office work. Many of the invoice copies she started looking through were also smudged with grease.

The invoices were generally kept in order by date, so the process of checking the alibi for John the Baptist's van went quickly. Ballard moved through the stack directly to the week in question and soon found a copy of an invoice for installation of a new transmission in a Ford Econoline van with the name John McMullen and the address of the Moonlight Mission on it. Ballard studied it and saw that the dates the van was in the shop corresponded with the blank squares on McMullen's calendar and covered the two days that Daisy Clayton was missing and then found dead.

Ballard looked around the office. She saw no copier. Leaving the McMullen receipt out, she returned the rest of the stack to the file drawer and closed it. She walked out of the office and into the garage. Zocalo was down in the trench with the other man. She squatted down next to the car they were working under and held out the grease-smudged invoice.

"Mr. Zocalo, this is what I was looking for. Can I take it and make a copy? I'll bring you back the original if you need it."

Zocalo shook his head.

"I don't really need to have it," he said. "Not for so long, you know. You just keep it. Is okay."

"You sure?"

"*Sí, sí,* I'm sure."

"Okay, thank you, sir. Here's my card. If you ever need my help with anything, you give me a call, okay?"

She handed a business card down into the trench and right away it was marked with a greasy thumbprint as Zocalo took it.

Ballard left the garage and stood next to her van. She pulled her phone and took a photo of the invoice Zocalo had let her keep. She then texted the photo to Bosch with a message.

Confirmed: JTB's van was in the shop when Daisy was taken. He's clear.

Bosch didn't respond right away. Ballard got in her van and headed toward Venice.

She caught the morning migration west and it took almost an hour to get to the overnight pet-care facility where she kept Lola. After she got her dog and took her for a short walk around the Abbot Kinney neighborhood, she returned to the van and drove over to the canals, Lola sitting upright on the passenger seat.

Public parking near the canals was at a premium. Ballard did what she often did when she visited Aaron. She parked in the city lot on Venice Boulevard and then walked into the canal neighborhood on Dell. Aaron shared one side of a town house duplex on Howland with another lifeguard. The other side of the duplex was also the home of lifeguards. There seemed to be a steady rotation of them moving in and out as assignments changed. Aaron had been there for two years and liked working

Venice Beach. While others aspired to assignments farther north toward Malibu, he was content to stay and therefore had the longest residency in the duplex, which was notable for its dolphin-shaped mailbox.

Ballard knew that Aaron would be home alone, since all lifeguards worked day shifts. She patted the dolphin on the head and led Lola through the gate by her leash. The sliding door on the lower level had been left half open for her and she entered without knocking.

Aaron was lying on the couch, eyes closed, balancing a bottle of tequila on his chest. He startled when Lola went over and licked his face. He grabbed the bottle before it fell.

"You okay?" Ballard asked.

"I am now," he said.

He sat up and smiled, happy to see her. He held out the tequila but she shook her head.

"Let's go upstairs," he said.

Ballard knew what he was feeling. Any death experience—whether it was a close call for oneself or involvement in the death of another—led to some kind of primordial need to affirm not having been vanquished from existence. That affirmation could turn into some of the best sex ever.

She pointed Lola to a dog bed in the corner. Aaron had a pit bull but he had apparently taken her to the kennel even though he had the day off. Lola dutifully climbed onto the round cushion, circled it three times, and finally sat down with a view of the sliding door. She would be on guard. There was no need to even close the slider.

Ballard went over to the couch, grabbed Aaron's hand, and led him toward the stairs. He started to speak as they went up.

"They took him off life support at nine last night after they got all the family there. I went over. I sort of wish I hadn't. Not a good scene. At least they didn't blame me. I got to him as fast as I could."

Ballard quieted him when they got to the bedroom door.

"No more," she said. "Leave that out here."

Thirty minutes later they were lying entwined and spent on the floor of Aaron's bedroom.

"How'd we get off the bed?" Ballard asked.

"Not sure," Aaron said.

He reached over to the tequila bottle on the wood floor but Ballard used her foot to push it out of reach. She wanted him to hear what she said next.

"Hey!" Aaron said, feigning upset.

"Did I ever tell you that my father drowned?" Ballard asked. "When I was a kid."

"No, that's awful."

He moved in closer to her to console her. She was turned and looking at the wall.

"Did it happen here?" Aaron asked.

"No, Hawaii," Ballard said. "That's where we lived. He was surfing. They never found him."

"I'm sorry, Renée. I—"

"It was a long time ago. I always just wished they had found him, you know? It was so strange that he just got on his board and went out there. And then he never came back."

They were silent for a long moment.

"Anyway, I was thinking about that with that guy yesterday," Ballard said. "At least you brought him in."

Hayes nodded.

"That must've been awful for you back then," he said. "You should have told me this before."

"Why?"

"I don't know. It's just sort of…you know, your father drowns at the beach and now you mostly sleep at the beach. You and me, with me being a lifeguard. What's that say?"

"I don't know. I don't think about it."

"Did your mother remarry?"

"No, she wasn't around. I don't think she knew for a long time."

"Oh, man. This story just gets worse."

He had his arm around her, just below her breasts. He pulled her against his chest and kissed the back of her neck.

"I don't think I'd be here doing what I do if things hadn't happened the way they did," Ballard said. "There's that."

She reached her leg out, hooked the tequila bottle, and slid it in so he could reach it.

But he didn't. He kept her in his embrace. She liked that.

BOSCH

23

Bosch waited for Lourdes in the Starbucks a block from the station. He sat at a tall bar table that allowed him to keep his left leg straight. He had just come from Dr. Zhang's and the knee was feeling good for the first time in two weeks. He knew that bending the joint might cut that relief short. That was inevitable with walking, but for now he kept it straight.

He had gotten Lourdes a latte and himself a straight black. They had agreed to meet away from the station after she did some preliminary intelligence gathering while he was getting needles stuck in his leg.

Lourdes arrived before the latte got cold.

"How's the knee?" she asked.

"Feeling pretty good at the moment," Bosch said. "But it won't last. It never does."

"Have you ever gotten a cortisone shot?"

"No, but I'm ready to try anything but a knee replacement."

"Sorry, Harry."

"Nothing to be sorry about. What did you find out?"

The night before, LAPD SWAT had moved in on the house Bosch and Lourdes had located in Sylmar and arrested four men, all SanFers gang members, and including one man who was found in a bed, suffering from a gunshot wound to the stomach. He was thirty-eight-year-old Carlos Mejia and he was the suspected shooter of Martin Perez. The other three were low-level gangsters most likely assigned to watch over Mejia and bring the doctor to him. All four were arrested on various gun and drug charges as well as probation violations.

Mejia was not charged yet with the Perez killing because the evidence was only circumstantial at the moment: he had been shot, and it was believed that Perez's killer had been shot. The upward trajectory of the wound trail through Mejia's lower intestine fit with the ricochet-in-the-shower theory as well. But it wasn't enough to take to the District Attorney's Office. The bullet had been removed from Mejia's gut and disposed of—there would be no ballistics match to the bullet taken from Perez's brain. However, the forensic team that processed the Perez crime scene had found that the blood spattered in the shower stall had come from two individuals—Perez and presumably his shooter after he caught the bouncing bullet. Confidence was high that a DNA comparison between Mejia's blood and that found in the shower would lead to a match and Mejia would be charged with murder. He was now in the hospital ward of the county jail while a rush was put on the DNA comparison.

The intel gathering that Lourdes had undertaken that morning was related to Mejia and any connections he might have with those who knew about the renewed investigation of the Uncle Murda case and that Martin Perez had flipped.

"I really hate this," Lourdes said. "What if we're wrong?"

"We make sure we aren't," Bosch said. "What did you find out?"

She opened a small notebook she always carried with her.

"Okay," she said, reading her notes. "I talked to my cousin

and a couple other guys in gang intel. They say Mejia is a SanFer OG known as El Brujo."

"What's that, 'sorcerer'?"

"More like 'witch doctor,' but it doesn't matter. He got the moniker because of his ability to find and get to people who supposedly can't be gotten to."

"Case in point, Perez. But somebody told him."

"I'm getting to that. The intel guys said that Mejia pretty much had his own set in the gang and would have been on equal footing with Tranquillo Cortez. So you can see how this is all cinching up. El Brujo hears somehow that Perez flipped and decides to take care of it for Cortez. End result, Cortez owes Mejia."

"Got it. The question is, how did he hear that Perez was flipping?"

Lourdes nodded and a painful frown creased her face again.

"What is it?" Bosch asked.

"Well," she said. "When the intel guys were talking to me, one of them says, 'Maybe you should talk to your buddy Oscar about El Brujo. He grew up with him.' I said, 'Oscar Luzon?' to confirm, and they said, 'Yeah, Luzon.' They said Oscar and Mejia went all the way back to Gridley."

Bosch knew that Gridley was an elementary school on 8th Street.

"So, was this connection in the gang book?" Bosch asked.

Because of the unavoidable connections between some home-grown SFPD officers and local gangs, the department had a registry known as the "gang book" in which officers named acquaintances in the gangs. It allowed the officers to avoid suspicion should the connections become known through the course of investigations, wiretaps, and street gossip. The book was also a resource for gang intel officers when they wanted to target a particular gang member. If there was a connection in the book, it could be exploited, by using the officer to initiate communication with the gang member or even cross paths with him in a seemingly coincidental way.

"No, they said Luzon never put it in the book," Lourdes said. "They only knew because they have class photos from all the schools in the city going back to the seventies. They have photos of Luzon and Mejia in the same classes at Gridley and then Lakeview. But a few years ago, when they asked Oscar why he never put it in the book, he said it was because he didn't really know Mejia."

"Did they believe him?" Bosch asked.

"Well, they accepted it. The question is, do we believe it?"

"The same class through elementary and high school, and Luzon says they didn't know each other? No, I don't believe it."

Lourdes nodded. She didn't believe it either.

"So, how do we do this?" she asked.

"We need to talk to him," Bosch said.

"I know that, but how?"

"Does he still take his gun off when he works at his desk?"

"I think so."

They needed to separate Luzon from his weapon before they confronted him. They didn't want to risk his harming them or himself.

Luzon was a muffin top. He cinched his belt tight around a growing waistline, creating an overflow roll of bulk that circled his body. This caused him to remove his sidearm when he worked in his pod so that the arm of his desk chair didn't drive the hard-edged weapon into his side. He usually placed the gun in the top drawer of his desk.

"Okay, we draw him out without his gun," Bosch said. "Then we brace him."

"But he always takes his gun when he leaves the office," Lourdes said. "It'd be a violation if he didn't."

"We get him over to the old jail, to come see me."

"That could work. We just need the reason."

They were both silent as they thought about a way to draw Luzon across the street from the station without his gun.

Soon they concocted a two-part plan. But it would involve the police chief's cooperation. This was not a deterrent, because they knew they could not carry out any confrontation with Luzon without alerting command staff. They finished their coffees and walked back to the station, going directly to the chief of police's office and asking for an audience.

Chief Valdez was not happy with what Bosch and Lourdes told him but agreed that an investigation had to be carried out. The chief was particularly pained because seventeen years before, when Luzon came into the department, Valdez had been his training officer. They had been close at one time.

"He knew several SanFers," Valdez said. "He grew up with them. And it worked in our favor. We would stop and talk to these guys and we always picked up good intel we shot back to the gang team."

"Look, Chief, we're not accusing him of being a double agent," Bosch said. "He could have been used or tricked and he might not even be the source. That's what we have to talk about with him. But the bottom line is, he never put Mejia in the book—and Mejia took out our witness."

"I get it, I get it," Valdez said. "It has to be done. What's your plan?"

It was simple. The chief would have his secretary call Luzon to his office to pick up some paperwork relating to a training day scheduled for the next month. It was likely that Luzon would not clip on his firearm just for a short jaunt down the hall from the detective bureau. While he was picking up the paperwork from the secretary, the chief would step out of his office to say hello. He would then ask Luzon to take a printed memo over to Bosch in the old jail. The direct route to the jail would not be through the detective bureau. The plan pivoted on the idea that Luzon would proceed directly to Bosch—without going out of his way back to his desk to pick up his weapon.

They also allowed for a quick abort if the chief saw that Luzon was armed or if Luzon cut back to the detective bureau to retrieve his gun before leaving the station and crossing the street.

"Now, does he carry a backup?" Valdez asked.

"If he does, it's not registered," Bosch said.

"We checked the registry," Lourdes said.

Department regulations allowed an officer to carry a boot gun or some other backup weapon as long as it was on an approved list of firearms and the officer notified command staff and entered the details in the weapons registry.

"Did you ever know him to carry a throw-down?" Bosch asked.

"No, never," Valdez said.

"So do we do this?" Bella asked.

"We do it," Valdez said. "But Bella, I want you over there with Harry. As backup."

"Got it," she said.

An hour later they went forward with the plan. Lourdes confirmed that Luzon was at his desk and was not wearing his weapon before she sent Valdez the go-ahead text. The chief then told his secretary to summon Luzon, and when the detective left the bureau, Lourdes confirmed that he had left his weapon behind. She then headed out the side door and crossed the street to the old jail.

Bosch was sitting at his makeshift desk in the old drunk tank when Luzon walked in carrying a memo from the chief with the schedule for the upcoming training days. He put it down on the old door that Bosch used as a desktop.

"That's from the chief," he said. "Asked me to drop it by."

"Thanks," Bosch said.

Luzon turned to go back.

"Did you hear about Sylmar last night?" Bosch asked.

Luzon reversed himself and was facing Bosch again.

"Sylmar?" he asked. "What about it?"

"They got the guy who hit our witness," Bosch said.

Luzon just looked at him, revealing nothing.

"He took a shot in the gut himself," Bosch said. "So he's not doing too good. They're hoping to stabilize him and have him ready to talk in a day or two."

"Good," Luzon said. "I'm going back to the bureau."

He once more moved toward the cell's exit.

"That doesn't worry you, Oscar?" Bosch asked.

Luzon once again turned back and looked at Bosch.

"What's that supposed to mean?" Luzon asked.

"It was your buddy the witch doctor, Carlos Mejia," Bosch said. "And I lied. He's already talking and he gave you up. Said you told him about Martin Perez."

"That's bullshit."

Lourdes stepped out of the next cell down and into the hallway that ran in front of the old cells. She took a position behind Luzon. He felt her presence and turned to see her.

"What the fuck is this?" he said.

Bosch stood up.

"You know what it is?" he said. "This is your chance to get out in front of this. Tell us what happened, what you did, and maybe there's a way out for you."

"I didn't do anything. I told you, this is bullshit."

"You're playing it wrong, man. You're giving him the leverage. They'll lock in his story and come for you."

Luzon seemed to freeze. His eyes went blank as he tried to figure out his next move. Bosch said nothing. Lourdes said nothing. They waited.

"All right, look," he finally said. "I made a mistake. You two weren't saying shit about what the search warrant at the garage was about. I thought maybe I could come up with something that would help. All I did was ask him what that place had to do with the SanFers. That's it. He figured everything out from there."

"That story is what's bullshit," Bosch said. "How'd he find Perez in Alhambra?"

"I don't know, but it wasn't me. You're the one who got Perez killed. Don't look at me now."

"No, man, it was you. You told Mejia. And the thing is, he's going to give you up in a heartbeat as soon as they offer him a deal."

Luzon stared at Bosch as he realized that Mejia wasn't talking—yet—and that he had fallen for the oldest cop bluff in the book. He turned to Lourdes as if for help. Bosch was an outsider in the department, but Lourdes was not. He looked to her but the cold set of her eyes showed he would get no sympathy from her.

"I want a lawyer," he said.

"You can call one as soon as you're booked," Bosch said.

He came around the desk as Lourdes pulled her handcuffs off her belt. He put his hand on Luzon's shoulder and directed him toward the hallway where Lourdes was waiting. He walked him through.

"Hands behind your back," he said. "You know the drill."

Bosch gripped Luzon by the elbow and turned him to face away from Lourdes. At that moment, Luzon brought his hands up and shoved Bosch into the cell's bars. He then rushed into the cell and with both hands slid the door shut with a heavy metal clang. He quickly pulled the chain and padlock through the bars into the cell and locked the door.

"Oscar, what are you doing?" Lourdes said. "There's nowhere to go."

Bosch had lost his balance against the bars. He righted himself and reached into his pocket for his key ring. It had the padlock key on it.

But the key ring wasn't there and he looked through the bars and could see it on his desk. He looked at Luzon, who was pacing in the cell, a man looking for options where there weren't any.

"Oscar, come on, settle down," Lourdes said. "Come out of there."

"The key's on the desk, Oscar," Bosch said. "Unlock the door."

Luzon acted like he didn't hear them. He paced back and forth a few times and then abruptly sat down on the end of the bench that ran almost the length of the cell. He bent over, put his elbows on his knees and dropped his face into his hands.

Bosch leaned over to Lourdes and cupped his hands around her ear.

"Go out into the yard and get a bolt cutter," he whispered.

Lourdes immediately headed down the corridor in front of the cells to the door that led to the Public Works yard. That left Bosch looking through the bars at Luzon.

"Oscar, come on," he said. "Open the door. We can work this out."

Luzon was silent, face in his hands.

"Oscar?" Bosch said. "Talk to me. You want me to get the chief in here? I know you two go way back. You want to talk to him?"

Nothing, and then without a word Luzon dropped his hands and stood. He reached to his neck and started to pull off his tie. He then climbed up onto the bench and reached up to the cell's ceiling, where there was a metal grate over an air vent. He pushed the skinny end of his tie into the grate and worked it back out of the next opening.

"Oscar, come on, don't do this," Bosch said. "Oscar!"

Luzon knotted the two ends of the tie together and then twisted the loop into a figure eight. He stood on his toes to get his head through the makeshift noose and then without hesitation stepped off the end of the bench.

24

Bosch and Lourdes waited in the hallway. Only the chief of police and family members were allowed back into the critical care unit. For the most part they sat quietly and drank coffee from paper cups out of a machine. After two hours Chief Valdez emerged with the news.

"They say he only went a couple minutes without oxygen to the brain, so he should be all right," he said. "It's a waiting game on that. The bigger concern is the skull fracture from when he hit the ground when the grate gave way."

Bosch had witnessed and heard the impact when Luzon's swinging body brought the iron grate down and the back of his head hit the end of the bench. Like a high diver hitting the board after a flip.

"Is he conscious?" Lourdes asked.

"He was but then they went into surgery," Valdez said. "They say he's got a subdural hematoma and they had to evacuate it, which means they drilled a fucking hole in his skull to let the blood and pressure out."

"Shit," Lourdes said.

"Anyway, I want a full report on what happened in that cell

213

and everything that led up to it," Valdez said. "How did it go so far sideways, Harry?"

Bosch tried to compose an answer.

"He took me by surprise," he finally said. "He must have known that that was the way some drunks did it back in the day."

"Everybody knows that," Valdez said. "You should have been prepared for it."

Bosch nodded. He knew Valdez was right.

"It's on me," Bosch said. "But are we going to charge him? I have the whole thing on my phone. He tipped Mejia. He put it in terms of a mistake, but he's responsible."

"I'm not worried about that right now," Valdez said. "We'll look at that later."

Bosch could see that the chief was having trouble concealing his anger about the whole thing.

"Bella, why don't you go back to the station and start in on the paper," Valdez said.

"Roger that," Lourdes said.

Valdez stood there and was awkwardly silent as he waited for Lourdes to leave.

"See you guys back there," she said.

Valdez watched her go down the hall toward the elevator alcove. When he judged she was far enough away, he spoke.

"Harry, we need to talk."

"I know."

"I'm going to ask the Sheriff's Department to come in and take a look at this and how it was handled. I think an outside review would be a good thing."

"I can save you the trouble, Chief. I fucked up. I know it."

"You know as a reserve you don't have the same protections the full-timers do."

"I know. Are you firing me?"

"I think you should go home and let the Sheriff's Department take a look at this."

"I'm suspended, then."

"Whatever. Just go home, Harry, and take a break. When and if the time is right, you'll be back."

"When and if…Okay, Chief. I'll do that. I'll send Lourdes the audio from the cell."

"That would be good, yeah."

Bosch turned and walked away, heading down the hallway in the direction Lourdes had gone.

He knew there was a very low chance that he would be back working for San Fernando after this. He thought about going by the city complex and gathering a few files and personal things from his office in the old jail but then decided against it. He just drove home.

He returned to a quiet house. He checked the porch first but there was no sign of Elizabeth. He then went down the hallway to her room and found the door open. The bed had been made and there were clean, folded towels on the bureau. He checked the closet. There were no clothes on the hangers and no sign of the suitcase she had used.

She was gone.

Bosch pulled his phone and called the number of the cell phone he had given her.

After a few seconds he heard its ring inside the house and found the phone left with a note on the dining room table. The note was brief.

Harry, you are a good man.
Thank you for everything.
I'm glad I got to know you.
Elizabeth

A wave of emotion immediately went through him. He had to admit there was at first relief. Elizabeth had been right that her staying with him was damaging his relationship with his daughter. There was also the relief from the pressures of living with an addict, of not knowing when she might stumble or what would cause it.

But then that feeling was crowded out by concern. What did Elizabeth's leaving mean? Was she going home to Modesto? Or was she going back to the addiction she had worked for months to leave behind? She had not had a single relapse in that time and Bosch had thought she was getting stronger every day.

Bosch had to consider that she had found clarity of mind and the access it gave her to guilt over her daughter's death too difficult to continue to live with.

Bosch opened the sliding door and walked out onto the back deck of the house. He looked down on the freeway and the wide expanse of the city beyond it to the mountains that rimmed the Valley. Elizabeth could be out there somewhere.

He pulled his phone and ducked back in and away from the freeway hiss to make a call to Cisco Wojciechowski. They had not spoken in at least two months, since the last time Cisco had checked in on Elizabeth's progress. He was a private investigator who worked for Mickey Haller, a defense attorney who was also Bosch's half-brother. That had put him into Bosch's orbit and he had been instrumental in getting Elizabeth Clayton straight.

Even more than Bosch, Wojciechowski was responsible for Elizabeth's recovery. He had seen her through the immediate withdrawal from the grip of oxycodone. Formerly addicted himself, he had walked and talked her through it, monitored her every minute at first, then by hour and then by day. She had followed that detox with a one-month stint in a more traditional rehab center. After she moved into the room offered by Bosch, Cisco was her weekly monitor. The check-ins didn't start to drop off until Elizabeth hit the three-month mark without a relapse.

Now Bosch told him that she was gone without much notice or any indication of where she was going.

"She answering her phone?" Cisco asked.

"She left it here," Bosch said.

"That's not good. She doesn't want to be tracked."

"What I was thinking."

They were both silent for a while.

"If we take the worst-case scenario, she's decided to go back to the life," Bosch said. "The question is, where would she go?"

"Does she have money?" Cisco asked.

Bosch had to think about that. In the last two months, Elizabeth had gotten bored when Bosch went to work at the SFPD. Bosch let her use his credit card to install an Uber account on her phone. She had asked to take over the duties of shopping for food and household products. He had given her cash for that. Between the credit-card number and the possibility that she could have put aside small amounts from the grocery money, he had to assume she had the wherewithal to get back to Modesto or to buy her way back into addiction.

"Let's say she does," Bosch said. "Where would she go?"

"Addicts are creatures of habit," Cisco said. "She'd go back to where she scored before."

Bosch thought about the place he had rescued Elizabeth from the previous year. A clinic that was little more than a pill mill with examination rooms crowded with the items stolen and offered in trade by addicts. When he found her, Elizabeth had only herself to trade.

"The place I took her from—this so-called clinic in Van Nuys—has got to be closed by now," he said. "My old partner from Hollywood detectives is now with the state medical board. He was there and saw that place. He was going to shut them down."

"You sure?" Cisco asked. "Sometimes these doctors get a slap on the wrist and just open up across the street."

Bosch recalled Jerry Edgar talking about how difficult it was to put charlatan doctors and pill mills out of business permanently.

"Let me call you back," he said.

Without waiting for a reply, he disconnected and went to his contacts screen. He called his former partner, and Edgar picked up right away.

"Harry Bosch," he said. "The man who said he would stay in touch but waited a lot of months to actually do it."

"Sorry, Jerry, I've been kind of busy," Bosch said. "I've got a question for you though. Remember that clinic where we found Elizabeth Clayton last year?"

"Yeah, Sherman Way."

"You said you were going to close that down. Did that happen?"

"Wait a minute, I said I was going to try to close it down. It's not an easy thing to do, Harry. I told you about how—"

"Yeah, I know, a lot of red tape. So, you're telling me that seven months later that place is still operating?"

"I opened a file, did the work, and submitted it. The license to practice is under what we call administrative review. I'm waiting on the board to act on it."

"So in the meantime, that guy we saw in there, that guy masquerading as a doctor, is still in there writing scrips."

"I haven't checked but that's probably the case."

"Thanks, Jerry, that's all I needed. I gotta go."

"Harry—"

Bosch disconnected. Before calling Cisco back he pulled his wallet and dug out the credit card he had given to Elizabeth to set up her Uber account. He called the phone number on the back and asked the service specialist to read him a list of his most recent charges. Other than an Uber charge from that morning, all the purchases had been his own.

Bosch grabbed the phone Elizabeth had left behind on the dining room table. He opened the Uber app and was greeted with a template for rating the driver who had picked Elizabeth up that morning. Bosch gave him five stars, then tapped the My Trips link and was taken to a map that showed the morning's ride and the address of the destination. Elizabeth had obviously called for the Uber, then left the phone behind when the car arrived. The destination was the Greyhound bus terminal in North Hollywood.

It would seem that Elizabeth had left the city on a Greyhound bus, but Bosch was familiar with the area, having worked cases over the years that took him to the bus terminal and its surroundings, and he knew the neighborhood had a high transient population, many of whom were drug addicts, and had several clinics and mom-and-pop pharmacies that catered to them.

Bosch called Wojciechowski back.

"The place I pulled her out of is still in business," he said.

"But I just traced an Uber she took this morning to the bus station in North Hollywood. She could be back in Modesto by now. Or..."

"Or what?" Cisco prompted.

"You talked about addicts returning to the places they know. The area around the bus terminal is pretty gritty. Lots of clinics, lots of pharmacies, lots of addicts. There's a park there next to the one seventy where they hang."

There was a moment of silence before Cisco responded.

"I'll meet you there," he said.

BALLARD

25

After spending the day with Aaron Hayes and Lola, Ballard headed downtown for a preshift dinner with Heather Rourke, the helicopter spotter, at the Denny's outside the entrance to Piper Tech, on whose roof the LAPD air unit was located.

It had become a routine for Ballard and Rourke to meet once or twice a month before their respective shifts. A connection had grown between them. They both worked graveyard and more often than not Rourke was Ballard's partner in the sky, running as both lookout and backup. Their first meal together had been offered by Ballard as a thank-you after Rourke had spotted a hooded man waiting in ambush for Ballard when she responded to a burglary call. The suspect turned out to have been previously arrested by Ballard for an attempted rape. He was out on bail, awaiting trial, and had made the phony burglary call hoping that it would be Ballard who responded.

Rourke had picked up a heat signature on the air unit's camera screen and radioed a warning down to Ballard. The hooded man was arrested after a short foot chase. Rourke was able to direct Ballard back to a duffel bag the man had thrown while running. It contained a complete rape package—duct tape, handcuffs, and snap ties. After this latest arrest, the man was deemed a danger to the community and denied bail.

When Ballard and Rourke got together, they mostly gossiped about the department. Ballard had early on told Rourke about her fall from grace at Robbery-Homicide Division, but in subsequent meetings she listened more than she talked because she largely worked alone and mostly encountered the same group of officers on the Hollywood late show. It was a closed environment that produced little in the way of new department intel from dinner to dinner. Rourke on the other hand was part of a large unit that supported eighteen helicopters—the largest police air force in the country. Veteran officers gravitated to the unit because the hours were steady and it included a hazard bump on the salary scale. She heard a lot in the break room from officers with connections all over the department and was happy to keep Ballard up to speed. It was a sisterhood of two.

Ballard always ordered breakfast there because it seemed like a meal that was impossible to mess up. Denny's was their choice because it was more convenient to Rourke and was part of Ballard's ongoing thank-you for the warning about the hooded man. Also, both women were fans of the movie *Drive* and it was at this location that the film's female lead worked as a waitress.

Now Ballard told Rourke about her involvement in the investigation of the nine-year-old murder of Daisy Clayton and her meeting Harry Bosch. Rourke had never met him or heard of him.

"It's weird," Ballard said. "I like working with him and think I can learn a few things. But at the end of the day, I don't think I can trust him. It's like he's not telling me everything he knows."

"You gotta be careful of those guys," Rourke said. "On the job and off."

Rourke was in her green flight suit, which went well with her red-brown hair, kept short like most of the other female coppers Ballard knew. She was petite and no more than a hundred pounds, which must have been a plus in an air unit where weight was a factor in lift and fuel consumption.

Rourke was more interested in hearing about Ballard's other cases, and the ground-side story of the incidents she had been involved in from above, so Ballard told her about the dead woman whose cat ate her face and the young Peeping Toms on the roof of the strip bar.

When it was time to go, Ballard picked up the check, and Rourke said the next one was hers.

"Call me if you need me," Rourke said, her usual goodbye.

"Fly like an eagle," Ballard answered with hers.

Once in her van, Ballard's goodbye to Rourke reminded her of the man called Eagle who had gotten baptized on the same night as Daisy Clayton. She had forgotten to follow up on him and planned to do it as soon as she returned to Hollywood Station and could access the moniker files in the department's database.

She checked her phone to see if she had gotten a call from Bosch during dinner. There were no messages and she wondered if he would turn up tonight. She headed up the 101 to the Sunset exit and got to Hollywood Station two hours before the start of her shift. She had wanted to get there before PM watch went off duty. She needed to talk to Lieutenant Gabriel Mason, who worked PM watch and who had been a sergeant nine years ago and assigned as Hollywood Division liaison to the department's GRASP program.

Since Hollywood was busiest during PM watch, which

roughly ran from three p.m. to midnight, there were two lieu-
tenants assigned to supervise the shift. Mason was one of the two
and Hannah Chavez was the other. Ballard did not know Mason that well, because her limited experience with PM watch
had been with Chavez. She decided that the straight-on approach would be best.

She found him in the break room, with deployment calendars
spread out on a table. He was a bookish-looking administrator
with glasses and black hair parted sharply on the left side. His
uniform looked crisp and new.

"Lieutenant?" Ballard said.

He looked up, annoyed with the interruption, but then his
scowl disappeared when he saw Ballard.

"Ballard, you're in early," he said. "Thanks for responding."

Ballard shook her head.

"I don't understand," she said. "You wanted to see me?"

"Yeah, I put a message in your box," Mason said. "You get it?"

"No, but what's up? I was actually going to ask you something."

"I need you to do a welfare check."

"During graveyard?"

"I know it's unusual, but there's something hinky going on
with this one. Comes from the tenth floor. A missing guy, hasn't
responded to phone calls or social media in a week. We've gone
by a few times today and his roommate says he's out every time.
Not much we can do, but I figure if you knock on the door in
the middle of the night, the guy's going to be home or not. And
if not, then we go to the next step."

The reference to the tenth floor meant the OCP—Office of
the Chief of Police—on the tenth floor of the Police Administration Building.

"So, who's the guy?" Ballard asked.

"I Googled him," Mason said. "Looks like his father's friends with the mayor. A high-dollar donor. So we can't let it drop. If he's still not home tonight, send a report to Captain Whittle and he'll report to the OCP about it. And we'll be done with it or not."

"Okay. You have the name and address?"

"It's all in your box. And I'll put it on the activity report for your lieutenant."

"Got it."

"Now, you wanted to see me about something?"

He pointed to the chair across the table from him and Ballard sat down.

"I'm working a cold case from '09," she said. "Teenage runaway selling it on the streets was found dumped in an alley off Cahuenga. Her name was Daisy Clayton."

Mason thought for a moment and then shook his head.

"Not ringing any bells," he said.

"I wasn't expecting it to," Ballard said. "But I asked around. Back then you were the division liaison for the GRASP program."

"Jesus, don't remind me. What a nightmare that was."

"Well, I know the department dumped the program when the new chief came in, but what I'm wondering about is what happened to all the Hollywood crime data."

"What? Why?"

"I'm trying to get a handle on this girl's murder and I thought it would be good if I could get a look at everything that was happening in the division that night or that week. As you can tell, we don't have a lot, so I'm grasping at straws a bit."

"Who's 'we'?"

"Just a figure of speech. So do you know where all the data went when the GRASP program ended?"

"Yeah, it went down the digital toilet. It was purged when the new administration wanted to go another way."

Ballard frowned and nodded. It was a dead end.

"Officially, at least," Mason said.

Ballard looked at him. What was he saying?

"I was the guy who had to collate and send all the data downtown. There was a guy we called the 'GRASP guru.' He wasn't a sworn officer. He was this computer genius from USC who came up with the whole thing and sold it to the chief. All the data went to him and he did all the modeling."

Ballard started to get excited. She knew that guys like the one Mason was describing were proprietary about their work and accomplishments. The order may have come down to end the program and spike the data, but there was a chance the civilian whose baby it was had kept records of the program.

"Do you remember his name?" she asked.

"Yeah, I should. I worked with him every day for two years," Mason said. "Professor Scott Calder. Don't know if he's still there but at the time he was on sabbatical from the Computer Science school."

"Thanks, L-T. I'll find him."

"Hope it helps. Don't forget about that welfare check."

"I'm going to my box now."

Ballard got up but then sat back down and looked at Mason. She was going to risk turning what could be the start of a solid relationship with a supervisor into something fraught.

"Something else?" Mason asked.

"Yes, L-T," Ballard began. "Last night I was working during PMs and busted a guy on a burglary. I was working solo and I called for backup. It never came. The guy made a move on me and I put him down but he wouldn't have had the chance if I'd had the backup."

"I was the one who took your call when you used the private line to ask where the troops were."

"I thought so. Did you find out what happened?"

"I'm sorry. I didn't. I got caught up in some stuff. All I know was there was no call on the board. There must have been a fuckup between the com center and the watch office. We never were copied. I heard no backup call go out."

Ballard looked at him for a long moment.

"So you're saying the problem wasn't at Hollywood Station. It was at the com center."

"Near as I can tell."

Mason sat silently. He did not offer to follow up. He wasn't going to rock any boats. It was clear that it was Ballard's decision whether to pursue it.

"Okay, thanks, Lieutenant," she said.

Ballard got up and left the room.

26

Ballard used her password to enter the department database and then began a search of the man who signed "Eagle" on his photo at the Moonlight Mission. The database contained a moniker file, which carried thousands of nicknames and aliases amassed from crime reports, arrest records, and field interviews.

"Eagle" turned out to be a popular moniker. She got 241 initial hits. She was then able to chop this down to sixty-eight by limiting her search to white males thirty-plus years old. She had the nine-year-old photo she had borrowed from the mission to guide her. The man depicted looked to be mid- to late twenties and that would put him over thirty now. She refined the search further by eliminating possibles who were over forty.

She was left with sixteen names and set to work pulling up reports and photos of the men. She quickly eliminated men who looked nothing like the man in the photo provided by John the Baptist. She hit pay dirt with the eleventh man she looked at. His name was Dennis Eagleton and he was thirty-seven years old. Mug shots from multiple arrests between 2008 and 2013 matched the face of the man in the photo from the mission.

She pulled up and started printing all reports in the database regarding Eagleton. He had a record of numerous arrests for

drugs and loitering and only one incident of violence, an aggravated assault charge in 2010 that was knocked down to simple
battery. Ballard even found a digitized field interview report
written by Tim Farmer in 2014 — his last full year on the job.
The summary section included Farmer's unique take on the
Hollywood streets and this particular denizen.

> *This is not the first nor the last time we will cross paths with
> "Eagle."*
>
> *A deep, cancerous river of hate and violence courses
> through his veins.*
>
> *I can feel it, see it.*
>
> *He waits. He hates. He blames the world for its betrayal of
> all hope.*
>
> *I fear for us.*

Ballard read Farmer's take twice. It was written five years after Daisy Clayton's murder. Could the pulsing, waiting violence
that Farmer saw in Eagleton have already been let loose in 2009?
Rather than seeing the future, had Farmer also seen the past?

Ballad spent the next half hour trying to locate Eagleton, but
she found nothing. No driver's license, no recent arrests. The
last known record of him had been the FI card Farmer had
filled out. He had stopped Eagleton and questioned him when
he was seen loitering around the Metro entrance on Hollywood Boulevard near Vine. In the blank marked "Occupation"
Farmer had written "panhandler." There were now no indications as to whether Eagleton was alive or dead, only that he had
gone completely off the electronic grid.

It was now after midnight and time to conduct the welfare
check Lieutenant Mason had assigned Ballard. She used a

BOLO template to put together a wanted-for-questioning sheet on Eagleton that would be distributed at all roll calls. After including screen grabs of his three most recent mug shots, she sent the package to the printer and signed off the computer. She was ready to go.

Her first stop was the watch office to drop off the BOLO sheet with Lieutenant Munroe and to tell him she was leaving the station to handle the welfare check. Munroe said the officers assigned to patrol in the neighborhood in question were finishing up a minor call but he would send them to her location as soon as they were clear.

The missing man was named Jacob Cady. His home was in a four-story condominium building on Willoughby just a block from the West Hollywood border. Ballard pulled over against a red curb and looked around for her backup. She saw nothing and used her rover to check with Munroe, who said the patrol unit had not cleared their call.

Ballard decided to give it ten minutes before she went in alone. She pulled her phone and checked her texts. There had been no response from Bosch to her message about John the Baptist and none to a text she had sent earlier to Aaron Hayes to check on his well-being. She didn't think she should text him again, for fear she might wake him up.

She checked her email next and saw that the blind email she had sent to Scott Calder with the standard USC address had already been answered. She opened it to find that she had reached the correct Calder and that he would be happy to meet early the next morning in his office to discuss the LAPD's defunct GRASP program. He gave his office location in the Viterbi building on McClintock Avenue and said he had an opening in his schedule at eight a.m.

After ten minutes, there was still no sign of a backup unit. Ballard decided to check out Jacob Cady's online profile. In just a few minutes she was able to determine that he was the twenty-nine-year-old son of a City Hall player of the same name who held several city maintenance contracts. The son apparently didn't want any part of the father's business and described himself on Facebook as a party planner. The photos on Facebook revealed a jet-set lifestyle for the young Cady. It looked like he favored Mexican resorts and the company of men. He was tan and trim with feathered blond hair. He liked form-fitting clothing and Tito's vodka.

Twenty minutes after arrival, Ballard got out with her rover and headed toward the entrance to the condo building. She radioed the watch office and reported that she was going in solo.

The documents left in her mailbox by Lieutenant Mason said that Cady owned the two-bedroom condo and rented space in it to a roommate named Talisman Prada. On the two prior welfare checks by patrol officers, Prada had answered the door and said that Cady had met a man in a bar two nights before and gone home with him. But this did not explain why Cady was no longer answering texts, email, or phone calls. Or why his car was parked in a reserved spot in the condominium's underground garage.

Ballard pressed the buzzer at the gate three separate times before a sleepy voice answered.

"Mr. Cady?"

"No, he's not here."

The connection was ended. Ballard buzzed again.

"What?"

"Mr. Prada?"

"Who's this?"

233

"The police. Will you open the gate?"

"I told you, Jacob is not here. You woke me up."

"Again, Mr. Prada, this is the police. Open the gate."

There was a long beat of silence before the gate buzzed, and Ballard pulled it open. She checked the street for the backup unit and saw nothing. She looked around the entry area. There was a rack of mailboxes with a shelf below it where some unclaimed newspapers were left. Ballard grabbed one and used it to prop open the gate for the backup officers, if they ever arrived. She entered and, while waiting for the elevator, used the rover to check on them. This time Munroe said the car was on the way.

Ballard took the elevator to the third floor. Down the hallway to the right she saw a man standing in front of the open door to a unit. He was wearing silk sleeping pants and no shirt. He was small but muscular with jet-black hair.

Ballard headed toward him.

"Mr. Prada?" she asked.

"Yes," the man said. "Can we get this over with? I'd like to get back to sleep."

"Sorry for the bother, but there's still no word from Jacob Cady. It's been forty-eight hours since we got the report and this is now a criminal investigation."

"Criminal? What is criminal about a guy shacking up with somebody?"

"We don't think that's what's going on. Can you step into the apartment so I can enter?"

Prada walked back inside and Ballard entered after him. She assessed him as she walked in. He was no more than five five and 125 pounds. It was clear he had no weapon on him. She left the door open and Prada noticed.

"Do you want to close that, please?" he asked.

"No, let's leave it open," Ballard said. "A couple uniform officers are coming."

"Whatever. Look around. He's not here. Just hurry, please."

"Thank you."

Ballard stepped into the living room and did a 180 sweep. The condo was nicely decorated in a modern style. Gray-washed wood floors, armless sofa and chairs, glass coffee table. Everything carefully coordinated like a picture in a magazine. The adjacent dining room featured a square table with stainless-steel legs and matching chairs. The wall beyond was hung with a 10 x 6 painting consisting of black slashes on a field of white.

Prada spread his arms to prove the point that Cady was not there.

"Satisfied?"

"Why don't you show me the bedrooms?" Ballard said.

"I mean, don't you have to have a warrant to conduct a search?"

"Not on a welfare check. If Mr. Cady is hurt or needs help, we need to find him."

"Well, you're looking in the wrong place."

"Can I see the bedrooms?"

Prada showed her through the home, and as she expected, there was no sign of Jacob Cady. She pulled her mini-light out of a pocket and used it to check the closet in the bedroom Prada said was Cady's. It was full of clothing, and there was an empty suitcase on a shelf. Stepping back out she noticed that the bed was crisply made and unslept in.

Prada's bedroom was more lived in, with the bed unmade and clothes hanging over a chair in front of a makeup table Ballard would've expected to see in a woman's room. The closet door was open and clothes were piled on the floor inside.

"Not all of us are as neat as Jacob," Prada said.

Ballard heard voices from the living room and turned toward the door.

"Coming out," Ballard called down the hallway.

Ballard and Prada returned to the living room and were met by Officers Herrera and Dyson. Ballard gave a nod.

"Glad you could make it," she said.

Prada spoke impatiently before either officer could respond.

"Are we finished now?" he asked. "I'd like to get some sleep. I have appointments tomorrow."

"Not quite," Ballard said. "I have to fill out full reports this time. Can I see your driver's license or passport, please?"

"Is that really necessary?"

"Yes, sir, it is. I'm sure you want to keep cooperating. It's the quickest way to get us out of here."

Prada disappeared back down the short hallway toward his bedroom. Ballard nodded to Herrera to follow and watch.

Ballard assessed the living room again. It had been carefully composed but something didn't seem right. She realized that the area rug was too small for the space and the furniture and that its abstract design of overlapping gray, black, and brown squares clashed with the striped pattern of the furniture's upholstery. She checked the adjacent dining room and noticed for the first time that there was no rug under the square table with stainless steel legs.

"What are you thinking here?" Dyson whispered.

"Something's not right," Ballard whispered back.

Prada and Herrera returned to the living room and Herrera handed Ballard a driver's license.

"I want you to know that my lawyer has filed the paperwork to officially change my name," Prada said. "I was not lying. I'm a DJ and I need a better name."

Ballard looked at the license. It had been issued in New Jersey, and the photo matched Prada but the name on it was Tyler Tyldus. Ballard put the flashlight down on the coffee table next to a small sculpture of a woman's torso. She pulled a small notebook and pen from her pocket and wrote down the information from the license.

"What's wrong with Tyler Tyldus?" she asked as she wrote.

"No imagination," Prada said.

Ballard checked the date of birth and saw that he had been lying about his age as well. The documents left for her had him at twenty-six years old. The DL said he was twenty-two.

"What are your appointments tomorrow, Mr. Prada?" she asked.

"Personal business," Prada said. "Nothing that concerns the police."

Ballard nodded. She finished writing and handed the license to Prada. She then handed him one of her business cards.

"Thank you for your cooperation," she said. "If you hear from Mr. Cady, please call me at that number and ask Mr. Cady to call me as well."

"Of course," Prada said, his voice friendlier now that he saw the end of the intrusion in sight.

"You can go back to sleep now," Ballard said.

"Thank you," Prada said.

As she waited for Herrera and Dyson to head to the door, Ballard looked down at the area rug. She saw what first looked like an imperfection in the design, a place where the material had knotted in manufacture. But then she realized it was just an indentation. The rug had been switched from the dining room so recently that the depression left by one of the legs of the table remained apparent.

Prada followed them to the door and closed it behind them. Ballard heard him turn a deadbolt.

The three women were silent until they got in the elevator and closed the door.

"So?" Dyson said.

Ballard was still holding her notebook. She tore the page out with the info on Tyler Tyldus and handed it to Herrera.

"Run that name and see what comes up," she said. "I'm going to call a judge. I want to see what's under that rug in there."

"Couldn't you just look?" Herrera asked. "Exigent circum-stances."

Ballard shook her head. Using exigent circumstances was a tricky thing and you didn't want it to come back and bite you on a case.

"EC refers to the missing man and possible danger to him," Ballard said. "You don't look under a rug for a missing man. You look under a rug for evidence. I'm going to call a judge, and that way there are no issues down the road."

"Is there a car we should be looking for?" Herrera asked.

"Patrol supposedly looked at it on the first welfare check," Ballard said. "Opened the trunk too. It's in the garage under-neath. But I'll include it in the warrant and we'll check it again."

"You think you have enough for a warrant?" Dyson asked.

Ballard shrugged.

"If I don't, I left my flashlight up there," she said. "I'll go back and wake him up."

27

Superior Court Judge Carolyn Wickwire was Ballard's go-to. She wasn't always the night-call judge but she liked Ballard and had given her a cell number, telling her she could always call day or night. Wickwire had been a cop, then a prosecutor, and was now a judge in a long career inside the justice system. Ballard guessed that she had persevered through her own share of misogyny and discrimination every step of the way. Though Ballard had never mentioned the obstacles she herself had encountered and overcome, some were known in the law enforcement community, and she believed Judge Wickwire was aware of them and empathized. There was a kinship there and Ballard wasn't above using it if it helped move things along on a case. She called Wickwire from the building's entry vestibule and woke her up.

"Judge Wickwire, I'm sorry to wake you. It's Detective Ballard, LAPD."

"Oh, Renée, it's been a while. Are you all right?"

"Yes, it has, and I'm fine. But I need to get a telephonic search warrant approved."

"Okay, okay. Just hold on a minute. Let me get my glasses and wake up a bit."

Ballard was put on hold. While she waited, Herrera came over, having just run Prada's name through the MDT terminal in her patrol car.

"Can you talk?"

"While I'm on hold. Anything?"

"Just some TVs back in New Jersey and New York. Nothing serious."

Traffic violations. Ballard knew they would not help her get a search warrant approval from the judge.

"Okay," she said. "I still need you to stick around if I get this. Can you find out if there's an on-site manager?"

"Roger that," Herrera said.

She headed off just as Wickwire came back on the line.

"Now, what do we have here, Renée?"

"This is a missing persons case but I think there's foul play involved and need to get into the missing man's condominium and the common areas of the building. It's complicated because a person of interest in the disappearance is the missing man's roommate."

"Are they a couple or just roommates?"

"Just roommates. Separate bedrooms."

"Okay. Tell me what you got."

Ballard recounted her investigation, putting the facts in an order that would intrigue the judge and build toward a conclusion of probable cause. She said Jacob Cady had now been missing for forty-eight hours and was not responding to any communication, ranging from his cell phone to his business website. She told the judge that the man living in Cady's condo had given a false name but left out Prada's explanation that he was in the process of legally changing it. She said Prada had expressed a reluctance to cooperate, leaving out that he had been awakened by her at one a.m.

Lastly, she mentioned the rug and her suspicion that it had been moved to cover up something.

When she was finished, Wickwire was silent as she digested Ballard's verbal probable cause statement. Finally, she spoke.

"Renée, I don't think you have it," she said. "You have some interesting facts and suspicions but no evidence of foul play here."

"Well, I'm trying to get that, Judge," Ballard said. "I want to find out why the rug was moved."

"But you have the cart before the horse here. You know I like to help you when I can, but this is too thin."

"What would you need? The guy's not texting or tweeting, he's not driving his car, he's not handling his business. It looks like he left all his clothes behind. Something's clearly happened."

"I'm not arguing that. But you have no indication of what happened. This guy could be on a nude beach down in Baja where he doesn't need a change of clothes. He could be in love. He could be in a lot of things. The point is, there's a person living in his domicile and you do not have the right to search that domicile without probable cause."

"Okay, Judge, thank you. I'm probably going to call you back after I get what you need."

She disconnected the call. Dyson was standing there.

"No on-site management," she said.

"Okay," Ballard said. "See if you and Herrera can get down into the garage and take a look around."

"Did you get the warrant?"

"No. I'm going up for my flashlight. If you don't hear from me in about ten, come on up."

"Roger that."

Ballard took the elevator back to three and knocked on Jacob Cady's door. After a few moments she heard movement inside and then Prada's voice through the door.

"Oh my god! *What?*"

"Mr. Prada, can you open the door?"

"What do you want now?"

"Can you open the door so we don't have to talk so loudly? People are sleeping."

The door was flung open. The anger was clear on Prada's face.

"I know people are sleeping. I want to be one of them. What is it now?"

"I'm sorry. I left my flashlight. I think it might be in Jacob's closet. Could you get it?"

"Jesus Christ!"

Prada turned and headed toward the hallway that led to both of the condo's bedrooms. Ballard noticed that Prada had now put on a T-shirt with a pink silhouette of a whale on it.

The moment Prada was out of sight, Ballard moved into the living room and went to the coffee table. She grabbed her flashlight from where it was partially hidden by the torso sculpture and pocketed it. She then stepped back and lifted a cushioned chair off the corner of the area rug. She put the chair down quietly on the wood floor, then stooped and flipped the corner of the rug back as far as was possible, laying it over the coffee table.

Ballard squatted down and looked at the floor. The gray-washed wood had been bleached of its stain in a pattern of semi-circular swipes. Someone had scrubbed this area of the floor with a powerful cleanser. Ballard noted the seams between the planking. It was a tongue-and-groove floor, meaning there was a good chance that residue from whatever had been cleaned up could have seeped down into the subflooring.

Ballard felt the heavy footfalls of Prada approaching. She flipped the carpet back down, then stood and quickly swung the chair back into place just as he entered the room.

"Nothing," he said. "It's not there."

"Are you sure?" Ballard said. "I know I had it in that closet."

"I'm sure. I looked. You can look if you want to."

"I'll take your word for it."

Ballard pulled the rover off her belt and keyed it twice before speaking into it.

"Six-Adam-Fourteen, did one of you pick up my flashlight in the apartment?"

Prada threw his hands up in dismay.

"Couldn't you have asked them first before waking me up again?" he said.

Ballard kept her hand depressed on the rover so that she was still transmitting.

"Calm down, Mr. Prada," she said. "Do you mind if I ask you one last question and then I'll get out of your hair?"

"Whatever," Prada said. "Just ask it and go."

"What happened to the living room rug?"

"What?"

Ballard had seen the tell when she asked the question. A moment of surprise in his eyes. It was Prada who had moved the rug.

"You heard me," she said. "What happened to the rug?"

"The rug is right there," Prada said, like he was talking to an imbecile.

"No, that's the dining room rug. See, it still has the marks from the legs of the table. You moved it in here because you got rid of the rug that was in this spot. What happened to it? Why'd you have to get rid of it?"

"Look, I've had enough of this. You can ask Jacob all about the rugs when he comes back and you see that there's nothing wrong."

"He's not coming back. We both know that. Tell me what happened, Tyler."

"That's not my name. My name is—"

Prada suddenly charged across the room at Ballard, raising his hands like claws as he aimed for her throat. But Ballard was ready, knowing her words might push him toward extreme measures. She turned and pivoted, sidestepping the rush like a bullfighter while bringing her hand holding the rover up and behind his back. She drove the heel of the radio into his spine and tripped him with her leg. Prada went down face-first into the corner of the room. Ballard dropped the radio and pulled her sidearm. She planted a foot on his back and pointed her weapon at his head.

"You try to get up and I'm going to put a hole in your spine. You'll never walk again."

Ballard felt him tense and test the pressure of her foot. But then he relaxed and gave up.

"Smart boy," she said.

As she was cuffing him and reciting the rights advisory, she heard the elevator door open and then running steps as Herrera and Dyson rushed down the hall.

Soon they were in the condo and by Ballard's side.

"Get him up and put him in a chair," Ballard ordered. "I'm going to have to call homicide."

The two officers moved in and grabbed Prada by the arms.

"He was going to kill me," Prada suddenly announced. "He

wanted my business, everything I've worked for. I fought him. He fell and hit his head. I didn't want him to die."

"And that's why you rolled him up in a rug and dumped his body somewhere?" Ballard asked.

"No one would have believed me. You don't believe me now."

"Did you understand the rights I recited to you?"

"He was going to cut me into pieces."

"Stop talking and answer the question. Do you understand the rights I just recited? Do you want me to say them again?"

"I understand, I understand."

"Okay. Where's Jacob Cady's body?"

Prada shook his head.

"You'll never find it," he said. "I put it in a dumpster. It's wherever the trash goes. And it's what he deserves."

She stepped out into the hallway to call Lieutenant McAdam, the head of the Hollywood Division detective bureau and Ballard's real boss, even though she rarely saw him. She had to directly inform him of any case of this magnitude. She took a guilty pleasure in waking him up. He was a strict nine-to-fiver.

"Hey, boss, it's Ballard," she said. "We've got a homicide."

28

When Ballard returned to the detective bureau after handing off the Jacob Cady case to a West Bureau homicide team, she found Harry Bosch ensconced at the desk he had used the night before, going through a box of field interview cards.

"Don't you sleep, Bosch?" she said.

"Not tonight," he said.

Ballard saw the coffee cup on the desk. He had helped himself in the break room.

"How long have you been here?" she asked.

"Not long," Bosch said. "I was out looking for somebody all night."

"Find him?"

"Her, and no, not yet. What have you been up to?"

"Working a homicide. And now I have to do the paperwork, so I won't be looking at any shake cards today."

"No problem. I'm making progress."

He held up the handful of cards he had put to the side for closer study later. She was about to say that there was a problem in him coming into the station and working the case alone, but she let it go. She pulled out a seat and sat down at a desk in the same pod as Bosch.

After logging into the computer, Ballard started writing an incident report that she would send to the team that took over the Cady case.

"What was the case?" Bosch asked. "The homicide."

"It's a no-body case," she said. "So far, at least. Started as a missing persons and that's why I was called in. Got a guy who admits killing the man, cutting up the body, and putting it all in a dumpster. Oh, and he says it was self-defense."

"Of course he does."

"We checked with the building manager—the dumpster got picked up yesterday, so they'll be going out to the landfill today as soon as they figure out who the trash hauler was and which dump they use. One of the few times I'm glad I don't get to see a case all the way through. The two guys that caught it were not too happy."

"I had a no-body case once. Same thing. We had to go to the dump but we were a week behind it. So we spent about two weeks out there. And we found a body but it was the wrong one. Only in L.A., I guess."

"You mean you found a murder victim but not the one you were looking for?"

"Yeah. We never found the one we were looking for. We went out there on a tip anyway. So maybe it never happened. The one we found was a mob case and we eventually cleared it. But those two weeks out there, I didn't get the smell out of my nose for months. And forget about the clothes. I threw everything away."

"I've heard it can be pretty ripe at those places."

She went back to work, but less than five minutes went by before Bosch interrupted again.

"Did you ever get a chance to check on the GRASP files?" he asked.

247

"Matter of fact, I did," Ballard said. "Supposedly they were all purged, but I got a line on the USC professor who designed the program and helped implement it. I'm hoping he kept the data. I have an appointment at eight with him, if you're interested."

"I'm interested. I'll buy you breakfast on the way."

"I won't have time for breakfast if I don't get the paperwork filed."

"Got it. I'll shut up."

Ballard smiled as she went back to work on the report. She was in the summary section, where she was typing out Tyldus's self-serving statements—he was being booked under his current legal name—after he was arrested and realized that he needed to try to talk his way out of a murder. His fervent plea of self-defense lost credibility when the forensics team called to the apartment pulled up the bathtub drain trap and found blood and tissue. Then Tyldus admitted cutting the body up and bagging the parts in plastic trash bags—an extreme measure for a self-defense killing.

It made Ballard feel bad for Cady's parents and family. In the next hours and days they would learn that their son was presumed dead, dismembered, and buried somewhere amid the garbage at a landfill. And Bosch's story about an unsuccessful search for a body in a landfill concerned her. It was critical that they find Cady's body so that injuries aside from dismemberment could be analyzed in concert with the details provided by Tyldus. If the injuries on the body told a different story, it would be Jacob's way of helping to convict his killer.

Despite what Ballard had said about being glad she was not seeing the case through to the end, she intended to volunteer to help look for Jacob. She felt the need to be there.

Ballard's shift ended at seven but she got her reports emailed to the West Bureau detectives an hour before that and she and Bosch headed downtown early. They ate breakfast at the Pacific Dining Car, an expensive LAPD tradition across the street from the Rampart Division station. They didn't talk much about the current case. Instead, they filled each other in on their histories in the LAPD. Bosch had bounced around a lot in the early years before spending several years in Hollywood homicide and finishing his career at RHD. He also revealed that he had a daughter who went to college down in Orange County.

Mention of the daughter prompted Bosch to pull out his phone.

"You're not going to text her now, are you?" Ballard asked. "No college kid is awake this early."

"No, just checking her location," Bosch said. "Seeing if she's at home. She's twenty-one now and I thought that would lessen the worry, but it's only made it worse."

"Does she know you can track her?"

"Yeah, we made a deal. I can track her and she can track me. I think she worries about me as much as I worry about her."

"That's nice, but you know that she can just leave her phone in her room and you'd think she was there."

Bosch looked up from the phone to Ballard.

"Really?" he said. "You had to plant that seed in my head?"

"Sorry," Ballard said. "Just saying if I was a college kid and my dad could track my phone, I don't think I'd carry it all the time."

Bosch put his phone away and changed the subject.

As promised, Bosch picked up the tab, and they headed south toward USC. Along the way, Ballard told Bosch about Dennis Eagleton and his being picked up by the Moonlight Mission bus on the same night as Daisy Clayton. She said there wasn't much of a tie between the two beyond that, but Eagleton was a dirtbag criminal and she wanted to interview him if he could be located.

"Tim Farmer talked to him," she said. "He wrote a shake in 2014, said 'Eagle' was filled with hate and violence."

"But no real record of violence?" Bosch asked.

"Just the one assault that got pled down. The dirtbag only did a month in county for splitting a guy's head open with a bottle."

Bosch didn't respond. He just nodded as if the story about Eagleton's light punishment was par for the course.

By eight a.m. they were at the office door of Professor Scott Calder at the University of Southern California. Calder was in his late thirties, which told Ballard he had been in his twenties when he designed the crime tracking program adopted by the police department.

"Professor Calder?" Ballard said. "I'm Detective Ballard. We spoke on the phone. And this is my colleague Detective Bosch."

"Come in, please," Calder said.

Calder offered his visitors seats in front of his desk and then sat down himself. He was casually dressed in a maroon golf shirt with USC in gold over the left breast. He had a shaved head and a long beard in the steampunk style. Ballard guessed that he thought it helped him fit in better with the students on campus.

"LAPD should never have disbanded GRASP," he said. "It would have been paying dividends right now if they had kept it in place."

Neither Ballard nor Bosch jumped to agree with him and Calder began a brief summary of how the program arose from his studies of crime patterns in and around USC after a spate of assaults and robberies of students just blocks from campus. After collecting data, Calder used statistics to project the frequency and locations of future crimes in the neighborhoods surrounding the university. The LAPD got wind of the project and the police chief asked Calder to take his computer modeling to the city, starting with three test areas: Hollywood Division because of the transient nature of its inhabitants and the variety of crimes that occurred there; Pacific Division because of the unique nature of crimes in Venice; and Southwest Division because it included USC. A city grant financed the project, and Calder and several of his students went to work collecting the data after a training period with officers in the three divisions. The project lasted two and a half years, until the chief's five-year term was up. The police commission did not retain Calder afterward. A new chief was named and he killed the program, announcing a return to good old-fashioned community policing.

"It was a shame," Calder said. "We were just starting to get our successes. GRASP would have worked if given the chance."

"It sounds like it," Ballard said.

She could not think of any other words of sympathy, as she had her own beliefs about the predictability of crime.

Bosch said nothing.

"Well, we appreciate the historical perspective on the program," Ballard continued. "What we're here for is to ask if you kept any of the data from it. We're investigating an unsolved murder from '09, which was the second year of GRASP. So it was up and running and collecting data. We thought it would be helpful if we had sort of a snapshot of the entire crime picture in Hollywood on that night, maybe the whole week of the murder."

Calder was silent for a moment as he considered Ballard's question. Then he spoke carefully.

"You know that the new chief purged all the data when he

killed the program, right?" he said. "He said he didn't want it to fall into the wrong hands. You believe that?"

The bitter tone that had come into Calder's voice revealed the anger he had stored for nearly a decade.

"That seems a bit contradictory to the department's keeping all kinds of other records," Ballard offered, hoping to separate the current investigation from political decisions she had nothing to do with.

"It was stupid," Bosch said. "The whole decision was stupid."

Ballard realized that Bosch was the way to win Calder's cooperation. He answered to nobody. He could say whatever he wanted and especially what Calder wanted to hear.

"I was told by the police department that I had to purge my own data storage on the project," Calder said.

"But it was your baby," Bosch said. "I'm guessing you didn't purge it all, and if I'm right, you might be able to help us solve a murder. That would be a nice little fuck-you to the chief, right?"

Ballard had to hold back a smile. She could tell that Bosch was playing this perfectly. If Calder had anything, he was going to give it up.

"What specifically are you looking for?" Calder said.

"We'd like a forty-eight-hour read on every crime in the division centered on the night our victim was grabbed off the street," Ballard said urgently.

"Twenty-four hours before and twenty-four after?" Calder asked.

"Make it forty-eight on both sides of it," Bosch said.

Ballard pulled out her notebook and tore off the top page. She had already written the date down. Calder took it and looked at it.

"How do you want this—digital or print?" he asked.

"Digital," Ballard said.

"Print," Bosch said at the same time.

"Okay, both," Calder said.

He looked back at the paper with the date on it, as if that alone held some great moral weight.

"Okay," he said. "I can do this."

29

C alder said he needed a day to retrieve the hard drive on which he had kept the GRASP data. It wasn't at the school but at a private storage facility. He said he would call as soon as he had the material ready for pickup.

Ballard had driven them both in her city car so they wouldn't have to worry about legit parking both their private cars, but before they left, Bosch asked to be dropped off at the nearby Exposition Park.

"Why?" she asked.

"I've never seen the shuttle," he said. "I thought I'd check it out."

The decommissioned space shuttle *Endeavour* had been flown to L.A. six years earlier, slowly moved through the streets of South-Central, and put on permanent display inside the air and space center at the park.

Ballard smiled at the thought of Bosch in the air and space museum.

"You don't seem like a space-travel guy, Harry."

"I'm not really. Just want to look at it to know it's really true."

"You mean you're a conspiracy-theory guy, then? Like the space program was a hoax? Fake news?"

"No, no, not like that. I believe it. It's just kind of amazing, you know, to think we could send those things up, circle the planet, fix satellites, and do whatever they were doing and we can't fix things down here. I just wanted to see it once, ever since they brought it here. I was…"

He trailed off like he was unsure he should continue.

"What?" Ballard prompted.

"Nah, I was just going to say, I was in Vietnam back in '69," Bosch said. "Way before you were even born, I know. And on this one day, I had just gotten back to base camp on Airmobile after a hairy op where we had to clear the enemy out of a tunnel system. That's what I did over there. Tunnels. It was late morning and base camp was completely deserted. It was like a ghost town because everybody was sitting in their tents, listening to their radios. Neil Armstrong was about to walk on the moon and they all wanted to hear it…

"And it was the same thing, you know? How did we put a guy up there bouncing around on the moon when things were so fucked up down here? I mean, that morning during the op…I had to kill a guy. In the tunnel. I was nineteen years old."

Bosch was looking out his window. He almost seemed to be talking to himself.

"Harry, I'm really sorry," Ballard said. "That you were put in that situation at that age. At any age."

"Yeah, well…" Bosch said. "That's the way it was."

He didn't say anything further. Ballard could feel the fatigue coming off him like a wave.

"You still want to see the shuttle?" she asked. "How will you get back to your car at the station?"

"Yeah, drop me off. I can grab a taxi or an Uber after."

She started the car and drove the few blocks over to the park.

They didn't speak. She got him as close as she could to the giant building that housed the shuttle.

"I'm not sure they're going to be open yet," Ballard said.

"It's okay," Bosch said. "I'll find something to do."

"After this, you should go home and get a nap. You seem tired, Harry."

"That's a good idea."

He opened his door, then looked back at Ballard before getting out.

"Just so you know, I'm done at San Fernando," he said. "So I'm fully committed to the Daisy case."

"What do you mean 'done'?" Ballard asked. "What happened?"

"I sort of messed things up. My witness getting killed, that's going to be on me. I didn't do enough to protect him. Then things happened yesterday between me and the guy who leaked it and I got suspended by the chief. Being a reserve, there are no protections so…I'm just done. That's it."

Ballard waited to see if he would say more but he didn't.

"So…the woman you were looking for all night," she said. "That wasn't part of that case?"

"No," Bosch said. "That was Daisy's mother. I came home and she'd split. Sorry you never got the chance to talk to her."

"It's okay," Ballard said. "You think she went back to the life?"

Bosch shrugged.

"I hit all her familiars last night," he said. "Nobody had seen her. But those were only the places I knew of. She could have had others. Places to score and crash. People who would take her in. She might've just hopped on a Greyhound and split, too. That's what I'm hoping. But I'll keep looking when I can."

Ballard nodded. That seemed to be the end of the conversation but she wanted to tell him something. Just as he started to get out, she spoke.

"My father went to Vietnam," she said. "You remind me of him."

"That right?" Bosch said. "He live here in L.A.?"

"No, I lost him when I was fourteen. But during the war, he came to Hawaii on...what was it called, furlough?"

"Yeah, or liberty. I went to Hawaii a few times. They didn't let you go back to CONUS, so you could go to Hong Kong, Sydney, a few other places. But Hawaii was the best."

"What was CONUS?"

"Continental United States. They didn't want you going back to the mainland because of all the protests. But if you worked things right in Honolulu, you could sneak onto a flight in civvies and get back to L.A."

"I don't think my dad did that. He met my mother in Hawaii and then after the war he came back and stayed."

"A lot of guys did that."

"He was from Ventura originally, and after I was born, we would visit my grandmother there—once a year—but he didn't like coming back. He saw it like you do. A fucked-up world. He just wanted to camp on the beach and surf."

Bosch nodded.

"I get that. He was smart and I was the fool. I came back and thought I could do something about things."

Before Ballard could respond, Bosch got out of the car and closed the door. Ballard watched him walk toward the building where they kept the space shuttle. She noticed a slight limp in his walk.

"I didn't mean it like that, Harry," she said out loud.

30

By the time Ballard switched vehicles, drove out to Venice, picked up Lola, and got to the beach it was midmorning and the wind had kicked up a two-foot chop on the surface that would make paddling a challenge instead of the therapy she usually drew from it. As much as she needed the exercise, she knew she needed sleep more. She pitched her tent, posted Lola at the front, and crawled in to rest. She thought about her father as she trailed off, remembering him straddling his favorite board and telling her about Vietnam and about killing people, putting it the way Bosch had put it, saying he'd had to do it and then had to live with it. He wrapped all of his Vietnam experiences into one phrase, *"Sin loi."* Tough shit.

Four hours later her watch vibrated her awake. She had been in deep, and waking was slow and disorienting. Finally, she sat up, split the tent flaps with her hand and checked on Lola. The dog was there, sunning herself. She looked back at Ballard with expectant eyes.

"You hungry, girl?"

Ballard climbed out of the tent and stretched. She checked the Rose Avenue tower and saw Aaron Hayes in the nest, gazing out at sea. There were no swimmers out there.

"Come on, Lola."

She walked down the sand toward the lifeguard tower. The dog followed behind her.

"Aaron," she called up to the tower.

Hayes turned and looked down at her from his perch.

"Renée. I saw your tent but didn't want to wake you up. You doing all right?"

"Yeah. What about you?"

"You know, back on the bench. But pretty quiet today."

Ballard glanced out toward the water as if to confirm the paucity of swimmers.

"You want to grab dinner tonight?" he asked.

"I think I have to work," Ballard said. "Let me make a call and see what's what, then I'll let you know."

"I'll be here."

"You have your phone?"

"Got my phone."

He was breaking a rule, having a personal phone with him while in the tower. A scandal had rocked a rescue crew up the coast a year before when a texting lifeguard missed seeing a drowning woman waving for help. Ballard knew Aaron would not text or take calls, but he could play back messages without taking his eyes off the water.

She walked back to the tent, pulled her phone out of the pocket of her beach sweats, and called the number given to her by Travis Lee, one of the homicide detectives who took over the Jacob Cady case that morning. He answered and she asked what the status of the case was. Lee had remarked to her early that morning that it was an unusual set of circumstances for him and his partner Rahim Rogers. They came into the case with the admitted killer in custody, thanks to

Ballard, and the detective work would be in finding the remains of the victim.

"We traced the truck that made the pickup on the dumpster," Lee said. "It first went to a sorting center in Sunland, then what was not picked out for recycling was dumped at the landfill in Sylmar. Believe it or not, it's called Sunshine Canyon. We're putting on moon suits now and about to start picking."

"You have an extra moon suit?" Ballard asked.

"You volunteering, Ballard?"

"I am. I want to see it through."

"Come on, then. We'll fix you up."

"I'll be there in an hour."

After packing up and dropping Lola at doggy day care, Ballard took the 405 freeway directly north, through the charred hills in the Sepulveda Pass and into the Valley. She called Aaron along the way and left a message telling him dinner was not going to happen.

Sylmar was at the north end of the Valley and Sunshine Canyon was in the armpit created by the intersection of the 405 and 14 freeways. Ballard could smell it long before she got to it. Slapping a name like Sunshine Canyon on a landfill was typical iconography. Take something ugly or horrible and put a pretty name on it.

Upon arrival, Ballard was driven out to the search site on an all-terrain vehicle. Lee and Rogers and a forensics team were already using what looked like ski poles to pick through an area of refuse that had been cordoned off with yellow tape. It was about thirty yards long and ten wide, and Ballard assumed that this was the spread of refuse from the garbage truck that had picked up Jacob Cady's condo dumpster on its route.

There was a table under a mobile canopy set up by the foren-

sics team on the dirt road that skirted the landfill's drop zone.
Extra equipment was spread across it, including plastic hazmat
coveralls, breathing masks, eye guards, glove and bootie boxes,
hard hats, duct tape, and a case of bottled water. A barrel next to
the table had extra search picks, some of which had orange flags
attached for marking finds.

Ballard was dropped off with an advisory from the ATV's
driver that hard hats were required to be worn in the debris
zones of the landfill. She put on a breathing mask first. It didn't
do much to cut the odor but it was comforting to know it might
cut down on the intake of larger particulate garbage. She pulled
a moon suit on over her clothes next and noticed that none of
the searchers on the debris pile had pulled the hood up on their
hazmat suits. She did, tucking her midlength hair completely
into the plastic and pulling the slip line that tightened the hood
around her face.

She put on gloves and booties and then used the duct tape to
seal the cuffs of the suit around her wrists and ankles. She put
on the eye guard and topped the outfit off with an orange hard
hat with the number 23 on both sides of it. She was ready. She
grabbed one of the picks from the barrel and started crossing the
debris toward the other searchers. There were five of them in a
line, working their way up the search zone.

Because they had not pulled up their hoods, Ballard easily
identified Lee and Rogers.

"You guys want me to squeeze into the line here or do something else?" she asked.

"Is that you, Ballard?" Lee said. "Yeah, squeeze in. Better
chance we don't miss anything."

Lee moved left and Rogers moved right, making room for
Ballard to join the line.

"Black plastic bags, Ballard," Rogers said. "With blue pull straps."

"Got it," Ballard said.

"Everybody, this is Renée," Lee said. "She's the one we have to thank for being here today. Renée, this is everybody."

Ballard smiled though no one could see it.

"My bad, I guess," she said.

"No, your good," Rogers said. "If not for you, that shitbird from New Jersey might've gotten away with it. And they told us here that if we had come two, three, days from now, we would never have been able to isolate a drop zone like this. We got lucky."

"Now let's hope we get lucky again," Lee added.

They moved slowly, each step sinking a foot or more into the debris, using the steel picks to dig down through the garbage. Line integrity was loose as sometimes a searcher would stop to use his or her hands to clear debris.

At one point Lee became concerned about the time and asked the others to pick up the pace. They had at least four hours of sunlight left but if they started finding body parts, a crime scene investigation would be initiated and he wanted to conduct it in daylight.

An hour after Ballard joined the search, they found the first body parts. One of the forensic techs uncovered a black plastic bag and ripped it open with her pick.

"Here," she called out.

The others gathered around the find. In the ripped bag were a pair of feet and lower legs, cut just below the knee. While the tech took photos on her phone, Rogers started back toward the equipment table to get a pick with a flag. The search would continue after marking the first find. Lee pulled his phone and started the Medical Examiner's Office rolling to the scene.

The next piece of evidence found was the rug from the living room. Ballard came across it in her search channel. It was sitting near the top of the pile but disguised by a ripped bag of what looked like garbage from a Chinese restaurant. The rug had been loosely rolled up. It was pulled out of the debris and unrolled to reveal a massive blood stain but no body parts.

Ballard was marking the find with a flagged pick when Kokoro, the criminalist who found the first black bag, called out that she had found two more. Again there was a grim gathering around these. One contained Jacob Cady's head, the other his arms.

Cady's face showed no sign of trauma and was composed, eyes and mouth shut, almost as if he were asleep. Kokoro took more photos.

The arms showed trauma beyond the obvious damage of being severed from the body. There were deep lacerations on both forearms and on the palms.

"Defensive wounds," Rogers said. "He held his hands up to ward off an attack."

"We've got a righteous murder case," Lee said.

They marked the location of these finds with flags and pressed on. By the time the van from the Medical Examiner's Office and a crime scene team arrived, they had found two more bags containing the rest of the body and a third that contained the large knives and hacksaw that had been used during the dismemberment. Jacob Cady had been completely recovered for burial. It was one thing that would not have to haunt his family.

Ballard backed out to the table under the canopy, lowered her mask, and drank half a bottle of water in one pull. Lee came over as well. The searchers had moved out of the refuse so the coroner's investigators and crime scene photographer could document everything.

"What a wonderful world," Lee said.

"What a wonderful world," Ballard repeated.

Lee opened a bottle of water and started gulping it down.

"Where are you with Tyldus?" Ballard asked.

"We got him on tape telling his self-defense story," Lee said. "I've seen enough here to know it won't hold up. He's going down."

"What about the victim's parents? How much have you told them?"

"We told them that we had a guy in custody and they should prepare themselves. We didn't get into the details of it yet. Now we will."

"Glad it's not me."

"Why we get the big bucks. So you were in RHD a while back, right?"

"A few years, yeah."

Lee didn't say anything further, leaving the question of what happened hanging like landfill stink in the air.

"I didn't go to the late show by choice," Ballard said. "But it turns out I like what I'm doing."

She left it at that. She took another drink from the water bottle and then pulled the breathing mask back into place. It felt like the mask and everything else was useless. The stench of the landfill was invading her pores. She knew that when she was finished here, she would shoot down the 118 freeway to Ventura and her grandmother's house, where she planned to spend at least a half hour under the shower while double-washing her clothes. She was going to run the hot-water heater dry.

"I guess I'm out of here, Travis," she said. "You've got the remains and I've got to get cleaned up before my shift."

"Yeah, good luck with that," Lee said.

He thanked her for volunteering and used a radio to call for
an ATV to take her down to the parking lot and her van.

Lee went back into the pile to join his partner and monitor
the investigation. As she waited for her ride, Ballard watched
the two coroner's investigators start to unfold a body bag. She
hoped they had brought more than one. She turned from the
scene and looked west. The sun was about to drop behind the
ridge of the debris pile. The sky was orange above Sunshine
Canyon.

BOSCH

31

Bosch's phone buzzed. The screen said UNKNOWN CALLER but he guessed it was Bella Lourdes again. The last two times, he had let the call go to message and she had left him voice mails saying she wanted to talk about his suspension and his taking the bullet for the Luzon plan they had both signed off on and taken part in. But Bosch didn't want to talk about any of that yet.

He took another gulp of black coffee and kept his eyes on the entrance to the clinic on Van Nuys Boulevard. There had been a steady flow of activity there for the past two hours but Bosch had not seen Elizabeth Clayton among those wandering in and out. It would be eight p.m. soon and the clinic was due to close.

He checked his texts again. He had sent a message to his daughter, inquiring about his coming down on the train for a breakfast or a dinner, maybe even an Angels game over the weekend, but it had been forty minutes and there was no response. He had her schedule and knew she didn't have night class but she could be studying in the library with her cell phone turned off. He thought about what Ballard had said about her not carrying the phone when she didn't want to be tracked. He wondered if this was one of those times.

He opened up the tracking app on his phone, but before he could locate his daughter, the phone buzzed with another call. This time, the ID wasn't blocked and he took the call.

"Renée, what's up?"

"Hey, Harry, where are you at?"

He could tell she was driving.

"Van Nuys," he said. "I'm watching a pain clinic, looking for Elizabeth."

"I thought you said you tracked her to North Hollywood," Ballard asked.

"I did but I was there last night. No sign. Tonight I'm watching a clinic she went to before. Maybe she'll show. Where are you? Sounds like a freeway."

"The 101 coming in from Ventura."

She told him about the landfill dig and the need to clean up at her grandmother's house.

"Am I going to see you later tonight at the shop?" she asked.

"Unless something happens here, I'll be by," Bosch said.

"I got a message from Professor Calder. He said he has the GRASP files on a thumb drive for us. He'll have it with him at the school tomorrow. I'll head back to USC after my shift if you're interested in joining. We can print out hard copies for you."

"Yeah, count me in for all of it."

"Okay. Maybe I'll get lucky tonight and have a quiet shift and then I'll be able to finish off the shake cards."

"Good luck."

Ballard disconnected and Bosch went back to watching the pain clinic.

He wasn't sure why he was doing it. Despite Elizabeth's previous connection to Dr. Ali Rohat, the shady doctor who ran the place, there were thousands of clinics in the Los Angeles area. She could be at any of them or none. He guessed he was doing it to be doing something. The alternative was to go home to an empty house and wonder about her.

He'd take his chances on a long shot. Besides, concentrating on the clinic kept some of the darker thoughts about his recent mis-cues out of the front of his mind. He knew that he was putting off a critical self-evaluation of his recent moves, an evaluation that might conclude with his deciding that he was unfit to do the work anymore. That would be his call to make, but he knew he set his standards higher than any other person he'd come across. If he be-lieved it was time to retire, then that would be it.

His phone buzzed again. It was an unknown caller. This time he decided to get the conversation with Bella Lourdes over with. He took the call.

But it wasn't Bella Lourdes.

"Hey, asshole."

He didn't recognize the voice. It had a Spanish accent and he placed the age at mid- to late thirties. It had some weight to it.

"Who's this?"

"Doesn't matter. What matters is that you are fucking with the wrong people."

"Which people is that?"

"You'll find out, muthafucker. Real soon, too."

"Cortez? Is this Cortez?"

The caller disconnected.

Bosch had received many threats over the years. Most of them were anonymous like this one. Receiving it gave him no pause. He had to assume the caller was Cortez or a member of the San-Fers. And that would explain how the caller had his private cell number. Bosch had written it on the business card that had been given to Martin Perez and then ended up slotted between his teeth after his murder. It was another in a lengthening line of missteps Bosch had made recently, beginning with his acquiescing to Perez's not wanting protection and ending with Luzon's getting the drop on Bosch and locking him out of the cell so he could try to kill himself.

He decided to call Bella Lourdes back and tell her about the threat. Threats were rarely carried out, but he thought there should be a record of this one should it prove to be the exception. He got her while she was still in the office doing accumulated paperwork.

"I've been trying to reach you all day, Harry."

"I know. I've been busy and just got the chance to call. What's up?"

"At some point we need to talk about Luzon and this bullshit suspension, but at the moment, there's something more important. The gang guys picked up some intel today. The SanFers put a hit out on you."

Bosch was silent for a long moment, thinking about the threat he'd just gotten.

"Harry, you there?"

"Yeah, I was just thinking. How good is the intel?"

"They said it was good enough to want to warn you."

"Well, I just got an anonymous call on my phone. My cell. Guy threatened me."

"Shit, did you recognize the voice?"

"Not really. Coulda been Cortez, coulda been anybody. But why call and tip me off if the hit is legit? That doesn't make sense, does it?"

"No, not really, but you have to take this seriously."

"Think they know where I live?"

"I have no idea. Maybe you should stay away from there to be safe."

Bosch saw a woman with a bandanna around her head come out of the clinic and start walking south on Van Nuys. She had the same thin build as Elizabeth but she had turned from Bosch's direction so fast that he was unable to confirm whether it was her. The bandanna hid her hair color and length.

"Bella, I need to go," he said. "Keep me posted. I think it's all talk, but let me know if you hear different."

"Harry, I think you need—"

Bosch disconnected and started the car. He drove slowly down the street, keeping his eyes on the woman. She was almost to the end of the block now and Bosch planned to go past her, pull to the curb, and then get out to see if it was Elizabeth. He realized that he had concentrated so much on finding her that he wasn't sure how he would handle things once he did.

As the woman got to the corner, she turned and Bosch lost sight of her. His plan to identify and confront her on the well-lit Van Nuys Boulevard now changed. He sped up and made the same turn the woman had. Immediately he saw her standing with two men in the shadows of a closed paint store. One of the men had his hands cupped and the woman was placing something in them. Bosch still could not get a good look at her face. He pulled to the curb directly in front of them.

Immediately one of the men ran off toward an alley perpendicular to Van Nuys. The woman and the remaining man stood frozen. Bosch's old Cherokee did not resemble a police vehicle in any way. He jumped out, grabbing a mini-light from the center console, and held his hands up so they could see them over the roof of the Jeep.

"It's all right. I just want to talk. Just want to talk."

As he came around, Bosch saw the man pull something from a back pocket and use the woman's body as a blind. Bosch could not tell if it was a gun or knife or pack of cigarettes. But in his experience, if you had a gun, you showed a gun.

Bosch stopped six feet from them, his arms still raised.

"Elizabeth?"

He peered into the darkness. He could not tell and she didn't answer. His hands still over his head, he snapped on the light and put the beam on her.

It wasn't Elizabeth.

"Okay, sorry, wrong person," Bosch said. "I'll leave you alone now."

He started backing away.

"Damn right, it's the wrong person," the man said. "What the fuck you doing, runnin' up on people like that?"

"I told you, I'm looking for somebody, okay? I'm sorry."

"I coulda had a gun, you fucking idiot. I coulda blown your shit away."

Bosch reached under his jacket and snapped his gun off his belt. He held it barrel up and took a step back toward the couple.

"You mean like this?" he said. "This what you have?"

The man dropped whatever he was holding and raised his hands.

"Sorry, man. Sorry," he called out.

"Put that damn thing away," the woman yelled. "We ain't hurting nobody."

Bosch looked down at the pavement and saw what the man had dropped. It was a plastic pill crusher. They were about to turn the pills she got at the clinic into powder for snorting. Bosch had carried a crusher just like it while working undercover the year before.

All at once he was struck by how pitiful the lives of the two people in front of him were. He wondered how Elizabeth could have gone back to this. He put his gun back into its holster and returned to the door of the Cherokee, the two addicts watching him.

"What are you, some kind of cop?" the woman yelled.

Bosch looked at her before getting in.

"Something like that," he said.

He got in, dropped the transmission into drive, and peeled off.

He decided to call it a night. If Elizabeth was out there on her own, she would no longer have Bosch looking for her. He headed home, resigned to the idea that he had done what he could for her. He would continue to look for her daughter's killer, but finding Elizabeth would no longer be a priority.

He picked up tacos at the Poquito Más on Cahuenga and then went up the hill to his house. The plan was to eat, shower, and put on fresh clothes. He would then head to Hollywood to read shake cards with Ballard.

The house was dark because he had forgotten to leave any lights on. He came in through the kitchen door and grabbed a bottle of water out of the refrigerator before heading out to the back deck to eat his dinner.

As he crossed the living room, he noticed that the sliding door to the deck was halfway open. He stopped. He knew he hadn't left it that way. He then felt the muzzle of a gun against the back of his head.

An image of his daughter went through his mind. It was from a few years ago, of a moment when he had been teaching her how to drive and told her she had done well. She smiled proudly at him.

BALLARD

32

Ballard had the kind of night she had been waiting for all week. No calls for a detective, no calls for backup, no officer-needs-assistance calls. She spent the whole shift in the detective bureau and even ordered food delivered to the front desk. This gave her time to focus and power through the remaining field interview cards.

The pickings were thin in the first two boxes in terms of pulling cards for follow-up investigation. Ballard put only two in the stack that had been accumulating from the start of the project. But the third box produced five cards, including three that she felt should immediately go to the top.

Three weeks before the murder of Daisy Clayton, two officers had stopped their car and inspected a panel van that was parked illegally in front of a red curb on Gower south of Sunset. When they approached, they heard voices from within the van and saw light inside. There were windows on the rear doors and they noticed a makeshift curtain had fallen partially open behind one of them. Through the narrow opening they saw a man and woman having sex on a mattress while a second man videoed them with a camera.

The officers broke the party up and checked the IDs of all

three of the van's occupants. They confirmed with the woman—who had a record of prostitution arrests—that both the sex and the videoing of it were consensual. She denied that any money had changed hands or that she was engaged in prostitution.

No arrests were made, because there was no crime the three-some could be charged with. Under the law, officers could make an arrest for lewd behavior only if it was witnessed by the public and a citizen reported being offended. The three were let off with a warning and told to move on.

Three individual shake cards were filled out. What Ballard keyed on—besides the van—was that one of the men had the words "porno actor" under his name. He was listed as Kurt Pascal, twenty-six years old at the time and living on Kester Street in Sherman Oaks.

From the few details that were on the shake cards, Ballard drew the likely conclusion that the officers had interrupted a porno shoot in the van. Pascal and the cameraman, identified as Wilson Gayley, thirty-six, had paid prostitute Tanya Vickers, thirty-one, to perform in the van. Ballard took it a step further and envisioned a night three weeks later when they picked up another prostitute for filming and then found out after the fact that they had committed a crime because she was underage. One solution to their problem would be to eliminate the prostitute and make it look like the work of a sexual sadist.

Ballard knew it was all supposition. Extrapolation upon extrapolation. But something about the scenario held her. She needed to run with those three shake cards and knew just where to start.

She looked up at the wall clock and saw that the shift had gone by quickly. It was already five a.m. and she realized that Bosch had not shown up, as he had said he would. She thought about calling him but didn't want to wake him if he had instead decided to get a full night's sleep.

Ballard looked at the three shake cards spread on the desk in front of her. She wanted to dive right in on them but she had an allegiance to Bosch and how he said the review of the cards should go. She moved to the final box and started looking through more cards.

Two hours later she had finished going through the last box. She had pulled no cards. Bosch still had not shown up. She checked her phone to see if she had somehow missed a call or text from him but there was nothing. She wrote him a text instead.

I'm heading to USC in 30—you coming?

She sent it and waited. There was no immediate reply.

Ballard went back to work and used the next half hour before leaving to run the three names from the van through the computer in an attempt to get current addresses and legal status. She determined that, over the four years that followed the van incident, Tanya Vickers was arrested nine times for prostitution and drug offenses before she died of a heroin overdose at age thirty-five.

The porno actor, Kurt Pascal, had no record and was still listed in Department of Motor Vehicle Records as living on Kester in Sherman Oaks, but the record was old. The driver's license had expired two years ago without being renewed.

The cameraman, Wilson Gayley, was also unaccounted for. In 2012 he was sentenced to prison after being convicted of intentionally infecting a person with a sexually transmitted disease. He spent three years in prison and completed a year on parole. He then dropped off the grid. Ballard could find no record of him having a driver's license in any state.

Ballard had her work cut out for her, but it was now eight a.m. and she was supposed to meet Professor Calder at USC in thirty minutes to pick up the GRASP data. She couldn't miss the window of time he had given her, because he had a three-hour computer lab starting at nine.

She put the four boxes of FI cards on top of the file cabinets that ran the length of the bureau, grabbed a rover from the charging station, and headed out the back door.

It was after eight by the time she pulled out of the parking lot, and Ballard felt no concern about calling and waking Bosch. But her call went straight to his voice mail.

"Bosch, it's Ballard. What happened to you? I thought we were doing this together. I'm on my way to USC. Call me. I found some shake cards I really like."

She disconnected, half expecting Bosch to call her back right away.

He didn't.

Ballard looked up a number in her phone and called it. Beatrice Beaupre was a director of adult films as well as a previous performer. All told, she had almost twenty years in the business. Ballard knew her because the year before she had rescued Beaupre from a man with plans to kill her. In that regard Beaupre owed Ballard, and she was calling now to collect.

Ballard knew that at this hour Beaupre was either wrapping up a night's work at her studio out in Canoga Park or she was asleep and dead to the world.

The call was answered after one ring.

"What?"

"Beatrice, it's Renée Ballard."

Beaupre was known by several different names in the porno field. Few people called her by or even knew her given name.

"Ballard, what are you doing? I was about to crash. Been working all night."

"Then I'm glad I got you beforehand. I need your expertise."

"My expertise. What, you want to try bondage or something?"

"Not quite. I want to run a few names by you, see if anything clicks."

"Okay."

"First one is Kurt Pascal. He's supposedly a porn actor. Was, at least, nine years ago."

"Nine years ago. Shit, the industry's turned over twice in that time. People come and go—no pun intended."

"So you don't know him."

"Well, I know these guys by their stage names and that ain't no stage name. Let me get to my computer. See if he's in the database under his real name."

"What database is that?"

"Adult casting. Hold on."

Ballard heard typing and then:

"Pascal? P-A-S-C-A-L?"

"That's what I have, yeah."

"Okay, yeah, he's here. I don't recognize the photo, so I would say I never worked with him. What did he do?"

"Nothing. Does it say where he lives?"

"No, nothing like that. It's got his management listing and then age and body details. He's a ten hard, which explains why he got into the business and apparently stayed. He's thirty-five and that's kinda old for the game."

Ballard thought for a moment about what would be the best way to connect with Pascal. For the time being she moved on.

"What about a guy named Wilson Gayley?" she asked. "He might be a cameraman."

"Is that a performing name?" Beaupre asked. "I don't make gay porn, so I wouldn't know him."

"No, it's a real name. I think."

"You think."

Ballard heard typing.

"He's not in the database," Beaupre said. "But it kinda rings a bell. You know, a guy with a name for gay porn but who's in the straight game. Let me ask around."

"He went to prison about five years ago for intentionally infecting someone with an STD," Ballard said.

"Oh, wait a minute," Beaupre said. "That guy?"

"What guy?"

"I think it's him. There was a guy back around that time that was mad at a girl—a performer—because she'd talked trash or something about one of his partners. So he hired her for a scene and put himself in it. She ended up getting syph and that forced her out of the business. She went to vice because somebody told her that the producer—sounds like this Gayley guy—did it on purpose. Like he knew he had it when he fucked her. And then vice made a case. They got his medical reports and stuff. Proved he knew it, and he went to jail."

"Have you heard of him since then? He got out a couple years ago."

"I don't think so. I just remember that story. It's about the scariest thing that can happen in this business."

Ballard knew she had to pull the files on Gayley to confirm

Beaupre's story. But it sounded like they were talking about the same man.

"On the first guy, Pascal," she said. "You could hire him for a shoot through that database?"

"I would send his management a message checking on availability," Beaupre said.

"Would there be like an audition or something?"

"No. In this business, you look at his reel, which the manager will send me, and you either hire him or you don't. He gets three hundred a pop. It says it right here in the database."

"Can you hire him for a shoot today?"

"What are you talking about? What shoot?"

"There is no shoot. I just want to get him to your place so I can talk to him."

There was a pause before Beaupre responded.

"I don't know, Ballard. If it gets out I did this for the cops, it might hurt me, being able to hire people in the future. Especially with that management group. It's one of the big ones."

Now Ballard paused, hoping her silence would communicate what she didn't want to say: *You owe me, Beaupre.*

The strategy worked.

"Okay, I guess I could claim innocence," Beaupre said. "Say I thought you were a valid producer or something."

"Whatever you need to do," Ballard said.

"What day?"

"How about today?"

"Same-day booking is kind of suspect. Nobody does that."

"Okay, what about tomorrow?"

"What time?"

"Nine o'clock."

"At night, right?"

"No, morning."

"Nobody works in the morning."

"Okay, tomorrow afternoon, then."

"Okay, I'll book him for four o'clock and let you know. And then you'll be here?"

"I'll be there."

They disconnected. Ballard then tried Bosch again and once more the call went directly to message.

It was as if Bosch's phone had been turned off.

33

Traffic was a bear getting down to USC. Even with her city car allowing her access to a no-parking zone on campus, Ballard didn't get to Professor Calder's office until he was locking the door to go to his lab.

"Professor, I'm sorry I'm so late," she said to his back. "Any chance I can pick up the GRASP data?"

Ballard realized she had adopted the imploring tone of a student. It was embarrassing.

Calder turned and saw it was her and unlocked his door.

"Come in, Detective."

Calder put a backpack down on a chair and went behind his desk, where he stayed standing while opening the middle drawer.

"You know, I don't know why I'm doing this," he said. "The LAPD did not treat me well."

He took a thumb drive from the drawer and held it out across the desk to Ballard.

"I know," she said. "It was the politics of the moment."

She took the drive from him and held it up.

"But I can assure you," she said. "If this helps us catch a killer, I will make sure people know it."

"I hope so," Calder said. "You'll have to print hard copies for your partner yourself. It's the end of the semester and it turns out I don't have the budget or the paper."

"Not a problem, Professor. Thanks."

"Let me know how it goes."

When Ballard got back to the car, no more than ten minutes after leaving it, there was a parking ticket under the windshield wiper.

"Are you kidding me?" she said.

She yanked the envelope out from under the windshield wiper and did a complete circle, looking for the parking enforcement officer who had issued it. There were only students on their way to classes.

"It's a fricking cop car!" she yelled.

Students stared at her for a moment but then moved on. Ballard got in the car and tossed the envelope onto the dashboard.

"Assholes," she said.

She headed back toward Hollywood. She had to decide what to do next. She could turn in the city ride, get her van, and head to the beach to follow her routine of paddling and then sleeping. Or she could keep moving on the case. She had fifty-six field interview cards that needed a second look. And she had the GRASP files, which represented a new angle of investigation.

She had not been on the water in two days and knew she needed the exercise and the equilibrium it would bring to her being. But the case was calling to her. With the FI cards narrowed and the GRASP data in hand, she needed to keep case momentum going.

She pulled her phone and called Bosch for the third time that morning. It once again went straight to message.

"Bosch, what the fuck? Are we working together on this or not?"

She disconnected, annoyed that there was no way to do an angry hang-up with a cell phone.

As she slogged through heavy traffic, her annoyance with Bosch dissipated and turned into concern. When she got back to Hollywood, she headed north on Highland into the Cahuenga Pass. She knew Bosch lived in the pass. He had given her his address so she could talk to Elizabeth Clayton. She didn't remember the number but she still had the street.

Woodrow Wilson Drive edged the mountain over the pass and offered clipped views between houses that held their ground on steel-and-concrete pilings. But Ballard wasn't interested in the views. She was looking for the old green Cherokee she had seen Bosch driving earlier in the week. Her hope was that Bosch didn't have a garage.

When she was three curves from the top of the mountain, she spotted the Jeep parked in a carport attached to a small house on the view side of the street. She drove past and pulled to the curb.

Ballard went to the front door and knocked. She stepped back and checked the windows for an open curtain. There was nothing, and no one answered. She tried the door and it was locked.

She moved to the carport and checked the side door. It too was locked.

Back out on the street, she walked to the other side and studied the house from afar. She thought about the way Bechtel, the art thief, had gotten in to steal the Warhols. She saw that the carport was supported by a cross-hatched ironwork with squares she judged to be large enough to use as footholds.

She headed across the street again.

Just as she had done three days before, Ballard climbed up to the roof and then crossed it to the rear edge. Every house with a view had a rear deck and she wasn't disappointed by Bosch's home. She checked a gutter for the strength of its moorings, then gripped it with both hands and swung down to the deck. She dropped the remaining three feet without a problem.

Something was definitely strange. The slider was open wide enough for her to slip inside without having to push it further. She stood in the middle of a small, sparsely furnished living room. Visually, nothing seemed wrong.

"Harry?"

No answer. She stepped further in. She noticed an odd food smell.

There was an alcove with a dining room table and a wall of shelves behind it that contained books, files, and a collection of vinyl records and CDs. On the table she saw an unopened bottle of water and a paper bag from Poquito Más, its sides stained with grease. She touched the bag and bottle. Both were room temperature. The bag was open and she looked down into it. She saw wrapped food items and knew the food had gone uneaten for a long time and was the source of the smell in the house.

"Harry?"

She said it louder this time but that didn't change the lack of response.

Stepping into the entryway by the front door, she looked into the galley kitchen that led to the carport. Nothing seemed amiss. She saw a set of keys on the counter.

She turned and walked down the hallway toward the bedrooms. A series of thoughts rushed through her mind as she moved. Bosch had said Elizabeth Clayton had mysteriously moved out. Had she come back to harm him? To rob him? Had something else gone wrong?

Then she thought about Bosch's age and the way he had limped away from her car to the space center. Was she going to find him collapsed in the bed or bathroom? Had he pushed himself too far with lack of sleep and exhaustion?

"Harry? It's Ballard. You here, Harry?"

The house remained silent. Ballard nudged open the door of a bedroom that obviously was Bosch's daughter's room, with posters and photos on the walls, stuffed animals on the bed, her own phonograph, and a thin collection of records. There was a framed photo on the night table of a young girl hugging a woman. Ballard assumed it was Bosch's daughter and her mother.

Across the hall was another room, with a bed and a bureau. All very basic and spartan. Elizabeth's room, she guessed. A communal bathroom off the hallway was next. And then the master bedroom, Harry's room.

Ballard entered and this time only whispered Bosch's name, as if she expected to find him asleep. The bed was made with a military precision, the spread tightly tucked under the edges of the mattress.

She checked the bathroom to finish the search but she knew Bosch was gone. She turned back and walked all through the house and out onto the deck. The last place she needed to check was the steep embankment below the cantilevered house.

The arroyo down below was overgrown with heavy brush and acacia and scrub pine trees. Ballard moved up and down the length of the deck, changing her angles of view so she would be able to see all of the ground below. There was no sign of a body or any sort of break in the natural shape of the canopy of branches.

Satisfied that the house and grounds below were clear, Ballard folded her arms and leaned down on the railing as she tried to decide what to do. She was convinced something had happened to Bosch. She checked her watch. It was now ten o'clock and she knew the detective bureau at Hollywood Station would be in full swing. She pulled her phone and called her boss, Lieutenant McAdam, on his direct line.

"L-T, it's Ballard."

"Ballard. I was just looking for the overnight log and couldn't find it."

"I didn't write one. It was a slow night. No calls."

"Well, that's one in a million. Then what's up?"

"You remember I put on the overnight earlier this week that I'm working the cold case with the girl who got snatched nine years ago?"

"Yes. Daisy something, right?"

"Right, yeah. And I was working it with Harry Bosch."

"Without my permission, but yeah, I know Bosch was in on it."

"He had the watch commander's permission. Anyway, here's the thing. Bosch was supposed to come in this morning and go through old shake cards with me and he didn't show."

"Okay."

"Then we had an appointment with a guy at USC and Bosch didn't show for that either."

"Did you call him?"

"I've been calling him all morning. No answer. I'm now at his house. The back door was open, there's uneaten food from last night just sitting on the table, and it doesn't look like his bed has been slept in."

There was a long silence as McAdam considered everything

Ballard had said. She thought he was on the same concerned wavelength as her, but when he finally spoke, it was clear that he wasn't.

"Ballard, are you and Bosch…involved in some way beyond this case?"

"No. Are you kidding me? I think something happened to him. I'm not—He's missing, Lieutenant. We need to do something. That's why I'm calling. What should we do?"

"All right, settle down. My mistake, okay? Forget I said anything. So, when exactly was he supposed to show up on this thing?"

"There wasn't an exact time. But he said he'd be in early. I was looking for him around four or five."

Again, silence.

"Renée, we're talking about six hours at the most here."

"I know but there's something wrong. His dinner's sitting on the table. His car's here but he isn't."

"It's still too soon. We have to see how it plays out."

"Plays out? What are you talking about? He was one of us. LAPD. We need to put out a bulletin, get it on RACR at least."

RACR, pronounced *racer,* was an internal text alert system through which messages could be sent to the phones of thousands of officers at once.

"No, it's too soon," McAdam said. "Let's see what happens over the next few hours. Text me the address and I'll send a car up there after lunch. You're done for the day."

"What?" Ballard said.

There was exasperation in her voice. McAdam wasn't seeing what she was seeing, didn't know what she knew. He was handling this wrong.

"You're done, Renée. I'll send a car up later to check on

Bosch. We've got to give this at least twelve hours. I'll call you later when we know more. It's probably nothing."

Ballard disconnected without acknowledging McAdam's order. She was afraid that if she said anything further it would be in a high-pitched voice that was near hysterical.

She kept her phone out and looked up the number for the San Fernando Police Department. She made the call and asked to be transferred to the detective bureau. A woman answered but identified herself too quickly for Ballard to pick up the name.

"Is Harry Bosch there?"

"No, he's not. Can someone else help you?"

"This is Detective Ballard with the LAPD. Can I speak to his partner, please? This is urgent."

"We don't have partners here. It's interchangeable. We—"

"I need to talk to whoever he was working with last—on the gang murder where the witness was killed."

There was a pause before there was a response.

"That was me. How do you know about that case?"

"What was your name again?"

"Detective Lourdes. How do you—"

"Listen to me. I think something's happened to Harry. I'm at his house now and he's not here and it looks…it looks like he might have been taken."

"Taken?"

"We were supposed to meet early this morning. He didn't show. His phone's turned off and he's not here. He's got uneaten food on the table from last night, the bed is still made, and his back door was open."

"Okay, okay, you need to listen to me now. We got intel yesterday that the SanFers had put a hit out on Harry because they know he was building a case against one of their OGs. Today we were working on it. But last night I warned Harry. I told him. So, is there any chance that he just went into hiding?"

A sharp pressure started building in Ballard's chest. It was dread.

"I — No, that's not what it looks like here. His keys are on the table. And his car's here."

"Maybe he thought the car could be tracked. Look, I'm not trying to downplay this. If you're saying this looks involuntary, then we'll call out the troops on this end. Have you talked to his daughter?"

Ballard suddenly realized that Bosch had revealed something to her during the course of the week that might be helpful.

"No," she said. "But I will now. I'll call you back."

She disconnected the call.

34

Ballard moved back into the house to conduct a different kind of search. She needed a phone number for Bosch's daughter. In the master bedroom, she had seen a small desk like the ones found in a hotel room. She went there and started looking through drawers until she found one containing checkbooks and rubber-banded stacks of envelopes.

One stack was all telephone bills. She quickly opened the envelope on top and saw that Bosch had a family plan where he paid for two cell phones on one account. One she recognized as his number, and the other she assumed was his daughter's. She next opened the checkbook and looked through the registry until she came upon a record of a check for four hundred dollars to Madeline Bosch.

She had what she needed and made the call. It rang through to a message, which didn't surprise her, since Bosch's daughter would have no reason to recognize her number.

"Madeline, this is Detective Ballard with the LAPD. It's very important that you call me back as soon as you hear this. Please call me back."

She gave her number even though the girl's phone would have captured it. She then disconnected, put everything back in the drawer, and got up from the desk. Bosch had mentioned in passing that his daughter went to Chapman down in Orange County and was just an hour or so away. She was considering a call to the school's security office to see if Madeline Bosch could be located, but then her phone buzzed and the screen showed the number she had just called.

"Madeline?"

"Yes, what's going on? Where's my father?"

"We're trying to find him and we need your help."

"Oh my god, what happened?"

"Don't panic, Madeline. Is that what you go by? Madeline?"

"It's Maddie. Tell me what happened."

"I'm not sure. He missed two appointments with me and I can't reach him. I'm at his house now and his car is in the carport and there's food on the table but he's not here. When did you hear from him last?"

"He, uh, texted me last night. He asked about getting together this weekend."

"Are he and your mother divorced? Would he be in touch with—"

"My mother's dead."

"Okay, sorry, I didn't know. This is where I need your help. Your dad told me that you two had a deal. He could track your phone if you could track his. I think his phone is off at the moment but I want you to pull up your tracker and tell me where the last tracking point on it is. Can you do that?"

"Yes. I just need to—I'll put you on speaker while I..."

"Go ahead."

Ballard waited and eventually Maddie spoke.

"Okay, it only goes up to eleven forty-two last night. Then it stops."

"Okay, that's good. What's the location of the phone?"

There was silence as Maddie checked the location. Ballard hoped it wasn't the house. That would not advance things at all.

"Uh, it's up in the Valley. A place called the Saddletree Open Space."

Ballard's heart sank. It sounded like a place to dump a body.

"Can you be more specific?" she asked, trying not to reveal her thoughts in the tone of her voice. "Can you widen the screen or something?"

"Hold on," Maddie said.

Ballard waited.

"Um, it's, like, near Sylmar," Maddie said. "The nearest road to the spot is Coyote Street."

"Can you hang up, take a screenshot, and text it to me?"

"Yes, but why was he up there? What is—"

"Maddie, listen to me. We need to hang up so you can send me the screenshot. I need to get that to the right people so we can see if your father is there. I know you're scared and this is an awful kind of call to get. But I need to go now. I will call you back as soon as I know something. Okay?"

Ballard thought she could hear the girl crying.

"Maddie?"

"Yes, okay. I'm hanging up."

"One other thing. I know that if you are anything like your dad, you're going to send me the screenshot and then get in a car and head up here. Don't do that. You have to stay away from your house, okay? It may not be safe."

"Are you kidding me?"

"No, I'm not. I need you to stay away until you hear from me or your father, okay?"

"Okay."

"Good. Send me the screenshot."

Ballard disconnected. She knew that Heather Rourke was probably sleeping, but that didn't matter. She called her friend and, surprisingly, the call was answered right away.

"What are you doing awake, Renée?"

"Still working, and I have a situation. I need a flyover up in the Valley. Who do you think would do it for me?"

"That's easy. Me."

"What?"

"I'm working an OT shift and have the Valley today. We're about to go up. Where in the Valley?"

"Sylmar area. How long until—"

"Thirty minutes. What exactly are you looking for?"

"We're looking for a missing police officer. I'm going to text you a screenshot of the location we have on a map. The area's called the Saddletree Open Space. I need to know what's there. Any houses, structures, whatever. And if there's nothing there…look for a body."

"You got it. Get that screenshot to me."

"As soon as I have it, I'll send. Keep this off the radio if you can. Use my cell to make contact."

"Roger that."

Ballard disconnected just as the screenshot from Maddie Bosch came through. She forwarded it to Heather Rourke and started moving through the house, realizing that it might become a crime scene. She left the back slider open and went out the front door and locked it behind her.

She didn't get a clear signal on her phone until she took Woodrow Wilson back down into the pass and started north on the 101 freeway. Then she called Lourdes back at San Fernando PD.

299

"Do you know anything about the Saddletree Open Space?"

"Uh, I don't even know what that is."

"It's just north of Sylmar off a road called Coyote Street. We traced Bosch's phone to a spot there last night about midnight. Then it went dead. I have an airship about to fly over and tell us what's there. I'm on my way."

"I'm closer. I can get up there now."

"Wait for the flyover. We don't know what's up there. It could be a body but it could be a trap."

"Jesus Christ."

"If you people knew there was a hit out on him, why wasn't he protected?"

"He turned it down. I don't think he took it seriously. We still don't know if it has anything to do with this. He might be up there camping and there's no cell service."

"Maybe, but I doubt it. I want to keep my phone free. I'll call when I hear something on the flyover."

"I'm here and, look, Harry saved my life once and…"

She didn't finish.

"I get it," Ballard said.

She disconnected.

The late-morning northbound traffic was light and Ballard made good time. She took the 101 to the 170 and then the 5 before dropping onto surface streets at Roxford. She checked her phone screen repeatedly, but there was nothing from Rourke on the fly-over. Ballard even leaned over to look up through the windshield to see if she could spot the helicopter moving against the backdrop of the mountains that rimmed the Valley. There was nothing.

As she was crossing San Fernando Road, she got a call from Rourke instead of a text. There was no sound of the chopper's engine in the background and she grew livid.

"You're still at Piper Tech?"

"No, we have a pad we can use at the Davis."

Ballard knew the department had a training facility near Sylmar named after former chief Edward Davis.

"You did the flyover? Was there anything up there?"

Ballard could hear her own voice drawn tight by the tension of the moment.

"No body," Rourke said. "But about a hundred yards further north into the scrub from the spot on that screenshot you sent me, it looks like there's some kind of an abandoned kennel or animal-training facility. There are a couple of sheds and training rings. But no vehicles, no sign of life."

Ballard exhaled. At least Bosch's body wasn't lying out there in the sun.

"Can it be accessed?" she asked.

"Might be tough on the suspension," Rourke said. "Looks like there was a washout on the dirt road up there."

"Did you take any photos?"

"Yes. I'm about to send but I thought I should talk to you first."

"No problem."

"Do you want us to stay close?"

"I think I'm about fifteen out on a ground search. If you can fly backup, I wouldn't turn it down."

"Okay, we're here till we get a call."

"Roger that."

Ballard disconnected and called Lourdes back. She told the San Fernando detective what the results of the flyover were and invited her to meet at the terminus of Coyote Street and then conduct a ground search of the last known location of Harry Bosch's phone.

"I'm on my way," Lourdes said.

BOSCH

35

The sound of the helicopter overhead gave Bosch hope. But it made the man watching him panic. Bosch had tried to break through to him all night, asking him his name, asking him to loosen the bindings and if he could allow him out of the cage to stretch his cramped legs. Asking if he really wanted the killing of a cop hanging over him.

But the man had said nothing. He just stared at Bosch and on occasion pointed his gun at him through the cage. Bosch knew that was a hollow threat. He was being kept alive for something else. Or someone else. Bosch guessed it would be Tranquillo Cortez.

The man had the hardened stare of a convict and the prison tattoos to go with it. Faded blue ink. Bosch saw none of the symbols associated with the SanFers—no VSF, no 13—such as he had seen on every SanFer he had encountered during his time with the SFPD. That included Tranquillo Cortez.

Bosch had all night to put things together and had come out of it sure that this man was Mexican Mafia, *eMe,* and that Cortez might have gone outside the SanFers to conduct what could be a rogue operation. Abducting a cop was a big move that would put massive pressure on the VSF. Killing a cop was even bigger pressure. Cortez wanted deniability.

It had taken three men to abduct him from his home, four counting the driver of the Jeep that took him up the rugged hillside to this grim destination, and now, for the past four hours, just one silent man to guard him. Every minute that passed felt like an hour, every hour like a day. Bound and crammed into a dog cage, Bosch contemplated his impending death. In the Jeep he had picked up enough of the conversation in Spanish to understand that he was ultimately going to be fed to the dogs. But it was not clear whether that was a figure of speech. And if not, it was not clear whether that would happen while he was still alive or not.

Through it all he was haunted by only one thing. His daughter. Not having had final words with her. Not being able to watch her prosper as an adult. It tore him up to think that he would never see or speak to her again. Guilt overtook him as he acknowledged that he had squandered the past several months as Maddie's father trying to save a woman who didn't want to be saved. In the darkest hours before dawn, hot tears of regret had rolled down his cheeks.

But then came the sound of the helicopter directly overhead. In a moment, it changed things for both Bosch and the man guarding him. Bosch had been at enough crime scenes and officer-needs-help calls over the years to recognize the high-pitched engine whine of the powerful Bell 206 JetRanger. He knew that the craft circling above the shed was an LAPD chopper and that they might already be looking for him. It gave him hope that he might see his daughter again and have the chance to make things right.

For the silent guard, the same sound bred terror and the fight-or-flight instincts that come with it. He went to the door, slivered it open, and looked up into the sky. Sighting the craft, he confirmed what Bosch already knew. He turned from the door and came to the cage, raising the barrel of his gun.

Bosch put his hands up as well as he could in the cramped space and spoke in rudimentary Spanish.

"You kill a cop, they'll never stop hunting you."

The man hesitated. Bosch kept speaking. He had no formal training in the language, just what he had picked up over a lifetime of working the streets, and from partners like Lucia Soto and Bella Lourdes.

"What will Tranquillo say? He wants me alive. You're going to take that from him?"

The man stood frozen, the gun still pointed at Bosch.

In his early life Bosch had spent fifteen months in Vietnam. Not a day went by in that time that he didn't hear helicopters. It was the background music of the war. Hiding in the elephant grass, waiting for a dustoff, he had learned early how to read their sound for distance and location. He could now tell that the airship flying above them was spiraling in increasingly larger circles.

His guard moved back to the door and looked out. He sensed what Bosch had, that the helicopter was making a wider turn. Then the sound changed again. It became muffled and Bosch knew the craft had flown behind the crest of the mountain. The shed was out of its sight.

The man with the gun turned and looked at him for a long moment, deciding what to do. Bosch knew he was deciding his life. He kept their eyes locked.

The man suddenly turned and pushed the door open further. He looked out and up toward the sky. The sound of the chopper was still distant.

"*Sali!*" Bosch yelled. "*Ahora!*"

He hoped it was "Go now!" or something close.

The man shoved the door all the way open, filling the shed with blinding light. He slid the gun into the waistband of his pants and moved back into the corner where a green motorbike was leaning against the rusting steel wall. He jumped on it, kick-started it, and then shot through the open door.

Bosch's eyes adjusted and he exhaled. He listened. The airship was coming around on another turn, clearing the mountain and getting louder.

With the interior of the shed now brightly illuminated, Bosch shifted his position in the cage, studying every corner and joint for weakness. He knew it was impossible to know if the airship was looking for him, simply conducting a training exercise, or just circling over a coyote. It was true that his abductors had made a mistake last night in not checking him for a phone until they were transferring him from a van to the Jeep, but Bosch knew he could not rely on anyone to save him but himself.

He had to work quickly and find a way out of the cage. It was only a matter of time before the man on the motorbike came back.

BALLARD

36

Ballard waited for Bella Lourdes by the Coyote Street gate to the fire road leading up into the hills and the abandoned animal training compound. She was looking at the aerial photos Heather Rourke had texted her and deciding whether it would be better to approach the compound on foot or by attempting to drive a vehicle up the rugged fire road.

The compound was not far up and was in an open area that would prevent an unannounced approach by car. She decided she would go on foot and call in the airship if a show of LAPD force was necessary.

When Lourdes arrived, she had a partner with her. She identified him as Detective Danny Sisto and, recognizing Ballard's concern, vouched for him as someone Bosch himself would implicitly trust. Ballard accepted her assurance and brought them both up to date on the situation. She showed them the photos from the airship's flyover.

"Okay, I think I know the connection here," Lourdes said.

"What?" Ballard asked.

Lourdes looked at Sisto for confirmation when she spoke.

"A couple years ago, there was a big Animal Control bust up here," she said. "This place was like a training center for animals used in film and TV but it had been abandoned for years. The SanFers discovered it and they were running cock-fights and dog fights up here. Animal Control got wind of it and shut it down."

"I remember that," Sisto said. "It was a big story. I think you guys were part of it."

This last part he said to Ballard, meaning that the LAPD had joined Animal Control in shutting down the illegal activities at the compound. Ballard remembered nothing about the events or the media attention it got. But the confirmation that this was a place the SanFers knew about and had used previously was im-portant. She knew they were in the right place.

Sisto pointed at her phone, which still had an aerial shot of the compound on the screen.

"We're going to search the structures, right?" he asked. "Do we have a warrant? This is still private property, abandoned or not."

"We don't have time," Ballard said.

"Exigent circumstances all the way," Lourdes said.

Looking at the photos, they identified two trails in addition to the fire road that led through the brush and up to the com-pound. Before they headed up separately, Ballard called Rourke, explained the plan, and told her to stand by. The airship was still on the ground at the nearby LAPD training facility and Rourke assured her that it was ready to respond.

Ballard disconnected and looked at Lourdes and Sisto.

"Okay, let's go find Harry," she said.

Ballard had chosen the most direct route to the compound — the fire road. She stayed close to the tall brush that lined it but had the easier climb and the quickest time to the clearing where the compound was located.

At the final bend before the clearing, she started to hear a loud banging sound coming from the direction of the compound. It was intermittent. Five or six heavy impacts and then silence. After a few seconds it would start again.

Ballard pulled her phone to call or text Lourdes but saw she no longer had cell service. She had left the rover in the car since she wanted to keep this operation off the air. Each of them would have to approach on their own now, not knowing the progress of the others.

Ballard reached the clearing, pulling her gun and holding it at her side as she approached the first of two rundown structures. She turned the corner of the front building and saw Lourdes emerge from a trail to her right. There was no sign of Sisto.

Ballard was about to signal Lourdes over so they could clear the first building, when the banging started again. She could tell that it was coming from the other, smaller building set at the back of the clearing. Ballard pointed toward it. Lourdes nodded and they moved in the direction of the sound.

There was a wooden door on rollers that had been slid open four feet. It gave Ballard and Lourdes an angle on the inside of the shed but the structure was rectangular and its full interior could not be seen from outside.

As they got within a few feet of the opening, the banging stopped.

They froze and waited. It didn't start again. Looking at the open door, Ballard spoke loudly.

"Harry?"

After a moment of silence:

"In here!"

Ballard looked at Lourdes.

"Hold cover. I'll go in."

Ballard entered the structure gun up. It took a moment for her eyes to adjust and then she turned to her right. The far wall of the shed was lined with rusting kennels, two stacked rows of four. Bosch was sitting in the third cage on the upper row, knees pulled up to his chest in the small space. Through the steel fencing, Ballard could see that his hands and ankles were tied. There was blood on his shirt and a laceration on his upper left cheek, just below a swollen eye.

Ballard swept the rest of the space with her weapon to make sure.

"It's clear," Bosch said. "But they'll probably come back soon."

He raised his bound feet and kicked at the door of the kennel, creating the banging sound Ballard had heard from outside the shed. His fruitless effort to break free and escape.

"Okay, hold on, Harry, and we'll get you out," she said. "What's your status? Do we call an RA?"

"No RA," Bosch said. "I'm good. Couple of bruised ribs, my legs cramping like hell. I probably need stitches under my eye. They didn't want to beat me up too bad before Tranquillo got here with his dogs."

Ballard didn't think Bosch would go for the rescue ambulance. Not his style. She moved close to the cage and studied the padlock holding it closed.

"They didn't leave the key hidden around here, did they?" she asked.

"Not that I saw," Bosch said.

"I could shoot the lock but the ricochet might hit you."

"Only works in movies."

"Bella? All clear."

Lourdes entered the shed then.

"Harry, you okay?" she asked urgently.

"I will be as soon as you get me out of here," Bosch said. "My knee's killing me."

"Okay, I'm going back to the car," said Ballard. "I think we can put a crowbar through the loop and twist it off."

Bosch looked at Ballard through the fencing.

"Sounds like a plan," he said. "Did you send the helicopter up here?"

"Yeah," Ballard said.

Bosch nodded his thanks.

"I'll be right back," Ballard said.

Sisto was standing in the clearing, his back to the shed and maintaining a watch. Ballard passed by him on her way to the road down to the vehicles.

"Did you clear the other structure?" she asked.

"All clear," he said.

"I'm going to need you in a few to twist off a lock."

"I'm ready. Is he okay?"

"He will be."

"Great."

As she was heading down the fire road, her phone regained service and a text from Rourke came through. She was checking in and wanting an update. Ballard called her and told her to continue to stand by. As soon as Bosch was free, they would need to make a decision on what to do: set up a trap for his captors should they return, or clear out and proceed in another way.

She retrieved the crowbar from her city car's roadside emergency kit, grabbed the rover out of the charging dock, and headed back up the fire road. Halfway up she heard the rat-a-tat sound of a dirt bike behind her. She turned and saw a rider on a lime-green bike come to a stop on Coyote Street and look up at her. He was wearing a matching helmet with a darkly tinted visor. They stared at each other for a few seconds before the rider turned the wheel and walked the bike into a U-turn before taking off.

Knowing that the first option of waiting for the return of the captors was now moot, she called Rourke on the radio and ordered the airship back into flight. She asked Rourke to circle the compound as a backup measure, keeping an eye out for the lime-green dirt bike.

Ballard was out of breath from hustling up the hill to the shed. She handed the crowbar to Sisto like she was passing a baton and he took it inside the shed while she trailed behind. She bent over and put her hands on her thighs and watched as Sisto threaded the crowbar through the loop on the cage door. He then turned the bar and the loop popped off its weld points. He opened the door and Ballard came over and joined Lourdes in carefully helping Bosch out and lowering him to his feet on the dirt floor. Lourdes opened a pocket knife and cut the bindings off his hands and feet.

"Standing up feels good," he said.

He painfully tried a few steps, putting an arm around each woman's neck.

"I think we need an RA, Harry," Lourdes said.

"No, I don't need that," Bosch protested. "I can walk. Just let me..."

He dropped his arms from them and hobbled toward the doorway on his own. The sound of the airship off in the distance was coming closer.

"Call them off," Bosch said. "These guys might be coming back. We can take them then."

"No, I blew it," Ballard said. "They know we're here. Lime-green dirt bike?"

Bosch nodded.

"Yeah, him."

"He saw me when I went back for the crowbar. Saw the cars."

"Shit."

"Sorry."

"Not your fault."

Bosch walked out into the clearing and looked up at the sun. Ballard watched him. She guessed that during the night, he might have come to the grim conclusion that he'd never see the big orange ball again.

"Harry, let's go get you looked at and get some stitches on that cheek," Lourdes said. "Then we'll go over gang books and draw warrants for every one of the motherfuckers you identify."

Ballard knew that the SFPD must have extensive photo books of known members of the SanFers. If Bosch made IDs of those who had revealed themselves to him during the night, then they could make arrests.

"I don't think they were SanFers," Bosch said. "I think Tranquillo called in the *eMe* for this. Probably made sure all of his boys had alibis for the night."

"And Cortez never showed up?" Lourdes asked.

"Nope. I think he was coming by today. With his dogs."

Bosch turned to Ballard.

"How did you find me?" he asked.

"Your daughter," Ballard said. "The tracking app on your phone."

"Did she come up?"

"No, I told her to stay away from the house."

"I have to call her. They took my phone and crunched it."

"You can use mine as soon as it gets service."

Lourdes pulled her phone and checked it, then held it up.

"Two bars," she said.

She handed Bosch the phone and he punched in a number. Ballard only heard his side of the conversation.

"Hey, it's me. I'm okay."

He listened and then continued in a calming voice.

"No, really. I got a little roughed up but no big deal. Where are you?"

Ballard read the relief on Bosch's face. Maddie had listened to her and stayed away from the house.

"My phone got crunched, so if you need me, call this number for Detective Lourdes," he said. "You can also call Detective Ballard. You have that number, right?"

He listened and nodded, even though his daughter wouldn't see it.

"Uh, no, she's gone now," he said. "She left a couple days ago. We can talk about that later."

He then listened for a long time before making a final response.

"Love you, too. I'll see you soon."

He disconnected the phone and handed it back to Lourdes. He looked shaken by the call, or maybe the realization of how close he had come to losing everything.

Bosch spoke to Lourdes and Sisto.

"I'll come in tomorrow to look at the *eMe* book," he said. "I just want to go home now."

"You can't go home," Ballard said quickly. "It's a crime scene. So is this. We need to run this by the book: call out Major Crimes, find out how they got to you. How they got to your house."

"And you need stitches," Lourdes said.

Ballard saw the realization break on Bosch's face. He had a long day ahead of him.

"Fine, I'll go to the ER. And you can call out the troops. But I don't want to be here anymore."

Bosch started unsteadily walking toward the dirt road leading down. His limp was more pronounced than when Ballard had seen it before.

She saw him look up at the airship passing overhead. He raised his arm and sent a thumbs-up as a thank-you.

37

By the time Ballard was released by the detectives from Major Crimes it was almost six and she had not slept in more than twenty-four hours. With her next shift starting in five hours it was not worth driving down to the beach or out to her grandmother's house in Ventura in rush-hour traffic. Instead, she drove south to Hollywood Station. She left her city ride in the parking lot, got a change of clothes out of her van, and then took an Uber to the W Hotel on Hollywood Boulevard. She knew from many previous stays there that they gave a deep law enforcement discount, had a dependable room service menu, and were liberal about checkout time. There was a cot at the station in a storage room known as the Honeymoon Suite, but she knew from experience she couldn't sleep there. Too many intrusions. She wanted comfort, food, and solid sleep in the limited time she had.

She got a room with a northern view of the Santa Monica Mountains, the Capitol Records Building, and the Hollywood sign. But she closed the drapes, ordered a salad with grilled chicken, and took a shower. A half hour later she was eating on the bed, bundled in an oversize bathrobe, her wet hair slicked back and down her neck.

Her laptop was open on the bed and distracting her from what was now less than four hours of available sleep time. But she couldn't help herself. She had downloaded the GRASP files from the thumb drive Professor Calder had given her that morning. She had told herself she would make only a quick survey of the data before going to sleep but the shower had helped push back her fatigue and she became transfixed.

What had drawn her attention initially was that there was a murder in the division just two nights before Daisy Clayton was abducted and murdered. This case was quickly cleared by arrest, according to the data.

Ballard was unable to enter the department's database remotely but was able to access two brief *Los Angeles Times* reports on the case in the newspaper's murder blog, which documented every murder that took place in the city. According to the first story, the killing had occurred in a tattoo parlor on Sunset called ZooToo. A female tattoo artist named Audie Haslam was murdered by a customer. Haslam owned the shop and was working a solo shift when someone entered, pulled a knife and robbed her. Haslam was then walked into a back room used for storage and stabbed multiple times during a brutal struggle. She bled out on the floor.

Ballard's excitement over a possible connection to the Clayton case was quickly doused when she read the second story, which described the arrest of the suspect, a motorcycle gang affiliate named Clancy Devoux, the following day after police matched a bloody fingerprint from the scene to him. Devoux had several vials of ink and an electric tattoo needle in his possession. Investigators found the victim's fingerprints on the vials. They also found a fresh tattoo of a skull with a halo scabbing over on Devoux's forearm. He had apparently come into the shop as a customer and the robbery-murder occurred after Haslam had given him a tattoo. It was not clear if the murder was an impulsive act brought on by something Haslam did or might have said or Devoux's plan all along.

According to the follow-up report, Devoux was being held without bail in the Men's Central Jail. That meant he was in custody on the night Daisy Clayton was taken. There was no way he was a suspect in the second murder. Deflated, Ballard still made a note to pull the murder book on the case. Her thinking was that there might be names in the book of people who were in Hollywood at the time and who might have information on the Clayton case. It was a long shot, she knew, but one that might need to be taken.

There were five rapes reported in the four-day span of the GRASP data and Ballard paid careful attention to these as well. She pulled up whatever information she could on her laptop and determined that two of the rapes were classified as assaults by strangers. The other three were considered rapes by acquaintances and not the work of a predator stalking women he didn't know. One of the stranger cases occurred the day before the Clayton murder and one took place the day after. It appeared from the digest summaries in the GRASP data that they were not the work of one man. There had been two sexual predators.

Ballard typed the case numbers from the murder and the two rapes into a file request form and emailed it to the archives unit. She asked for expedited delivery of the files but knew that the priority would be low because she was looking for cold files— a closed murder case and two rapes that were now beyond the seven-year statute of limitations.

After sending the email, Ballard felt her excitement wane and her fatigue return. She closed her laptop and left it on the bed. After setting her phone to sound an alarm in three hours, she slipped under the bedcovers, her robe still on, and fell immediately to sleep.

She dreamed that someone was following her but disappeared each time she turned around to look behind her. When the alarm woke her, she was in a deep stage-four sleep and disoriented as she opened her eyes and didn't recognize her surroundings. It was the thick terry cloth of the robe that finally brought it all back and she realized where she was.

She ordered an Uber and got dressed in the fresh clothes she'd brought from her van. The car was waiting when she took the elevator down and walked out to the hotel's entrance.

Harry Bosch's abduction made the sergeant's report at roll call. It was mentioned since it had occurred in his home, which straddled the line between Hollywood and North Hollywood divisions, and that home was now posted with uniformed and plainclothes officers from Metropolitan Division in an attempt to dissuade Tranquillo Cortez from sending more men to abduct Bosch again.

Otherwise the briefing was short. A cold front had moved across the city from the ocean, and lower temperatures were one of the best crime deterrents around. Sergeant Klinkenberg, a longtime veteran who kept himself in shape and wore the same size uniform as he did on graduation day from the academy, said things were slow out on the streets of Hollywood. As the troops were filing out, Ballard made her way against the flow of bodies heading to the door and up to Klinkenberg, who remained behind the lectern.

"What's up, Renée?" he asked.

"I missed the last couple of roll calls," Ballard said. "I just want to check to see if you guys put out the BOLO I gave Lieutenant Munroe about the guy named Eagleton."

Klinkenberg turned and pointed to the wall where there was a corkboard covered with Wanted flyers.

"You mean that guy?" he said. "Yeah, we put that out last night."

Ballard saw her flyer for the man who called himself Eagle on the board.

"Any chance you can give it another pop next roll call?" she asked. "I really want this guy."

"If it's as slow as tonight, then no problem," Klinkenberg said. "Get me another stack and I'll put it out."

"Thanks, Klink."

"How's Bosch? I know you were involved in that."

"He's good. He got roughed up and cracked a few ribs. They finally persuaded him to stay the night at Olive View up there. With a guard on the door."

Klinkenberg nodded.

"He's a good guy. He got a rough deal around here but he's one of the good ones."

"You worked with him?"

"As much as a blue suiter can work with a detective. We were here at the same time. I remember he was a no-bullshit kind of guy. I'm glad he's okay and I hope they catch the fuckers who grabbed him."

"They will. And when they do, he and whoever was part of it will go away for a long time. You grab one of us, you cross a line, and that message will go out loud and clear."

"There you go."

Ballard went downstairs to the detective bureau, where she set up at a desk near the empty lieutenant's office. The first thing she did was go online and connect to the live cams at the pet-care center where she had left her dog. It had been more than twenty-four hours since she had seen Lola and she missed her greatly. Ballard had always thought that when she rubbed the dog's neck or scratched her hard head, she got more fulfillment out of it than Lola did.

She located her on one of the camera screens. She was sleeping on an oval bed. A smaller dog had pushed in and curled up on the bed with her. Ballard smiled and immediately felt the pang of guilt that came every time she caught a case that took over her schedule and required leaving Lola at pet care for extended periods. She had no qualms about the level of care. Ballard checked the cameras often and paid for extra things like walks around the Abbot Kinney neighborhood. But Ballard could not help wondering if she was a bad pet owner and if Lola would be better off being put up for adoption.

Not wanting to dwell on the question, she killed the connection and went to work, spending the next two hours of her shift going through the FI cards put aside for special attention and backgrounding the individuals who had caught the notice of patrol officers in Hollywood in the months surrounding the murder of Daisy Clayton.

At shortly after two a.m., she got her first callout of the night, and spent the next two hours interviewing witnesses to a brawl that had broken out at a bar on Highland when the bouncer had attempted to clear the place at closing time and a group of four USC students had objected because they still had full bottles of beer. The bouncer was cut across the back of the head by one of those bottles and was treated at the scene by paramedics. Ballard took his statement first, but he could not say for sure which of the four students had wielded the bottle he was struck with. After securing his confirmation that he wished to press charges against his attacker, the LAPD released him to the paramedics, who transported him to Hollywood Presbyterian. Ballard next spoke to a bartender and the establishment's manager before moving on to the students.

The students were locked two apiece in the back seats of patrol cars. Ballard had purposely put the two boys who looked the most scared together and had secretly left her digital recorder on the front seat where they couldn't get it. It was a ploy that every now and then produced an unintended confession.

When she pulled the recorder out this time, she got the opposite of a confession. Both of the young men were angry and scared that they were going to be arrested when neither of them had thrown the bottle at the bouncer.

That left the two in the other car, whom Ballard had not covered with a recorder. She took them out one at a time to be interviewed. The first student denied that he had instigated the brawl or hit the bouncer with the bottle. But when confronted with the twenty-six-beer bar tab they had amassed, he acknowledged that he had overconsumed and was talking trash to the bartender and the bouncer when closing time was announced. He apologized to Ballard for his behavior and told her he was willing to do it to the bar's staff as well.

The interview with the last student went differently. He announced that he was the son of a lawyer and was fully aware of his rights. He said he would not be waiving his rights or talking to Ballard without an attorney present.

When finished, Ballard conferred with Sergeant Klinkenberg, who was the on-site patrol supervisor.

"What do you think?" he asked. "Somebody's gotta go for

this, right? Otherwise, these little college pissants will just come back up here and do it again."

Ballard nodded as she looked down at her notebook to get the names right.

"All right, you can kick Pyne, Johnson, and Fiskin loose," she said. "Book Bernardo—he's got the shaved head and thinks his lawyer dad will save him. And make sure the three you let go aren't driving."

"We already asked," Klinkenberg said. "They Ubered."

"Okay, I'll paper it as soon as I get back to the barn and drop it by the jail."

"It's a pleasure doing business with you."

"Likewise, Klink."

Back at the bureau it took Ballard less than an hour to write up the incident report and the arrest warrant for Bernardo. After leaving the paperwork with the records clerk, she checked the watch office clock and saw she was down to the last two hours of her shift.

She was dead tired and looking forward to sleeping five or six hours at the W. The thought of sleep reminded her of the dream she'd had in which she felt there was someone following her. It made her turn around as she walked down the empty back hallway to the detective bureau.

There was no one there.

38

The phone call came in at noon, waking Ballard from another deep trench of sleep. The hotel room was dark with the blackout drapes drawn closed. The screen of her phone glowed. It was a number she didn't recognize, but at least it wasn't blocked.

She took the call, her voice cracking when she said hello.

"Ballard, it's Bosch. You asleep?"

"What do you think? What number is this?"

"It's a landline. I haven't replaced my cell yet."

"Oh."

"You had to work last night? Even though you spent the day saving my ass?"

"I wasn't on the clock when I did that, Harry. Where are you? Still at Olive View?"

"No, got released this morning. Six stitches, two cracked ribs, and otherwise a clean bill of health. I'm at San Fernando PD."

"Did they pick up Tranquillo yet?"

"Not yet, but they think they got him surrounded. SIS is sitting on a house in Panorama City where they think he's holed up. Belongs to his aunt—the one that was married to Uncle

Murda. They're in deep cover, waiting for him to make a move, and then they'll scoop him up."

The SIS was the LAPD's elite surveillance squad that was called in to shadow violent offenders. They carried high-powered weapons and engaged in military-style follow maneuvers. Ballard also knew that SIS tactics had been questioned for decades by the media and law enforcement critics from across the country. Many of their surveillance jobs ended in deadly shoot-outs. The SIS kill count topped all other divisions and units in the department.

"Okay," Ballard said. "Let's hope they do."

"So, what's on the schedule for today?" Bosch asked, changing the subject.

"Technically, I'm off, but my partner's not back till Monday and I could use the OT. I was going to work. But my number-one priority is to get up and go see my dog. She probably hates me by now."

"You have a dog?"

"Yup."

"Nice. So you see the dog, then what? Where are we on the shake cards?"

It didn't sound to Ballard like Bosch was a dog person.

"I've gone through the finalists and you are welcome to back-read me on them if you want," she said. "I cleared about twenty and prioritized the rest. I have an appointment at four today with one of the men at the top of the list."

"An appointment?" Bosch asked. "What do you mean?"

Ballard told him about the shake cards involving the officer who happened upon a porno shoot in a van. She said the two priority names were Kurt Pascal and Wilson Gayley.

"I know somebody in the business," she added. "She set up a

casting meeting with Pascal. He was the one having sex in the van. I'm going to—"

"Where's the meet?" Bosch asked.

"Canoga Park. She has her own studio. I met her last year on—"

"You shouldn't go on your own. I'll go too."

"You have Tranquillo Cortez to worry about."

"No, I don't. I'm just sitting here waiting. But my car's still at my house. Can you pick me up on the way?"

"Sure. Give me a couple hours to go see my dog."

"Anything on the GRASP files?"

"Yeah, I picked them up yesterday before the shit hit the fan with you. The professor gave me a thumb drive. I printed hard copies for you before I left work this morning."

"Good. Did you take a look?"

"Not a deep dive. I did see there was a murder two days before Daisy. But the suspect was in custody before Daisy disappeared."

"We should probably look at it anyway."

"I ordered the book last night. Before heading up to you, I'll see if it's landed."

"Sounds like a plan."

"Good."

"And Renée?"

"Yes?"

"You saved my life yesterday. When I was in that cage…all I could think about was my daughter and her being alone…and all the things I was going to miss being with her for…anyway, thank you. It's not much but…yeah, thank you."

Ballard nodded.

"You know what I was thinking about, Harry? I was thinking about all the cases that would never get solved if you were gone. You still have work to do."

"I guess. Maybe."

"I'll see you in a few hours."

Ballard disconnected and rolled off the bed. She started getting ready to go see her dog.

39

Bosch was waiting in front of the SFPD headquarters when Ballard pulled up in her van. He eyed the boards on the roof racks as he approached and opened the door. Ballard noticed that the bruise under his eye was now a deep purple and he had a row of butterfly sutures on his upper left cheek.

Bosch got in and checked out the back of the van while pulling his seat belt over his shoulder.

"Is this like a Scooby-Doo van or something?" he asked. "The surfboards and stuff?"

"No," Ballard said. "But I thought if I brought my city ride, our guy might see it and rabbit before the interview."

"You have a point."

"Besides, it saved me having to go into the station. I called to check on the ZooToo murder book and it hasn't landed yet. On Saturdays they cut the courier runs in half."

"'ZooToo'?"

"It was the name of the tattoo shop where the murder went down."

"Got it."

"So, do you think it was wise to be standing out in front of the police station like that?"

"If you're not safe at a police station, then where are you safe? Anyway, how do you want to handle this guy?"

Ballard had been thinking about that for the thirty minutes it took her to get from Hollywood to San Fernando.

"This guy isn't going to know what this is about," she said. "So I'm thinking we identify ourselves upfront and draw him in with the Good Samaritan play."

"'Good Samaritan play'?" Bosch said.

"Come on, you must've done it a million times. Make the guy think he's helping the police. Draw him in and lock in his story, then turn it upside down. He goes from hero to zero."

Bosch nodded.

"Got it," he said. "We always called that the rope a dope."

"Same thing," Ballard said.

They discussed the play further as Ballard drove across the north end of the Valley toward Canoga Park, the community where more than half of the world's legally sanctioned pornography production was located.

They arrived at Beatrice Beaupre's unmarked warehouse twenty-five minutes before Kurt Pascal was due. Beaupre opened the studio door. She was black with startling green eyes that Ballard thought were probably contacts. The short dreadlocks were new since Ballard had last seen her. She looked past Ballard at Bosch and frowned.

"You didn't tell me you were bringing somebody," she said.

"This is my partner on the case," Ballard said. "Detective Harry Bosch."

Bosch nodded but remained quiet.

"Well, just as long as we're clear," Beaupre said. "I run a business here and I don't want any trouble. To me, a man means trouble. We already have one coming in, so you, Harry Bosch, you chill out."

Bosch held his hands up in surrender.

"You're the boss," he said.

"Damn right," Beaupre said. "Only reason I'm doing this and putting my neck out is because your partner saved my skinny ass from death's door last year. I owe her and I'm going to pay up today."

Bosch looked at Ballard with a raised eyebrow.

"She saves more people than John the Baptist," he said.

The joke fell on deaf ears with Beaupre but Ballard stifled a laugh.

They walked past the door to the room Ballard remembered as being Beaupre's office and continued down a hall, passing a framed poster for a movie called *Operation Desert Stormy,* which depicted porn star Stormy Daniels straddling a missile in a bathing suit. Ballard scanned the credits for Beaupre's name but didn't see it.

"Was that one of your movies?" she asked.

"I wish," Beaupre said. "All of Stormy's flicks are in big-time demand. I put the poster up for appearances, you know. Doesn't hurt if people think you have a part of that action."

They entered a room at the end of the hallway that was carpeted and had a stripper pole on a one-foot-high stage. There were several folding chairs lined against one wall.

"This is where we do casting," Beaupre said. "But most of the time it's for the women. Men, we go off reels and reps. But I figure this is where you should talk to the guy. If he shows."

"Do you have reason to think he won't?" Bosch asked.

"It's a flaky business," Beaupre said. "People are unreliable. I don't know anything about this guy. He could be a flake and a no-show. He could be right smack on time. We'll see. Now I got a question. Am I supposed to be in here with you all?"

"No, that's not necessary," Ballard said. "If you can send him back here when he arrives, we'll take it from there."

"And no blowback on me, right?" Beaupre said.

"No blowback on you," Ballard said. "We have you covered."

"Good," Beaupre said. "I'll be in my office. The intercom buzz will go to me and then I'll bring him to you."

She left the room, closing the door behind her.

Ballard looked at Bosch and tried to gauge what he was thinking about the setup. She couldn't read him and was about to ask if he wanted to change the interview plan, when Beaupre stuck her head in through the doorway.

"Imagine that, this guy's an early bird," she said. "You two ready?"

Ballard nodded at Bosch and he nodded back.

"Bring him in," he said.

Ballard looked around at the room. She quickly started moving chairs, putting two side by side and facing a third in the center.

"I wish we had a table," she said. "It will feel weird without a table."

"It's better without one," Bosch said. "He can't hide his hands. They tell a lot."

Ballard was thinking about that when the door opened again and Beaupre led Kurt Pascal in.

"This is Kurt Pascal," she said. "And this is Renée and…is it Harry?"

"Right," Bosch said. "Harry."

Both Ballard and Bosch shook Pascal's hand and Ballard signaled him to the single chair. He was wearing baggy polyester workout pants and a red pullover hoodie. He was shorter than Ballard had expected and the baggy clothes camouflaged his body shape. His long brown hair was streaked with a slash of red dye and tied up in a topknot.

Pascal hesitated before sitting down.

"You want me to sit or do you want to see my stuff?" he asked.

He hooked his thumbs into the elastic band of his pants.

"We want you to sit," Ballard said.

She and Bosch both waited for Pascal to sit first, then Ballard sat down. Bosch remained on his feet, leaning his hands on the back of the empty folding chair so he could cut off any move Pascal made toward the room's door.

"Okay, I'm sitting," Pascal said. "What do you want to know?"

Ballard pulled her badge and held it up to him.

"Mr. Pascal, Ms. Beaupre doesn't know this but we're not really movie producers," she said. "I'm Detective Ballard, LAPD, and this is my partner, Detective Bosch."

"What the fuck?" Pascal said.

He started to stand. Bosch immediately took his hands off his chair and stood straight, ready to keep Pascal from the door.

"Sit down, Mr. Pascal," Ballard ordered. "We need your help."

Pascal froze. It seemed to be the first time in his life that anyone had asked him for help.

He then slowly sat back down.

"What's this about?" he asked.

"We're trying to find a man—a dangerous man—and we think you might be able to help," Ballard said. "You have a past association with him."

"Who?"

"Wilson Gayley."

Pascal started to laugh and then shook his head.

"Are you fucking with me?" he asked.

"No, Mr. Pascal, we're not fucking with you," Ballard said.

"Wilson Gayley is dangerous? What did he do? Run a stop sign? Flip off a nun?"

"We can't share the details of the case we're working. It's a confidential investigation and anything you tell us will be confidential as well. Do you know where he is at the moment?"

"What? No. I haven't seen that guy in a couple years, at least. Somebody had a party for him when he got out of prison, and I saw him there. But that was like three years ago."

"So you have no idea where he is these days?"

"I have an idea where he isn't and that's in L.A. I mean, if he was here, I would have seen him around, you know?"

Pascal shoved his hands into the front pocket of the hoodie. Ballard realized he could hide his hands even without a table.

"How did you know Wilson Gayley in the first place?" Bosch asked.

Pascal shrugged like he was not sure how to answer.

"He was making street movies," he said. "Shorts. He had a name for them. It was like a series. I think it was called *Hollywood Whores* or something like that. He hired me in a room like this after seeing my package, you know? And then we went driving around, and he'd pay street girls to get in and fuck me while he filmed it. That was how I got my start in the business, you know?"

Ballard and Bosch stared at him for a long moment before Ballard continued the questioning.

"When was this?" she asked.

"I don't know," Pascal said. "Ten years ago. Thereabouts."

"What kind of vehicle did you use?" Bosch asked.

"Vehicle? It was a van," Pascal said. "It was an old VW like they had on that show *Lost*. People always made that connection. Two-tone. White on the top, blue on the bottom."

"And the women? Who talked them into getting in the van?" Ballard asked.

"That was him mostly," Pascal said. "He had a silver tongue. He used to say he could sell matches to the devil. But there was no shortage of women who would get in. Most of them were pros, anyway."

"Prostitutes," Ballard said.

"That's right," Pascal said.

"Were some of them runaways?" Ballard asked.

"I suppose so," Pascal said. "We didn't really ask a bunch of questions, you know? If they got in the van, they got paid, and they knew what they had to do."

"Underage girls?" Ballard tried.

"Uh…no," Pascal said. "That would be illegal."

"It's all right," Ballard said. "Ten years ago—the statute of limitations has passed. You can tell us."

Ballard's statement about the statute of limitations wasn't exactly true but it didn't matter. Pascal wasn't going there.

"No, nobody underage," he said. "I mean, we checked IDs but somebody here and there could've had a phony, you know what I'm saying? Not our fault if they were lying."

"How often did you do this?" Bosch asked.

"I don't know," Pascal said. "A couple times a month. He'd call me up when he needed me. But he was going out with different guys on different nights. To have variety in the product, you know?"

"You know any names of those other guys?" Bosch asked.

"No, not really," Pascal said. "Been a long time. But Wilson would."

"But you don't know where he is?"

"No, I don't. Scout's honor."

He pulled his right hand out of the hoodie's front pocket and held it up as if to show his sincerity. Ballard noticed that he was getting happy feet—involuntarily shaking his foot as he got increasingly nervous about the interview. She was sure Bosch had picked up on it as well.

"Did you ever see Gayley get mad or upset with any of the women in the van?" Ballard asked.

"Not that I remember," Pascal said. "So, all these questions. What's this all about? I thought you wanted me to help with an investigation or something."

"You are helping," Ballard said. "I can't tell you how because of the case, but you are definitely helping. The thing is, we really need to locate Gayley. Are you sure you can't help us with that? Give us a name. Somebody else who knows him."

"I got no names," Pascal said. "And I really need to go."

He stood up again but Bosch took his hands off the back of his chair once more and moved a few steps toward the door to block Pascal's angle to it. Pascal immediately read the situation and sat back down. He slapped his palms down on his thighs.

"You can't hold me like this," he said. "You haven't even given me my rights or anything."

"We're not holding you, Mr. Pascal," Ballard said. "We're just talking here, and there's no need for rights at this stage. You're not a suspect. You are a citizen aiding the police."

Pascal reluctantly nodded.

"I'm now going to show you some photos of individuals and I want to see if you recognize any of them," Ballard said. "We want to know if any of these women were ever with Wilson Gayley."

From her briefcase Ballard pulled out a standard six-pack — a file with six windows cut into it and displaying six photos of different young women. One of the photos was a shot of Daisy Clayton that Ballard had gotten out of the online murder book. It was a posed shot taken at her school in Modesto when Daisy was in the seventh grade. She was smiling at the camera, makeup covering acne on her cheeks, but she looked older than her years and there was already a distant look in her eyes.

Another photo was a mug shot of Tanya Vickers, the prostitute who had been with Pascal and Gayley on the night they had been rousted by the cops and their shake cards were written. While their interaction probably amounted to just that one night, including her photo was intended as a test of Pascal's veracity.

Ballard flipped the cover of the file back and handed it to Pascal.

"Take your time," Ballard said.

"I don't need to," Pascal said. "I don't know any of them."

He reached out to hand the file back but Ballard didn't take it.

"Look again, Mr. Pascal," Ballard said. "It's important. Did any of those women ever get into the van with you and Gayley?"

Pascal withdrew the file and impatiently looked again.

"You know how many women I've fucked in ten years?" he asked. "I can't remember every — maybe her and maybe her."

"Which ones?" Ballard asked.

Pascal turned the file and pointed to two of the photos. One was Vickers. The other was Daisy Clayton.

Ballard took the file back and pointed to the photo of Daisy.

"Let's start with her," Ballard said. "You recognize her from the van?"

"I don't know," Pascal said. "Maybe. I can't remember."

"Think, Mr. Pascal. Look again. How do you recognize her? From where?"

"I told you. I don't know. It was from back at that time, I guess."

"She got into the van with you and Gayley?"

"I don't know. Maybe. I've fucked about a thousand women since then. How am I supposed to remember them all?"

"It must be difficult. What about her?"

She pointed to the photo of Vickers.

"Same thing," Pascal said. "I think I remember her from back then. She mighta been in the van."

"Where in Hollywood would Gayley stop the van to pick up women for his films?" Ballard asked.

"All over the place. Wherever the whores were, you know?"

"Santa Monica Boulevard?"

"Yeah, probably."

"Hollywood Boulevard?"

"Sure."

"How about Western Avenue? Was that a place you stopped?"

"Most likely—if that's where the pros were working."

"Do you remember specifically stopping at Hollywood and Western to recruit women for the films?"

"No. Been too long."

"Do you remember the name Daisy from back then?"

"Uh…"

He shook his head. Ballard knew she wasn't getting anywhere. She went in a new direction.

"What was in the van?" she asked.

"You mean, like, inside the VW?" Pascal asked.

"Yes."

"I don't know. Stuff, you know? He always had a fucking carton of rubbers. He had to. And there was a mattress. All the seats were taken out and a mattress was on the floor. And he had extra sheets and all of that. Some costumes. Sometimes the girls would only work if they had on a disguise, you know?"

"How'd he store it?"

"He, uh, he had boxes and cartons and shit that he put it all in."

"What kind of cartons?"

"You know, like plastic containers for putting shit in."

"How big?"

"What?"

"How big were the plastic containers?"

"I don't know. Like this."

He used his hands to shape a box in the air in front of him. He delineated a square that was maybe two feet by two feet. It would be difficult to fit a body into such a space.

"I really gotta go now," Pascal said. "I have a wax at five. I've got work tomorrow."

"Just a few more questions," Ballard said. "You've been very helpful. Do you know what happened to the van you and Mr. Gayley used?"

"No, but I doubt it's around anymore. It was a real piece of shit back then. What else?"

"The films you made in the van with Mr. Gayley, do you have copies?"

Pascal laughed.

"Fuck, no. I wouldn't keep that shit. But it's all gotta be out there somewhere on the internet, right? Everything's on the net."

Ballard looked at Bosch to see if he had any questions. He gave a quick head shake.

"Can I go now?" Pascal said.

"Do you have a driver's license?" Ballard asked.

"No, I don't drive anymore. I Uber."

"Where do you live, then?"

"Why do you need that?"

"In case we have follow-up questions."

"You can call my agent. He'll find me."

"You're not going to give me your home address?"

"Not if I don't have to. I don't want it in some police file somewhere, you know?"

"What about your cell-phone number?"

"Same answer."

Ballard stared at him for a long moment. She knew there would be many ways to find Pascal later. She wasn't worried about that. The moment was more about cooperation and what his refusal meant in terms of her suspicions about him. It was also the moment when she needed to make a decision. If she wanted to shift things and go at him hard with questions about Daisy Clayton and his possible involvement with her murder, then she would need to advise him of his rights to have an attorney present and to choose not to speak to the police. Considering the reluctance to talk that Pascal had already shown, such an advisement would most likely bring the interview to an abrupt end and put Pascal on notice that they considered him a suspect.

She decided it was too soon for that. She hoped Bosch was on the same page with her.

"Okay, Mr. Pascal, you can go now," she finally said. "We'll find you if we need to."

40

Ballard and Bosch didn't discuss the interview until after they thanked Beatrice Beaupre for her help and got back into the van.

"So?" she asked.

"I'd put him on the long-shot list," Bosch said.

"Really? Why?"

"I think if he had anything to do with Daisy, he wouldn't have said what he said."

"What do you mean? He didn't say shit."

"He picked out her picture. Not a good move if he and Gayley killed her."

"Nobody said the guy's a genius. He makes his living with his dick."

"Look, don't get upset. I'm just giving you my reaction. I'm not saying he's in the clear or we should drop it. I'm just saying I didn't get the vibe, you know what I mean?"

"I'm not upset. I'm just not ready to move on from these guys yet."

She started the van's engine.

"Where to?" she asked. "Back to San Fernando?"

"You mind taking me to my house?" Bosch asked.

"Is it safe?"

"Supposedly they put a car on it. I'm just going to get some fresh clothes and my Jeep. Be good to get mobile again. You going that way?"

"Not a problem."

Ballard backed out of the parking slot in front of the warehouse and drove off. She headed south on surface streets, wanting to avoid the freeways at this point in the day. As she drove, she thought about Bosch's take on Pascal and the interview. She had to decide if her suspicions were based on solid underpinnings of circumstantial evidence or simply her hopes that a creep like Pascal would be guilty because society would be better off without him. After a while she had to admit to herself that she may have let her feelings about Pascal and what he did for a living skew her judgment of things. Her way of acknowledging this to Bosch was indirect.

"So, there's still some of the culled shake cards to go through and run down," she said. "You going to be around tonight? We could split them up."

"Hey, I'm not telling you to drop Pascal," Bosch said. "Let's do a deep dive on Gayley. We locate him and see if what he says matches up with Pascal. We get them telling different stories and we might have something."

Ballard nodded.

"We can do that," she said.

They drove in silence for a while, with Ballard thinking about next moves in trying to locate Gayley. She had only scratched the surface in her prior search.

Bosch directed her to take a shortcut on Vineland up into the hills. It would lead them to Mulholland Drive and that would take them to his street.

"So, have you figured out how they knew where you lived?" Ballard asked. "The men who grabbed you, I mean."

"Nobody knows for sure," Bosch said. "But once Cortez was wired in through Luzon, he could have had people on my tail since early in the week. I drove home with them on me."

"Is Luzon the cop who set you up?"

"He was the leak that got my witness killed. How much he knew about setting me up is not yet determined."

"Where is he?"

"The hospital. He tried to kill himself. He's still in a coma."

"Wow."

"Yeah."

"So, the SIS setup on Cortez—how'd they get PC if Luzon's in a coma and nobody else is talking?"

"You don't need probable cause to watch somebody. And if he flushes, they have a reason to pull him over. Child support. He's got a judgment against him for three kids and a standing subpoena from a children's court judge."

That darkened the picture for Ballard. If the SIS was operating without probable cause to arrest Cortez, then following and pulling him over would seemingly have only one purpose; to see if he made the wrong move.

She dropped that part of the conversation. In a few minutes she turned off Mulholland onto Woodrow Wilson Drive. Then, as they came around the last bend before his house, Bosch leaned tensely forward and released his seat belt.

"Damn it," he said.

"What?" Ballard asked.

There was a patrol car parked in front of the house. There was also a Volkswagen Beetle. As she got closer, she could read the Chapman sticker on the back window.

"Your daughter?" she asked.

"I told her not to come up," Bosch said.

"So did I."

"I've got to send her back, get her out of here."

Ballard pulled her van to a stop next to the patrol car and showed her badge to the officer behind the wheel. She didn't recognize him and saw that the car's roof code was from North Hollywood Division. They lowered their windows at the same time.

"I've got Harry Bosch here," Ballard said. "He's got to pick up some things inside."

"Roger that," the officer said.

"When did his daughter arrive?"

"A couple hours ago. She drove up, showed me her ID. I let her go in."

"Roger that."

Bosch got out of the car and checked up and down the street for any vehicles or anything else that didn't belong. He looked back in at Ballard before closing the door.

"Are you going into the station from here?" he asked.

"Not yet," Ballard said. "I'm heading downtown and taking the spotter from the airship yesterday to dinner. I called in a favor on that flyover."

"Hold on, then. Let me go in and get some money. I want to buy dinner."

"Don't worry about it, Harry. We just go to the Denny's by Piper Tech. It's not a big deal."

"Really? What about something nicer? Let me send you over to the Nickel Diner. I know Monica there. I'll call and she'll take good care of you."

"Denny's is good, Harry. Convenient. It's right across from Piper."

Bosch nodded toward his house.

"I've got to deal with my daughter and then I have something else to do," he said. "But I want to meet this guy sometime—the spotter. To say thanks."

"It's not necessary and it's not a guy. She was just doing her job."

Bosch nodded.

"Well, tell her thanks for me," he said. "The sound of that chopper—it changed everything."

"I'll tell her," Ballard said. "You coming by the station later to help me look for Gayley?"

"Yeah, I'll get by later on. Thanks for the ride."

"Anytime, Harry."

She watched him cross in front of the van and go to the front door. He had to knock because his keys were one of the things left behind when he had been abducted. Soon the door was opened and Ballard caught a glimpse of a young woman as she grabbed Bosch into an embrace and closed the door.

Ballard stared at the door for a few seconds and then drove off.

BOSCH

41

Bosch hugged his daughter as tightly as she hugged him. It made his cracked ribs sing with pain but he didn't care.

He heard the door close behind him and looked over her head pressed against his shoulder at the slider to the deck. It was still open a couple of feet, the way the intruders had left it. There was black fingerprint dust on the glass. He was reminded that the house had been processed as a crime scene.

He brought his hands up to his daughter's shoulders and pulled back from her so he could look into her eyes.

"Maddie, you were told not to come up here," he said. "It's not safe yet."

"I had to come up," she said. "I couldn't just stay down there when I didn't know if you were all right."

"I told you. I'm fine."

"Are you crying?"

"No. I mean—I have two cracked ribs and when you hug...you really hug."

"I'm sorry! I didn't know. But look at your face. You're going to have a scar."

She reached toward his face but he caught her hand and held it.

"I'm too old to worry about scars," he said. "It doesn't matter. What matters is you can't stay here. I'm not even supposed to stay here. I was just coming for the Jeep and to get some of my own clothes."

"I thought those looked weird," she said, nodding toward the ill-fitting suit he was wearing.

"I borrowed clothes from another cop," Bosch said.

"Where will you go?" she asked.

"I don't know yet. I'm waiting to see if they pick up the guy who was behind all of this."

"Well, when is that?"

"There's no telling. They're looking for him."

"Why did this happen, Dad?"

"Maddie, look, I can't tell you about case stuff. You know that."

He saw a determined look enter her eyes. She was not going to let him stonewall her with case protocol.

"Okay," he said, "all I can tell you is that I was working on a cold-case murder that was a gang-on-gang killing and I tracked down a guy who was a witness to part of the planning. That led to the suspect and somehow that suspect found out I was onto him. So he had his guys grab me and they pushed me around a little, but nothing really happened because I got rescued. And that's it. End of story. Now you need to go back down to school."

"I don't want to," she said.

"You have to. No choice. Please."

"Okay. But you have to answer the phone. I came up because you don't answer and I always think the worst."

"The landline? I wasn't even staying here. And I told you when we talked yesterday that my cell phone was smashed."

"Well, I forgot."

"I'll get a new one first thing tomorrow and then I'll take every call from you."

"You'd better."

"Promise. How's your gas?"

"It's fine. I filled up on my way."

"Good. I want you to get going because it's going to get dark soon. You should be south of downtown before it gets dark."

"Okay, okay, I'm leaving. You know, most dads like their daughters to be around."

"Now you're just being a smart guy."

She grabbed him and pulled him into another painful hug. She heard his breath catch and quickly detached.

"I'm sorry, I'm sorry. I forgot!"

"It's okay. It's just sore. You can hug me anytime. You have the landline number. When you get to your house, call that and leave a message that you're home and safe. I'll be checking the line."

"You have to clear it first. I already left about ten messages today."

"Okay. Did you bring anything up with you?"

"Just myself."

Bosch touched her arm and led her toward the front door. Outside they walked to the Volkswagen. Bosch nodded to the officer in the patrol car. He scanned up and down the street again to check if he could see what he wasn't supposed to see. This time he even checked the sky before returning his attention to his daughter.

"How's the car?" he asked.

"It's good," she said.

"A couple more up and backs and I'll get the oil changed and the tires checked."

"I can get all of that done."

"You're busy."

"So are you."

This time he hugged her despite the penalty to his ribs. He kissed the top of her head. His heart hurt worse than his ribs, but he wanted her far away from him right now.

"Remember to leave a message on the house line so I know you're home," he said.

"I will," she promised.

"Love you."

"Love you."

Bosch watched her drive off and around the bend. He headed back into the house, nodding once more to the patrol officer with the thanklessly boring job in the car out front. At least he had a car to sit in and wasn't posted at the front door.

When he got back inside, Bosch went directly to the landline in the kitchen and pulled a business card out of his pocket. He called Lieutenant Omar Cespedes, who ran the SIS squad working the Cortez case. He didn't bother to identify himself when Cespedes picked up.

"You should have told me she came up to the house."

"Bosch? Couldn't do it. You know that. Besides, you got no phone. How am I supposed to tell you anything?"

"Bullshit," Bosch said. "You were using her as bait."

"That's totally wrong, Harry. We wouldn't do that, not with a cop's kid. But if we had told you she was coming up, then you would have called her and turned her around. That happens and it's a giveaway. We don't do giveaways and you know that. We play it as it lays."

Bosch calmed a bit as he came to understand the logic of the answer. Cespedes had a team watching Maddie—just as he had a team on Bosch and on the spot where Tranquillo Cortez had supposedly gone underground. If there was any sort of deviation in Maddie's moves—like a U-turn on a trip up to L.A.—then it could tip someone else who might be watching or tailing her.

"Are we okay?" Cespedes said into the silence.

"Just let me know when she gets back safe to her house."

"Not a problem. Check your mailbox on your way out."

"Why?"

"We put a phone in there for you. So next time we can contact you when we need to. Don't use it for anything else. It's monitored."

Bosch paused as he thought about that. He knew that every move the SIS made was monitored and analyzed. It came with the territory.

He changed the subject.

"What's the latest with Cortez?"

"Still underground. We're going to goose him after it gets dark, see what that gets us."

"I want to be there."

"Not going to happen, Bosch. Not how we work."

"He was going to feed me to his dogs. I want to be there."

"And that is exactly why you won't be. You're emotionally involved. We can't have that cluttering things. You just keep that phone handy. I'll call you when the time is right."

Cespedes disconnected. Bosch was still bothered but not too much. He had a plan for crashing the SIS surveillance.

Bosch retrieved the messages on the landline and started clearing them one by one. They went back weeks and most were inconsequential. He rarely used the landline anymore and let the messages pile up over time. When he got to the messages his daughter had left yesterday, he couldn't bring himself to delete them. Her emotions were raw, her fear for him real. He felt terrible about what she had just gone through but knew the messages were too pure to lose. The last one had no words. It was just Maddie's breathing, hopeful that he would simply pick up and rescue her from her fears.

After hanging up he called his own cell number. The phone had been destroyed but he knew the number would still be active and collecting messages. Nine had accumulated over the last thirty-six hours. Four were from his daughter and three were from Ballard, all left when his whereabouts were unknown. As with the landline messages, Bosch did not delete these. There was also one message from Cisco, saying he had nothing new to report on Elizabeth and asking Bosch whether he did. The last message, which had come in only an hour before, was from Mike Echevarria, and it was a call Bosch didn't want to get.

Echevarria was an investigator with the Medical Examiner's Office. Bosch had worked many homicide scenes with him and they were professionally, if not personally, close. Bosch had called him the night he was out looking for Elizabeth Clayton to see if she was in the morgue. She wasn't but now Echevarria had left a message—just asking Bosch to call him back.

He got right to the point when Bosch returned the call.

"Harry, this woman you've been looking for? I think we have her here under a Jane Doe."

Bosch dropped his chin to his chest and leaned against the kitchen counter. He closed his eyes as he spoke.

"Tell me," he said.

"Okay, let's see," Echevarria said. "Female, midfifties found in the Sinbad Motel on Sunset Boulevard two days ago. She's got the R-I-P tattoo on her rear shoulder that you described with the name Daisy."

Bosch nodded to himself. It was Elizabeth. Echevarria continued.

"Autopsy won't be till Monday or Tuesday but all signs point to opiate overdose. According to the summary, she was found on the bed by the manager. She had paid for one night and he was going to shoo her out. Instead, he found her dead. Had her clothes on, body on top of the sheets. No foul play suspected. No homicide callout. Signed off on by a patrol sergeant and M.E. staff on scene."

"She didn't have ID?"

"No ID in the room – that's why I didn't connect it when you called. A lot of these people hide their stuff outside their rooms because they're afraid of getting ripped off after they fix and pass out or whatever. She have a car?"

"No. What about pills? Any extra pills?"

"An empty prescription bottle. The prescription scratched off. They do that too. In case they get popped. It protects the doctor, because as soon as they hit the streets again, they're going to see that same doctor. Creatures of habit."

"Right."

"Sorry, Harry. Sounds like you knew her."

"I did. And it's better knowing than not knowing, Mike."

"Any chance I can get you down here to make a formal ID? Or I could shoot you a picture."

Bosch thought about that.

"I'm not on a cell. How about I come in tomorrow?"

"Tomorrow's good. I'm off Sundays but I'll let them know."

"Thanks, man."

"Talk to you, Harry."

Bosch hung up and walked through the house and out to the deck. He leaned on the railing and looked down at the freeway.

He was not fully surprised by the news about Elizabeth but was still taken aback. He wondered whether the overdose was intentional. The empty pill bottle indicated she had taken everything she'd gotten.

The details made no difference either way to Bosch, because he considered her death a murder. It was a nine-year-old murder, and whoever had taken Daisy had also taken Elizabeth. Never mind that the killer had never met or even seen Elizabeth. He took everything that mattered away from her. He had killed her just as plainly as he had killed her daughter. Two for the price of one.

Bosch made a promise to himself. Elizabeth might be gone now but he would renew his efforts to put a name to the killer. He would find him and make him pay.

He went back into the house, closed the slider, and walked down the hall to his bedroom. He changed clothes, dressing in dark pants and shirt and adding an old army-green jacket. He threw some backup clothes and toiletries into a duffel bag because he didn't know how long it would be until he could return.

He sat down on the bed and picked up the landline. He dialed Cisco Wojciechowski's number from memory and got it right. The big man answered after four rings, a cautious tone in his voice, probably because he didn't recognize the number.

"Yeah?"

"Cisco, it's Bosch. I've got bad news on Elizabeth."

"Tell me."

"She didn't make it. They found her in a motel room in Hollywood. Looks like an OD."

"Shit..."

"Yeah."

They stayed silent for a long moment before Cisco broke the silence.

"I thought she was stronger, you know? That week I spent with her—her breaking it off cold—I saw something. I thought she could go the distance."

"Yeah, me too. But I guess you never know, right?"

"Right."

After a few more minutes of small talk, Bosch thanked him for all he had done for Elizabeth and finished the call.

He went back down the hall to the closet next to the front door, where there was a steel gun box. His abductors had taken his firearm but Bosch had a spare weapon, a Smith & Wesson Combat Masterpiece, the six-shot revolver he had carried as a patrol officer almost forty years before. He had cleaned and maintained it regularly ever since. It was in a clip-on holster now and Bosch attached it to his belt under the jacket.

The keys to the house and Cherokee were on the kitchen counter where Bosch had left them two nights before. He exited the house through the front door and pulled the phone Cespedes had left for him out of the mailbox. He took another look around the street, checking for the surveillance, but saw nothing beyond the marked car from North Hollywood Division. He went into the carport, where the Cherokee awaited.

As he drove down the hill he thought about Elizabeth and her fatal sadness. He realized that the long wait for justice had been too long and not enough to keep her alive. And that his effort to help her ultimately hurt her. Getting her sober only made the pain sharper and less bearable. Was he just as guilty as the unnamed killer?

Bosch knew he would carry that question for a long time.

42

Cespedes had purposely not given him the exact location of the surveillance set up on Tranquillo Cortez's hideout in Panorama City but Bosch knew enough from sitting in SFPD briefings to be able to find the neighborhoods considered to be SanFer strongholds in the area. And with his plan, a general knowledge was all that was needed. He dropped down out of the hills and headed north into the Valley, traveling through Van Nuys and up into Panorama City.

The light was leaving the sky and the streetlights were coming on. He passed tent communities and drab industrial buildings colored with graffiti. When he got to Roscoe Boulevard he turned east, and it wasn't long before the SIS phone was buzzing in his pocket. He didn't take the first or second call. He turned into a large apartment complex where there were no rules about storing furniture and refrigerators on the balconies. He drove the length of the parking lot before turning around and driving back through. He saw young Latino men watching from a few of the balconies.

The third time the phone buzzed he took the call.

"Bosch, what the fuck are you doing?" Cespedes demanded.

"Hey, Speedy," Bosch said, using the nickname he had

heard SIS officers use for their boss. "Just taking a drive. What's up?"

"Are you trying to fuck this up?"

"I don't know. Am I?"

"You need to get out of here and go home."

"No, I need to get in the car with you. If tonight's the night, I want to be there."

"What are you talking about, tonight being the night?"

"You slipped. You said you were going to goose Cortez tonight. I want in."

"Are you nuts? I told you we don't do things that way. Christ, you're not even LAPD anymore, Bosch."

"You could make up a reason to have me. I could be the spotter. I know what Cortez looks like."

"That would never wash. You're not part of this operation and you're compromising it."

"Then I guess I'll just continue my one-man search for Cortez. Good luck with yours."

Bosch disconnected and pulled back out onto Roscoe. He hit the turn signal as soon as he came up on another apartment complex. His phone buzzed again before he got to it. He took the call.

"Don't turn in there," Cespedes said.

"You sure?" Bosch asked. "Looks like the kind of place where Cortez might hide out."

"Bosch, keep going. There's a gas station on the right down at Woodman. I'll meet you there."

"Okay, but don't keep me hanging."

This time it was Cespedes who disconnected.

Bosch did as instructed and kept driving. At Woodman Avenue he pulled into a gas station and parked by a broken air pump at the edge of the property. He kept the car running and waited.

After three minutes a black Mustang hardtop with smoked windows streaked into the station and pulled in next to Bosch's car. The passenger-side window lowered and Bosch saw Cespedes behind the wheel. He had dark skin and a gray crew cut. The angular cut to his jaw seemed perfect for a man who led a team of hard chargers and sharpshooters.

"Hey, Speedy," Bosch said.

"Hey, asshole," Cespedes said. "You know you are fucking up a solid operation here."

"Doesn't have to be that way. Am I riding with you or not?"

"Get in."

Bosch exited the Jeep and locked it. He then got into the Mustang. It was a tight squeeze because of an open laptop sitting on a swivel mount attached to the dash. The screen was angled toward Cespedes, but once Bosch was in his seat, he turned the mount so he could see the screen. It was quartered into four camera views of Roscoe Boulevard and an apartment building. Bosch recognized the complex he had been about to turn into when Cespedes agreed to allow Harry to ride with him.

"You got cameras on your cars?" Bosch asked. "I guess I was getting close."

He pointed at the apartment building on one of the camera views. Cespedes abruptly turned the screen back toward himself.

"Don't touch," he ordered.

Bosch raised his hands in acknowledgment.

"Put on your seat belt," Cespedes added. "You don't leave this car unless I tell you to. Got that?"

"Got it," Bosch said.

Cespedes dropped the Mustang into reverse and pulled out of the slot next to the Jeep. The car then shot forward and back toward Roscoe.

Two blocks down, he pulled to the curb in a spot where there was a view of the apartment complex that the cameras on the other cars were focused on. Cespedes canted his head back and spoke toward the ceiling of the car.

"Sierra two, show me back at OP one."

Bosch knew there was a microphone behind the visor, probably activated with a foot switch on the floor. Standard surveillance gear. A series of clicks from other cars followed. Cespedes had observation-point one. The others had views from other angles on the apartment complex.

Cespedes turned to Bosch.

"Now we wait," he said.

Bosch understood why they were waiting for darkness. The night always favored the followers. Cars became headlights, unrecognizable in the rearview mirror. Drivers became silhouettes.

"How are you going to goose him into moving?" Bosch asked.

Cespedes was quiet a moment and Bosch knew he was deciding how much to tell Bosch. The SIS was a very insular group within the department. Once officers transferred in, they never transferred out. They cut off relationships and contact with old partners and friends in the department. In the fifty-year history of the unit, there had only been one woman ever assigned to the team.

"Foothill gangs has a deep-cover snitch," Cespedes said. "He got us the cell number of a shot caller on the same level as Cortez. We hijacked the cell and sent Cortez a message about a must-attend meet regarding you, Bosch, at Hansen Dam. We're hoping that does the trick."

Cespedes had just described at least two things that were compromising, if not outright against department protocol, not to mention illegal—if hijacking the phone had been done without a warrant. He was attempting to draw Bosch in and make him complicit in what might go down later. If Bosch didn't object now, he couldn't claim innocence afterward.

And that was all right with him.

"Why Hansen Dam?" he asked.

"The truth?" Cespedes said. "No cameras up there."

He turned to look at Bosch. It was another moment where Bosch could either raise a flag or go along.

"Good plan," he said, putting himself all in.

The SIS held a unique position in the LAPD. Often investigated by outside agencies ranging from the FBI to the media to civil rights groups, often sued by the families of the suspects shot, routinely labeled a "death squad" by outraged attorneys, the unit enjoyed a completely opposite reputation within the rank and file of the department. Infrequent openings in the unit brought hundreds of applications, including from those willing to drop pay grades just to get in. The reason was that, more so than any other unit, this was seen as true police work. The SIS took violent offenders off the board. Whether they were taken alive didn't matter. They took out shooters, rapists, serial killers. The ripple effect of crimes *not* committed because of SIS captures and kills was unquantifiable but huge. And there wasn't a cop on the force who wouldn't want to be part of that. Never mind all the outside critics, the investigations, and the lawsuits. This was to serve and protect in its rawest form.

Bosch felt no choice but to go all in. Tranquillo Cortez had not played by the rules. He'd had his men take Bosch from his home, from the place his daughter often slept. There can be no greater crime against a police officer than to threaten his family. You do that, and all bets are off. So when Bosch called it a good plan, he meant it, and he hoped that one way or another the threat from Tranquillo Cortez would be over before midnight.

43

At 8:10 p.m., the Mustang's radio came alive with one call after another reporting that the target—Tranquillo Cortez—had been spotted and was on the move. Interpreting the radio code used by the SIS officers, Bosch deduced that Cortez was with an unidentified bodyguard/driver and had gotten into a white Chrysler 300 with a lowered suspension. The car had illegally smoked windows that made it impossible to identify those behind the glass.

The Chrysler was eastbound on Roscoe, and Cespedes let the entourage of SIS vehicles go by before putting the Mustang in play. Still, he hung back to see if Cortez had initiated any countersurveillance techniques such as a long-lead follow car. When he was satisfied there was none, he pulled into traffic to catch up to the others. His role as commander of the unit was to hang behind and be ready to move up into one of the corners of the floating-box surveillance surrounding the Chrysler should one of the four cars rotating positions be made by the suspect or otherwise taken out of commission.

Bosch heard over the radio that the Chrysler had turned north on Branford, which would lead directly into the park and golf course at Hansen Dam. Bosch listened as units identified themselves over the radio as Advance, Backdoor, and Outrigger One and Two and kept a running report on the moving surveillance. The voices were calm and slow, as if they were describing a golf match on TV.

"Where are we going in the park?" Bosch asked.

"The golf course parking lot," Cespedes said. "Should be empty right about now. Can't play golf in the dark, right?"

Bosch had asked the question as an attempt to get Cespedes talking about the plan. They were about a mile from the park and Bosch didn't know what the tactical strategy would be once they reached the takedown spot.

"It's going to come down to a choice," Cespedes said. "It always does."

"What do you mean?" Bosch asked. "What choice?"

"To live or die. The plan is always about containment first. We will put him into a situation where he knows he isn't getting out of the box. He then has a choice. Go out on his feet or on his back. It's amazing how many times these guys make the wrong choice."

Bosch just nodded.

"This is the guy who had you abducted," Cespedes said. "From the place your daughter calls home. Then he was going to torture you and feed your body to his dogs."

"That's right," Bosch said.

"Sounds like a movie I saw once."

"I heard somebody say that. I missed it."

"Yeah, well, we need to teach these people that the movies aren't real life. Bring a little truth to the situation, you know what I mean?"

"I do."

"How's the case against him going?"

367

"Nowhere. We got a guy in a coma—a cop. If he comes out of it and talks, then maybe we make a case."

"But you never saw Cortez, right? When you were in the cage."

"No."

"So in other words, you don't have shit. If we take him in on this bullshit child support thing, you get a shot at talking to him and you gotta hope that, first, he doesn't lawyer up and, second, he says the wrong thing and craps on himself."

"That's about right, yeah."

"Well, then, let's hope he makes the wrong choice tonight."

The radio came alive a few moments later with reports that the Chrysler carrying Cortez was entering the Hansen Dam Recreation Area. Two of the surveillance cars from the floating box had entered ahead and were in layup positions waiting for the Chrysler to enter the felony-stop trap.

"We got a decoy car in the lot," Cespedes told Bosch. "A Ford pickup like the guy whose phone we used drives. Cortez goes to it, we move in."

Bosch nodded. By leaning into the center console of the Mustang he was able to get an angle on the laptop screen and watch the four dash cameras from the surveillance cars. He noticed that two cars were moving in traffic, not having entered the park yet, and two were static. The view on these was now set to infrared. One angle was simply down a driveway next to a building that Bosch assumed was the golf course clubhouse. The other looked across a parking lot at a pickup truck backed into a space at the far end of the lot.

"Is there a delay on these screens?" he asked.

"About two and a half seconds," Cespedes said.

"Recording?"

"Recording."

The radio went from an overlapping of voices reporting the movement of the target to complete silence for nearly thirty seconds before the trap was sprung.

Soon Bosch saw the Chrysler enter the parking lot in one of the static camera angles. But it stopped dead before approaching the pickup.

"What's he doing?" Bosch asked.

"Just being cautious," Cespedes said.

Cespedes then went on the radio.

"Give him a wink, Jimmy."

"Roger that."

On the dashcam from the follow car in the lot, the pickup's headlights blinked twice. Bosch noticed that all four of the camera views were static now and on infrared.

"You got a guy in the pickup?" Bosch said, stating the obvious.

Cespedes held up a hand for silence. Now was not the time to give Bosch the play-by-play. He went back on the radio.

"Now bail, Jimmy. Get out of there."

The Chrysler started moving toward the pickup. Bosch saw no indication that anyone had gotten out of the Ford. Cespedes timed the Chrysler's approach, factored in the delay on the cameras, and then stomped on the radio transmit button on the floor of the car.

"Now! All units—go!"

All four camera views started moving and closing in. Far behind, Cespedes picked up speed and the Mustang entered the park. The car bounced on the uneven roadway as they sped toward the golf course but Bosch couldn't take his eyes off the laptop screen. He gripped his armrest with one hand and the laptop mount with the other in an effort to hold it steady and watch the action as it played out.

The four surveillance cars closed in on the Chrysler as it pulled into a slot next to the pickup. Bosch could see as the cameras got closer that the truck was backed up to an ivy-draped wall. There would be no escape that way.

The four follow cars moved in, their dashcams revealing that they had a classic spread formation on the Chrysler. It was trapped with its nose against a wall and four cars with armed officers fanned behind it across a 120-degree arc.

The camera angles overlapped and Bosch could see SIS officers using the open doors of their cars as cover and pointing weapons at the Chrysler. There was no sound but Bosch knew they were yelling and demanding the surrender of the men inside.

Bosch could see two officers in combat stances moving to the left and right of the SIS cars to further contain the Chrysler but still keep an angle that would clear them of any cross fire.

For ten seconds, there was nothing. No movement from the Chrysler. Its smoked windows were up but the high-powered beams of the SIS cars cut through and Bosch could make out the silhouettes of the two men inside.

The Mustang entered the parking lot and sped toward the confrontation. Bosch glanced up to get his bearings but then looked back down at the camera screens. It was then that the front doors of the Chrysler opened simultaneously.

Bosch first saw the hands of the passenger come out of the car, held high and open as Tranquillo Cortez emerged to surrender. He was wearing the same flat-brimmed Dodgers hat he had worn on the day they met.

The driver followed but held only his left hand up as he emerged.

The Mustang had pulled behind one of the follow cars and was now close enough for Bosch to hear the tense voices from the officers. He looked over the laptop to watch the action play live.

"Hands!"

"Both hands!"

"Hands up!"

And then the warning turned to alarm.

"Gun! Gun!"

Bosch could only see the driver's head and shoulders because one of the SIS cars was between them. He looked down at the laptop screen and to the camera angle showing the driver's side of the Chrysler. The driver, a stocky man who had to twist his body to step out of the car, was emerging, turning and bringing his right arm up in a swinging motion. When his arm cleared his body, Bosch saw the gun.

A tremendous volley of shots seemed to come from all around him.

Tranquillo Cortez paid for his bodyguard's bravado and suicidal decision to wield the gun. Cortez was centered in the killing ground and was fair game. Both men were hit repeatedly as fire continued from the eight shooters fanned around them. The Chrysler's windows shattered and the men on either side of it went down. Cortez had actually turned, possibly seeking cover, and went face-first back into the car. His body then fell out, and he was left leaning against the door sill, head down. His hat never came off.

Only when the gunfire stopped did Bosch look back up from the laptop screen. Through an angle between the open doors of two of the follow cars, he could see Cortez, the front of his white shirt soaked in blood. His head jerked as his body seized. For the moment, he was still alive.

"Stay in the car, Bosch," Cespedes yelled.

He jumped out and ran between two of the cars and through the heavy smoke of the gunfire. He followed two of his men, who were cautiously approaching the Chrysler with guns trained on the men on the ground. Bosch went back to the laptop, turning it fully toward him now because the view was better.

There was a gun on the ground next to the bodyguard's body. One of the SIS officers kicked it away and then leaned down to check the body for a pulse. He made a hand signal, a flat line, indicating the bodyguard was dead.

Cortez was pulled down flat on the ground and an officer knelt next to him. Even on the infrared screen, it was clear he was breathing. Cespedes was on the screen now, already talking on a cell phone. Bosch assumed he was calling for rescue ambulances or making notifications to command staff.

Bosch wanted to get out of the Mustang and enter the scene, but he remained as ordered in the car. If it appeared that Cespedes had forgotten him, he would get out. He saw Cespedes disconnect from a call and make another.

Bosch looked at the screen and saw the same action again, remembering that the feed to the laptop was delayed. He looked at the keyboard, located the left arrow, and pressed it. The video on the screen started rewinding. Bosch held his finger on the button until the images reversed past the shooting and the two SanFers were still in the white Chrysler.

He replayed the fatal confrontation, tapping the reverse button intermittently to slow down the playback or to entirely replay moments. He wasn't sure how to set the playback to slow motion. He focused on the camera angle on the upper-left corner of the screen. It was an almost straight-on view of the driver emerging from the car with one hand up.

He focused on the driver's right arm as it moved out of the shadows of the car. As the arm came up from behind his torso, Bosch could see the gun. But the hand was not grasping it by the grip. The driver was holding the weapon but it was not in a ready-fire grip.

Then Bosch saw an impact on the car as a bullet hit the door frame and fragmented. The first shot. It had come before the gun could have been clearly seen and the driver's intentions made apparent. Bosch took his finger off the keyboard and let the rest of the shooting play out. He looked up through the windshield and saw Cespedes walking toward the Mustang. He quickly put his finger on the forward arrow and sped the playback, catching it up to real time just as the SIS boss opened the passenger-side door.

Cespedes leaned in.

"He's circling but conscious if you want to say anything to him," he said.

"Okay," Bosch said. "Yeah."

Cespedes backed away and Bosch got out. They walked between two of the SIS cars and to the passenger side of the Chrysler. A heavy pall of smoke still hung in the air.

Cortez's eyes were open and looked fearful. Blood was on his tongue and lips and Bosch knew his lungs had likely been riddled with fragmented lead. Harry was shocked by how young he looked. The man who had sneered and postured in the *lavandería* parking lot a few days before was gone. Cortez now looked like a scared boy in a baseball cap.

Bosch knew it was not the time to say anything, to play the victor or to taunt him with vengeful words.

He said nothing.

Cortez said nothing as well. He locked eyes with Bosch and

373

then moved his arm and reached a bloody hand to the cuff of Bosch's pants. He grabbed hold of it as though he might be able to hang on to life and keep from being pulled into the waiting darkness.

But after a few seconds he lost his strength. He let go, then closed his eyes and died.

BALLARD

44

Ballard spread the final shake cards out on a table in the break room. There was more room here than on a borrowed desk in the detective bureau. She was waiting for Bosch. She had been through the cards and done the electronic backgrounding. It was time to work these in the field. If Bosch got in before it was too late, they could possibly knock off a few during the night. She wanted to text or call him to say she was waiting but remembered that he had no phone.

She was sitting there, staring at the cards, when Lieutenant Munroe came in to get a cup of coffee.

"Ballard, what are you doing in so early?" he asked.

"Just working on my hobby case," she said.

She didn't look up from the cards and he didn't look up from his prepping of his coffee.

"That old murder of the girl?" Munroe asked.

"The girl, right," Ballard said.

She moved two cards across the table to the lesser-priority side.

"What's it got to do with that tattoo artist?" Munroe asked. "That one was solved."

Now Ballard looked over at Munroe.

"What are you talking about, L-T?" she asked.

"Sorry, I guess I was being snoopy," Munroe asked. "I saw a murder book in your mail slot when I was going through the records retention box. I took a quick look. I remember that one, but they got the bad guy on it pretty quick, from what I can remember."

The ZooToo book. Ballard had been waiting on it but had forgotten to check her slot when she had come in from dinner.

"They did clear it," she said. "I just wanted a look at it. Thanks for letting me know it's there."

She walked out of the break room and down the back hallway to the mail room, where every officer and detective in the division had an open slot for internal and external deliveries. She pulled the plastic binder out of her slot.

Munroe was gone when she got back to the break room. She decided to review the murder book there so she would not have to leave the spread of shake cards unattended. She sat down and opened the binder.

The design of a murder book was consistent across all department homicide squads. It was divided into twenty-six sections—crime scene reports, lab reports, photos, witness statements, and so on. The first section was always the chronological record, where the case investigators logged their moves by date and time. Ballard flipped back to section sixteen, which contained the crime scene photos.

Ballard pulled a thick stack of 3 x 5 photos out of a plastic pocket and started looking through them. The photographer had been thorough and clinical. It seemed that every inch of the tattoo parlor and the murder scene had been documented in the bright, almost overexposed prints. In 2009 the department was still using film, as digital photography had not yet been accepted by the court system because of concerns about digital tampering.

Ballard moved quickly through the photos until she reached those taken of the victim's body at the center of the crime scene. Audie Haslam had put up a fight. Her arms, hands, and fingers were all deeply lacerated with defensive wounds. Eventually, though, she succumbed to her larger and more powerful attacker. There were deep stab wounds in her chest and neck. Blood completely soaked the ZooToo tank top she was wearing. Arterial spray had splashed all four walls of the small storage room the killer had pushed her into. She died on the polished concrete floor with one hand clasping a crucifix on a chain around her neck. Incongruously, the tattoo artist had no tattoos herself, at least none that were visible to Ballard in the photos.

Murder was murder, and Ballard knew that every case deserved the full attention and effort of the police department. But Ballard was always struck by the murder of a woman. Most times the cases she reviewed and worked were exceedingly violent. Most times the killers were men. There was something deeply affecting about that. Something unfair that went beyond the general unfairness of death at the hands of another. She wondered how men would live if they knew that in every moment of their lives, their size and nature made them vulnerable to the opposite sex.

She stacked the photos and slid them back into the pocket of section sixteen. She then went to section twelve, which was dedicated to the suspect. She wanted to see a photo of the man who had killed Audie Haslam.

In his booking photo, Clancy Devoux stared at the camera with dead eyes and an expression that seemed devoid of human empathy. He was unshaven and unclean and one eyelid drooped farther than the other. A straight, thin-lipped mouth was set in a smirk of defiance rather than an expression of guilt or apology. He was a hardened psychopath who had probably hurt many before the killing of Audie Haslam brought his run to an end. Ballard guessed that most of those victims—whatever the crimes—were women.

A printout of his prior record substantiated this. He had been charged numerous times going back to his juvenile days in Mississippi. The crimes ranged from drug possession to multiple aggravated assaults and an attempted murder. The list did not denote the gender of the victims but Ballard knew. Devoux was a woman hater. You didn't stab a woman in the back room of a tattoo parlor as many times and with as much ferocity as he had without building toward it over years. Poor Audie Haslam was at the wrong place at the wrong time. She had probably set her own death in motion with the wrong word or a judgmental look that set Devoux off.

A notation on the pocket of section twelve said that Devoux was sentenced to life in prison without parole for the murder in the tattoo parlor. He would never hurt a woman again.

From there Ballard went to the section containing the statements of witnesses in the case. There was no witness to the actual murder, because the killer had waited until he was alone in the shop before robbing and murdering Haslam. But the investigators had run down and talked to other customers who had been in the shop that night.

Ballard took out a notebook and started writing down the names of the witnesses and their contact information. These were all denizens of the Hollywood night circa 2009 and they might be useful to interview if they could be located now. She realized that one of these witnesses, a man named David Manning, sounded familiar. She put the murder book aside and looked over the shake cards she had spread out for Bosch's perusal. She found Manning.

According to the witness statement, Manning had been in the tattoo shop less than two hours before the murder. He was described as a fifty-eight-year-old ex-smuggler from Florida. He lived in an old RV he parked on different streets in Hollywood on different days of the week. He was a frequent visitor to ZooToo because he liked Audie Haslam and liked to add to the prodigious collection of tattoos that sleeved both his arms. From reading between the lines of the statement, which had been written before the investigation focused on Clancy Devoux, it appeared to Ballard that Manning was an early person of interest in the Haslam case. He had a record, albeit one without violence, and was one of the last people to see her alive. He was actually in police custody and being interviewed when the results of fingerprint analysis from the crime scene came in and put the investigation in a different direction.

Much of the information on the shake card matched that on the witness statement. The shake card had made the final cut with Ballard because of Manning's RV. It fell in with the van category that Ballard and Bosch were interested in. The card had been written seven weeks before the Clayton and Haslam murders when an officer had inspected the RV parked on Argyle just south of Santa Monica and told Manning it was illegal to park the recreational vehicle in a commercial parking zone. At the time, the LAPD was not shy about rousting the homeless and keeping them moving. But since then, a series of civil-rights lawsuits and a change in leadership in City Hall had led to a revision of that practice, and now bullying the homeless was practically a firing offense. Consequently, there was almost no enforcement of laws with them, and someone like Manning would be allowed to park his RV just about anywhere he wanted to in Hollywood as long as it was not in front of a single-family home or a movie theater.

The officer who had rousted Manning in 2009 had filled out a field interview card with information garnered from their short conversation and his Florida driver's license. When Ballard had run Manning's name and birth date through the database as she prepped the cards for Bosch, she had determined that he now had a California license but the address on it was unhelpful. Manning had followed a routine tactic of using a church address as his own in order to get a California license or identification card. Though the address was a dead end, the RV registered to Manning should not be too hard to spot if he was still living in the area.

Ballard now picked up the Manning shake card and moved it over to the row of cards that she believed warranted a higher priority of attention. The fact that he knew, liked, and might have been obsessed with a woman who was murdered two days before Daisy Clayton was in her estimation worth checking out.

Ballard wanted to talk to him. She opened her laptop and went to work on an information-only bulletin on Manning. The bulletin was an informal BOLO with instructions: If Manning or his RV is spotted, do not roust or arrest, just contact Ballard 24/7.

She printed out the page, which included a description and plate number for the RV, and then walked it back down to the watch office to give to Lieutenant Munroe. When she got there, Munroe was standing with two other officers in the middle of the room and looking up at the flat-screen mounted high on the wall over the watch commander's desk. Ballard could see the logo of channel 9, the local twenty-four-hour news channel, and a reporter she recognized doing a live stand-up with the flashing lights of several police vehicles behind her.

Ballard walked up beside them.

"What's this?" she asked.

"Police shooting in the Valley," Munroe said. "Two bangers down for the count."

"Is it SIS? The Bosch surveillance?"

"They're not saying anything about it on this. They don't know shit yet."

Ballard pulled her phone and texted Heather Rourke, the airship spotter.

You over this thing in the Valley?

No, south end tonight. Heard about it. 2Ks. Is it the Bosch thing? SIS?

Sounds like. Checking.

She still had no working number for Bosch. She stared at the screen, watching the activity behind the reporter but not listening to what she was saying until she finished with her exact location.

"Reporting live from the Hansen Dam Recreation Area."

Ballard knew that meant Foothill Division and, most likely, SanFers. It had to be the Bosch case, so she knew she would probably not be seeing him tonight.

She went back to the break room, stacked the shake cards according to priority, and then carried them and the ZooToo murder book back to the detective bureau. She checked the clock and saw that her shift didn't start for an hour. She considered for a moment driving up to the Valley and crashing the SIS shooting scene. She felt proprietary about the case, considering her part in the rescue of Harry Bosch.

But she knew she would be kept on the fringe. The SIS was a closed society. Bosch would be lucky if they even let him under the yellow tape.

She decided not to go and instead opened the murder book again to complete her review. She turned to section one, the chronological record. This was as close as she would get to riding along on the investigation. The chrono was a step-by-step accounting of the case detectives' movements.

She started at the beginning, from the moment they were called out from home and sent to the tattoo parlor. The case was carried by two detectives assigned to the Hollywood homicide squad before it had been dissolved and cases from the division were folded into West Bureau homicide. Their names were Livingstone and Peppers. Ballard knew neither of them.

The chrono, like the murder book, was shorter than what Ballard had seen in other murder books, including those she had prepared herself during her time in the Robbery-Homicide Division. But this was not a measure of the effort by Livingstone and Peppers. It was because the case so quickly came together. The detectives were moving forward and thoroughly when forensics handed them a suspect on a platter. A bloody fingerprint from the rear storage room of the shop was connected to Clancy Devoux. He was quickly located and picked up, a broken knife believed to have been the murder weapon was recovered in his possession, and the case was considered closed in less than twenty-four hours.

All murder cases should go so easily, Ballard thought. But

they usually don't. A girl gets snatched off the street and murdered, and nine years go by without so much as a clue to her killer. A woman gets brutally slashed with a knife in the back room of her business, and the case is closed in a day. There was no rhyme or reason to murder investigation.

After the arrest, the entries in the chronological record started tapering off as the case shifted from investigation to preparation for prosecution. But one entry in the log gave Ballard pause. It came in forty-eight hours after the murder and twenty-four hours after Clancy Devoux was arrested. It was an innocuous entry added simply for thoroughness. It said that two nights after the murder, at 7:45 p.m., Detective Peppers was notified by the watch sergeant at Hollywood Division that a crime scene cleaner named Roger Dillon had found additional evidence on the ZooToo case. This was described as a broken piece of knife blade that had been on the floor of the storage room but had been completely covered by the pool of blood that had flowed from the victim and then coagulated around her body. The two-inch blade had apparently gone unnoticed by the detectives and forensic techs.

Peppers wrote in the log that he asked the watch sergeant to dispatch a patrol team to go to the tattoo parlor, take the blade from Dillon, and bag it as evidence. Peppers, who lived more than an hour from Los Angeles, said he would pick up the evidence in the morning.

Ballard stared at the log entry for a long time. As far as the ZooToo case went, it was strictly housekeeping. She knew that if the blade matched the broken knife recovered during the Devoux arrest, then detectives had another piece of significant evidence against the suspect. She wasn't bothered by the seeming gaffe made by the crime scene team. It was, in fact, not

385

unusual for evidence to be missed or left behind at a complicated and bloody crime scene. Spilled blood can hide a lot.

What gave Ballard pause was the cleaner. By coincidence, Ballard had met Roger Dillon earlier in the week, when he had discovered the burglary of the Warhol prints from the house on Hollywood Boulevard. She still had the business cards he had given her in her briefcase.

The log entry documented that Dillon had called about the broken blade at 7:45 on the same night Daisy Clayton disappeared. It meant that Dillon had been working in Hollywood on Sunset Boulevard just a few hours before. Ballard had seen his work van earlier in the week and had gotten only a quick glimpse inside it, but she had seen inside others like it at other crime scenes. She knew Dillon had chemicals and tools for cleaning. And he would have containers for the safe transport and disposal of biologically hazardous materials.

All in a moment, Ballard knew. She had to look at Roger Dillon.

45

Ballard went to her locker to store the shake cards and the Haslam murder book. She then pulled out the fledgling murder book Bosch had started putting together on the Clayton case. She sat on a bench in the locker room and opened it up, immediately flipping to Bosch's report on the plastic container manufactured by American Storage Products. He listed the sales supervisor he had talked to as Del Mittleberg. Ballard almost jumped up off the bench with joy when she saw that Bosch, thorough detective that he was, had listed both Mittleberg's office and cell numbers.

It was after ten. She called the cell and it was answered with a suspicious hello.

"Mr. Mittleberg?"

"I'm not interested."

"This is the police, don't hang up."

"The police?"

"Mr. Mittleberg, my name is Renée Ballard. I'm a detective with the Los Angeles Police. You recently talked with a colleague of mine named Bosch about containers made by American Storage Products. Do you remember?"

"That was a couple of months ago."

"Correct. We are still working that case."

"It's ten fifteen. What is so urgent that this couldn't—"

"Mr. Mittleberg, I'm sorry, but it is urgent. You told Detective Bosch that your company made some direct sales of the containers to commercial accounts."

"We do, yes."

"Are you at home, Mr. Mittleberg?"

"Where else would I be?"

"Do you have a laptop or access to sales records involving those commercial accounts?"

There was a pause while Mittleberg considered the question. Ballard held her breath. The case had been full of long shots. It was about time one of them paid off. If Dillon operated a business that ran close to the line—she remembered he had commented about competition—then he might be just the kind of man to seek a direct-sale discount from a manufacturer.

"I have some access to records," Mittleberg finally said.

"I have the name of a company," Ballard said. "Can you see if they have ever been a customer of ASP?"

"Hold the line. I'm going to my home office."

Ballard waited while Mittleberg got to his computer. She heard a partially muffled discussion as he told someone that he was talking to the police and he would be up as soon as he was finished.

"Okay," he then said directly into the phone. "I'm at my computer. What's the name of the company."

"It's called Chemi-Cal Bio Services," Ballard said. "Chemi-Cal is broken into two—"

"No, nothing," Mittleberg said.

"You spelled it with a dash?"

"Nothing beginning with C-H-E-M."

Ballard felt deflated. She needed something more in order to go all in on Dillon. Then she remembered the truck she had seen on the day they met on Hollywood Boulevard.

"Okay, try just CCB Services, please," she said urgently.

She heard typing and then Mittleberg responded.

"Yes," he said. "A customer since 2008. They order soft plastics."

Ballard stood up, holding the phone tight against her ear.

"What kind of soft plastics?" she asked.

"Storage containers. Different sizes."

Ballard remembered Bosch giving her the ASP container he had bought. It was still in the trunk of her city ride.

"Including the twenty-five-gallon container with the snap-on top?"

There was a pause while Mittleberg checked the records.

"Yes," he finally said. "He ordered those."

"Thank you, Mr. Mittleberg," Ballard said. "One of us will follow up with you during business hours."

She disconnected and went back to her locker. She put the murder book back on the top shelf and opened her briefcase, retrieving one of the business cards Dillon had given her. His company had an address on Saticoy Street in Van Nuys.

When Ballard entered the watch office, Munroe was still looking up at the TV screen.

"Anything new?" she asked.

"Not much," Munroe said. "But they did say the dead guys were persons of interest in an abduction case. It's gotta be the Bosch thing. You hear from him?"

"Not yet. I'm heading out to do an interview on my hobby case. Might not be back for roll call."

Ballard stared at the screen for a moment. It was the same reporter on another stand-up.

"If Bosch happens to show up here, can you give him this? He'll know what it means."

She handed him the card with Dillon's name and business address on it. Munroe looked at it disinterestedly and then put it into one of his shirt pockets.

"Will do," he said. "But stay in touch, Ballard, okay? Lemme know where you are."

"You got it, L-T."

"And if I need you on a call, the hobby case goes back on the shelf and you come running."

"Roger that."

Ballard doubled back to the detective bureau and grabbed a rover out of the charging station and the keys to the city ride. She left out the back door into the parking lot.

Ballard took Laurel Canyon Boulevard over the mountain and then down into the Valley. It was near midnight when she turned down Saticoy and into an industrial sector lined with warehouses and fleet lots near the Van Nuys Airport.

Chemi-Cal Bio Services was in a warehouse park called the Saticoy Industry Center, where manufacturing and service businesses were lined side by side in duplicate duplex warehouses. Ballard drove down the center lane and by Dillon's business and then out the other side of the industrial park. It looked like none of the businesses were open this late at night. She found parking on a side street and walked back.

Dillon had only a small sign on his warehouse. It wasn't the kind of business that drew customers who were either walking or driving by. His was the kind of service you found through internet searches or recommendations from professionals in the same arena—detectives, coroners, forensic specialists. The sign was on the door next to the side-by-side garage doors. The building was freestanding but literally no more than two feet away from the identical structures on either side of it.

Ballard knocked on the door, though she did not expect any sort of response. She stepped back and looked up and down the access lane, checking to see if her knock on the hollow metal had aroused any interest.

It had not.

Ballard stepped over to the thin channel between CCB and its neighbor to the north, a building with no sign or other identifiers on it. The alley, if it was big enough to be classified as such, was unlit. Ballard poked a flashlight into the space and saw it was strewn with debris but passable. At the far end, which Ballard guessed was eighty feet away, there was no gate or other obstacle.

Ballard tentatively stuck one foot into the slim opening. She kicked away a pile of old and dusty breathing masks that she could only imagine had come from CCB.

Another step in and then there was no longer anything tentative about her advance. She moved quickly down the passage, concrete block walls on either side of her, toward the opening ahead. Remembering the old movie gag about the walls closing in on the hero, she thought herself into a bout of vertigo and had to put a hand out on one of the walls for support and to keep her balance.

She stumbled out of the narrow opening and into a rear alley and bent over, hands on knees, and waited for the dizziness to pass. When it did, she straightened up and looked around. It was the cleanest alley she had ever seen. No debris, no junk, no impromptu storage of old vehicles or anything else. Each unit had its own neatly kept and closed trash bin that was secured inside a concrete corral. Ballard opened the bin behind CCB and found it empty except for a couple of crumpled to-go bags and several empty coffee cups. Ballard expected there to be bloody mop heads and other debris from cleaning crime scenes, but nothing like that was here.

There was a single rear door with just CCB painted on it. Ballard checked it but it was locked with a deadbolt. She knocked anyway to complete the due diligence but did not wait by the door for a reply she was confident wasn't coming. Moving back into the narrow passage between the buildings, she shone the light up the walls to the slim slice of night sky. The roofline was about twenty feet up. Because the warehouse was windowless, she knew there was a strong possibility that there would be a skylight on the roof to allow in natural light as well as ventilation.

Ballard put the end of the flashlight in her mouth and then a hand on each of the walls of the two buildings she stood between. She then raised her left foot and angled it against one wall, using the mortar line between two of the concrete blocks to find a shallow toehold. Pressing her hands against the wall and gripping the upper edges, she raised herself up and brought her right foot against the opposite wall, angling it until it found purchase. She was wearing rubber-soled work shoes favored by professionals who worked a lot on their feet. They were chosen for comfort over style, and they grabbed the edges of the mortar lines well.

Ballard slowly started climbing the walls of the passage between the two buildings, using her weight to counterbalance her body and to keep from falling. The ascent was slow and it was toward a complete unknown, but she pressed on, pausing once when she heard a car in the entrance lane of the industrial park. She quickly grabbed the flashlight out of her mouth and switched it off. She was halfway up the climb and could do nothing but hold still.

The car out in the lane drove by the passage without stopping. Ballard waited a moment, then turned the flashlight back on and started climbing again.

It took ten minutes to reach the top and then Ballard put her arm over the parapet around the roof of the CCB warehouse and carefully pulled her body over and onto the gravel rooftop. She stayed on her back for almost a minute, catching her breath and staring at the dark sky.

She rolled onto her side and got up. Brushing off her clothes, she knew that she had burned through another suit. She was planning to take Monday and Tuesday off once her partner returned. She would complete all her laundry errands then.

Ballard looked around and saw that she had been wrong about there being a skylight on the roof. There were actually four of them—two over each garage bay—plastic bubbles shining in the moonlight. There was also a steel exhaust chimney that rose six feet above the roofline. The diffuser at the top was coated black by smoke and creosote.

Ballard inspected the skylights, moving from one to another with her flashlight, stepping around a pool of standing water that covered part of the roof. There were no lights on in the CCB warehouse below, but it didn't matter. Visibility with the flashlight was limited. It appeared that each of the once-clear plastic bubbles had been haphazardly sprayed with white paint from the inside.

This was curious to Ballard. It appeared to be a move designed to keep anyone from looking down at activities below. But there were no taller buildings in the area with views through the skylights. Ballard thought about the boys caught earlier in the week attempting to glimpse naked women through the skylights of a strip club. Here, the attempt at skylight privacy seemed unwarranted.

Each of the skylights was hinged on one edge and could presumably be opened from within. This was the moment of decision. She had certainly already trespassed on private property but she would be crossing a more important line if she took things further. It was a line she had crossed before.

She had no direct evidence of anything but plenty of circumstantial facts that pointed the needle toward Dillon. She had the fact that the crime scene cleaner was in Hollywood with his van and his chemicals and cleansers on the night Daisy Clayton was taken. And she had the fact that he had ordered storage containers with the same brand mark that had ended up on the victim's body, and in the size that would have been used to store and bleach it. The circumstances of the murder pointed to a killer who knew something about law enforcement and took the effort to rid the body of potential evidence to an extreme level.

She knew she could call Judge Wickwire, her go-to, and run these things by her in an effort to establish probable cause. But in her mind she could hear the judge's voice saying, "Renée, I don't think you have it."

But Ballard thought she did have the right man. She decided she had come this far and was not turning around. She reached into a pocket and took out a pair of rubber gloves. Then she started checking the skylights.

Each of the rooftop bubbles was locked, but one of them felt loose on its frame. She moved around it, stepping in the water that had accumulated around its rear edge. The standing water was apparently a longtime problem. The moisture had worked its corrosive magic on the skylight's hinges.

Ballard put the light in her mouth and reached down with both hands to the frame. She pulled up and the hinge screws gave way, coming out of the wet plaster abutment below the frame without protest. She pushed the skylight up until it rolled back on its rounded surface and into the water.

She pointed her light down and was looking at the flat white top of a box truck parked in the bay directly below the opening.

Ballard estimated that it was a drop of no more than eight feet.

46

Ballard lowered herself through the roof opening and hung for a moment by her hands before letting go and falling to the roof of the truck. She hit it off balance and fell onto her back, momentarily stunning herself and leaving a dent on the truck's roof.

After lying still and recovering for a few seconds, she crawled toward the front of the truck, slipped down onto the cab, and then climbed down the side of it, using the sideview mirror and door handle as toeholds and grips.

Once she was on the concrete floor, Ballard checked the warehouse's doors to see if she would have a quick escape route if needed. But the deadbolts on both front and back doors required a key on the inside as well.

With her flashlight in hand, she located a panel next to the front door with what she believed were the garage door switches, but like the doors, these required a key to operate. Ballard realized that she was going to have to figure out how to get up and out through the skylight or somehow break down one of the doors. Neither was a good choice.

Below the garage-door panel was a row of light switches that were not key controlled. She flicked them up and two rows of overhead fluorescents came on, brightly lighting the warehouse. She stood there for a long moment, studying the layout of the place. The two side-by-side parking bays took up the front half of the warehouse, while the rear half was dedicated to the storage of supplies and a small office area with a couch. In the corner opposite the office was an incinerator for burning the biologically hazardous materials collected at crime scenes.

One of the parking bays was empty, but there were fresh oil drips on the floor where a truck would normally sit. Ballard knew that the truck backed into the other bay was not the one she had seen earlier in the week when she had met Dillon. It was painted differently, with the full name of the company on the driver's-side door and not the large CCB across the side panel. It was older, had low air in its tires, and appeared to her to have been sitting in disuse. It seemed to put the lie to what Dillon had said about having two trucks and four employees ready to go 24/7. He apparently was a one-man operation.

It all added up to Ballard realizing that the truck Dillon currently used was out there somewhere, and she had no idea if he was on a job and could arrive back at the warehouse at any time or if he simply took his work truck home at night. It didn't seem to Ballard that it would go over well with fellow residents to park a biohazard truck in the neighborhood. But Ballard had not seen any personal car that could belong to Dillon parked near the warehouse.

She decided to move quickly with her search and started with a survey of the desk standing against the wall near the rear door of the warehouse. Ballard scanned for any information or notation about a job that might give her an idea of where Dillon and the truck were. But after finding nothing, she moved on, attempting to open the desk's file drawers to see if there were any historical records regarding the purchase of supplies from American Storage Products.

The drawers were locked and that ended her search of the desk.

The warehouse was neat and orderly. Against the wall opposite the incinerator were large plastic barrels containing cleaning and disinfecting liquids with hand pumps for filling smaller containers for use on individual jobs. There were shelves stacked high with empty plastic containers. Ballard checked these for size and the ASP logo that had left a mark on Daisy Clayton, but there was nothing that would be large enough to contain her body and nothing with the logo. She realized that she had neglected to ask Mittleberg the time frame of the orders from CCB that he had seen on his computer.

There was a small bathroom with a shower and it looked like it had been recently cleaned. She opened the medicine cabinet and found routine first-aid materials on its shelves.

Next to the bathroom was a closet in which Ballard found several white jumpsuits on hangers, *CCB* embroidered on the left breast pocket of each, and *Roger* on the right—further evidence that Dillon's claim of fielding four employees was self-aggrandizement.

Ballard closed the closet and stepped over to the incinerator. It was a square stand-alone appliance with stainless-steel sidings and an exhaust pipe going straight up through the ceiling. The front was double-doored, and a matching stainless-steel staging table was positioned in front of it.

Ballard opened one of the doors of the burning chamber and the other opened automatically with it. She pointed the beam of her flashlight inside and got a sharp kickback of reflecting light. The interior panels of the chamber were so clean as to be shiny, and it looked like the ash trap below the flame bars had been vacuumed after its last use. The incinerator looked brand-new. She could see a gas pilot light burning blue in the back corner.

She closed the incinerator doors and turned around. She saw no shop vac or any other kind of vacuum that could have been used to clean it. She then remembered seeing equipment in the truck Dillon had driven to the job site earlier in the week and assumed that he carried both wet and dry vacuums with him.

This thought drew her focus to the truck parked in the second bay. It was the last place for her to search. It had been backed into the warehouse and she was staring at the two double doors of the rear compartment.

Ballard next checked the license plate. The registration sticker was two years out of date. It was clear this truck was not part of CCB's active fleet.

She pulled back a handle that disengaged upper and lower locking pins on the doors and pulled one of them open. She stepped back to swing it to the side and saw that the truck might have been taken out of service but it was being used as storage. It was full of cleaning and containment supplies packaged in bulk. A tower of twenty-four-packs of paper towel rolls, five-gallon containers of soap, a trash can full of brand-new mops, plastic-wrapped cases of aerosol cleaners and air fresheners. Leaning against one side of the interior was a thick stack of cardboard boxes that needed to be folded into shape for use.

It was essentially a wall of supplies that blocked her view into the truck. There was a handle mounted just inside the door. Ballard grabbed it and pulled herself up, using the truck's rear bumper as a step. The inside of the truck was shielded from the fluorescents. Ballard used her light to cut through the shadows and look farther in. She quickly realized that the supplies were stacked at the back of the truck only as a blind and that there was an open space behind them. She shoved the trash can and mops in and out of the way and moved into the truck to look.

On the floor there were some old food wrappers, napkins, and fast-food bags strewn around a thin mattress that looked like it had been taken from a folding cot. A dirty blanket and pillow were thrown haphazardly on top of it and a battery-operated lantern was on the floor. Ballard moved the blanket with her foot and exposed a metal loop bolted to the floor of the truck. She squatted down and looked closely at it, saw the scratch marks on the interior of the loop, and knew it could be used to handcuff or chain a person to the mattress. She noticed that there was a slightly sour smell to this area of the truck. It told Ballard someone had recently been inhabiting this space.

Ballard suddenly knew that it was the scent of fear. She had recognized it in herself before. She had heard of dogs trained to track it. Ballard knew she was in a place where someone had trembled and feared for her life.

Something on the floor next to the mattress caught her eye and Ballard leaned farther down to look. On closer examination, she realized it was a broken fingernail that had been painted pink.

The truck suddenly started shaking as a sharp metallic sound engulfed the warehouse. Ballard's first thought was earthquake, but then she quickly identified it as one of the aluminum garage doors rolling up. Someone was about to enter.

She killed the flashlight, pulled her weapon, and thought about quickly climbing out of the truck. But that would put her out in the open and exposed. She held her place and listened. She heard the high idle of a truck engine but no movement.

Then the engine revved and the vehicle entered the garage. After Ballard judged that it was in the bay next to her, the engine was killed.

Again, for several seconds there was only silence. Ballard didn't even hear the sound of anyone getting out of the cab. And then the ratcheting sound of the garage door began again, this time as it was lowered.

Ballard listened intently, her ears her only tool at the moment.

She had to assume that the driver of the truck was Dillon. She listed three things in her mind that he could have noticed upon his arrival. The lights of the warehouse were on, one of the out-of-service truck's back doors was standing open, and there was a missing skylight above. She had to assume that Dillon would notice all three and be aware that there had been a break-in. It remained to be seen if he thought the intruder had come and gone or was still in the warehouse. If he called 9-1-1, Ballard knew she would probably be arrested and her career would be over. If he chose not to call, then he would be confirming that he didn't want police in the warehouse because of the things that had gone on in here. She flashed on the incinerator, its exhaust pipe coated black on the roof from use but its burning chamber spotlessly cleaned and vacuumed.

Ballard looked down at the thin mattress on the floor. She wondered if she would ever know who had been in this dark place and shivered under the thin blanket. Who had broken her nail trying to find an escape route. Her anger toward Dillon began to grow to the point of no return. To the killing place she knew she carried inside.

Ballard heard the door of the other truck open and its occupant climb out and drop to the concrete floor. Her only view out to the warehouse was through the open door at the back of the truck she was in, and that gave a tight angle of the space beyond. She waited and listened, trying to pick up Dillon's footsteps and movements but hearing nothing.

Suddenly the back door of the truck she hid in was slammed shut, plunging Ballard into darkness. She heard the handle on the outside turn and the locking pins at the top and bottom of the door snap into place. She was locked in. She gripped her gun in one hand and the flashlight in the other, but chose to stay in darkness, thinking it might keep her ears sharper.

"Okay, I know you're in there. Who are you?"

Ballard froze. Though she had spoken to Dillon only once before, she knew it was his voice.

She said nothing in return.

"Looks like you broke my skylight pretty good. And that makes me mad because I don't have the money for that."

Ballard pulled her phone and checked the screen. She was basically in a metal box inside a concrete box and she had no service. And the rover she had taken from the station was sitting in the mobile charger in her car two blocks away.

Dillon started pounding on the door, a sharp metal-on-metal sound.

"Come on, talk to me. Maybe you agree to pay the damages and I don't call the cops. How about that?"

Ballard knew that there was no way he was going to call the police. Not with what she had found in the truck. She needed to put that in her favor. She started to make her way toward the truck's back doors. She had the gun. Most burglars don't carry firearms, because it increases prison time if they are caught. Dillon would not anticipate her having one.

She startled when he hit the door again.

"You hear that? I've got a gun and I'm not fucking around.

You need to tell me you are ready to come out with your hands where I can see them!"

That changed things. Ballard stopped moving forward and slowly crouched down to the floor in case Dillon started shooting through the thin steel skin of the truck. She held her weapon in a two-handed grip and was ready to approximate the origin of shots and fire back.

"Okay, fuck it. I'm opening the door and I'm just going to start shooting. It'll be self-defense. I know lots of cops and they'll believe me. You'll be dead and I'll—"

There was a loud bang on the back door of the truck—this one not metal-on-metal—and Dillon didn't finish the threat. This was followed by the sound of metal clattering on the concrete. Ballard assumed that it was Dillon's gun skittering across the floor. She knew at this point that there was a second person out there.

The handle on the truck's back door was turned and the upper and lower locks released. The door opened, flooding the inside of the box with light. Ballard kept in a low crouch, using the trash can and mops as a blind. She raised her weapon to ready position.

"Renée, you in there? It's all clear."

It was Bosch.

BOSCH

47

Bosch helped Ballard out of the back of the truck and down to the ground. The man he had hit with his gun was still on the floor and unconscious. Ballard looked at him after climbing down.

"Is that Dillon?" Bosch asked.

"It's him," Ballard said.

She turned and looked at Bosch.

"How did you find me?" she asked. "I thought maybe you were up at the SIS scene."

"I was but I got out of there because you and I were supposed to work," Bosch said. "But when I got to Hollywood you were gone. I talked to Money and he gave me the card you left."

Bosch pointed to the man on the floor.

"I pull up here and he was opening the garage. I could tell that something was wrong by the way he was hesitating and looking around before driving in. I figured that you were inside. I snuck in behind his truck before he brought down the door."

"Well, I guess we're even then. You saved me."

"You had your weapons. You would have taken care of things, I think."

"I don't know about that."

"I do. When I said 'weapons,' I meant more than your gun. I know what you can do."

Bosch looked down at Dillon's body, still unconscious and prone on the floor.

"I don't have cuffs," Bosch said.

"I do," Ballard said.

She stepped forward, taking the cuffs off the back of her belt.

"Hold on a second," Bosch said.

He moved toward the shelves where supplies were stocked and stopped to pick up Dillon's gun and snug it into his waistband. He then grabbed a roll of duct tape and came back.

"Keep your cuffs," he said. "Let's do it this way."

"Why?" Ballard asked. "We have to call it in."

"'We'? Not you. You get out of here. I'll handle it."

"No. I'm not going to let them blame you for what I did. If anybody gets fired, it's going to be me."

Bosch spoke as he used the tape to bind Dillon's wrists and then feet.

"I can't get fired. I don't have a job, remember? You need to go now and leave all this to me."

"What about evidence? There's a mattress and food wrappings in the truck. I found a pink fingernail. He didn't stop with Daisy Clayton."

"I know. He just got better at it."

He glanced over his shoulder at the incinerator, and then back up at Ballard.

"I bet he didn't have this place back then—with Daisy," he said. "Or that incinerator."

Ballard nodded somberly.

"I wonder how many," she said.

Bosch took strips of tape and put them across Dillon's mouth and eyes.

"I'm going to try to find that out as soon as you're out of here," he said.

"Harry…" Ballard said.

"Go now. Go back to the station and ask Money if I ever came by. Say you never saw me."

"You're sure about this?"

"I'm sure. It's the only way. When I have everything ready, I'll call it in to Van Nuys Division. And I'll let you know. No blowback on you. If they get mad at someone, it will be me, but they'll have to think real hard about that if I offer them this guy in a package wrapped in audiotape."

"What tape?"

"I've got a tape recorder in my car."

Dillon suddenly groaned and shook his body. He was coming to and realizing his situation. He tried to yell something through the tape that was gagging him.

Bosch looked at Ballard and put a finger on his mouth for silence, then twirled it in the air. It was time for her to get moving.

Ballard pointed to the locked door at the front of the warehouse and made a signal like she was turning a lock with a key. Bosch nodded and leaned down next to Dillon's body. He started checking his pockets for keys. Dillon loudly objected, yelling nonsensically through the duct tape.

"Sorry, buddy," Bosch said. "Just checking the pockets for weapons and other bad things."

He pulled out a set of keys and signaled Ballard to follow him, then unlocked the door and walked her out. He saw his car where he had left it parked in front of one of the other warehouses down the line. He spoke quietly to Ballard.

"Keep your eye on him for a second while I pull my car up and grab some gloves and the recorder. Just stay here by the door."

"Will do," Ballard whispered.

Bosch walked off. Ballard stopped him.

"Harry."

He looked back at her.

"Thanks."

"You already said that."

"That was for before. This is for you taking the weight on this."

"What weight? It'll be a breeze."

He headed off toward his car. Ballard watched him go.

48

Bosch was alone with Roger Dillon now. He had him propped up against one of the big barrels full of cleaning solvents. Bosch had forcefully pulled the tape off his captive's mouth, eliciting loud cries of pain and subsequent cursing. He'd left his eyes covered.

Before yanking the tape, Bosch had moved around the warehouse, planning and prepping for the interview. He had pulled the chair away from the desk and set it five feet away from Dillon, front and center. He had cut the tape around Dillon's ankles and spread his legs on the concrete floor.

Bosch put two metal mop buckets on the floor on either side of his chair. One had two inches of water in it. Into the other he had poured a bottle of sulfuric acid that he had found on one of the storage shelves.

He then sat down in front of Dillon.

"Are you awake now?" Bosch asked.

"What the fuck is this?" Dillon answered. "Who are you?"

"Doesn't matter who I am. Tell me about Daisy Clayton."

"I don't know what or who you're talking about. Untie me right the fuck now."

"Sure you do. Nine years ago? The child hooker on Sunset

you grabbed from out front of the liquor store? She had to be your first, I'm thinking, or one of your first. Before you had this setup, back when you had to worry about where and how to get rid of the bodies."

There was a momentary pause in Dillon's response that told Bosch he had thrown a strike.

"You're crazy and you're going to jail," Dillon said. "All this—illegal. Doesn't matter what I tell you. I could say I killed Kennedy, Tupac, and Biggie Smalls and it wouldn't matter. This is all illegal search and seizure. I'm not even a cop and I know that. So just call it in, motherfucker. Let's get this over with."

Bosch leaned back in the desk chair. It squeaked.

"One problem with all of that," he said. "I'm not a cop. I'm not here to call anything in. I'm here for Daisy Clayton. That's it."

"Bullshit," Dillon said. "I can tell. You're a cop."

"Tell me about Daisy."

"Nothing to tell. I don't know her."

"You grabbed her that night. You took her."

"Whatever, man. I want a lawyer."

"There are no lawyers here. We're past that."

"Then do what you gotta do, bro. I'm not saying shit."

His chair squeaking, Bosch reached down to the bucket containing the acid. He carefully lifted it and moved it to a spot between Dillon's spread legs.

"What are you doing?" Dillon asked.

Bosch said nothing. The fumes from the acid did the talking.

"Is that the sulfuric?" Dillon asked, panic rising in his voice. "I can smell it. What the fuck are you doing?"

"What's it matter, Roger?" Bosch said. "You say I'm a cop, right? I won't do anything to hurt you. Not if it's illegal."

"All right, okay, I believe you. You're not a cop. Just get that stuff away from me. You don't want to fuck with it. The fumes alone can—Wait a minute. What did you pour it into? It eats through metal. You know that, right?"

"Then I guess we don't have a lot of time. Daisy Clayton. Tell me about her."

"I told you—"

Dillon suddenly abandoned his argument and started screaming *"Help!"* at the top of his lungs. Bosch did nothing and after twenty seconds Dillon stopped, knowing the effort was useless.

"Ironic, huh?" Bosch said. "You designed and built this place so nobody could get out and nobody could hear anybody's calls for help. And now…here we are. Go ahead, keep on screaming."

"Look, please, I'm sorry," Dillon said. "I'm sorry if I upset you. I'm sorry if I ever did any—"

Bosch reached out with his foot and slid the bucket a few inches closer to Dillon's crotch. Dillon tried to lean back but there was no place for his body to go. He turned his face to the right.

"Please," he said. "The fumes. It's getting in my lungs."

"I read a story in the newspaper once," Bosch replied. "It was about this guy who got sulfuric acid spilled on his hands. He quickly put his hands under a faucet to wash it off and that only made it hurt worse. Water more than doubles the pain, but if you don't flush the acid it will eat right through your skin."

"Jesus Christ," Dillon said. *"What do you want?"*

"You know what I want. I want the story. Daisy Clayton. Two thousand nine. Tell me the story."

Dillon kept his face turned away from the fumes.

"Get it away!" he cried. "It's burning my lungs."

"Two thousand nine," Bosch said as he sat back in the chair and it squeaked again.

"Look, what do you want?" Dillon said. "You want me to say I did it? Fine, I did it. Whatever it is, I did it. So let's just call the cops. I know you're not a cop but let's call the cops and I'll tell them I did it. I promise. I'll tell them. I'll tell them I did the others, too. As many as you want. I'll tell them I did them all."

Bosch reached into his pocket for the mini-recorder he had retrieved from his car.

"How many others?" he asked. "Tell me their names."

He hit the record button.

Dillon shook his head and then kept it turned away from the bucket.

"Jesus," Dillon said. "This is crazy."

Bosch put his thumb over the microphone.

"Give me a name, Dillon. You want to get out of here, you want me to call the cops, give me a name. I can't believe you if you can't give me a name."

He freed the microphone.

"Please, let me go," Dillon said. "I won't tell anyone about this. I'll just forget about it. Just let me go. Please."

Bosch gave the bucket another push with his foot. It was now touching the inner seam of Dillon's jeans. He covered the microphone again and whenever he spoke.

"Last chance, Roger," he said. "You start talking or I start walking. I leave the bucket and maybe it burns through and maybe it doesn't."

"No, you can't do this," Dillon said. "Please. I didn't do anything!"

"But you just said you did the others. Which is it?"

"All right, whatever. I killed them. I killed them all, okay?"

"Tell me their names. Tell me one name, then I can believe you."

"That Daisy girl. Her."

"No, I gave you that name. You have to give me a name."

"I don't have any names!"

"That's really too bad."

Bosch stood up as if to leave. The chair squeaked, underlining his intentions.

"Sarah Bender!"

Bosch stood still. The name had a slight resonance but he couldn't place it. He put his thumb on the mic.

"Who?"

He released his thumb.

"Sarah Bender. She's the only name I know. I remember her because that one made the papers. Her father didn't give a shit about her until she was missing, then it was boo-hoo all over the news."

Thumb on.

"And you killed her?"

Thumb off.

Dillon nodded quickly.

"She was out front of a coffee shop. I remember because it was only a block from the LAPD station. I grabbed her right under their fucking noses."

Thumb on.

"What did you do with her afterward?"

Thumb off.

Dillon nodded in the direction of the corner where the incinerator was located.

"I burned her."

Bosch paused.

"What about Daisy Clayton?"

"Her too."

"You didn't have the burner then."

"No, I was working out of my own garage then. Just getting the business started."

"So, what did you do?"

"I cleaned her. With bleach. I didn't have my acid permits yet."

"You used your bathtub?"

"No, I put her in one of my bio containers. With a top. I filled it with bleach and left it like that for a day. Rode around with it while I worked."

"Who else besides Daisy and Sarah?"

"I told you. I can't remember their names."

"What about the most recent one? The girl with the pink fingernails. What was her name?"

"I don't remember."

"Sure you do. You had her in the back of that truck. What was her name?"

"Don't you see? I never asked her name. I didn't care. Their names didn't matter. Nobody missed them. Nobody cared. They didn't count."

Bosch stared down at him for a long moment. He had what he needed in the way of confirmation. But he wasn't done.

"What about their parents? Their mothers—did they count?"

"Most of the girls out there? I got news for you, their parents didn't give a shit about them."

Bosch thought about Elizabeth Clayton and her sad end. He put it all on Dillon. He pocketed the recorder and reached down to the bucket. He picked it up, ready to dump its fiery contents over Dillon's head.

Even blinded by the tape, Dillon knew the decision Bosch was making.

"Don't," he said pleadingly.

Bosch reached down to the bucket of water. He quietly lifted it and put it down between Dillon's legs, making sure to slosh the liquid. He then put the bucket of acid down to the side.

"Jesus, be careful!" Dillon exclaimed.

Bosch picked up the roll of duct tape and started wrapping tape around Dillon and the barrel, making sure he could not get up or go anywhere. He did two turns around Dillon's neck, leaving him the ability to keep his face turned from the bucket. When he was finished, he tore off a small piece of tape, pulled the recorder from his pocket, wiped all sides and buttons against his shirt, then taped it to Dillon's chest.

"You sit tight now," he said.

"Where are you going?" Dillon demanded.

"To get the police, like you asked."

"And you're just going to leave me here?"

"That's the plan."

"You can't do that. Sulfuric is very volatile. It could eat through the bucket. It could—"

"I'll be quick."

Bosch patted Dillon on the shoulder in a supportive way. He then picked up the bucket containing the acid and walked toward the door he had unlocked for Ballard. He left it unlocked behind him.

Outside, Bosch walked into the narrow passageway between Dillon's warehouse and the one next door. He poured the acid out on top of the accumulated debris and discarded the bucket there as well. He then exited the passage and walked toward his Jeep.

49

Van Nuys Division was less than a mile away. Bosch drove there. This was not because he had any intention of speaking to the police in person, but because it was the only place he knew of in the area that still had operating pay phones. There was a bank of them at the bottom of the stairs below the station's main exit—placed there as a convenience for inmates who were released from the station's jail and needed to call loved ones or lawyers for pickup.

Bosch no longer had the SIS phone. Cespedes had asked for it back when Bosch announced that he was leaving the Cortez shooting scene and catching a ride with a patrol officer back to his car.

Next to the phone bank, there was also a change machine but it took only five-dollar bills. Bosch had two calls to make but reluctantly cashed a five into twenty quarters. He first called Ballard's number from memory and she answered right away.

"He admitted to Daisy and to others," he said. "Too many for him to even remember."

"Jesus," Ballard said. "He just told you all of this? Who were the others?"

"He only remembered one name, and that was because it made news and there was some heat at the time. Sarah Bender, you remember her? Her dad was some kind of a big shot, according to Dillon. I remember the name but can't place the case. I want to use it as the control case. I brought up Daisy but he brought up Sarah Bender. If we can confirm it, we—"

"We can. Confirm it, I mean. Sarah Bender's dad has that club on Sunset—Bender's on the Strip. There's usually a line out the door."

"Right. I know it. Down near the Roxy."

"Sarah disappeared about three years ago. George Bender went very public, hired private eyes to find her. Supposedly he even went to the dark side for help when he didn't think the LAPD was seriously looking for her."

"What's that mean, the 'dark side'?" Bosch asked.

"You know, he had connections outside the law working on it. Mercenary types. There was a rumor that his backers in the club were organized crime. When his daughter went missing, that became part of the investigation, but it didn't pan out. I think the official line was that she was a runaway."

"It may have looked that way but she wasn't a runaway. Dillon grabbed her outside a coffee shop."

"I remember the father also put up a reward. They started getting sightings all over the country. People who wanted to cash in. Eventually it all went away and now it's just another L.A. mystery."

"Well, mystery solved. He said he killed her, put her in the incinerator."

"Motherfucker. How'd you get him to tell you about her?"

"Doesn't matter. He did and I didn't feed him the name. He came out with it. He said her and Daisy. The rest he couldn't remember by name. Not even the woman with the pink finger-nails."

There was a pause before Ballard spoke.

"What did he say about her?"

"Nothing. He said he never knew her name in the first place, let alone forgot it."

"Did you ask when he grabbed her?"

"No. I guess I should have."

"I think it was recent. When I was in the back of that truck…I could smell her fear. I knew that's where he kept her."

Bosch didn't know how to respond to that. But it fed into the frustration and anger growing in him. The more he thought about it, the more he regretted dumping out the sulfuric acid on the ground and not Dillon's head.

Ballard spoke again before he could.

"Is he still…"

"Alive? I'll probably regret it the rest of my life but, yeah, he's alive."

"No, it's just…never mind. What will you do with him now?"

"I'll call it in, let Van Nuys sort it out."

"Do you have him on tape?"

"Yes, but it won't matter. Inadmissible. They'll have to start over, build a case. I'll tell them to start with the inside of that truck. Fingerprints, DNA."

There was a long pause as they both contemplated how their illegal actions had imperiled any sort of traditional way of bring-ing Dillon to justice.

Ballard finally spoke.

"Let's hope something's there," she said. "I don't want him walking free again."

"He won't," Bosch said. "I promise you that."

More silence followed as they considered what Bosch had just said.

It was time to hang up, but Bosch didn't want to. He realized it might be the last time they would speak. Their relationship had been held together by the case. Now the case was over.

"I need to make the call," Bosch finally said.

"Okay," Ballard said.

"I guess maybe I'll see you around, okay?"

"Sure. Stay in touch."

Bosch hung up. It was a weird ending. He jangled the change in his hand as he thought about how to handle the call that would send investigators to Dillon's warehouse. He needed to protect himself but wanted to make sure that the call created an urgent response.

He dropped quarters into the phone's slot but then his intentions were hijacked. Thoughts of Elizabeth Clayton hit him, and a deep grief washed over him as he imagined her sad ending, alone in a seedy motel room, empty pill bottle on the bed table, haunted by the ghost of her lost daughter. Then he remembered Dillon's dismissal of his victims as women and girls who didn't count or matter and suddenly he was filled with anger. He wanted revenge.

When the dial tone pulled him out of his dark reverie he punched in 411 and asked the operator for the number of Bender's on the Strip.

He was about to drop in more quarters to make the call when caution pushed through the red glare of vengeance. He turned and looked up into the overhang of the police building. He counted at least two cameras.

He hung up the phone and walked away.

Bosch moved through the government plaza toward Van Nuys Boulevard, where he had parked the Jeep. He popped the back hatch and reached in for his bad-weather attire, a Dodgers cap and an army jacket with a high collar that offered protection from wind and rain. He put them on, closed the hatch, and crossed the street to a row of twenty-four-hour bail bonds offices. At the end of the row was a pay phone attached to the side wall of the building.

He pulled his hat down and his collar up as he approached. He dropped in quarters and made the call, checking his watch while he waited for it to ring. It was 1:45 a.m. and he knew the clubs on the Sunset Strip would close at two.

The call was answered by a woman whose voice was engulfed by a background of loud electronic music.

"Is there an office?" Bosch yelled. "Give me the office."

He was put on hold for nearly a minute before a male voice answered.

"Mr. Bender?"

"He's not here. Who's this, please?"

Bosch didn't hesitate.

"This is the Los Angeles police. I need to speak to Mr. Bender right now. It's an emergency. It's about his daughter."

"Is this bullshit? The guy's been through enough with you people."

"This is very serious, sir. I have news about his daughter and need to speak with him right now. Where can I reach him?"

"Hold on."

He was put on hold for another minute. And then another male voice came on the line.

"Who is this?"

"Mr. Bender?"

"I said, who is this?"

"It doesn't matter who this is. I'm sorry to be so blunt with news that is so bad. But your daughter was murdered three years ago. And the man who killed her is sitting in a —"

"Who the fuck is this?"

"I'm not going to tell you that, sir. What I'm going to do is give you an address where you will find the man who killed your daughter waiting for you. The door will be unlocked."

"How can I believe you? You call up here out of the blue, won't give your name. How do I —"

"Mr. Bender, I'm sorry. I can't give you any more than what I have. And I need to do it now before I change my mind."

Bosch let that hang in the darkness between them for a bit.

"Do you want the address?" he finally asked.

"Yes," Bender said. "Give it to me."

50

After supplying Bender with the Saticoy address, Bosch hung up without a further word. He left the phone and started across the deserted boulevard, back toward his car.

A collision of thoughts went through his head. Faces came too. Elizabeth's face. And her daughter's—known to him only in photos. Bosch thought about his own daughter and about George Bender losing his, and the blinding grief something like that would bring.

He realized then that he had put Bender on a path that would simply trade a momentary urge for justice and vengeance for another kind of guilt and grief. For both of them.

In the middle of the boulevard, Bosch turned around.

He went back to the pay phone for one final call. He dialed a direct line to Valley Bureau detectives and asked for the investigator working the late show. He got a detective named Palmer and told him that there was a killer left bound and waiting for him in a warehouse on Saticoy. He said there was a recorder with a confession on it that should jump-start an investigation and prosecution. There was evidence in the back of a truck in the warehouse as well.

He gave him the exact address and told him to hurry.

"Why's that?" Palmer asked. "Sounds like this guy isn't going anywhere."

"Because you've got competition," Bosch said.

BALLARD AND BOSCH

EPILOGUE

Bosch came out of the glass doors of the Medical Examiner's Office and found Ballard waiting for him, leaning on the front wall.

"Is it her?" she asked.

Bosch nodded somberly.

"But I knew it would be," he said.

"I'm sorry," Ballard said.

He nodded his thanks. He noticed that her hair was wet and slicked back. She noticed him noticing.

"I was on my board this morning when you left the message," she said. "First time I've been able to get out on the water after my shift in a while."

"You took the Scooby-Doo van?" he said.

"I did," she said.

They started walking down the steps toward the parking lot.

"You check the newspaper this morning?" Ballard asked.

"Not yet," Bosch said. "What did they have?"

"They had a story about the SIS thing up in the Valley. But it happened so late they didn't get many details in. There will probably be a fuller story online today and in the paper tomorrow."

"Yeah. SIS means headlines. They'll be all over it for days. Anything about Dillon?"

"Not in the paper. But I got a call last night from Valley Bureau."

"What did they say?"

"They were looking for guidance on the Daisy Clayton case—they knew I had been working it. They said they picked up a guy who they think was good for her killing, among others. They were tipped to him by someone calling himself a concerned citizen. Like Batman or something. Identity unknown."

"Did they say whether they can make a case?"

"They said the taped confession was no good but otherwise they had enough probable cause to get a judge to give them a search warrant for the truck inside the warehouse."

"That's good. Hopefully, they'll find—"

"They already did. Prints and DNA. If they get matches to any missing women, then Dillon goes down. Probably not for Clayton, though. That'll be a long shot after so many years."

"I guess all that matters is that he's taken off the board."

Ballard nodded.

"Funny thing," she said. "While they were at the warehouse, a car pulls up and then takes off. The guy I'm dealing with, Detective Palmer, he has patrol chase the car down and guess who's in it?"

"No idea," Bosch said.

"George Bender and a couple bouncers from his joint on the strip. Sarah Bender's father—who we had just talked about last night."

"Strange."

"Even stranger is that he says he was told by an anonymous caller that the guy in the warehouse killed his daughter. They check his trunk and find a chain saw. Just sitting in his trunk. A frickin' chain saw."

Bosch shrugged but Ballard wasn't finished.

"Makes me think this Batman guy was trying to play both ends against the middle," she said. "Palmer even said that his caller told him to hurry because he had competition. So I'm glad you called me today, Harry, because I wanted to ask you what the fuck you were doing last night."

Bosch stopped so he could turn and face her. He shrugged.

"Look, I was following the plan and then I started thinking about Elizabeth, okay?" he said. "It's like he murdered her too, if you ask me. So I got angry and I made a call. But then I corrected it. And everything turned out okay."

"Barely," Ballard said. "It could easily have gone the other way."

"And would that have been so bad?"

"That's not the question. The question is, is that how we do things?"

Bosch shrugged again and continued toward his car.

"Was that why you wanted to meet?" Ballard said. "To explain calling Bender?"

"No," Bosch said. "I actually wanted to talk about something else."

"About what?"

"I was thinking that we worked pretty well together. Like, we were a good team on this."

They stopped at the Cherokee.

"Okay, we were a good team," Ballard said. "What are you saying?"

Bosch shrugged.

"That maybe we keep working on cases together," he said. "You know, you find them, I find them. I'm outside, you're inside. We see what we can get done."

"And what then?" she said. "You do your Batman thing and decide who we call at the end of the case?"

"No, I told you. It was a mistake and I corrected it. That won't happen. You can call the shots on that stuff, if you like."

"What about money? I get paid and you don't? We split my check? What?"

"I don't want your money or anybody else's. My pension's probably higher than your paycheck anyway. I just want what you've got, Renée. Not too many have it."

"Not sure I know what you're talking about."

"Yes, you do. You know. You have that thing—maybe one in a hundred have it. You've got scars on your face but nobody can see them. It's because you're fierce. You keep pushing. I mean, I'd be dog food right now if it wasn't for what you've got. So let's work together. Let's work cases. Badge, no badge, it doesn't matter. I'm past all of that now anyway. I don't know how much time I've got left, but whatever I have, I want to use it to go out there and find people like Dillon. And one way or another, take them off the board."

Ballard had her hands in her pockets. She was looking down at the asphalt when Bosch said all those things about her. Things she knew were true. Especially about the scars.

She nodded.

"Okay, Harry. We can work cases. But we bend the rules. We don't break them."

Bosch nodded back.

"That sounds right," he said.

"Where do we start?" she asked.

"I don't know. Just call me when it's time. I'll be around."

"Okay, I'll send up a signal."

They shook hands on it and went their separate ways.

ACKNOWLEDGMENTS

The author wishes to acknowledge those who contributed large and small to this novel. Chief among them is Detective Mitzi Roberts of the Los Angeles Police Department. Also, former and current detectives Rick Jackson, Tim Marcia, and David Lambkin provided great insight and detail.

A cast of editors led by Asya Muchnick were an indispensable part of the process and included Bill Massey, Emad Akhtar, and Pamela Marshall.

The Connelly Cabal of trusted readers helped sculpt the book, and they include Linda Connelly, Jane Davis, Terrill Lee Lankford, Heather Rizzo, Henrik Bastin, John Hougton, and Dennis Wojciechowski. Anyone who helped bring this story to the page is gratefully acknowledged.

Many thanks to all.

ABOUT THE AUTHOR

Michael Connelly is the author of thirty-one previous novels, including the #1 *New York Times* bestsellers *Two Kinds of Truth,* *The Late Show,* and *The Wrong Side of Goodbye.* His books, which include the Harry Bosch series and Lincoln Lawyer series, have sold more than sixty million copies worldwide. Connelly is a former newspaper reporter who has won numerous awards for his journalism and his novels and is the executive producer of *Bosch,* starring Titus Welliver. He spends his time in California and Florida.